To J
for all his love and support.

CHAPTER ONE

'FITTER, THINNER, RICHER,' BRUCE proclaimed, topping up glasses in readiness for Big Ben booming out its televised chimes.

'Ditto,' a couple of the guests agreed.

'With knobs on,' added a third.

'I will remember to put out the wheelie bin every Friday morning.'

'My viewing of The Simpsons will be restricted to twice a week.'

I smiled. Was watching The Simpsons such a sin? I've stopped making resolutions. Year after year I had vowed to quit smoking and year after year I had failed, until finally I recognised the futility. And now I was departing one year content with my personal life and at peace, and entering the next in the same way. It had not always been so. Okay, there were a few minor gripes – like wishing I looked thirty-five, rather than fifty-five, could afford a home-help and was a millionairess to boot – but I had no nail-biting anxieties, no serious complaints.

'Whenever Joan farts in bed, I shall banish her to the spare room. Which means she'll spend most of her time there,' guffawed a man who had been tossing down brandies all evening, and received a murderous look from his wife.

As on previous occasions – some in the distant past, but mainly in more recent times – I was celebrating New Year's Eve at the home of my best friend, Jenny, and her husband, Bruce, in the company of mutual friends and several of their neighbours. Earlier twelve of us had sat down to a delicious four-course dinner with all the trimmings. Jenny is an heroic cook.

Jenny has also given up on new leaves because, time and

again, she had resolved to lose weight and it hadn't happened. Like me with the cigs, come mid-January she invariably succumbs to the delights of Cadbury's flakes, chocolate digestives and their ilk. Though she isn't *that* fat, just 'cuddly', but it continually bothers her.

'Next year will see me – us – becoming richer,' Jenny declared brightly. 'Once I'm a working girl.'

Bruce laughed. 'Be realistic, my love. Whatever you might manage to earn will make zero difference to our lifestyle.'

Patronising twit, I thought. Although we go back decades, Bruce and I have never clicked. I've tried to like him, but he's not my sort – too much the in-charge husband and boring with it. Equally, I'm not his sort – overly independent, I guess.

'You'll change your tune once she's bringing in the cash,' I told him, but my words were lost beneath the first *boing* from the great clock tower.

Jenny hasn't worked – as in gone out to work and been paid – for twenty-eight years, since she became pregnant with William, her eldest, but after spending the autumn brushing up on her typing, attending computer workshops and practising on her daughter's p.c., as from 1st January – in eleven more *boings* – she will be actively job-hunting. I'm rooting for her, but Bruce is anti. He makes fun of her wanting to be, in his words, 'a dogsbody in an office'.

'With luck, I'll be richer, too,' I said to Jenny, who was stood beside me. 'Once Eric departs and I take over, which could be sooner rather than later.'

I am chief reporter at *The Dursleigh Siren,* the local weekly newspaper, while Eric is the editor. A lazy, uninspired, shambolic editor.

'Doesn't he have a couple more years to go until retirement?' she asked, as the *boings* progressed.

'In theory, but yesterday Mr Pinkney-Jones, the proprietor, came in and as he left I overheard him say something to Eric about 'time for a change at the top'.' I grinned. 'So –'

Boing. Boing. Final *boing.*

Glasses were raised. 'Happy New Year!' The shouts rang

out. 'And many of them!'

Fireworks were exploding on the television screen when a tweed-jacketed arm slithered around my waist and I was turned to face a russet-haired man with jug ears and a toothy smile. My heart sank. It was Russell. I had been placed next to him at dinner.

The placement was strategic. As had been all previous placements beside lone males. Jenny harbours the eternal hope that I will hit it off with lone male, fall – whoosh! – head over heels in love, marry and live happily ever after. But Russell, a financial consultant and acquaintance of Bruce, had spent the entire meal detailing the intricacies of share options. Utter fascination for him; made me itch to thrust my celery sticks up his excitedly quivering nostrils before slumping into a deep, deep sleep. Ever since we'd risen from the table I had been socialising with other guests, all established two-by-twos, in a desperate attempt to avoid him, but at regular intervals he had appeared. And here he was again.

'Happy New Year, Carol,' he yodelled, and kissed me.

The kiss was pink-rubber-lipped and sloppy, like being snogged by a turbot.

'We must get together sometime,' he declared.

My smile fell into the rictus category. I had no serious complaints with my *status quo*? Wrong!

Later, when my middle-aged suitor and the other guests had departed, and I was ferrying dirty glasses through to the kitchen, I got Jenny on her own.

'There's a New Year's resolution I would like you to make,' I told her. 'I will not try to fix Carol up with any more unattached males.'

'You didn't care for Russell?'

''Fraid not.'

'He did seem a touch... intense.'

'He was. So no more fixing. Please, Jen. *Pleeease*. I do not want, do not need, have not the slightest inclination to be partnered off with anyone. Understand?'

She sighed. 'Alright. Unless,' she added, with a smile, 'he

3

happens to look like George Clooney.'

'Not even if he *is* George Clooney!'

'You'd change your mind,' she said.

What I needed, I thought as I climbed into bed in the early hours, was a walker, a poodle faker, one of those debonair, anonymous types who do duty as escorts to film actresses and high society divas. A man I could trot out from time to time as my current interest – red-hot lover understood – but with no strings attached. Someone who'd be willing to accompany me to dinner parties, village am-dram productions, any 'twosome' events and who looked the part and would act the part, following my instructions to the letter.

'Flirt with me, gaze in adoration, converse brilliantly with all and sundry without revealing any personal detail, then lie low until I call you again.'

Not so much a wolf in sheep's clothing as a sheep in wolf's clothing.

Be a divorced woman and it is automatically assumed, *in toto,* that you must be in want of a man. Even if you've been on your own for aeons, are happy with your single status and have reached an age which is politely termed 'mature'. You would think that after years of trying and failing to pair you off with Mr Wonderful, people would get the message that your independence is a choice and not a session in purgatory, or at least suffer battle fatigue. On the contrary. The longer you spend *sans homme,* the more doggedly determined they seem to become. And the less attractive are the Mr Wonderfuls. Or am I too picky?

'We thought we'd invite Jeremy,' – or Norman or Phil – friends, invariably female, say, dredging up a pot-bellied widower, twitchy bachelor, or divorced liver-spotted uncle as a potential beau.

'Found yourself a bloke yet?' the thrice-married Jezebel in the Post Office wants to know, with irritating regularity.

'Getting any nooky these days, princess?' the dustbin man enquires whenever our paths cross, and winks.

But an on-call escort would mean no more jug-eared bores,

no more queries about my sad lack of a sex life, no more heavy hints from family, friends and shop assistants that it was high time I got cracking. An escort seemed the ideal solution and if he could fix a wonky loo and ferry a regular load of empties down to the bottle bank, so much the better. Trouble was, how to find one? If you're famous and beautiful or filthy rich and well-connected, and live in Hollywood or Monte Carlo, they're probably beating down your door. Otherwise – what's in it for him?

Hiring a guy from an agency had crossed my mind, briefly. But the prospect of forking out hard cash didn't appeal and when a trawl of the Net for 'male escorts' produced shots of butt-naked hunks sprawled over leopard skin sofas and adverts for 'the ultimate adult experience' – no thanks. It's not that I'm anti-sex – anything but – I just prefer it to evolve naturally.

I could, I suppose, buy a blow-up Bertie doll, sit him in my car beside me on dark nights, speed along the High Street and when people comment, act coy. People would comment. Work on a local paper in a smallish community and it's amazing how many folk know you, or know you by sight and notice you. And, as a reporter, I'm well aware of how rumours fly, can be exaggerated and embellished. How thistledown fiction hardens overnight into cast-iron fact.

'So you've shacked up with the landed gentry/millionaire banker/ageing pop star who lives in the area,' the Post Office Jezebel would say enviously. 'And he makes love non-stop/is buying you real diamonds/will be whisking you off in his Lear jet to his private Caribbean island next month.'

'Hear you're walking bandy-legged these days, princess,' the dustbin man would remark, and leer.

'Don't be so secretive, I'm dying to meet him,' Jenny would declare.

But if a red light flashed at the pedestrian crossing, I was forced to halt and someone looked closer at my inflated passenger with his merry, fixed, half-moon smile…

Time for a rethink.

CHAPTER TWO

As I HAD FEW grumbles with my personal circumstances, so my working life pleased me, too. I've always been passionate about journalism and while working on *The Dursleigh Siren* I had pinpointed plenty of local issues, aired subjects which had prompted readers' responses, interviewed all manner of interesting folk. Admittedly Eric's lackadaisical attitude riled me and, at times, had had me damn near headbanging in frustration, yet, on the plus side, it meant I had freedom. Freedom to make my own choices, freedom to follow my own instincts, freedom to develop a busy but satisfying routine.

Then Eric exited and Steve Lingard arrived.

Eyeing the guy one Tuesday morning in March, I did not feel kindly disposed towards him. Firstly, because he was sat in the editor's office at *The Siren*, behind the editor's desk in the editor's high-back chair – where *I* should have been sitting. Secondly, because he looked brisk, critical, impatient. A new broom set to sweep clean and make all the changes which I would have made. Third, because the binning of his predecessor's pub-counter sized ashtray indicated he did not smoke. I, of course, do. And as the general office is designated a 'no smoking' area, whenever I had come in to speak to Eric I had been able to wallow in nicotine heaven.

After his late December visit, the proprietor had kept clear of *The Siren*. I had decided I must have misinterpreted his reference to 'a change at the top' when, mid-February, Eric had dropped a hint that he could be leaving. As it had seemed correct to go through the motions, I had promptly applied for the editorship and, to my surprise and indignation, been refused. This was due to the fact that, unbeknownst to me, Eric's replacement had already been lined up, but also thanks to the proprietor's inherent belief that women are nature's also-rans. Fine in the kitchen, in the nursery, in a négligée. In charge? Forget it.

'You're a valued employee, Carol, and we've been so fortunate to have you,' Mr Pinkney-Jones had said, speaking in his plummy voice and smiling his latex smile. 'But the editor's position is really a man's position. You wouldn't want the rough and tumble. The responsibility.'

'Yes, I would,' I informed him. 'I do.'

I not only wanted the job, ravenously, I had *expected* it. Lying in bed at night, I had imagined myself rejigging the paper with expertise and to wide acclaim. Being interviewed on radio and television, in high demand as a journalistic guru. Becoming an icon. Okay, I'm pushing it, but given the chance I could have, would have, shone. It was not to be. Mr P-J had blithely ignored my insistence, my arguments, even my shameful attempt at a girly, wide-eyed plea, and brought in Steve Lingard.

I studied the man who had been transferred from *The Ringley Bugle,* another in the group of six local weekly papers which includes *The Siren.* During his tenure *The Bugle's* sales had increased by an astonishing thirty-five per cent, which was why the proprietor considered him to be a wunderkind – and expected him to work the same miracle again. Although Eric had spoken begrudgingly of Steve Lingard, who, he said, had been held up as a shining example, I had never met him. Mr P-J does not encourage rapport between his various staffs. Probably scared we might compare grievances, band together in a workers' army and revolt.

'He's tall, dark and handsome. A regular Captain Cool,' Eric had muttered, when I'd asked what Steve Lingard was like. But men have different ideas to women on what constitutes good looks – for example, Tom, my ex, used to rave about the 'delectable Cher' – and my description of the new editor was tall, dark and grim. Edging on the severe.

Did I want to work with him, for him, under him? No thanks. So should I ask for a transfer to another paper in the group? Mr P-J would agree. While he may not see me as an overlord, he recognised that I was a hardworking professional.

I could also study the journalistic 'situations vacant' columns in general. Yet why should I put myself through all the turmoil of changing jobs? If anyone shovelled their belongings into a bin bag and pedalled off to the blue horizon, it ought to be Steve Lingard. Admitting defeat. Tail between legs. Soonest. Then I could do such a fantastic job of holding things together and creating my own initiatives that Mr P-J would be forced to abandon his sexist views. Or perhaps I should sue for discrimination?

'Residents' meeting to protest about mobile phone mast. Seven-thirty tonight in the village hall,' Steve Lingard said, in no-nonsense, whip-cracking mode. 'Tony, I need a full report on what happens, together with a photograph of the proposed site, quotes from the chief protestors and comment from the phone company. Around nine hundred words.'

'Nine hundred!' Tony looked shell-shocked.

He was not enamoured of our new boss, either. Tony, who usually covers sports, road accidents and court cases, which are considered a male domain, is a younger – thirty-nine to be exact – version of Eric, in that he bumbles along and doesn't overstretch himself. The change at the top threatened to ruin this. However, Melanie, the bosomy graduate who is the latest addition to our reporting team, replacing another easy-going Friar Tuck, had been making eyes at Steve Lingard since the moment he arrived. While she could be involved in a move to seduce and curry favour, she makes eyes at virtually any male who ventures within allurement distance – even if she is in her early twenties and, in this case, the male looked to be in his mid to late forties.

'Nine hundred,' Steve Lingard confirmed. 'Masts are the current hot issue and this could develop.'

'I usually cover evening meetings,' I said.

'Carol covers any events at weekends and on Bank Holidays, too,' Tony told him, at speed.

'She's divorced and lives on her own, so she doesn't mind,' Melanie gratuitously explained.

Sharp grey eyes met mine. 'That true?'

8

'Yes, yes and yes,' I replied, wondering if the noble saddo should add that her carnal desires had gone unrequited for the past five years and she had a hole in the toe of her tights.

The golden boy had arrived on Monday, spent the day reading, scrutinising, investigating and, wasting no time, had summoned us three reporters to a 'planning meeting'. Eric, who had been shunted out and pensioned off – though he claimed to have opted for early retirement – had never aspired to planning meetings. A mistake maybe, for neither had he increased the circulation figures nor won a Scoop of the Year award. His good fortune had been in attending the same public school as Mr Pinkney-Jones, a connection which had allowed him to coast for years and push *The Siren's* expenses claims to the limit. Mr P-J, who had inherited the newspapers from an uncle, was none too bright, far too lax and not too interested. Though, so I've been told, he greatly welcomed the increased profits which Steve Lingard's success at *The Bugle* had generated. Instead of viewing the papers as a pesky albatross slung around his neck, Mr P-J had belatedly realised they could be a cash cow. And now came close to genuflecting whenever he saw his benefactor.

'So you wrote the previous pieces on protests about phone masts,' Steve Lingard said, sounding surprised, 'and objections to a skateboarding park and –'

'The uprising over advertisement hoardings beside the river. Plus reports of council meetings and Neighbourhood Watch and healthcare discussions,' I listed, with what was intended to be crisp authority. If he rated as Captain Cool, I could play Princess Pert. 'I did. And I'm happy to go along tonight.'

'Do that. But keep an eye out for anything… untoward.'

'You're referring to Councillor Vetch, who is pals with the phone company chairman and who could be in receipt of a backhander, arguing in favour of the mast?'

He cast me a quizzical look. 'You're aware of the situation?'

'I am, and I'll be on the alert. Ron Vetch might profess to

9

be twenty-four carat dependable, but it's my suspicion he could've been on the take for years.'

What I didn't reveal was that the councillor was also pals with Eric, who had deleted comments in my earlier reports which had hinted at doubts about his friend's integrity. When I had objected, Eric had blathered on about the dangers of provoking a libel case and how he dared not risk the paper being dragged into court. I could have said he was talking piffle and that the intrepid hackette knew the score and wasn't so irresponsible, but we had had several battles on-going and I had felt disinclined to start another. Battling with Eric could be as frustrating as juggling soot.

'This afternoon Iced Kidneys are making a video at Pondsby Place,' Steve Lingard continued, naming a nearby National Trust property. 'Carol, would you attend and –'

'Who or what are Iced Kidneys?' I demanded.

I resented being allocated work. I had always run my own regime and did not appreciate being sent off to monitor some itsy-bitsy video shoot. He'd have me doing a survey of bus shelters next!

'They're an indie band influenced by 'crunk and B', and they've had two number ones in the charts this year already,' Melanie explained excitedly.

'Oh.'

I don't know what indie music is, let alone 'crunk and B'. Once upon a time when my daughter was a teenager and we watched *Top of the Pops* together, I could name all the groups in the charts, plus their lead singers. Nowadays – zilch. Don't recognise the personnel nor the terminology. Though I am word perfect with almost every line of almost every song recorded by the Beatles and the Rolling Stones.

'You must remember 'Clock My Bling Bling?' Melanie said. The rest of us looked blank. She sang a snatch of something which sounded like a dirge. An Albanian dirge. We still looked blank. 'But could I do that story? To see them in real life, to speak to the guys would be bulls-eye.' Reaching into the canvas tote bag which she lugs around, she produced a newspaper cutting and showed us a picture of shaggy-haired youths in jeans with the crotch at knee level and back-to-front baseball caps. 'They're awesome,' she sighed.

I've never trusted 'awesome' and, for me, anyone who wears the peak of their cap over the nape of their neck has to be pea-brained and looks pea-brained. Even if it is the uniform of the day. There's only one thing worse, people with clip-on plastic sunshades for their glasses, who walk around with them raised. Oh, and men with ponytails, especially if they're over forty. Though that's a common grouse. And I do make exceptions if the men are dramatically good-looking.

'Please could I go?' the girl begged, thrusting out her pink-clad twin peaks and giving Steve a cutesy smile. 'Please, please, please.'

'Okay,' he said curtly, 'but make sure you get the facts correct and give people their right names spelled properly.'

She pulled at one of the long corkscrews of fair hair which dangle down over her eyes. 'I usually do.'

'Usually isn't good enough. You've had it far too easy here for far too long, but things are going to change.'

He may have been speaking to Melanie, but the warning went out, loud, clear and all encompassing. Smarten up, you lot, or else…

'At three p.m. today the Garth House Hotel is hosting a presentation to publicise the state-of-the-art health club and spa which they're opening to guests and exclusive membership,' Steve Lingard said, returning to his papers.

I arched a brow. 'Whoopy-do.'

'It may not be earth-shattering, but Garth House has advertised with *The Siren* for years so –'

'You know about that?' I said.

'I've done my homework – so a write-up would be politic. If you handle the health club –' he passed me a glossy brochure advertising it '– then Tony can spend time at the new traffic lights on the by-pass roundabout which are causing so many delays and which everyone's bellyaching about.'

Tony had been sucking on a Biro, but now he looked

11

baffled. 'Doing what?' he asked.

'Photographing the queues and conducting a survey on how long drivers are having to wait, together with irate comments,' Steve replied. 'Don't bother to claim a lunch. As well as cutting down on errors, we're cutting back on costs and expenses.' Sitting upright in the high-back chair, he eyed the three of us. 'Do you have any thoughts on stories or features? Some suggestions to brighten up the paper?'

'Suggestions?' Tony repeated, as if he had not heard the word before.

'Eric never wanted suggestions,' Melanie objected.

Our new boss gave a dry smile. 'Think of me as a learning curve.'

Was he attempting to establish that we were as lacklustre as he believed? Or could he be trying to pick our brains? He may have done his homework – I'd been surprised he also considered Councillor Vetch to be an iffy character – but he hadn't worked on *The Siren* for years nor did he live in Dursleigh. So should I help… or let him stew?

'Think!' he urged.

'The local hospice is holding a fun run next month,' I said. 'And in June there's a festival of football for kids. We could do features on them.'

As Mr P-J's darling Steve Lingard possessed the power to make life difficult for me, so it made sense to at least appear to be co-operative. Plus intelligent.

'*The Siren* hasn't done that before?'

'No.' I'd suggested both ideas to Eric the previous year, and the year before that, but, although agreeing, he had let them slide. 'We could publish photographs of the various teams. People get a buzz from seeing pictures of themselves, or their kids, in the paper. Or even from reading their names.'

He scribbled a note. 'Smart thinking.'

Was he being facetious, ironic or patronising? Or all three? Whichever, it wasn't smart thinking and he knew it. All I had done was read several editions of *The Ringley Bugle* and seen what he was up to. Like *The Siren, The Bugle* has a sizeable advertising section, plus a pull-out entertainment guide to what's going on locally which is syndicated, but the difference was in the news pages. *The Bugle's* twelve pages, as against our six, were sparkier and far more varied in content. While both papers have strong family values – no swear words, no nipple shots, nothing too graphically grisly – he had demonstrated those values by printing plenty of accounts and photographs of local events – the planting of a cherry tree in memory of a soldier who'd been killed in Iraq, children setting off on school trips, W.I. ladies with their flower arrangements.

'The chef at the local Italian won a best meal award recently,' Tony said. 'My wife and I go there sometimes in the evening,' he added, as if to emphasise that he did not dine courtesy of *The Siren.*

'So interview the guy, take his photo,' Steve told him. 'And while you're there, suggest that the restaurant advertises with us. The advertising needs to be boosted. But get out and about, make contacts, ask questions.'

'Charm old ladies,' I said.

Steve frowned. 'Sorry?'

'You wrote a tongue-in-the-cheek editor's column for *The Bugle* which had old ladies stopping you in the street to say how you'd made them laugh.' I, too, had done a little homework, in the form of a phone conversation with a Ringley reporter. A male reporter who had described Steve Lingard as 'a heavy-hitter, but a nice guy and a damn good editor.' I would've preferred to chat with a woman, who would have been more on my wavelength and more likely to pass on any gossip, but both of the women reporters had been out of the office. I had rung a couple more times, but frustratingly missed them again. 'Seems they fancied you rotten,' I said, wondering why such a grim-faced character should appeal.

'Yeah, I'm catnip to any female over seventy.'

'Which is why they tell you their family secrets.'

This reference was to his Scoop of the Year Award, when the geriatric mother of a government minister had chattily revealed to him that, after an unwise evening in the company of lap dancers, her son had decided to resign.

'Are you going to write an editor's column in *The Siren?*' Melanie enquired.

He nodded. 'That's the intention. Once I've got the hang of things. Any other suggestions?'

Silence.

In a couple of weeks the am-dram society was putting on performances of *The Master Builder* and I could have suggested we printed a piece on that, but I kept quiet. Didn't want to make his life too easy. I had also amassed a folder of ideas for possible stories, but I wasn't about to share that with him, either.

'Nothing?' he asked.

Tony and Melanie looked thoughtful. 'No,' they said, in unison.

I shook my head.

Steve Lingard frowned and checked his watch. 'Then that's it for now. I've arranged to meet a few folk to introduce myself –'

'Who?' I demanded.

He was on my territory *interfering* and I wanted to know. I deserved to know. Indeed, it would've been courteous if he had raised the idea with me first.

'Today I'm seeing the fire chief and later one of *The Siren's* freelancers, the guy who writes about antiques. If that's agreeable to you?' he asked, with a sardonic bow of his head.

I made myself look coolly back. 'It is,' I replied. Let's face it, I didn't have any choice.

'Praise the Lord. But I'll be back in the office mid afternoon. And I can always be contacted on my mobile, I've given you the number. If anything comes in which you think merits *The Siren's* presence, clear it with me first.'

'Yes, sir,' I said, and resisted the urge to salute.

Eric had not demanded that he be consulted, he had allowed me, left me, *trusted* me to do my own thing.

As Steve Lingard departed, the rest of us returned to our

desks in the general office. After agonising over how many drivers he would need to speak to in order to satisfy the new editor's idea of a survey – two, twelve, twenty? – Tony left for an early bar lunch to be bought at his own expense. He rarely missed lunch, washed down by a pint or two, which accounted for his jowls, beer barrel belly and tendency to nod off in the afternoons. Though it seemed unlikely he'd be doing much nodding off from now on.

Steve Lingard may not have said he considered us to be a dead loss trio, but it had been evident in his attitude. I was not a dead loss, I thought indignantly. I had been responsible for the major proportion of the news which filled the news pages. But did he know that? He had been surprised to realise I had written about the phone masts *et al,* so could Eric have claimed the reports as his? It was possible, correction highly probable; given Eric's erratic commitment to the gospel truth and the fact that he had rarely put my by-line on my work. Reckoned it would've looked like I wrote too much. Which, of course, I did. The ultimate underachiever and devious with it, Eric had shown little enterprise. He had preferred to let others – i.e. me – provide the drive, while he subbed their work in the comfort of his office. And studied the racing journals, placed telephone bets and chain-smoked.

'OHOC. OHOT. WLTM a WOCA with GSOH. That'd suit you.'

I looked across at Melanie. 'I beg your pardon?'

'Own house, own car. Own hair, own teeth,' she translated. 'Would like to meet a woman of a certain age with good sense of humour for a long term relationship. Interested?'

'No thanks. And you shouldn't be logging onto encounter sites and printing out details in company time and at company expense. Eric may have let you get away with murder, but Mr Lingard would not approve.'

'He isn't here.'

'Makes no difference.'

If she had a spare moment and, I suspected, whenever she was left in the office alone, Melanie scanned what seemed to be a never-ending scroll of lonely hearts 'males eager to contact females'. When I had asked why a girl in her twenties should need to forage for dates in such a way, I had been informed that 'everyone does it'. I'd also been informed that there are specialist sites catering for vegans, poets and herpes carriers. Wow!

Courtesy of the Net, Melanie had even gone speed-dating where, in the course of one evening and after sipping a free cocktail, the organisers had introduced her to eighteen members of the opposite sex and allotted her three minutes to talk to each. So much for romance! Whatever happened to old-fashioned courting?

Melanie had subsequently met up with two of the men and afterwards given me a detailed – too detailed – account of what had happened. While not wanting to go all the way on a first date and be viewed as 'easy', she had agreed to blow jobs. Crikey! In my youth, a lad would've considered himself fortunate if a girl had held his hand. Melananie had not, however, felt inclined to see either of the guys again. And vice versa.

'I am a well-mannered, healthy and intelligent businessman, looking for an older solvent lady who –'

'No!'

Melanie popped a Smint in her mouth. She sucks them continuously. 'Wouldn't you like to team up with a guy? There's a lot on offer for the silver surfer market.'

I stiffened. 'I am not a silver surfer.'

'You are nearly.'

I disagreed. To my reckoning, you don't rate as a silver surfer until you clock at least sixty, and more like sixty-five. I was a long way off that. A mere chick. A funky chick, too. But I wasn't prepared to argue the point. Not with someone who regards thirty as 'past it'.

'What I wouldn't like,' I said, 'is to fix to meet a guy over the Net and find myself lumbered with a well-mannered, healthy and intelligent serial killer. Or rapist.'

Melanie rolled her eyes skywards. 'That is so last

millennium. On-line dating is just window shopping. You chat for two or three weeks, then arrange a get-together in a public place. If you're sensible, it's perfectly safe. How about this one? JLFAS. Just looking for adulterous sex.'

I shuddered. I'm not saying my moral compass is superior to anyone else's, but I would never sleep with a married man.

'Spare me.'

CHAPTER THREE

THE SMALL FLAT WAS as glossy and immaculate as one of those show flats you see in colour supplement advertisements. All the polishable furniture gleamed, the carpets had been recently vacuumed and a vase of cerise carnations, which hadn't been there on my previous visit, stood on the coffee table. Everything which could be tidied away had been tidied away and the air hung with an aerosolled fragrance which, if inhaled sharply, promised to purge the sinuses.

'Nora's doing a good job,' I remarked, as I made the usual pot of Earl Grey. 'You wouldn't like to send her round to me?'

'Nora?'

Poking my head out of the tiny kitchen, I spoke to my father who was sitting on the sofa. Sat between plumped-up and neatly arranged cushions. 'Isn't she the lady who's doing your cleaning?'

'She was until last week, but now Em's taken over. Dab hand, she is. And Dilys is a dab hand in the food department. She's started making me my dinner. Seven p.m. prompt, it's on the table. And there's always a pudding.'

'I thought you preferred to get your own meals,' I protested. 'You said it wasn't any bother.'

'It isn't and I'm still seeing to my lunch, but Dilys was... persuasive.'

I raised my brows. Whenever a man was widowed or a lone man moved into the Bridgemont Retirement flats there was, so Gillian, the chatty house manager, had told me, fierce competition amongst the solo women to grab him.

'Forget feminism. They go crazy, offering to cook and clean and iron,' she had said, 'until one of them wins through. Then the winner is so damn smug, it's like she's landed Brad Pitt. Not some doddery old soul with National Health dentures.'

Within a few weeks of my mother's demise around eighteen months ago, my father had had volunteers dealing with his vacuuming and his laundry. He had, however, insisted on tackling the catering side himself – until now.

I poured out cups of tea and carried them into the living room. 'You gave Nora her marching orders?' I asked, handing him a cup.

'Yes, though I did it kindly. She was peeved, but Em was so eager I felt I had to give her a chance.'

'You're happy with her?'

'For now. And I'm happy with Dilys doing my evening meals, for now. And with Peggy who is my ballroom dancing partner.'

I saw a sparkle in his eye. 'You old devil,' I said, 'you're just stringing them along.'

He chuckled. 'I'm footloose and fancy-free, so why not?'

Sitting down, I tasted my tea. My mother, Muriel, had been scathing about the feminine interest which lone males inspired and had roundly condemned the women who had attempted to befriend them, calling them 'fast' and 'hussies'. If she knew that her 'darling George' was benefiting from their attentions and relishing every minute, she would be furious.

'You're early today,' my father said.

'I have an appointment later.'

After eating a quick sandwich in the office, I had driven over to see him. I did this twice a week. Eric had known of my visits and not minded, but if Steve Lingard knew would he be as accommodating? Not a chance; even though I only stayed for around thirty minutes and made a point of working half an hour extra to compensate.

'I see. Still it's just as well because I need to get showered and changed soon, ready for Winnie's bunfight.'

'Winnie is the one who's turning ninety?'

'That's right. She's having port for the gents and cream sherry for the ladies, plus sausage rolls, quiche slices and meringues. Not fussed about meringues myself, too crumbly. Gillian's decorating the lounge.'

19

I nodded. 'I saw the balloons when I came in.'

The residents' lounge was the scene of a multitude of events; including birthday parties, beetle drives and seminars on inheritance tax avoidance, run by a local accountant gunning for business. My father had religiously attended the latter. As a retired surveyor he may not possess millions, but he's keen on looking after what money he has. Keen as in he never uses a first class stamp.

The lounge was also the venue for send-offs. The only way anyone ever quit the Bridgemont flats was in their box, usually followed by a 'bites and drinkies' send-off organised by Gillian. They were a high spot and patronised by most of the residents. Some came out of sheer relief that they were still alive and vertical, others for the free drink, but many from affection for the deceased. My dear old mum had had a wonderfully warm send-off. The memory of it still touches me.

'Didn't realise you could buy them with ninety printed on, did you?' my dad said. 'The woman at the party shop told Gillian they make them for a hundred, too, though you need to order those.' Putting down his tea, he reached for a garment which was folded up at one end of the sofa and had obviously been placed there ready to show me. 'What do you think about this?'

The waistcoat he held up was silky, with vertical red and white stripes and a red satin pocket containing an extravagant white satin handkerchief. It had bookmaker's clerk written all over it. I grinned. For someone who, for years, had worn a dark brown knitted beneath his jacket, it seemed extreme.

'Wow! You got it from Jenny's shop?'

Jenny helps as a part-time assistant at a charity shop in the village and my father, who possesses a beady eye for value, often goes in there. He buys second-hand paperbacks and – to Jenny's amusement and my shame – will haggle if there's a tear in the cover or the pages are curled. Knocking the one pound price down to half delights him.

'No, I did not,' he said huffily. 'It's brand new and it cost a pretty penny. Dilys insisted on buying it for me.'

'This is the same Dilys who's doing your cooking?' There seemed to be so many women floating around, I thought I had better check.

'That's right. Dilys Langsdon. We got the waistcoat in Oxford Street. Went up on the train.'

'But you don't like shopping in London. For years you've said it's too busy, much too much of a hassle.'

'No, no, pet, that was your mother.'

'Is it wise to be accepting gifts from strange women?' I asked.

My mother would have strongly disapproved and I wasn't too keen on the idea myself. He was my dad, I thought protectively, and I resented outsiders smarming up to him.

'Dilys isn't strange and, besides, I gave her a gift, too.' The waistcoat was being carefully refolded. 'I bought her a nightie.'

This seemed an overly personal offering, but then I remembered the long-sleeved, high-necked tents which my mum had worn. Perhaps Dilys suffered from the cold, too.

'Wincyette?'

'Black chiffon with shoestring straps and a slit up the side. She looks good in it.'

I almost choked on my tea. To purchase black chiffon seemed bravura enough and uncharacteristically extravagant, but what was my seventy-eight-year-old father saying – that the woman had given him a fashion show? That they were going to bed together? It had to be a joke… didn't it? I wanted to ask, but we've never talked about sex – men of his generation don't discuss such things with their daughters – and I felt awkward now.

'You seem to like this Dilys,' I began cautiously.

There was no reason for him to joke nor, I supposed, any reason why they shouldn't be making mad, passionate love morning, noon and night. So long as you are capable and feel the urge, why should age be a veto? Yet the thought of an elderly parent 'at it' was… uncomfortable.

'She's good fun. Wicked sense of humour, a snappy dresser and game for anything. Lives on the third floor, has one of the larger balconies. She's recently had the place painted and decorated throughout. She –'

'Which is what you should do here,' I interrupted.

For at least a year before she died, my mother had been eager to have their flat freshly painted, but my father had insisted there was no urgency. In other words, he could not bring himself to spend the money.

'I'll get round to it, in due course. Dilys has a son, William, who's same as you,' he continued. 'Divorced and at a loose end.'

I gritted my teeth. Maybe I should procure a blow-up Bertie and drive with him past the retirement flats at night. Whatever time I arrived, the twitch of at least one curtain indicated a perpetual look-out and a glimpse of me plus male passenger would provoke gossip which would be certain to reach my father. Gillian refers to the residents of the thirty-six flats as 'one big family' and they are, in so much as everyone is zealously interested in everyone else – their state of health, financial situation, the activities of their offspring. And if the news contains a whiff of scandal, so much the better. Bridgemont residents are also united in their hatred of noise after eleven p.m. and dogs which wander in off the road and relieve themselves in the landscaped gardens.

'I am not at a loose end,' I protested, but he wasn't listening.

'Which reminds me, I won't be with you on Sunday. I'm taking Dilys out for a pub lunch. And although it's kind of you to call round twice a week, pet, I realise it must be a nuisance and from now on once a week will be sufficient.'

I felt a spurt of anger. My mother's death had left my dad lost and forlorn, and, initially, I had made a point of visiting every day – to try to cheer him, to see if he needed any washing or shopping done, to let him know he wasn't alone. Again Eric had been aware of my visits and had not minded. I had also suggested my father should come and stay with me at my house for a while, but he had refused. To my secret relief, for he expects to be waited on hand and foot, turns the television sound up high and then talks over it. But I had visited out of love and willingly, though I had always come round often. As their only child who lived near – my brother has been up in Scotland for years – my parents' welfare as they had grown older had seemed like my responsibility.

'They're very lucky, having you dashing around like a blue-arsed fly dancing attendance,' Gillian had said. 'There're several in here who only get to see their kids on rare occasions. And some who don't have kids and no visitors.'

Gradually, the visits to my father had settled into sometime on Tuesday and Thursday afternoons, with him coming for lunch at my house every Sunday. It was not always easy to find the time – and the regular Sundays meant me turning down invitations and were tying – but I had made the effort. And my dad, who frequently claimed that my visits were 'life-savers', had seemed so grateful.

'You want me to come on any special day?' I asked a touch tartly, for regardless of the fact that I worked, the Tuesdays and Thursdays had been chosen because they did not clash with his other pursuits, such as short mat bowls, ballroom dancing lessons – he had never set foot on a dance floor when my mother was alive – and whist. Thanks to Gillian's oft-stated desire to 'keep her old folks happy', there is a leisure pastime perpetually on tap at Bridgemont.

'Let's leave it open for now, but it would help if you could ring first, pet. In case Dilys and I have plans. Though I should be at home this Thursday.' The clock was eyed and his tea was being drunk with noticeable speed. Today I had not been offered a piece of the Battenburg cake of which he is so fond, not even a biscuit. 'There was a bit in one of the papers at the weekend about your Tom. Did you see it?'

I sighed. 'No.'

If ever a reference to my ex-husband should appear in the national press, my father can be guaranteed to spot it and to comment. And although eight years have passed since we were man and wife, he always speaks of him as 'your Tom'.

'It said how he was political editor of his paper right now, but top favourite for the overall editor's job when the present man retires in twelve months. Your Tom's done so well. Extremely well.'

'He has,' I agreed.

At the time of our separation, my mother's criticism of Tom was vitriolic and she had continued to badmouth him – out of her granddaughter's hearing – until she died. Although he had once basked in her favour, he had never been forgiven for 'running off with that floozie.' 'I think she ran off with him,' I had said, but my mother would make no concession. 'Then he should have resisted.'

My father, however, was not so hostile. He had enjoyed having a son-in-law whom he described as 'a top-notch journalist with his finger on the political pulse'. He had loved it when Tom had told him about conversations he'd had with various Prime Ministers and given him the low-down on M.P.s. Even now, it wouldn't surprise me if he still boasts about Tom.

And Tom was not all bad. Maybe it was to assuage his guilt, but when we divorced he'd been generous; splitting the proceeds from the sale of our Kensington apartment straight down the middle and then contributing extra cash to enable me to buy a house outright, furnish it and equip it with microwave, television, tumble-dryer – the essentials. He also keeps in regular touch with Lynn, our daughter, and, still, gives her sizeable cheques.

My dad boasts about me, too. I've squirmed with embarrassment when he's described me to other Bridgemont residents, in my presence, as 'an outstanding writer and a caring and loving girl'. But then, when we're alone, he spoils it by talking about other people's daughters who, according to him, are constantly arriving with home-made cakes and casseroles, who take their parents on expensive foreign holidays, whose Father's Day gifts stretch to Rolex watches – which beats a bottle of cheap gin from Sainsbury's hollow.

The clock was inspected again. 'Don't want to rush you, pet, but –'

'I'll go.' I took a last drink of tea. 'Dad, don't you think you should be careful about your friendships with these women?' I suggested.

He may not be able to get them pregnant, but I could foresee other kinds of trouble; catfights on the stairs, laxative in his morning coffee, accusations of sexual harassment.

'Why? I'm enjoying playing the field. And that's what you should do.'

I groaned. My father has spent the last eight years hoping that I would either marry again – to someone of status and thus provide him with a second son-in-law he could boast about – or produce a string of classy boyfriends. I had failed miserably on both counts. He's even daydreamed about Tom and me getting together again, regardless of the doting slick chick and their two sons. Mind you, I have to confess there was a time when I harboured idiotic yearnings in that direction myself, too.

'Or you should find yourself a special fellow,' he went on, as we walked to the door. 'Time's passing and you're not getting any younger. What do they call it – drinking at the Last Chance Saloon?'

'Thanks! And what about you?'

'It's different for men,' he said smugly. 'But you need to get a move on.'

Should I invent a boyfriend? I wondered. Should I claim to be seeing someone? But while it would get him off my back, it would also have him asking a thousand probing questions. About the boyfriend's job and salary, value of his house, if he owns any ISA's and how much he's paying into his pension fund. My father would've adored Russell. If he had known I'd met him he would have demanded a word-by-word report of his conversation, but at the first mention of 'share options' my brain had disengaged.

'Dad, I'm not interested.'

'You should be.'

'I'm perfectly happy on my own.'

He patted my hand, as if I was a misguided child, then kissed me goodbye. 'So you say.'

'It's true. I'm happy with my house, with my –'

I hesitated. I had been going to say 'with my job', but the work situation didn't thrill me at the moment.

'You'd be even happier if you had someone.'

'Would I? Does it follow? You may think so, but I enjoy my independence. In any case,' I added quickly, to stem a protest, 'I never see anyone I fancy.'

He grunted. 'You never look!'

Girls in their thirties might be desperately seeking Mr Right, or Mr Darcy, but I'd been there, done that and torn up the T-shirt for rags, I reflected, as I drove along. After an experimental and educational spell a few years back, I had accepted life as a born-again single and was at ease living by myself. Mistress of my own fate and a free spirit, able to do whatever I wanted when I wanted. Able to take charge of the TV remote control, weep over late night movies, shave my legs in the bath. Tom had complained bitterly about the latter. I missed the sex – missed it like mad – and having someone to scratch that inaccessible itch on my back, but I didn't miss ironing shirts or being forced to listen to endless moans about how, these days, so many politicians looked and sounded like third-rate car salesmen. Or the national indignity of having Prime Ministers who wore jeans.

'My life is fine,' I informed a squirrel which was standing, upright and still, on the distant grass verge. 'Honest.'

It was fine, yet there's no denying that a solo existence requires effort and, now and then, I do feel sorry for myself. When I see married couples who are relaxed and loving together, I can't help thinking how good it would be to have someone to grow old with. To share the trials and tribulations, the laughs, the holidays, the intimate thoughts. To cozily reminisce about past experiences. But after twenty-two years of what we had both agreed was a happy marriage, I had always assumed that someone would be Tom.

I had also assumed my father would remain forever faithful to my mother's memory. But then I'd never considered him to be a babe magnet – though he does have a full head of white hair, his own teeth, apart from a couple of bridges, and, despite arthritic twinges, he walks miles, executes a mean foxtrot – so Gillian has reported – and, on occasion, kicks a ball with his great-granddaughter. The idea of him 'playing the field' troubled me. He seemed destined to hurt the old ladies and could get hurt himself. So far as I was aware, he'd never looked at another woman when my mum was alive and now to–

'Oh no!' I yelped.

Anyone who travels Surrey's renowned leafy lanes will know from the scraps of fur and intestine regularly pancaked to the tarmac that the odds of running over a squirrel must be high. Squirrels do not halt at the kerb, look right, look left and proceed with care. Nor wait for a passing lollipop lady. Trustingly, foolishly, they dash straight beneath the wheels of your Ford Focus. Or this one had. It had remained still until I'd drawn level, then sprinted out, kamikaze style. Because squirrels look so delicate, I'd always imagined that if you ran over one – heaven forbid – you wouldn't feel a thing. Not true. I felt a bump, albeit a light one, and a crunch. The crunch was sickening. It turned my stomach.

Fearful the poor little creature would be writhing in its death throes, I risked a glance in my rear-view mirror. There was no movement. No blood and twitching guts, either. Just an inert ball of grey fur lying on the road. Had it passed on to an acorn-filled heaven or merely knocked itself out cold? Should I stop, go back and move it before another vehicle – maybe a Tesco lorry – thundered along to deliver a resounding *coup de grace*? Animal rights activists might insist there was no choice, but I wasn't sure if I could bring myself to pick up a lifeless, still warm body, nor did I fancy trying to shift it with my toe and getting scratched or rabidly bitten. Calling myself all kinds of a coward, I drove on to the hotel.

*   *   *

Originally an Elizabethan manor house and Grade Two listed, Garth House is an opulent chintzy place with four-poster beds, jacuzzis in the en-suites and nightly rates to make you wince. The grounds include a formal walled garden, nine-hole putting green and a helipad. Most guests are executive-level businessmen, living the good life courtesy of their companies. There are several high-ceilinged function rooms where wedding receptions, conferences and small-scale exhibitions are held. Time-share sharks sometimes bask there.

When I arrived, I sped straight to the Ladies. I was desperate for a pee. I had washed my hands and was looking at the wan face in the mirror – an assassin's face? – when I spotted two hairs. They were jet black, stiff and so *long*. I could swear they hadn't been there yesterday, so they must have grown overnight, sliding stealthily out in the dark. Grotesque invaders. Leaning closer to the mirror, I angled my chin. The hairs appeared to come from the same follicle, one shooting right, the other to the left, like aerials on a ghetto blaster. I've accepted that youth has become a fond memory – more or less – but this was a wake-up call. Old age looms, it yodelled. The buzzards are circling.

Some day! First Steve Lingard had stamped his authority, then my father had revealed himself as a closet Lothario, next I had pole-axed a squirrel and now bristles were sprouting from my chin. Fate had locked into the kick-ass mode.

I poked at the hairs. How did I remove them? There's everything in my bag from plastic toothpicks to an illegal pepper spray to squashed sachets of 'refreshing tissues' plundered from long-ago holiday flights, plus the essential chocolate lollies and Marlboro Lights, but no tweezers. The likelihood of ripping the hairs cleanly out with my fingers seemed remote, and painful, so all I could do was leave them and hope no one would notice, as I hadn't noticed when I'd made up my face that morning. Made it up in a hurry, as usual. I find it hard to resist that extra ten minutes in bed.

I was sprouting bristles, but what came next – a dowager's

hump, more warts than Oliver Cromwell, incontinence pants? Could my frantic dash to the loo denote a weak bladder destined to get weaker – or simply nerves brought on by my fears of a possible murder?

Still fretting about the squirrel – was it dead or alive, even now ought I to race back and rescue it? – I went out onto the thick-carpeted corridor. Hearing the distant rumble of conversation, I headed towards it. Double doors were half open, so I walked inside and found a glass of red wine being thrust into my hand.

'Thanks.'

'No problem,' said a foreign-sounding waiter, who was going the rounds with a tray. He nodded towards a long buffet table on one side of the room. 'Helpa yourself.'

The wine tasted like nectar. While I don't profess to be an expert, I can tell a good vintage and this rated high. Numero Uno, classy expensive stuff. The kind of wine which TV noses drool over as 'full-bodied', 'flirtatious', 'confident'. I was wondering why the Garth House management was being so generous – or had someone uncorked the wrong bottle? – when it dawned on me that the people who were gathered didn't look like aerobics aficionados. On the contrary. Most were elderly, portly and dressed in black. Nor was this the purpose-built wing designed to 'soothe the senses and release your physical potential' – according to the brochure. I hadn't joined the health club launch, I had wandered into a wake. Dumbo.

I ought to leave, but… the wine was doing wonders for my shattered nerves – and persuading me that my vision of galloping senility was an over-reaction – so I would, I decided, stay and finish the glass. I might be an intruder, but it would've been a crime to let such liquid pleasure go to waste.

I knew who had been buried at St. John's, Dursleigh's parish church, earlier that day and who would be the reason why so many pillars of the community had congregated – Duncan Kincaid. No residents' lounge 'bites and drinkies' for him, an up-market farewell in sumptuous surroundings was just his style. At one time, Mr Kincaid had owned a fair number of the shops along the High Street: the newsagent's, the bookshop, the bakery, the dry cleaner's, the ironmonger's and a tearoom which is now the Tandoori. Then, as he'd approached retirement age, the self-styled 'king of the village' had begun selling off his businesses, one by one, to the Patels. An act which had caused much muttered consternation amongst Dursleigh's less 'inclusive' denizens. We may be only twenty-five crow-winging miles from central London, but ethnic minorities are still minor.

'Have you heard the reason why Duncan had his heart attack?' a woman nearby said to her companion, in a cut-glass Surrey voice, a voice unhindered by volume control.

I was born and bred in Dursleigh and, apart from five years near Manchester and eleven in the cosmopolitan climes of Kensington, have lived here all my life, but I don't possess the blah-blah accent nor the piercing tones. They come with family money, private education and impenetrable self-confidence. Usually. The speaker oozed confidence. Short, with a corseted bosom you could bounce bricks off, and bouffant, stiff-lacquered silver hair, she was headmistressy. The type who marches around dispensing orders and laying down the law. I didn't recognise her, though others amongst the gathering were familiar. There was the lady mayor of the borough, our M.P., a Conservative, of course, several councillors, one of which was the dubious Mr Vetch, and an assortment of shopkeepers, including the Patel patriarch and his four tall, good-looking sons.

'No, Beryl. Do tell.'

'He was on the golf course with Peter and a couple more chaps when he claimed an eagle three on the long par five. Puffed out his chest and strutted. You know what Duncan was like.'

I did. I'd interviewed Duncan Kincaid a few years back when he had paid for a clock to be erected on the village green. A tubby sort wearing a blazer and tasselled loafers, with sparse strands of grey hair combed meticulously across his scalp, he had regarded himself as the big enchilada and taken great delight in telling me about his business acumen and the rip-roaring success he'd made of his shops, on and on and on. That said, the man had been affable and was generous. Always the first to put his hand into his pocket if funds were needed for the village football team or the brass band or some such thing. He had also been the founder, and mainstay, of the Dursleigh village fête which takes place every July.

'Duncan said he didn't want to boast, but wasn't he a clever fellow?' Beryl continued. 'Declared it had to be a cause for a celebration, a black-tie dinner at the Club House with him and her –' a scathing glance was cast across the room to an elegant blonde in a wide-brimmed black hat '– holding court. At that point Peter interrupted and told him he'd actually played four shots. Well, Duncan went wild. Called Peter a liar –'

'Never!'

'To his face. And vowed he'd always been jealous of him.'

This time the blonde received a look to kill. She was the widow, Tina Kincaid, Duncan's second wife. I've seen her emerging from dress shops – correction, fashion stockists – in Dursleigh, laden down with stiff parchment bags. And working on the paper, I get to hear the gossip.

Tina is slim, chic and perfectly packaged. A regular Barbie doll. She favours pastel trouser suits, with toning shoes and handbag, and wears her long straight hair tied back by a chiffon scarf which always, but always, matches her outfit. That some women devote vast chunks of their time and energy to their appearance never ceases to amaze me. I keep a couple of decent outfits for work – today I am in a black skirt suit with a lavender sweater and high heels. In all modesty, I have good legs and high heels are a vanity. If you've got it, why not flaunt it? But I would never go schlepping from one shop to another in search of a handbag to match the exact shade of a dress and, at home, I'm a slob. Tina Kincaid won't be a slob. She'll wear smart casual and full make-up, not pad around barefoot with a shiny face, clad in fraying chain store jeans.

'However,' Beryl went on, 'the other chaps backed Peter up. Confirmed Duncan had indeed taken four shots, but said four was excellent, to be applauded. Still Duncan insisted he'd only had three. When Peter tried to explain that he was mistaken, Duncan swore. Told him to –' she lowered her voice and I needed to strain to hear '– eff off and go stuff himself, and waved his five-iron around as if he intended to batter them all.'

'For heaven's sake!' exclaimed her companion.

'Then, all of a sudden, Duncan dropped to his knees and fell forward. One of the other chaps was Frank Carr, you know him, the doctor, now retired. He diagnosed a heart attack and asked Peter to summon an ambulance on his mobile. It's a Nokia, top of the range. You can send and receive emails on it. And there's an FM radio, plus digital music player. But it was too late. A minute or so later, Frank pronounced that the silly old fool was dead.' Placing her empty wine glass on a side table, Beryl repositioned a bucket-sized handbag on her arm. 'I suppose I'd better pay my respects. Do excuse me.'

As she made her way through the crowd – pausing to greet people, tracking the waiter to demand another glass of wine, helping herself to three prawn florets from the buffet table – I followed by a more circuitous route. Having eavesdropped this far, I wasn't going to miss out on what came next. You could say I was being nosey, though I prefer to think of it as the journalistic drive. As I wove my way through I needed to briefly acknowledge, and avoid, several people in the throng. Though I saw that Councillor Vetch, who had seen me, kept his distance. Could Eric have warned him of my suspicions?

Ron Vetch, who exudes a persistent bonhomie, claims to be a devoted family man. His election literature always carries a photograph of him with his wife and four children, arms around each other and smiling brightly. Yet I have been reliably informed that he treats his wife, who is a timid woman, like a skivvy. She rarely appears with him in public and she was not with him today.

Beryl reached the widow just as a couple who had been

voicing words of condolence were shifting into their goodbyes.

'You must come round for coffee,' the wife declared. 'Some day.'

Tina Kincaid nodded. 'Some day.'

Fat chance! A definite invitation would never be issued. You didn't need extra-sensory perception to know that the women in the room – the wives of Duncan Kincaid's golfing, Chamber of Commerce and Rotarian associates, he was a busy socialiser – disapproved of Tina. The glances she'd been receiving made it clear. Fifteen or whatever years ago when Duncan had married his 'child bride' as he'd called her, she had been slotted into the role of gold-digger and there she had stayed. If she had attempted to break down prejudice and encourage camaraderie, it hadn't worked. Though she may have thought 'bugger you lot' and remained aloof.

It wouldn't help that she was younger and left the wives standing in the looks department. With killer cheekbones, full lips and clear skin, Tina was decidedly pretty now and had been a beauty in her youth. When I had interviewed Duncan Kincaid he had talked proudly of how, in the past, she'd been on television.

'Went under the name of Tina Sinclair,' he'd said. 'Used to set the male population alight every Saturday evening at eight.'

I can remember seeing her. She was a hostess on a game show, displaying the prizes. Draped over a car bonnet in a slinky dress or smiling excitedly at a food mixer, that kind of thing.

The woman must be in her fifties now, same as me, but the wives, all seventy-plus, would regard her as a threat. With reason. A procession of men had been in attendance; soothing, stroking her back, an arm around her shoulders as they comforted. Were they visualising her as a merry widow and thinking that, after a decent interval had elapsed, they would sidle close and suggest getting closer? Despite hearing aids and walking with sticks, several had the air of randy old sods.

And Tina had lapped up their interest. Even when couples had come to speak to her, she had concentrated on the husbands and virtually ignored the wives.

'I want to offer my sympathy,' Beryl stated, standing four-square in front of Tina, 'and say that dear departed Duncan was an exceptional human being and an inspiration to us all.'

The two-faced bitch! Her nose should've shot out a mile. But why is it that whenever someone dies, they are instantly transformed into a saint? You can guarantee that, before *rigor mortis* has set in, friends and relations will rush to say how warm, kind, intelligent, talented, etc., the deceased was. It would be refreshing if, just once, someone would declare that so-and-so had been a complete pain and thank God they'd gone.

As Beryl gushed out tributes with passionate insincerity, Tina's attention began to stray. She examined her fingernails, which were lacquered a metallic ruby, smoothed the skirt of her black wool dress over the line of her hip, shot sly smiles at male admirers. Not quite the behaviour you'd expect from a grieving widow, though shock can have a strange effect.

'I was wondering about the house,' Beryl said, reaching the end of her diatribe.

'House?' Tina asked.

'Your house. It's a big place for one, so do you intend to move?'

'Move?' Tina repeated, as if stunned by the question.

It stunned me, too. Her husband had barely been placed six feet under and already Beryl was demanding to know her plans.

'If so, I trust you won't sell to developers who'll demolish it and build two in its place. These new monstrosities do lower the tone and can bring in people who are, frankly, riff-raff.'

Tina shook her head. 'I won't be selling.'

'Pleased to hear it,' Beryl declared, and with her fears put to rest, she said goodbye and walked away.

The Kincaid residence was in Thyme Park, which is one of the private gated estates which edge Dursleigh. With peaceful, tree-lined roads and large houses set in large gardens, some with tennis courts and swimming pools, it is recognised as a premier residential location. A leading professional golfer lived there for a while and current home-owners include the CEOs from a couple of major companies. Most of the houses were built in the Thirties, though a few, like the Kincaid property, date from Victorian times.

But, as in the area in general, there's an increasing trend to knock down older Thyme Park houses and replace them with multi-bedroomed, multi-bathroomed mansions which stretch from one boundary fence to the other. Or sometimes with two mansions. And recently I heard of a house in another part of Dursleigh where one old lady had lived which, when she'd died, had been demolished and sixteen starter homes erected on the land. 'Pack 'em in' building is happening more and more.

I was thinking that Tina would now be a wealthy woman when an elderly, upright man with U-shaped bags beneath his eyes, and a distinctly bulbous nose, arrived to speak to her.

'Poor girl, how're you feeling?' he asked.

'It hasn't really hit home yet,' she replied, her voice and expression suddenly touched with such fragile vulnerability that the accompaniment of wailing violins would have been appropriate.

'Quite a surprise, Duncan popping his clogs. Seventy-six is no age these days. Don't forget, I'm just over the fence and within calling distance so if I can be of any possible help in any possible way you mustn't hesitate to ask.'

Raising a hand, Tina caressed his cheek with her fingertips. 'You are so kind,' she murmured. 'So very, very kind.'

'I mean it.' He was in earnest. 'If I can be of any help in –'

'If *we* can be of help, Peter,' a voice said sharply.

It was Beryl, she had returned. So the man was Peter of the golf course saga, her husband and, it appeared, Tina Kincaid's next-door neighbour. Which explained the concern about Tina selling her house.

'If we can be of help,' Peter adjusted obediently, 'you must let us know.'

Tina smiled into his eyes. 'I will,' she assured him. 'I will.'

Beryl scowled, then gestured towards two boys, aged around eight and ten, who were making their way along the buffet table, picking up a vol-au-vent, sniffing it and putting it down, then picking up another. The words 'poo', 'gross' and 'fart' could be heard.

'At least you have your grandchildren to cheer you up,' she said.

'*Step* grandchildren,' Tina corrected, as if horrified by the thought of being mistaken for a grandmother.

I don't know why. For me, being a gran is one of the best things in my life and, if it's the age stamp which offends, you can be a grandmother when you're in your thirties. Of course, my granddaughter, Beth, is a little gem with good manners, whereas the boys looked thuggish, spawn of the devil types, and were in drastic need of discipline, which could be why Tina had rejected the connection.

'Managing on your own won't be easy,' Beryl continued. 'At your age.'

Tina's lips thinned. 'I'll survive.'

All of a sudden, heads swivelled, there was a whispering and a flurry of attention. A tall, well-dressed man had entered the room and was cutting an energetic path through the mourners, heading for the widow. I stared, blinked, did a double-take. It was Joe Fernandez, the household-name comedian. What was he doing here?

Joe Fernandez has had his own television show, off and on, for years, and, in his sixties, continues to be popular. He has an easy humour, can tap dance a little, play the piano, sing a little, and is a clever mimic. An all-round entertainer of the old school who has secured his place in the nation's affections. Seen in the flesh, he had aged well. He was still slim, with a thatch of dark hair, which must be dyed, but didn't look dyed, a perma-tan and a winning smile. Still the Latino heart-throb for women of a certain age. Not me. I've always found him too suave, too smooth, a little slippery.

When Tina saw him, she gave a squeal of delight. 'Joe!' she cried.

Then I remembered. Joe Fernandez had been the compère on the Seventies game show where Tina had acted as hostess. How kind, I thought, that after all those years, a big name and busy man like him would take the trouble to come here today and give her his support. A moment later, my cynical side kicked in. Perhaps it was a public relations exercise to show how caring slippery Joe really was. Perhaps the next person to enter the room would be a press photographer, trailed by a TV crew.

'Got delayed, so I couldn't make it to the church,' he said, as he reached his target. 'But I was determined to be with my favourite girl at her time of need.'

Wrapping her arms around him and lifting one high-heeled foot in a decidedly theatrical pose, Tina hugged him close. 'Thanks, Joe, thanks.'

Watching them, I was struck by their glamour and how they were both in such good shape. As if they worked out daily. That jogged my memory. Cripes, the health club presentation. It was the first job Steve Lingard had allotted me and I hadn't even showed up.

'All our equipment – bikes, treadmills, rowers – is linked to a computerised training programme that stores individual work-outs and recalls performance details. These can be accessed from anyplace in the world, which is a big bonus for those of our clients who travel.'

I had slunk into the pale wood lobby with its cantilevered glass roof to discover a small group massed and listening intently to the manageress of the health club who was in full flow. A swarthy well-built guy in a glued-on T-shirt and short shorts had emerged from behind a curved counter to hand me a glass.

'Thanks,' I'd whispered.

This time it was carrot juice. Ugh.

'We have three exercise studios, including one for t'ai chi, another dedicated to capoeira, a speciality, and the third for holistic classes such as Pilates. There's a sauna and steam room, a flotation tank, hot stone therapy –'

'Excuse me,' I said. 'What's capoeira?'

The manageress, a young blonde with a choppy bob, all mousse and highlights, flung an impatient look. She hadn't been pleased when I'd tiptoed in late, pink-faced from hurrying and hoping there wasn't the whiff of alcohol on my breath, and she was not pleased to be interrupted now.

'Capoeira –' She condescendingly spelled the word, which was just as well because I hadn't a clue. '– is the Brazilian martial art and dance form. Our practitioner comes from Brazil.' She smiled at Big Boy Testosterone who had provided the carrot juice. 'We're authentic here.'

'Is capoeira popular?' I asked. 'Do many people do it?'

Her smile narrowed. 'We're still establishing the nature of the requirement.'

As she rattled on; about how the health club would be taking the fitness-on-delivery concept to a new level, about them running classes for several different versions of yoga, about the café bar which would serve organic salads, I took notes. There was no real need – the glossy brochure provided adequate information – but note-taking not only made *me* look authentic, it would also prove to my new boss, should proof be needed, that I was trying hard. Though the thought of needing to prove anything to him rankled.

'If they wish to remain fit and healthy, exercise is essential for those in their later years,' the manageress announced, and I realised she was spearing her words in my direction.

Why? Could she have spotted my chin hairs? The smug cow. But her turn would come. No, it was because a quick glance around showed that I was the oldest person in the lobby. The rest were women in their thirties or early forties, at most, with a smattering of young men; presumably all dedicated to the naked narcissism of 'making it burn'.

But I am fit and healthy, and slim. I've always been slim. I can eat KitKats, crisps, toffee cheesecake, all the high cal stuff, yet never put on weight. Which irritates the hell out of Jenny. She says I'm so lucky and I suppose I am in that I must be blessed with the right genes – all my family tend to be slim. But nerves play a part, too. If I start to worry my appetite goes and I can worry about most anything: dictatorial editors, my father revealing a raffish side, the wellbeing of squirrels. When I divorced, the weight fell off and I became positively skeletal.

'People can lose more than a pound of muscle a year as they age, unless they exercise. That's regular exercise, under tuition,' the manageress added. 'Develop a keep-fit regime and, as the years progress, you'll be firmer and trimmer. You'll benefit.'

She had a point. Even though I am slim, of late I've noticed a tendency towards flab in the form of a blancmange belly and – horror of horrors – the dreaded kimono arms. My mother had them, though her term was 'bat wings', so it must be a family failing.

'Any questions?' the manageress enquired, reaching the end of her spiel.

A young woman asked about a crèche for kids. Yes, there was one, which allowed mothers to enjoy quality time unencumbered, though you needed to book in advance. Another queried the views of the instructors on deep stretching, breathing technique and muscle balance. Both question and answer were delivered in solemn quasi-holy tones and sounded like double-Dutch.

'How much is it to join the club?' I asked, thinking that maybe I should enrol.

Garth House is less than ten minutes from home and surely Steve Lingard wouldn't mind if I took an hour off twice a week? Not if I told him of all the unpaid overtime I've worked over the years, and still do. On second thoughts, he may well kick up. *Would* kick up. In which case I could come in the evenings, then treat myself to a plate of rabbit food for dinner.

'There's an initial joining fee of one thousand pounds, then the membership fee is two thousand pounds a year.'

What! Mercifully I didn't shriek my horror out loud. I may only have myself to support and be comfortable, but there was no way I could justify spending forty pounds a week on knees bend, arms stretch, ra-ra-ra. Yet, by now, embarking on some form of exercise was beginning to seem essential.

'And,' the manageress added, as though this could swing it, 'those who enrol within the next ten days will receive a free Feng Shui C.D.'

Big deal.

Five minutes later when I left the hotel, I was happy to note I felt absolutely no desire to micturate.

I travelled the same route back to the office. The road was clear. The squirrel had gone. Could it have picked itself up, dusted itself down and scampered blissfully off into the bushes? Or, the nightmare scenario, had that Tesco lorry appeared, the still-woozy squirrel becoming stuck to a tyre, meeting a torturous death revolving endlessly round and round?

CHAPTER FOUR

'WE SHOULD DO AN obituary on Duncan Kincaid,' Steve Lingard decreed. 'Alias Lord High and Mighty. Alias self-styled royalty. Alias pompous old git.'

'You knew him?' I asked.

'Several years ago, he put money into an art gallery in Ringley and hosted a grand opening where he lengthily pontificated, the champagne flowed and to which I was invited. We did a piece about it in *The Bugle* and he came in afterwards to thank me. And to tell me what a splendid chap he was and how his beautiful, much younger, wife – who adored him and couldn't leave him alone in bed – had been unable to attend the opening because she was at a health farm. 'Being made even more beautiful.' The art gallery didn't last long. It's one of those tanning studios now.'

'Duncan did have his good points,' I defended him, recalling how he had bragged of Tina 'never leaving him alone' to me, too. 'For years he was chairman of the fête committee –'

'This is Dursleigh's annual summer fête?'

'Right – and he worked hard to make it a success. He was also a master at distributing largesse. Gave generously to all kinds of groups, all kinds of people.'

'I believe he used to flash around wads of notes?'

'He did, which I thought was asking for trouble.'

'Perhaps you'd go along and speak to his widow?'

It was Friday afternoon, three days later, and the editor had summoned me into his office. I hadn't told him about gate-crashing the wake and swigging buckshee wine. Dingbat was not about to confess to faults to him. However, sod's law said that, sooner or later, someone would be sure to reveal my presence and then I'd need to come up with a snappy explanation. Like I'd been shadowing Councillor Vetch?

'You want me to write the obit?' I said.

It must have been because I was in his office, and the association of place with activity, but I was desperate for a smoke. In dire need. I looked around, hoping that a new, small ashtray might have been provided as a courtesy for visitors, but in vain. The office, which had previously been a cluttered mess, was tidier. The wobbly stacks of files had gone from the floor, the books which Eric had left lying around 'for easy reference' were back on the shelves, the desk top was orderly. 'Em of Bridgemont' perfection may not yet have been attained, but it was within striking distance.

The new editor was also far tidier in his personal appearance than the old. Eric had frequently sported food stains down the front of his open-necked shirt and had worn ancient corduroys which were thin at the knees, whereas his replacement arrived each morning in a clean shirt, tie and well-pressed trousers.

Steve Lingard nodded. 'The OAP brigade love them. We're short of space and I'd like to include a photo of Kincaid, so no more than four hundred.'

'You wouldn't prefer to send Melanie?'

It wasn't that I objected to doing an obituary – Duncan Kincaid had been a leading light – my objection was to being given instructions, down to the number of words.

'No thanks. She may have a B.A. in Medieval Literature and 38D boobs –'

I gave a silent groan. 'That right?'

Eric had been fascinated by the girl's chest, which was, I felt sure, the reason why he had employed her, and Tony, too, never missed a chance to ogle. I had despaired of them both and here was a third lascivious male.

'According to Tony. He seems to be a connoisseur.'

'A.k.a dirty old man.'

''Fraid so – but her piece on the indie band is ungrammatical, unstructured and too casual. Sloppy, in fact. She –'

'Melanie is sloppy because she's been allowed to be

42

sloppy,' I cut in. 'But this is her first job and if she's given tighter guidelines, she'll follow them.'

'You reckon?'

'I do. Tony would benefit from a stricter regime, too. What it needs is for him to be motivated, though kick-starting him could take time,' I said, and stopped. The telephone on his desk was ringing.

Steve answered it, then held out the receiver. 'For you.'

'Quick word,' the caller said, 'to let you know that Gifford's has been robbed.'

'Robbed!' I repeated, in surprise. 'When?'

Gifford's is the local jeweller's, a sedate, old-fashioned family establishment, and my caller was Roger, younger brother of a one-time schoolmate and friendly policeman. For years he has given me the nod on anything he thinks might be of interest to the paper. He tells me off the record and I, of course, never reveal his input. In return I've passed on various bits of info which, on occasion, have pointed the police in the right direction.

'Around half an hour ago. One guy with what appeared to be a wrapped up shotgun stood guard at the door, while two others smashed the display cabinets. They wore balaclavas and protective paper suits, and were armed with sledgehammers and machetes, which terrified the staff and a customer. They grabbed watches, rings, jewellery, then drove off in either a Ford Mondeo or a Vauxhall Vectra, the witnesses are divided.'

'Colour?'

'Blue or it could be green, again the witnesses, two old codgers, can't agree. Seems one has cataracts.'

'I meant the colour of the robbers.'

'White – and professionals. Knew exactly what they wanted and what they were doing. Traffic are keeping a look-out for what could be the getaway car, but haven't spotted anything yet. No one hurt, just frightened, shocked and talkative. Bye.'

'Bye.'

'Who's been robbed?' Steve enquired, as I replaced the

receiver.

'Gifford's, it's the jeweller's halfway along the High Street. Happened around thirty minutes ago.' I rose to my feet. 'I'd better get down there and –'

'I'll go.'

'You?' I protested.

'Me.'

'But Eric never did the nitty-gritty, no interviewing and –'

'You don't consider it's the editor's role? Sorry, but I like to keep my hand in.'

'Look, I received the info,' I began heatedly, 'and I know the Giffords, both father and son. I also know the two assistants, old dears who've been there since the year dot, so–'

'I'll cover it,' he said.

I glared. Although, like anywhere else, Dursleigh suffers its share of twenty-first century crime, this is mainly in the form of vandalism, car theft or drunken youths brawling. It was unusual for a shop to be attacked and a firearm flourished, which was why I was eager to get the story. A front page and detailed story which would have the entire village buzzing.

'You're another like Mr P-J, who believes women should know their place?' I demanded.

'No, I don't. And there's no need to be aggressive.'

I could have killed for a cigarette and I could've killed him. Stuck a paper knife into his heart and twisted it. Always supposing he had a heart.

'I'm not,' I snapped.

'With all due respect, you bloody are,' he said amicably. Or was it sarcastically? 'But I want to get to know Dursleigh and to become known in Dursleigh, and this seems an ideal opportunity. However, I promise not to make a habit of stealing your leads. Okay?'

I scowled at the place on the desk where the ashtray used to be and then I shrugged. 'Okay,' I agreed, in who-gives-a-monkey's tones.

'So if you would visit Mrs Kincaid. Please,' Steve said, and smiled.

I gawped. It was the first time I'd seen him smile and the smile which lit up his face was sexy, charming, pure manipulation. His full lips had curved, there were dimples in his cheeks, the grey eyes were warm. Now I understood why old ladies opened up to him. And, yes, when Captain Cool smiled he was handsome. Not male model handsome – his nose was a touch too big for that – but smoulderingly charismatic. Buggeration. But I refused to be cajoled. He had stolen the job I wanted and which I deserved. He was giving me orders. He was the enemy.

'Me, not Melanie? You're sure?'

'Positive. From what I hear, people are always happy to talk to you.'

'You mean I'm the motherly kind?' I asked suspiciously.

I could only be five or six years his senior – well, ten at a pinch – but did he regard me as old? An ageing matron? Another crone to be charmed? He should be so lucky. This gal was made of sterner stuff. It took more than a couple of dimples to reduce me to quivering jelly. A hell of a lot more.

Steve laughed. 'God, no! I just meant – well, you'll be *simpatico*. Would you go this afternoon?' He smiled again, another dazzler. 'I'd be eternally grateful.'

Up yours, matey, I thought.

'Will do,' I said, then added as a kick of defiance, 'as soon as I've finished the hospital waiting times write-up.'

I was damned if I'd be too much of a pushover.

The cars parked along one side of the High Street, combined with a delivery truck unloading on the other, had slowed the traffic to a crawl. Add drivers eyeballing the two police cars stopped outside Gifford's and the crawl resembled that of an infirm snail. There was no sign of Steve, who was doubtless buried in the depths of the shop charming the female assistants.

I turned up the radio where Tom Jones was singing 'Sexbomb'. I like his voice and his dirty laugh. I remember lusting after the young rough trade Tom, belting out songs in his string vest. Though nowadays a string vest seems so tacky. And Sir Tom ain't so young and handsome.

'Get a move on,' I instructed the traffic.

Thirty-odd years ago when I'd sat my driving test, the roads in Dursleigh were empty. Or so it appears in retrospect. But no more. Now at morning and evening peaks, a solid queue can stretch back along the river in one direction and out to the roundabout west of the village in the other. The roundabout with the new lights which had been installed to 'increase the traffic flow', but were creating deadlock, was the one where Tony had dutifully listened to ten feather-spitting drivers.

As I inched my way around a bend, I peered into a charity shop. I was looking for Jenny, then I remembered that this afternoon she was attending a job interview and, besides, she usually did morning stints. Be lucky with the job, Jen, I willed. Be lucky.

Once upon a time jumble sales in church halls dominated the second-hand market, but these have given way to car boots and charity shops. There are three shops in Dursleigh which, although everyone calls it a village, is more accurately a small town. With easy commuting into London and edging onto countryside, it is an affluent town with umpteen estate agents selling 'sought after' properties for one or maybe two million – selling them easily, so my daughter, who works in an estate agency, tells me – and many well-heeled residents. Yet all three charity shops prosper, thanks to mankind's eternal desire to grab itself a bargain. My dad isn't the only one with a frugal streak.

Looking ahead, I caught a glimpse of the river sparkling in the sunshine. The March day was bright, but cold. A brisk wind blew, ruffling the dangling fronds of the willows with their fresh lime-green shoots. I made a mental note to call in at the supermarket on my way home and buy food for the weekend.

As the snail-pace decelerated to a full stop, I helped myself to a mint humbug from the tube which I keep in the door pocket. Steve Lingard had been right, people usually are happy to talk to me. My theory is, it's because I listen. My mother used to say that people have two ears and one mouth because they should listen twice as much as they speak. She believed listening was an art. I am also interested. Interested in the story and interested in the individuals who're involved. I'm fascinated by what makes people tick. What drives them, what they care about, how they function.

What drove Steve Lingard? What made him tick? I wondered. To have been so successful at *The Bugle* he had to have been smart, dedicated... and ruthless? Was it the thought of achieving glory which provided his impetus or the simple satisfaction of a job well done? Might his drive centre on his own aggrandisement, with no consideration for others?

'At last,' I said. The traffic had begun to move.

I drove alongside the river, past the children's play area and around the green, where Field of Hope daffodils bobbed golden heads. Reaching Thyme Park, I turned in. Like so many other roads it had speed bumps, forcing me to slow, hurdle and accelerate, time and time again. The five-bar gate which opened onto the gravelled forecourt of the Kincaid house was closed, so I parked beyond it. Would my journey be worthwhile? After ringing and getting the answerphone – the 'so sorry, my wife and I are unable to take your call right now' message was spoken by Duncan – I had come on chance.

Climbing out of the car, I checked my bag. A somewhat battered black leather shoulderbag which is used whatever my outfit, whatever the season. I had my tape recorder, plus a notebook and pencil. The interview was the kind of colour-by-numbers exercise I can do in my sleep. Not that I minded. When I first joined *The Siren,* I had missed the excitement and tension of my London job as a news reporter with a popular broadsheet. I'd felt I was slumming it. I had longed for something *important* to happen, something which would set the journalistic vibes a-tingle. Like a plane carrying a royal making an emergency landing on the village green or a mysterious multiple murder or an international terrorist pitching up in a local pub. Then, one day, I had recognised that what I wrote about *was* important – to those involved. The problems may seem parish pump and ordinary, but they mattered to ordinary people. And pretty soon they had mattered to me. I was slumming it? Never.

What I did miss, and do still miss, is earning a decent salary. Reporters on small-town newspapers are not well paid – not if they work for Mr P-J – and although I don't have a mortgage and, like I've said, am comfortable, I miss being able to splash out on occasion and indulge myself. But if Steve Lingard could be persuaded to resign as editor and I took over...

'You'll need to cut back on your spending,' a man suddenly declared, in a carrying Hooray Henry voice.

'Yah, get rid of the love god and his personal services for a start,' jeered a second male.

Peering through the budding leaves of the beech hedge which edged the forecourt, I saw two men coming out of the house. Both wore dark suits and had fleshy features and shaven heads, like convicts – or the Mitchell brothers from *EastEnders*. But these brothers were Giles and Simon Kincaid, who may well consider those of us who watch soaps to be the lowest form of human life. Although I knew them by sight I hadn't seen them at the wake, but the small boys sniffing the vol-au-vents belonged to them, so they must have been there. No doubt keeping barge-pole distance from their stepmother who, the grapevine said, they had always resented for frittering away their inheritance and hated with a vengeance.

Their own mother, who had died a couple of years or so before Tina sashayed onto the scene, had been a stocky, talkative woman who helped out in the shops. She had dressed in navy Crimplene and shown a propensity towards a moustache.

The grapevine had also revealed that Duncan Kincaid had planned for his sons to follow him into his businesses, but after attending private schools and going to university, they had both refused.

'Considered shopkeeping was way beneath them and virtually said sod off,' I was told.

But although his dream had been dashed, Duncan had continued to bankroll the pair and later bragged about them being hotshots in their careers.

'Giles is an environmental officer, while Simon does something in the City,' my informant had said. 'Though whether they're as hotshot as Daddy claims – old buffer's given to exaggeration – is anyone's guess.'

'And you can stop buying designer clothes and forget about manicures, Botox injections and having your bikini line waxed,' Giles, the older and bulkier of the duo, went on. 'As for luxury holidays in the Indian Ocean and a new car every other year, lady, those days are history!'

He and his brother were stood on the porch and behind them, in the doorway, was Tina Kincaid. She wore a black trouser suit. Her face was pale and she was twisting her hands. She looked haggard.

'You – you tricked your father,' she accused. 'You've tricked me.'

Simon smiled, a crocodile smile. 'Prove it.'

'Ever since you got your claws into Pop you've been living the high maintenance life and you still have occupancy of the house – *our* house – until you croak, so quit bitching,' Giles snapped.

'Yah, thank your lucky stars,' Simon added.

'Your best piece of luck was in dazzling Pop,' Giles said scornfully, 'though how someone like you could ever've appealed to him, God only knows.'

'Someone like me?' she queried.

The crocodile smile came again. 'He told us about your white-trash family.'

Although Tina shifted uneasily, my knowledge of Giles said that, in his terms, 'white trash' meant people who flew economy class and hadn't received riding lessons as children. In other words, most of us.

'It's you two who are trash,' she countered. 'Your father

49

intended to leave the shares to me. He always said –'

'Old boy's dead and we're off,' Giles cut in. 'Bye.'

He marched down the steps, making for a bright red Aston Martin which was parked alongside a soft-top BMW and a large Mercedes. As he climbed into the driving seat, his brother came to open the gate. The car moved forward, Simon got inside and they roared off in the direction I'd come, not seeming to notice either the Focus or me.

I frowned. The Kincaid brothers made a gruesome twosome. They were men well-fed on self-importance like their father, but lacking his amiability and with a nasty hint of threat. The grapevine had told of a couple of occasions in their younger days when they had thrown their weight around and Duncan had needed to pay to hush things.

When I walked in through the open gate, Tina remained immobile. Her head was lowered and she seemed confused, as if she was finding it difficult to take everything in.

'What a pair of shits,' I remarked, drawing close.

Her head jerked up. She looked surprised by my presence and by my comment, then she gave a weak smile. 'They are. You heard what they said?'

'Everything.'

'I haven't had Botox injections,' Tina declared, lifting her hand to a brow which now seemed remarkably smooth.

I shrugged. Whether the woman had or not was of no concern to me and I certainly wouldn't condemn her. While injections or a face lift don't appeal – I'd be terrified of the procedure going wrong and ending up with a trout pout or that fright lady look – I'm a sucker for anti-ageing creams. Common sense says that lines which have been decades in the making are not going to vanish within weeks, or months, if ever, yet advertisements for a new cream invariably seduce me.

'How did they trick you, trick your husband?' I asked.

'Oh, a year or two ago they persuaded Duncan to put all the shares he owned into their names. They're my stepsons,' she began to explain.

'Giles and Simon, I know. Duncan didn't tell you what he'd done?'

'No. He used to talk for hours about his shares, how he'd made smart decisions and they'd greatly increased in value, so he must've forgotten.' Tina tweaked at the black chiffon scarf which fell over one shoulder. Her scarves were usually fresh and floaty, but this one hung like a dead snake. 'His memory had become... dodgy and sometimes he couldn't remember what he'd done from one minute to the next. Crazy old twit even forgot the names of close friends and I had to remind him.'

'Alzheimer's?' I asked, wondering if this explained why Duncan had erroneously claimed the eagle three – whatever that was – on the golf course and had been so furiously certain that he was right.

'The start of, I think. Giles and Simon had realised there were occasions when he didn't make much sense, couldn't see sense and they took advantage.' Tears welled in her blue eyes. 'They took advantage of an old man, of their own father who'd always done his best for them. Who thought they were little tin gods.'

'That's disgraceful. And they cheated you out of – how much were the shares worth?'

'Over six hundred thousand pounds.'

'Good grief!'

'Duncan had already given them their cash inheritances and he paid for their kids' posh schools.' Putting a hand to her brow, Tina swayed. 'But they're greedy.'

'Suppose I make you a cup of tea?' I suggested. The widow had dark shadows beneath her eyes and looked as if she hadn't slept in days. She also looked on the point of collapse. 'Or a stiff gin and tonic?'

'A gin sounds better. It's this way. Um, who are you?' she enquired, leading the way up the steps and into a cavernous wood-panelled hall, with a scuffed parquet floor covered by well-worn rugs.

'My name is Carol Webb,' I replied. I had wondered if she

might have noticed me at Garth House and remembered, but there had been no glimmer of recognition. Presumably I was the wrong sex. 'I'm a reporter with *The Dursleigh Siren* and –'

She swung round. 'A reporter!'

'Don't worry,' I said quickly. 'I'm not going to write about what I overheard or what you've told me. I know it's all confidential and I shan't broadcast it, I promise. I'm here because *The Siren* would like to print an obituary of your husband. I interviewed him once and we got along fine. I'd also like to say I'm sorry and I understand how devastated you must be feeling.'

I did understand. Until it happens to you, you don't realise how harrowing it is when someone you love dies. My mother's death had created such feelings of desolation inside me and for months I was bereft. And I still haven't recovered from the pain of a much earlier death I suffered. Don't think I ever will.

'Thanks,' Tina muttered.

'So how about me making you that g and t?'

She eyed me warily, then she nodded. I had, I knew, caught her at a weak moment. After the jibes and nastiness of her stepsons, she needed to be with someone sympathetic, needed to talk to someone sympathetic. Anyone. Later she might regret being so open about her husband and his finances, might regret inviting me in, but right now it was comfort. A thumb and a blanket.

'Please, and have one yourself. I've just returned from seeing the solicitors in London about Duncan's will. My stepsons brought me back,' Tina explained, as we went into a small kitchen with dark brown Formica worktops and a chipped enamel free-standing cooker from the Sixties. 'I only realised yesterday that Duncan's pension ended with him, but I'd taken it for granted the share portfolios were mine and I was going to sell them, quickly. But Giles and Simon have scuppered that idea.' She gave her head a bewildered shake. 'The only cash I have is about five hundred pounds which I found in Duncan's trouser pocket. But there are bills to pay.

The undertakers and Garth House, where we went after the funeral. The claret they served cost hundreds. Giles and Simon chose the wine, as they chose the hotel and invited all the people, but left it to me to settle up.'

And stung you regally, I thought.

'What about money in a bank account?' I said.

'Don't have an account. I just used to tell Duncan when I wanted to shop and he'd provide the necessary. He was so kind. There's a few thousand in his bank account, but it seems I can't have that until the will's gone to probate. Whatever that means. And until then –' her voice rose in a plaintive wail '– what am I going to do?'

'Sell something. Where're the glasses and the gin and tonic?'

'Glasses?' She looked blank. 'They're in there. I think,' she said, indicating an upper cupboard. 'Mrs B did everything in the kitchen, prepared the meals and our drinks, and she bought the food. But she's gone to work for Giles. Mrs B was our live-in housekeeper and –' the wail came again '– he's stolen her. Maybe – yes, the gin and the tonic are in here,' Tina decided, opening another cupboard and lifting out bottles. She delved into a large fridge/freezer, American style but ancient. 'Mrs B usually kept slices of lemon in the freezer.'

I poured the gin and tonics, added the frozen lemon, then handed her a glass. No wonder she was distressed. Her husband appeared to have worked along the lines of her 'not worrying her pretty little head' about money matters and she hadn't. The nay-sayers and Jeremiahs may have insisted she had married him purely for his wealth, but she was not the sharpest tool in the box when it came to finance.

'Let's get this straight,' I said. 'You have possession of the house for the rest of your life and then it passes to your stepsons?'

'Yes. Duncan and I had discussed it, and I'd agreed. It's in his will. I don't have any children, pregnancy can ruin the figure, so –' She made an aimless gesture.

'What about the contents, the furniture and such?'

I hadn't noticed anything which looked to be of value, but perhaps there were items the woman could sell. Antiques, silverware, a collection of Ming vases?

'It all stays and is for my use until I die. Though the things which are mine – clothes, shoes, jewellery – I shall leave... to someone,' she said, as if she had no idea who that someone might be. 'Giles and Simon have always hoped I'd fall out of a high window or under a bus, but now they'll be hiring a hit man.'

'You should watch your back,' I said wryly. Her stepsons would begrudge every single day Tina spent in the house and she could live for another thirty years. But the Thyme Park plot must be worth something in the million-pound bracket. 'The money from the shares was meant to support you?'

'Yes. Duncan said if I spoke to the bank manager he'd suggest the best way to invest it to give me a monthly income. But I don't own the shares, so there won't be any income. How will I manage? How can I manage now?'

Presumably, having ensured she was without funds, Giles and Simon intended to pressure her into a deal where she was paid off cheaply and they took possession of the property. She might currently have a roof over her head, but she would need to pay a sizeable amount of council tax for that roof, plus there would be regular outgoings for utilities and upkeep.

'Perhaps you could sell a car?' I suggested, recalling the vehicles parked on the forecourt.

'Yes! Duncan gave me the Mercedes for my birthday, but I found it a pig to park – I'm rubbish at parking – so he took it and bought me the Beemer instead. But the Merc's in my name so no problem there.' Looking cheerier, Tina swigged again from her glass. 'And when the car money runs out I could sell some jewellery. Duncan had a thing about buying me brooches and, to be honest, most are hideous. So old ladyish. So old-fashioned. Of course, he was much, much older than me, like a father really, and his taste was dated.'

'When you get the money from the car and for the brooches, put it into a bank account,' I told her. I don't usually go around issuing instructions to people I've just met, but she seemed to need looking after.

'I will.' Tina knocked back another mouthful. 'Duncan handled all the bills, but I'll have to pay them now. And I'll have to deal with everything else he dealt with, like locking up at night – he made such a fuss about that – and getting the car serviced and making sure there's enough air in the tyres. But I don't know how to fit the air machine at the garage onto the wheels, so –'

'So you read an instruction manual or you ask someone to do it for you. People are very kind,' I said, trying to quell her rising panic.

While I can't claim to be a whizz at 'blokey' things which require a drill or mechanical know-how – to my shame, after Tom and I split, I had had endless trouble opening the bonnet of my car – I am semi-proficient in most areas. And if there is something I can't manage, my dad will always help.

'Really?' she said uncertainly.

'Really. And if you have family living within shouting distance –'

'I don't. My father died when I was a child and my mother –' Tina broke off. She looked wistful. 'I'm all on my own.'

'Then you'll just have to grit your teeth and get on with it. It isn't that bad.'

She pouted, as if teeth gritting did not appeal. 'Are you on your own?'

I nodded. 'Divorced. Simon mentioned the love god. Who's he?'

'Max, my personal trainer. He comes twice a week and his personal services are work-outs, that's all. But he's a handsome guy with muscles to die for and –' she giggled '– he shocks the neighbours. I'm sure they think we spend our time smoking dope or getting up to other kinds of naughties.' Her expression sobered. 'Max costs twenty pounds a throw. He usually charges fifty, he's qualified and it's the going rate, but Duncan gave him money to buy mats and dumb-bells and a couple of exercise bikes, so he reduced the price for me.'

'Your husband and Max were friends?'

'Sort of. They met when Max was giving a fitness demo to the golf club ladies to try to drum up customers. He's an actor, but decided to do personal training in between jobs and was starting up. Max went into the bar afterwards, got talking to Duncan, explained he needed a sponsor and Duncan offered to help. Forty pounds a week seems a lot now,' she said, returning to her money problems, 'but I need to keep in shape. Extra weight adds years and –' She changed tack. 'Max also gives nutrition advice and lifestyle advice and, well, the guy just makes me feel so fantastic.'

'And if the Brothers Gruesome have suggested you get rid, that sounds all the more reason to keep him. Couldn't you get a couple of friends to join in the work-outs and so cut the cost?' I suggested.

'I guess Max'd go along with that. Would you be interested?'

'Me?' I said, in surprise.

I was a stranger and if she needed to ask a stranger to join her in the classes, then she couldn't have any close female friends. How odd. How sad. I have a cosy social circle. Some of the girls – these are fifty-something girls, you understand – I went to school with, others are chums I've made over the years.

'With one of your friends,' she said.

I thought fast; thought of how I would like to exercise and thought of Jenny who was forever fretting over her desire to lose some weight. I also thought of Steve Lingard, and how I would need to ask him if I could have the time off. Life had been so much simpler when there had only been Eric to deal with.

'Yes, though I'll need to check with her. And with my boss.'

'Do that, and I'll check with Max to see if he's agreeable. He comes Tuesday and Thursday mornings, nine to ten.'

'Sounds fine. I'll be in touch,' I said, and took out my tape recorder. 'Now about the obituary.'

My food shopping done, I waited in the checkout queue. Listening to Tina Kincaid talk about her husband, it had become clear how much she had depended upon him. He may have been a 'crazy old twit', yet now there was a gaping hole in her life. She seemed destined to seriously miss the cash and practical day-by-day support he had provided, but how much would she miss the actual man? Had she adored him, as Duncan had claimed, or was it his pampering which had appealed? Did it matter? If she had married Duncan because he was Old Man Moneybags, he had wed his 'child bride' because she was glamorous and made his friends pea-green with envy. It had been a mutually beneficial arrangement.

And where did sex come into things? *Had* it come into things? Duncan may have been quick to imply a vigorous lovelife, but Tina's reference to him being 'like a father' gave a different impression.

Whatever her feelings for her husband, one thing Tina genuinely did care about was getting old. But if you're a head-turner in your youth, it must be grim when your looks start to fade. Every line which appears will seem like graffiti. And if you believe your looks are your only asset, then your self-esteem is doomed to dwindle.

Age doesn't bother me. Not too much. Okay, I would've done a deal with Beelzebub to stick at twenty-nine, but I certainly don't intend to 'rage, rage against the dying of the light' for the rest of my life. What's the point when we all grow old and snuff it anyway? Funny thing is, while the face I see in the mirror is no spring chicken and my body's starting to succumb to the law of gravity, inside I don't feel any different to how I felt at forty. Or thirty. Granted, I don't care so much about people's opinions – I've realised that not everyone is going to like me and I won't like everyone – but basically I feel the same. There's no sense of approaching blue-rinsed oblivion or disappearing into a black hole when I reach sixty.

On the contrary, I reckon there's all to play for in my next decade. When I retire, I plan to write a book. A best-seller which will cover me in literary glory and earn vast royalties. And be made into a film starring either Richard Gere or Clive Owen or Johnny Depp – I haven't decided which yet – who will be knocked sideways by my talent and become a close and admiring friend.

Mind you, I rather fancy myself as a wacky old dame; telling smutty jokes in a loud voice, doddering around in white stilettoes and tight skirts, flirting outrageously with young men. When do you start bragging about your age? I wonder. And stop thinking about sex? In which decade does the libido decrease? Or doesn't it? I could ask my dad, but did I really want to hear his answer?

I focussed on the basket of the man ahead of me. We were in an 'eight items only' line, but he had ten. Should I point it out and object? The older I get, the bolshier I seem to become.

Jenny wouldn't complain. If some oaf barged through the 'eight items only' with a trolley piled high, she would stay silent. With Jen it's anything for a quiet life. She doesn't like conflict or confrontation. Also she always thinks the best of people and is forgiving, whereas I can nit-pick and criticise like crazy. I need to see her to ask if she's interested in the work-outs. There isn't time now – Bruce will be due home and won't welcome an unscheduled visitor – and Jenny is busy with her family at weekends.

She has two sons and a daughter. Victoria, the youngest, is on her gap year and is currently backpacking through Australia, but William and Patrick will be around. Although both work and neither lives at home any longer, at weekends they bring back their washing for 'good old Mum' to attend to, and expect her to cook them meals. Which she does. Full-scale meat or fish and two fresh veg meals, with a home-made dessert to follow. Jenny makes a wicked treacle tart, then spends the next few days eating up the left-overs and the double cream. Despite continually chastising herself.

I remember us as young wives together, in Sale, south of Manchester, where we first met, as neighbours. We used to push our pushchairs, talking nineteen to the dozen, and get whistled at by builders. I felt a pang. When was the last time I got whistled at? It was years ago. But wolf whistles are now politically incorrect. If women receive one, they're supposed to suffer panic attacks, loss of confidence, then take the perpetrator to court. Personally, I'd love to be whistled at again. I'd even settle for a bloke with defective vision.

Though I do still get eyed up by the opposite sex. Men will give me the once-over and smile, or sometimes make a flattering comment. Regrettably, the men who do this tend to be of the short, rotund and bald variety. And over fifty.

I would speak to Jenny on Monday, but if she was in favour of the work-outs I would not, I decided, ask Steve Lingard for his permission to take time off. I could fabricate a reason to be out of the office at the required times and the work-outs may be short-lived. The trainer could turn out to be a no-no or we could soon get fed up. Exercise is notorious for being deadly boring.

All of a sudden, the tinny strains of Grand Valse sounded, sending me rooting in my shoulder bag for my mobile. Around me, the more elderly shoppers cast impatient glances.

'Carol Webb here,' I said, wondering if Steve could be phoning, either to send me off on some new assignment or check up on progress with the Kincaid obituary. But I did not need checking up on. I had been producing the journalistic goods for long enough and could be trusted.

'It's me.'

'Hello, my love. How's it going?' Lynn, my daughter, was calling.

'Badly.' The word fell like a slab of lead.

'Why? What's happened? Is Beth alright?' I demanded, suddenly worried my little granddaughter might be ill.

There was no reason why she should be, but, you know how it is, you always think the worst. As Lynn is my only child – my only living child – so Beth is my only grandchild, and both are precious. Beth is the reason I carry a supply of chocolate lollies, in case I should come across her and Lynn in the village, by chance.

'She's fine. It's Justin. He rushed through dinner last night just so he could watch the stupid football on TV. Then he sat there for hours, swigging beer and shushing me if I dared say a word. And because the side he was supporting lost, he was in a foul mood afterwards. He stomped around –'

As I removed my goods from basket to conveyor belt, had them priced, packed them in a plastic bag and paid the bill, Lynn complained about her partner. She was still complaining as I returned to my car in the car park.

'Men can be like that sometimes,' I said, when she eventually paused for breath. 'You just have to accept it and think how good Justin is with –'

'You want me to be a doormat? Never. I've told him that that kind of behaviour isn't on.'

'Are you perfect?' I enquired. 'Don't you do things which annoy him? Of course you do.'

'I thought you'd be on my side,' Lynn said, and the line went dead.

I put the mobile back into my bag. I hadn't meant to hurt my daughter and I didn't want to fall out. Should I call her back? No, I'd let her calm down, see sense and ring later.

Ring and discover the crisis was over and she had forgiven him.

CHAPTER FIVE

MONDAY LUNCHTIME, I WENT to see Jenny. She also lives on one of Dursleigh's gated estates. With grass verges planted with trees it is attractive, but because the plots are smaller it doesn't possess quite the cachet of Thyme Park. Even so, soaring property prices mean houses there are rocketing in value. Bruce told me recently that their four-bedroom mock Tudor detached is worth more than twice what they paid for it seven years ago. And it was insanely Surrey expensive then.

'So, thanks,' he'd said, the pound signs virtually revolving in his eyes.

Jenny and Bruce came to Dursleigh due to me. When my marriage ended, I packed in my London job and moved back here. It was a comfort thing – even in my forties, I needed the unconditional, all-surrounding love of my mum and dad – but also a coward's retreat. I couldn't face the prospect of continuing to operate in the same journalistic circles as Tom, which would've meant hearing about him, if not actually seeing him. Divorce may have become commonplace, but I found it hard. I refused to mope when Lynn, who was away at university, was around, but alone in the house I used to sit with tears trickling down my face, hiding behind my hands. I wanted to kick things. Viciously. And howl in protest at the moon. *This was not supposed to happen to me.* Call me naïve, but I had believed that, like puppies, marriage was for life and not just for Christmas – or, in my case, not just for twenty-plus years.

Mind you, in public I acted upbeat and perfectly together. 'It's the way things go,' I used to say, and give a philosophical shrug. Others could be the broken-winged victim wife, not me. I'm sure most of my associates believed I was a cool cookie who had taken everything in her stride. It was only my parents and close friends like Jenny who knew the truth.

Jenny had suggested I go north and stay with them for a while, or she could come down to me at weekends. I had said thanks, but no thanks. Bruce would not have welcomed a lodger and would've hated being left alone to look after his kids.

Throughout the years when Tom and I lived in Kensington, Jen and I had kept in touch. We'd telephoned, sent photographs to keep each other *au fait* with our children growing up, and she and Bruce had come to stay with us – minus sprogs – for an annual weekend. For Jen and me, the weekends had been non-stop talkathons, whereas our husbands had struggled to find much to discuss. As a hard-pushed, and hard-pushing, political journalist, Tom had had scant interest in Bruce's tales of growing his own runner beans. While Bruce didn't give a damn about the latest government upheaval.

Then, unexpectedly and to his great delight, Bruce, who had worked for a bank, was headhunted by a firm of financial consultants. The firm's premises were in the south London suburbs – though they've since relocated to a swish custom-built office complex just a few miles from Dursleigh – and when Jenny and Bruce were wondering where to live, they stayed with me. They liked the village with its green and the river, and when I praised the local schools, decided to forget about living in the concrete jungle, a short commute for Bruce was acceptable. His 'golden hello' had included a preferential mortgage which meant they could afford a decent house in a decent location.

Having Jenny close again was good. Whenever I felt down, she'd cheer me up. When I needed to rant against Tom and the slick chick and the bloody injustice of life, she would listen and comfort – as she had listened and comforted during those other dire days long ago in Sale. In time my angst had ceased – even if there were still mornings when I'd wake up and be surprised and, yes, disappointed to find Tom wasn't beside me – and I'd realised that there is a future after marriage.

Now Jen and I get together about once a week; maybe for five minutes or maybe for an evening, it depends on what's happening. If Bruce is off on one of his business trips, we'll go to the cinema or Jenny will come round for a microwaved dinner and we'll talk. Part of the attraction is our differences. She reckons I'm sophisticated, daring, a bit of a hippy – if I am, it's only in comparison to her – and some of the things I say shock her. Whereas I respond to Jen's homeliness and reliability and, though I'm nowhere near as puritanical, I respect her strict moral code.

As someone who's been happily married to the same man for thirty years, was a virgin when she married him and has only ever slept with him, Jenny is a member of an endangered species. But I admire her, envy her stability and it's comforting to know that such people exist. Comforting to know long-term true love is still alive and kicking. And possible. My parents' age group had the knack, but many of my generation seem sadly lacking. And heaven help the next lot.

When I arrived I saw Jenny through the glass of the front door, making her way backwards down the stairs, wiping the skirting board. And this on a Monday when she would've changed the bed – she and Bruce sleep between fresh sheets each week – done the washing, half of which was probably already ironed, and tidied the house after the weekend. In addition to hating conflict, Jenny can't stand mess. So her windows gleam, the carpets are always spotless and nothing – no jackets, shoes, magazines – is left lying around. It's a joke with her kids that if they put something down for more than thirty seconds, Mum will clear it away. Though I have heard Victoria mutter about her being 'anal' and needing to 'get a life'.

I tapped on the door. 'Hello,' I mouthed.

'Come in, come in. Lovely to see you,' Jenny said, smiling and hugging me. 'Carol, you look terrific. I wish I could wear black leather trousers, but –' she sighed.

'You can.'

'You're being kind.'

'I'm not.' Actually I was, but if you can't be kind to your

friends it's a poor do.

'No, my bottom's too big and my legs are too short. Plus I need trousers with an elasticated waist.'

'Stomachs are a design fault,' I commiserated, when she looked down at her rounded tum.

'And some are faultier than others,' Jenny said ruefully. 'Will you have a coffee and a sandwich? A smoked salmon sandwich? I was just about to make one for myself.'

'Yes, please.'

It wasn't by chance I'd called in at lunchtime. I had done so many times before and Jenny had always produced something far more appetising than Pot Noodles or the door-step cheddar cheese baps sold by the baker.

'William loves smoked salmon, so I often buy some for the weekend,' she said, shunting me through to her granite work-topped, stainless steel-applianced kitchen, 'but he didn't appear. Couldn't spare the time. Remember I told you he was thinking of moving from his bed-sit to live with Becci in her flat? Well, that's what he was doing.' She looked pained. Jenny doesn't approve of people having 'partners' and 'living in sin', so for her son to go down that route is a major disappointment and worry. 'The only good thing is that the flat has a washing machine and tumble-dryer, so William will no longer arrive here carrying a huge load of dirty laundry.'

'Which will make it easier for when you start work,' I said, though I doubted the lad handling his own washing and ironing would last for long.

Following his father's example, William is not big on the domestic front. And Becci, his girlfriend with attitude, is not the type to do his washing for him. Jen lives in perpetual fear of the girl and when I met her, at one of Jenny and Bruce's dinners, she scared me half to death, too. A trainee solicitor, Becci burns with contrary opinions. She'll argue about everything from the judicial system, to the merit of lip gloss over lipstick, to which English county has the most woodland. I'd said Surrey, whereas she proclaimed it was West Sussex. For definite. I checked later and I was right, though, if we should meet again, I doubt I'll pluck up the courage to tell her.

'How did the interview go?' I asked.

Jenny switched on the coffee machine. 'Not well.'

I had guessed it hadn't. I knew that if she'd been offered the post of Personal Assistant – the latest term for secretary – with a local housebuilding firm, she would've telephoned me straight away to share the good news.

'What happened?' I said.

It was her third interview and she had told me about the others. How the jargon had had her floundering. How the emphasis had seemed to be on 'delving into her psyche'. How she'd been asked to talk about a matchstick for two minutes.

'I was one of six applicants and we'd been summoned *en masse*.' She took a multi-grain loaf from the breadbin. 'I was the oldest, by far, and the pair who interviewed us – Mandy, who was Head of Human Resources, and Damian, the Team Leader – seemed so aware of my advancing years that I don't know why they'd ever asked me to attend. Damian remarked on my not having been in paid employment since the late Seventies, which was before he was born. Made me want to reach for my Zimmer frame!'

'Perhaps they were frightened of being criticised as 'ageist' and sued, so you were the token oldie,' I suggested, only half joking.

'Could be. Before I started attending interviews, I wasn't particularly conscious of my age and I didn't consider fifty-three to be decrepit. I'd read that being in your fifties is fashionable, because it's our generation that has the spending money. And sixty is said to be the new forty, which makes us only thirty-something. But now I'm beginning to feel as if I've been around since Moses was a lad.' Jenny pulled a face. 'Anyhow, Mandy explained that after everyone'd been seen we should wait, then she and Damian would confer and announce their choice.'

'Sounds like taking part in *Pop Idol*.'

She smiled, buttering the bread. 'It was. The company operate a policy of all-week dressing down and Damian, who had that gelled spiky hair, was in a polo shirt and chinos, so he looked like someone from *Pop Idol*. Though a kid contestant, not a judge. I'm getting the hang of the lingo,' she went on, 'so I was able to trot out which packages I have. But they were keen on 'people skills' and 'communication skills'.

'Which are simple common sense.'

'Exactly. When I last applied for jobs, the main concern was shorthand and typing speeds, but these days they throw such oddball questions. Like 'what are you most proud of in your life?'

'To which you replied?'

'My children. Yes, the minute I'd said it I knew they'd been looking for something sexier,' she said, when I raised my brows.

'Such as going hang-gliding off Mount Everest or the time you'd arm-wrestled an alligator and won.'

'Similar.' She was laying slices of smoked salmon on the bread. 'They gave the job to a foul-mouthed girl in her twenties, who was wearing a skin-tight dress with one bare shoulder. And Mandy's comment to me as I left was that I hadn't been 'sufficiently pro-active'.'

'So at the next interview you'll go topless, scatter f-words like confetti and tell them about your days in the SAS?'

'You'd better believe it.'

'Are there any more interviews in the offing?' I asked, as we sat down at the table. A neatly set table, with linen placemats and napkins and milk in a jug.

'No, but I've posted off three more applications so keep your fingers crossed. And if you should happen across Bruce, remember that everything's hush-hush.'

'It is?' I spoke through a mouthful of sandwich. I was starving. 'Why?'

'Because now if I mention finding a job, he gets annoyed. He says he earns more than enough to keep us in considerable comfort, so what's the point. But he's missing the point. Although I've always been happy at home I feel as if I've spent my entire life being someone's wife or someone's mum and now –' she sighed '– I want to be myself and do my own thing. To earn my own money and have a measure of independence.'

'So you go for it, gal!'

'I shall, but I've decided to say nothing more about attending any interviews. I'll wait until I'm successful and hit him with it as a *fait accompli,* he'll be pleased for me then.'

Would he? Bruce has always run the show. Not in any domineering manner – he's an amiable guy – but he's the boss. And can be a touch lordly. Most of the time Jenny agrees with whatever he wants or suggests, though if she doesn't she doesn't argue. She lets him have his own way. I'm sure the reason he's opposed to her working is because, although he would never admit it, he believes that having a wife who stays at home and whom he supports imparts extra status. Being the sole breadwinner makes him king of the midden. Like my dad, Bruce also expects to be waited on hand and foot. Which he is. Jenny even packs his suitcase when he goes away, then gets chastised if he doesn't have the particular colour of shirt he wanted.

It was Bruce who landed Jenny with the charity shop sessions. One of his colleagues, now retired, had a wife who was active in cancer – shops, fairs, appeals – and the man had spoken of how desperate they were for help. Seems the average age of volunteers is seventy and charities have great trouble finding replacements because so many younger women work. Bruce had offered Jenny's services. He had offered without consulting her, which is typical. And she had uncomplainingly agreed, which, again, is typical.

'How're you getting along with your new boss?' Jenny enquired, as we ate.

'We're co-existing, just, but the man's a control freak. He insists on giving me orders, which I do not appreciate.'

'You won't. You've been a free agent for so long. But shouldn't an editor give his reporters orders?'

'Not when the reporter in question could teach him a thing or two!'

'Any sign of him becoming disaffected with working at *The Siren*?'

'Not yet, but it's early days.'

'He has to be better for the paper than Eric.'

I made a face. 'That's what Lynn says.'

'How is she?'

'Fine. Grumbling about Justin watching too much footie on the box, but she'll get over it.'

I had rung my daughter back and been treated to another roiling complaint which, thankfully, had been cut short because Beth had been eager to tell me about a police lady on a horse who had visited her playgroup. The children had been allowed to pat the horse which had proceeded to produce a steaming mound of manure, causing much giggling hilarity.

'Any mention of Lynn and Justin getting married?' Jenny said hopefully. She asks this every few months, has asked it for years, but my answer is always the same.

'None. Like you, I'd prefer them to marry, for Beth's sake. And yet does a ceremony and a piece of paper really make that much difference?'

'It makes a big difference,' she declared. 'Within five years of the birth of a child, fifty-two percent of co-habiting couples have broken up, compared with only eight per cent of married couples. Though eight per cent is bad enough. And it's common knowledge that children from one-parent families – usually without a father around as a role model – can suffer all kinds of emotional, educational and social difficulties.'

I felt flattened. 'Oh dear,' I said.

Jenny is full of facts, often surprising facts. It's the legacy of years of sitting at home and scrutinising *The Daily Mail* while she eats her lunch. She's also good on trivia, the showbusiness kind. She can quote the exact heights of Tom Cruise, Hugh Grant and Rob Lowe – poor guys are surprisingly short – knows Donald Duck's middle name – it's Fauntleroy – and that Charlie Chaplin once came third in a Charlie Chaplin look-alike contest. Not that this information is of the slightest use, but it's something she remembers. And she believes that if it is printed in the national press, it must be the copper-bottomed truth. Although I have advised her differently.

'Patrick's company has offered him a move to New York,' she said, in such an abrupt change of subject that I guessed she'd been thinking about William and Becci having a child out of wedlock – and hated the idea. 'It'd be a big promotion.'

'Will he take it?'

Patrick works for an international bank and already earns a high salary. He's loose-limbed and lanky, with the kind of floppy, pale brown hair which is usually seen on ponies. He was born a few months after my son and I've always had a soft spot for him.

'Probably. Bruce thinks he should. So when Victoria goes to university in September we'll be empty nesters with a vengeance,' she said, and frowned, as if unsure about this prospect of new-found freedom.

'Did you speak to Victoria at the weekend?' I asked.

'No, she didn't ring, though she usually does. I hope she's alright.'

'She will be. She can look after herself.'

She could, too. Not in any degree her mother's daughter, Victoria was tough, unafraid and sassy. Often cruelly sassy. On one occasion she'd told Jenny she had no neck, just a double chin, while on another she'd said she sounded like a barmaid out of *Coronation Street*. Poor Jen, the comments had really wounded.

'I suppose so.' There was a pause, then another change of subject. 'Have you changed your mind about going out on a date with Russell? He's obviously taken with you.'

Her conversational turns are always for a reason. Often to block out worrying thoughts. And chances were she was now imagining Victoria being kidnapped, raped or eaten by a shark. Like me, Jenny inevitably zeroes in on the worst possible scenario.

I shook my head. Although my New Year's Eve dinner partner had rung a couple of times since to suggest we meet, I had made an excuse. 'No, and I won't. As you know, he doesn't appeal. Last week I went to see a woman called Tina Kincaid,' I said.

Now it was me who was changing the subject, but I didn't relish another encouragement to think again about Russell because then, maybe, I'd experience a thunderclap which would weld us together, hearts, bodies and minds, for life.

'Tina the fashionista,' Jenny said. 'She used to be a model, then appeared in a show on television. Her husband was buried last Tuesday.'

'That's right. I'm writing his obituary. I wasn't aware Tina had modelled.'

'She was one of the top girls of her day. On the cover of *Vogue* and in high demand.'

'She could still model, she looks terrific.'

Jenny nodded. 'I was in the charity shop when her husband's funeral cortège went by and I saw her. You'd never think she's almost sixty.'

'That old?' I protested.

'We're not exactly light years away from the big Six-O ourselves,' Jenny said wryly, and poured cups of coffee. 'Do you ever look at a picture of someone in the paper and think 'grief, they're ancient', then discover you're older than they are?'

'Often.'

'Me, too. There's a theory that, as the decades progress, we all start to think we're fifteen years less than our actual age, and I reckon it's true. I find it hard to believe I'm in my fifties.'

'Yes, fifties means staid and clapped-out and sexless, until you hit them yourself. Then –' I shimmied my hips '– you realise fifties are vibrant with a capital V. How do you know how old Tina Kincaid is?'

'Because I remember reading about her being five years younger than Joe Fernandez and he's sixty-four. He was on television the other night, joking about the relevance of the Beatles' song. At one time there were rumours about him and

70

Tina Kincaid – Tina Sinclair, as was – getting married.'

'I thought he already was married?'

'He is, but it seems that when she joined his programme they began an affair. She'd recently been divorced from a husband who dealt in rare books, he was a highfalutin type, and Joe –' Jenny indicated quotation marks '– 'helped her to recover'.'

'I never knew that,' I said, though the comedian's appearance at the wake took on a different slant.

'They didn't advertise their affair, but it lasted a good number of years and then, suddenly, it was over. His wife suffered from an illness, ME or MS or something, can't remember, and the tale was that when it came to the crunch Joe couldn't bring himself to desert her.'

'Or didn't fancy the bad publicity that deserting an ill wife might bring.'

'Could be.'

'Then Tina chanced across Duncan Kincaid and – hey presto!'

'But was it by chance?' Jenny said. 'Or had she heard he had plenty of cash, knew he was a widower and recognised an opportunity? Seems she'd been living in Dursleigh for a while before they met, so –'

'She had?' I consider I'm well informed about the village, but I wasn't aware Tina had resided locally prior to her marriage. Nor that Duncan Kincaid was her second husband. 'How do you know all this?'

'Eileen, who works in the charity shop, told me. Eileen never stops talking. If she's not describing her and her husband's latest health scare – she's forever at the doctor's with some complaint or other, while he, poor soul, suffers from erectile dysfunction –'

'That must've been some description!'

Jenny grimaced. 'It was – she's recycling local gossip. She reckons there's something iffy about Tina Kincaid's background.'

'Iffy?'

'Eileen's convinced she has something to hide. Seems that when Tina and Duncan got married no one from her family attended and there's not been sight nor sound of a relative ever since.'

I recalled Giles Kincaid's 'white trash' remark. 'Eileen thinks Tina could've banished her family from the scene because they're down-market?'

'Down-market or they're all mass murderers or nudists, she hasn't a clue. She's just a busybody who loves to create tittle-tattle.'

'Tina told me her father died when she was little and her mother isn't around now, either. And if she was an only child –' I moved my shoulders.

'It must be sad to grow up without a dad and I can't imagine not having any family. True, my parents and sisters are up north, but we're forever telephoning or popping up and down to see each other. Poor woman, all alone with no one to care what happens to her.' Jenny gave a sympathetic sigh. 'And you're writing Duncan Kincaid's obituary?'

'It'll be in the paper this week, so long as Tina produces the photograph of him which she promised. Produces it by the end of today.' After the sandwich and coffee, a cigarette would have been perfect. I restrained myself. Jenny's is a non-smoking household and although she's never objected on the rare occasions when I have lit up – and doesn't complain when I light up in my own home – I'm conscious that she would rather I didn't. 'How do you fancy working out and becoming lean and mean?' I went on. 'Tina Kincaid has a personal trainer whom she'd like to share. I've said I might go along and she asked if I knew anyone else who would be interested.'

'So you immediately thought of me?'

I was about to say 'yes', then I realised that Jenny had bridled. It was alright for her to complain about being overweight, but she didn't welcome acknowledgement from elsewhere. I remembered how once I'd suggested she try Weight Watchers and received a surprisingly frosty look.

'No, no, I just wondered if it might seem like fun,' I

replied, acting so darn casual I almost slid off my chair. 'Personal trainers are all the rage and your street cred would soar with Victoria if you had one, or a third of one.' I told her the days and time. 'How about it?'

'Ever since New Year, Bruce has been using the gym at work,' she said. 'He's lost nearly a stone and on Saturday he bought himself a sports jacket from Balmour's.'

'Gee whizz!'

Balmour's is a gents' outfitters which has recently moved into Dursleigh, replacing a butcher who could no longer compete with the nearby superstores. They sell clothes which carry designer labels and designer prices.

Jenny smiled. 'He surprised me, too. I never thought he'd spend so much or be so trendy, but I must admit he looks good in the jacket.'

He would look good, especially slimmer. Bruce is boxy-shouldered and of medium height, with mid-brown hair greying at the temples. A slightly formal bloke of the 'decent honest citizen' variety.

'You want to watch it,' I said. 'New jacket, working on the pecs, losing the love handles – it's the giveaway sign.'

'Of what?'

'A cheating spouse. Of another woman, stupid!' I expected her to laugh. She didn't, she looked… anxious. But Bruce has never had a wandering eye, never been one for chatting up the girls, and Jenny told me that when Tom and I divorced he'd vowed he couldn't have coped with the hassle, so she was 'stuck with him for all eternity'. 'Just kidding,' I said.

Now she did laugh, though it was a synthetic laugh. 'I've seen much fatter women than me wearing leather trousers,' she announced. 'One or two who must've been at least a size 20.'

'You're what – a 16?'

'Right, and that's the average size for women in the U.K. these days. Marilyn Monroe was a size 16 when she sang 'Happy Birthday' to President Kennedy. I ought to cut down on the calories, but I feel I'm failing in my duty if there aren't home-made cakes and flapjack in the tin.'

'Rubbish!'

It is years since I've baked, let alone made pastry, and now I wouldn't know where to start.

'And Bruce will buy me Belgian chocolates as a regular treat. The times fit in with my hours at the shop, so I will come with you to Tina Kincaid's,' Jenny decided. 'But as soon as I get a job I'll need to stop.'

I nodded. 'Understood, old chum. Understood.'

Melanie wiggled her fingers in farewell. 'See you tomorrow.'

'See you,' I replied.

It was dead on five. The girl may be sloppy in her grammar, punctuation and spelling, but she was meticulous when it came to clocking-off. She often cut it fine arriving in the mornings, too. Yet she professed an earnest desire to be a reporter on a national paper and talked enthusiastically of *The Siren* as 'work experience'. The door clicked shut behind her, the thump of her clumpy shoes on the stairs receded and the general office fell silent. Tony had been sent off on a job by our new lord and master, and wouldn't be back.

The Siren occupies a rambling, pebble-dashed villa on a road off the High Street. The Advertising Department is downstairs and the Editorial upstairs. The general office is two rooms knocked into one and is open-plan, with screens to give privacy placed between each of the three work stations. The editor's office is out along the corridor, with a small interview room beyond it.

I was jotting down questions to ask an eighty-six year old 'fearless great-grandmother' who had sky-dived ten thousand feet to raise money for charity, when Steve Lingard came in.

'Would it be all right if I took an hour off on Tuesday and Thursday mornings to do a fitness class?' I heard myself ask, and could have kicked myself.

I had decided to say nothing, but inside me runs a seam of honesty which stubbornly, maybe stupidly, insists on playing fair. It's an honesty which has had me returning a hundred pounds to a bank clerk when he'd miscalculated and handed over too much, which means I take a taxi, rather than use my car, if I suspect I could be over the drink-drive limit, which demands I tell people in queues if they are ahead of me. My mother is to blame. She could spot a fib a mile off and never let me, or my brother, get away with one.

'I'm out on average two evenings a week for *The Siren*,' I continued, mustering my case, 'and –'

'No problem.'

'You don't object?' I said, in surprise.

Steve shook his head. 'I've been going through the back copies and you've contributed a hell of a lot of stuff. The greater proportion by far. And, whatever Eric may've claimed, I suspect it's been like that for years?'

'The cock croweth, but the hen delivereth the goods,' I quoted.

The back copies are the last three months' worth of original reports which are routinely filed and kept in case of complaints or if legal factors should come into play.

'I've also taken a look at the wages bill,' he continued, 'and it seems that you don't get paid overtime for the evenings nor for any weekend work.'

'Never have been.'

'So go ahead.'

'You're sure?' While I was grateful for his agreement, I hadn't expected it to come so easily.

'I'm sure. Are the fitness classes at Garth House?'

'No, at Tina Kincaid's with her personal trainer. She's asked me if I'd like to join her.'

'Maybe you'll be inspired to write about the craze for aerobics?' he suggested.

'Maybe. And –' I shone a sweet smile of entreaty '– maybe you'll allow me to use my own judgement on whether or not to follow up a story, without asking for your permission?'

'No can do,' he said. 'You must ask. We need to discuss.'

My smile switched to a glare. Who did he think I was, some thoughtless, careless two-bit junior?

'You may be *le grand fromage,*' I began, 'but –'

'Submission's not your strong point, is it? Look, Eric may not have given a damn, but for me –' Steve starfished a hand on his chest '– it's important to consider the content of each page and the issue as a whole, and to strike the right balance. Hence, before you rush hither and thither gathering stories, we must discuss.' He was all sweet reason. 'And I'm sure that nine times out of ten, we'll agree.'

'Huh!'

I could see the sense in what he said and knew that consulting him was good manners, but I resented it all the same. Resented it deeply.

'Did you hope to take over as editor when Eric departed?' he enquired.

'Yes, and I'd do a damned good job, but the powers-that-be were not in favour. Are you happy to be saddled with *The Siren?*' I retaliated. 'To be running yet another provincial paper, which may not necessarily respond to your loving touch? Don't you yearn for greater things?'

'Are you hoping I'll lose heart and quit, then you can take over?'

'You bet I am,' I said, being honest again.

'Tough shit, I'm here for the duration.'

I scowled. He sounded as though he meant it.

'When you've got the hang of things are you planning to get rid of Tony, Melanie and me, and replace us with favoured underlings from *The Bugle?*' I demanded.

'You think I have 666 tattooed on my scalp?'

'I thought I caught a glimpse above your left ear.'

'Thanks, but I'm not planning to get rid of anyone. Not yet. What I do plan is to put fire into bellies, Tony's and Melanie's. Though not yours, you're combustible enough. As for yearning for greater things, I happen to like running a provincial paper. In my younger days I worked on a national–'

'Which one?' He told me. 'I worked for the competitor,' I said.

'I know. I've read your c.v. But –'

'What about your c.v.?' I cut in.

'My first job was with a free daily London paper, then I went to the national. After eight years or so, I moved to Bristol and became deputy editor, later editor, for a local paper. I was settled there, until someone in the business suggested to Mr P-J that I'd make a good editor for *The Bugle*. The job offered a challenge and I like challenges.' He shrugged. 'But I've never regretted opting for a quieter life. Slightly quieter, with fewer late nights. More hands-on, which appeals. And one big advantage was that a couple of years ago when my wife and I split up, I could be around for my kids.'

'You're divorced?' *The Bugle* reporter had not mentioned this and I had simply assumed he was married.

'Same as you, again.'

'How many children do you have?'

'Two. A girl, Debbie, who's fourteen, and Paul, who is twelve. They come and stay over in my flat sometimes and actually –'

He broke off at the sound of high heels clattering up the stairs. A moment later, the office door swung open and Tina Kincaid came in. She looked around and saw me.

'Hello,' she said, then her gaze went to Steve. 'Hello,' she said again, but this time the word was lower, throatier, breathier. Soignée in a cream trouser suit worn with a jazzy cream, brown and purple top and cream skyscraper stilettos, she steered her way across the room towards us. 'You asked for a photograph to go with Duncan's obituary and I've brought a selection so that you can choose.'

Although the words should have been meant for me, she was smiling at Steve. Not just smiling, she was looking at him as if he was the most desirable hunk in the world. And he was smiling back, widely. The sap.

'This is Mrs Kincaid,' I told him.

'Call me Tina,' she said.

'Pleased to meet you, Tina. I'm Steve Lingard, the editor. New editor.'

She stepped closer to him. 'The man in charge,' she purred.

'May I say how sorry I was to hear about your loss.'

'Thank you.' There was the tragic bite of a lower lip. 'I'm not very good at being alone.'

'It can be hard at first,' he said.

'You're on your own, too?' she enquired, and made big eyes. Big brown eyes. Funny, I could've sworn her eyes were blue.

Steve nodded. 'Divorced.'

'Perhaps you should decide which photograph you think is suitable. There's one of me and Duncan on our wedding day which is good.' She giggled. 'At least, I think it is.'

'Let's have a look,' he said.

Tina glanced at the cream suede bag which she was holding, a lozenge shaped affair with a cane handle. 'There are rather a lot. If I could spread them out somewhere? Perhaps on your desk?'

'Good idea. Excuse us, Carol, will you? It's this way,' Steve said, and ushered her out to his office.

Great! It was me who had spoken to the woman and written the obituary, but I was not to be included in the photo choosing process. Normally, I wouldn't care. It was a minor decision which I'd be happy to leave to the editor. But today I felt rattled and now I began to understand why the wives of Duncan Kincaid's friends were not too keen on Tina. If there was a man around, did she always ignore the women? As for Steve; he was so pathetically predictable. Couldn't he recognise that her purring, the big eyes etc., was a well-rehearsed act?

I had returned to compiling my 'fearless great-gran' questions when footsteps sounded again on the stairs. This time, when the door opened, a young girl came in. She was clad in a denim jacket and the baggy, pocketed cargo pants which so many teenagers wear these days, wear at half mast. She had long dark hair and carried a sports bag.

'I'm looking for Mr Lingard. My father,' she said shyly.

'Come in.' I beckoned her forward. 'You must be Debbie.'

'That's right.' She grinned. 'Dad's told you about me?'

'He's mentioned you. And your brother. Your father's in his office, but there's someone with him so, if you'd like to wait a few minutes.' I indicated a chair beside me. 'Take a seat.'

'Thanks.' She sat down.

'I'm Carol, by the way. Carol Webb. I write for the paper.'

'I like to write, too,' the girl said. 'I write stories. Just for myself, though maybe some day I'll send one to a magazine.'

'You should. It's always worth a try. I started by writing stories when I was fourteen.'

'Did you?' She was full of interest. 'What kind of stories?'

'I remember one was about a girl singer in a pop group, called Natasha, who was madly beautiful with long blonde hair and who had all the boys fighting over her. She rescued a kidnapped baby while fighting off thugs, exploding tennis balls and a wicked ghost along the way. Of course, Natasha was me. Or how I would've liked to be.'

Debbie laughed. 'I write things like that sometimes, thought mostly I write about animals, pets of various sorts. Was your Natasha story published?'

'No, but it was good practice because eventually I did sell another one, then another. In time I had articles, usually humorous ones, accepted by newspapers and magazines and I decided I wanted to be a journalist.'

'Next time I come in here, if I brought one of my stories would you read it and tell me what you think about it? If it's any good?'

'With pleasure. And I'll be honest.'

'Thanks. I'm here because Mum has a fair meeting which could last until late, so Paul and I are spending the night at Dad's. Paul's at football practice, so he's going straight on from there, but I said I'd meet Dad here. Then he'll drive me over. And he'll take us to school in the morning.'

'What's a fair meeting?' I asked.

'Mum runs a stall selling New Age stuff and promoting crystal therapy at psychic fairs, and tonight the organisers are fixing next year's programme. The fairs are held all over the south of England. A few years ago, Mum 'saw the light' and became interested in astrology and the spiritual and crystals. She reckons crystals have healing properties and are a conduit for energy.' Debbie grinned. 'Dad thinks she's wacky. Mum's also become a vegan which is a real pain, so Paul and I love it when we stay with Dad. Tonight he's promised to do us bacon, egg and sausages. Yummy!'

'Your mother doesn't object to you eating that kind of food?'

'No. She knows Dad has different ideas to her and accepts that what he does in his own place is up to him. Dad's nifty at cooking. He used to cook sometimes when we all lived together and, if Mum was busy, he'd do the ironing.'

I thought of how, in over twenty years of marriage, Tom had never wielded an iron – and how Bruce probably wouldn't even know where the iron was kept. As for either of them making meals – big joke.

'Sounds the ideal husband,' I said.

'Mum used to think so. She still likes him, y'know. And he likes her. They had an amicable divorce.' The girl leant forward, speaking confidentially. 'Paul and I think they might get back together again, but don't say anything to Dad.'

'I won't,' I promised.

'He's stressy about the divorce. Feels guilty. Oh, hi, Dad,' she said, as Steve and Tina came into the room.

Tina was in the middle of telling him how much she approved of his choice of photograph, but he raised a hand in greeting.

'Hi.'

'I know Duncan would've been delighted,' Tina continued, slinging Debbie and me a quick glance before concentrating again on Steve. 'And he would've been delighted that you wanted to print his obituary. For him to be acknowledged in such a way – I'm really grateful.'

'Your husband was a leading member of the Dursleigh community,' he told her.

'You think so? Duncan would've been so proud and –'

Clasping Steve's arm, she gazed up at him. 'You are so kind.'

'It was Carol who wrote the obituary,' he said.

Tina spared me another quick glance. 'Thanks. I must go. Lovely to meet you,' she told Steve. 'Bye.' She crossed to the door which lead out to the stairs. 'Oh,' she said, suddenly remembering, 'I'll see you in the morning, Carol.'

'You will. With my friend, Jenny, just before nine,' I replied. I had been wondering if she would mention it. 'I assume Max is agreeable?'

'He is. Bye-bye, Steve,' she sang, and gave him a wave before she disappeared.

Debbie grinned. 'You've got yourself an admirer there, Dad. And she is rather glam. For someone that old.'

'She's a good-looking woman,' he said. 'Her husband died recently and the housekeeper's left, and she was telling me how difficult she finds it, just coping with simple things. Like working the washing machine and the cooker, and removing a spider from the bath – seems she gave up on that. She's also been having trouble with radiators not heating up, so I explained how to bleed them.'

Debbie wrinkled her nose. 'Sounds a bit of an airhead.'

'Maybe,' he said, 'but you can't help feeling sorry for her.'

'Talking of feeling sorry for people, I was wondering if you could give me a sub from next week's pocket money, please?' his daughter asked, and rose. With her cargo pants softly scuffing the wooden floor, she ambled over to him. 'Pretty please. There's a new teenage magazine just come out and every girl in my class has it, except me. This week's issue has a give-away make-up bag which is wicked.'

'How much?'

'Two pounds fifty.'

'Two pounds fifty for a kids' magazine?' he protested.

'I mean, like, hello!' Debbie said. 'Two pounds fifty is nothing.'

I grinned. 'When your father was a boy, you could feed a family of four for a week on two pounds. And magazines cost six pence. That's six old pennies.'

She pulled a face. 'So he's always telling us. Once he made such a fuss over the cost of an ice-cream. We'd gone down to Brighton and he told the girl in the kiosk it was daylight robbery. Like as if she fixed the price.' She sighed. 'Dad can be so *gay*.'

I looked at Steve. 'Gay?' I queried.

'Teenage speak for embarrassing.'

'They have the magazine in the newsagents around the corner,' Debbie said. 'I checked. But they're selling fast and if I'm the only person who doesn't have one –'

'I give up.' Putting a hand into his trouser pocket, Steve brought out coins. 'Here's three quid. Keep the change. And it's not a sub, it's a gift.'

Standing on tiptoe, Debbie kissed his cheek. 'You're the top of the pops. Be back in a minute.'

'Isn't parenthood fun?' I said, as the girl rushed out.

He groaned. 'She's becoming expensive. Last week it was nail polish she wanted, but not just one bottle, five, because each nail on her hand had to be a different colour. Kids!' he complained, then smiled. 'Forgive the ramblings of a grumpy middle-aged man. There are times when I remind myself of my father and he's the prototype for Disgusted of Tunbridge Wells.'

I began to clear my desk. It was time to go home. 'Debbie was telling me about your amicable divorce.'

Steve frowned. 'Kid's a blabber-mouth.'

'But it was amicable?'

He hesitated, as if unsure about talking about his personal life – or talking about it to me. Which was fair enough. We were not confidants. Nowhere near. In fact, we barely knew each other and, for much of the time, the situation between us could be described as unarmed combat.

'It was as amicable as any divorce can be, which –' he sighed '– isn't to say there haven't been times of anguish and utter despair.'

'Par for the course.'

'But, from the start, Annette and I agreed not to criticise,

82

never to dump blame on the other, so there's been no hostility for the kids to pick up on. And we're not hostile. We've never had any major rows or unpleasantness. This sounds so bloody hackneyed, but we simply grew apart.'

'Because your wife 'saw the light'?'

Steve nodded. 'When she started chanting 'om' as we waited in traffic and talking about 'embracing the universe' and 'rebirthing', I realised we no longer had much in common and it was time to call it a day.'

'There was no other woman?'

'No.'

'And you feel guilty?'

'About my marriage breaking down? About me deciding I wanted out? Yes. I accept I'm no madder, sadder or badder than anyone else, but – well, in divorce the kids always have a bumpy ride.' He frowned. 'I shan't get married again.'

I looked at him. To me, it seemed entirely possible that some eager spinster with a ticking biological clock could zoom in and persuade him to give matrimony a second shot. Or perhaps, as his daughter hoped, he and his wife might rekindle their love.

'Me, neither,' I said.

'I don't even fancy having another relationship, not a serious one.'

'Nor me.'

CHAPTER SIX

'LOOKING GOOD. AGAIN, A full body stretch and don't forget the arms and the legs. Fingers and toes. Stretch every last muscle, real slow. Man, yeah! Get with that funky beat.' Max clicked his fingers to the reggae pumping out from his boom blaster. 'Jenny, keep the tum tucked in. Navel against spine. Carol, breathe deeply and relax. Tina, you're hot today.'

Lying flat on my back on an exercise mat on the floor of Tina Kincaid's large conservatory, I took a deep breath. This wasn't the touch-the-toes routine that I had vaguely imagined, it was much more. We had begun with a warm-up, followed by what Max termed cardio-vascular work, which had meant us taking turns on an exercise bike, skipping and performing 'squat jumps' and 'jumping jacks'. Although I'd considered I was fit, the skipping had had me puffing and panting, but the last time I'd skipped rope was in a school playground. I had felt a real clodhopper attempting the jumps and Jenny hadn't been any better. What made it worse was that we were both wearing common-or-garden T-shirts and shorts which revealed our pasty white legs and would've brought cries of horror from the style police, whereas Tina – who performed perfectly – was in dedicated fitness gear of a sleek aquamarine halter-neck and cropped leggings. And full, expertly applied, make-up.

Now we had reached the cool down which signalled the end of the session.

Throughout it all, the young man had kept up a ceaseless stream of chat. He'd talked about raising energy levels and how exercise equals empowerment. Of the advice he could give us on everything from addictions to back pain to lack of confidence. There'd been American-style fluff of the 'get in touch with your inner self' variety and psychobabble quotes, such as 'a person's greatest emotional need is to feel appreciated' and 'if you can watch the world go by or boogie, I hope you boogie'.

'Sit up slowly, that's it, and widen those legs. Stretch the inner thighs. You feel the pull?' Max enquired, his smile zipping between the three of us.

The personal trainer was not as I had imagined, either. Tina had called him handsome which, with dark thickly-lashed eyes, a square jaw and even white teeth he certainly was, but I hadn't been prepared for his flamboyance. He stood around six foot four, was broad-shouldered, lean-hipped, with skin the colour of pale coffee and a head of thick dreadlocks. Long blonded dreadlocks. Three silver studs were embedded in one ear and he wore a black Lycra bodysuit which covered him from neck to ankle, yet appeared to reveal everything. I understood why he shocked the neighbours. You don't come across exotic Adonises like him moseying along the road too often.

'Right, babes, stand up slowly. Last stretch is the back stretch, with legs apart.' Max set his hands on his hips. 'Like this.'

As he leant back and bounced to the beat, I whispered to Jenny. 'Get a load of the lunchbox.'

She flushed beetroot. I don't know why, the guy couldn't hear what I'd said, though my grin and look may have indicated what I was talking about. If so, he wasn't fazed. And I would guarantee other women have done a lot more than whisper a comment.

'Thank you very much,' Jenny said politely, when the work-out ended a few minutes later.

Catching my breath, I wiped the sweat from my brow with a towel I'd brought. 'It was good.'

Sweat was pouring off me and Jenny; running down our cheeks, dripping inelegantly from the end of our noses – yet Tina's face was dry. Hadn't I read somewhere that Botox stopped perspiration? That you could even have injections in your armpits to block up the sweat glands?

'So you'll both be here again on Thursday?' Tina asked.

'I will,' I said, and Jenny nodded.

Walking over to the boom blaster, Max switched it off. Silence. Blessed silence. Then the telephone rang.

Tina's face lit up. 'Excuse me,' she said, and sped away. The conservatory was off the living room where the telephone was located, so we heard her squeal of delight when she answered. 'Joe!'

She was given to squeals and, I had noticed, used a breathy little girl voice whenever men were around. She'd spoken that way to Peter and Joe Fernandez at the wake, with Steve yesterday, and again this morning with Max. She seemed to regard the trainer as a deity on high; smilingly grateful if he praised her and nodding sombre acknowledgement of his Slick Willy quotes.

I had also noticed that Tina's eyes were blue, not brown. The office lights must have cast a curious tint the other day.

'We need to talk terms,' Max declared. 'It'll be one hundred pounds for an initial assessment, but the session fee is as you've fixed with Tina, which you must realise is dirt cheap.'

'A hundred pounds?' I protested. There had been no mention of this earlier and I felt certain Tina knew nothing about it.

'Cash, Thursday. Don't choke on your pretzel. It's a quarter my usual fee and not much to change your life. Exercise makes you better today than you were yesterday. It strengthens the body, relaxes the mind and toughens the spirit.' He paused, as if expecting me to marvel at his wisdom. 'From your shortage of breath, I'd say you're a smoker. A twenty fags a day smoker. Correct?'

I towelled off more sweat. He was too accurate. 'Near enough.'

'If you want to stop and, babe, you know you should, I can help. Likewise with you,' he said, turning to Jenny. 'If you lost some weight you'd feel better and look better. Get rid of the chubby cheeks and emphasise those bewitching eyes, and you'll be a stunner.'

She gave an awkward smile, as if wondering if he was taking the mickey. But Jenny is pretty and if she slimmed down, would be even prettier. She has an open, cheery face and curly mid-blonde hair, streaked with increasing strands of grey. I tint away the grey – my hair is dark brown and it's straight – but so far she has resisted. Seems Bruce is scathing about women who dye their hair. A daft attitude, if you ask me, when so many do and, half the time, you can't tell. Plenty of men wield the dye bottle, too. Including, I felt sure, the russet-haired Russell.

'Me, a stunner?' Jenny said warily. 'I don't think so.'

'I do. And you should accept compliments, accept them with grace and pride. If you want to slim that bod keep a diet diary for five days – just eat normally and list everything – then I'll check it out and advise, as part of the assessment. Do you take any regular exercise?' Max asked, speaking to both of us. We shook our heads. 'Then you should put time aside each day to go through some of the exercises we've done here, plus you should walk whenever possible, instead of using the car. Unleash the goddess within.' He cocked a brow. 'I guess that hundred pounds is beginning to seem like good value?'

Jenny nodded, smiling and won over. 'I'm happy with it.'

'How about you?' he asked me. 'Come on, babe, I have to eat, plus I'm saving up to finance my own health club. Though at the rate I'm going it'll take some time, unless I can find a backer.'

'I understood you were an actor,' I said.

'I am, but two strings to my bow, y'know.'

I hesitated. I don't like to be unfairly separated from my hard-earned cash, yet his offer of an assessment lured. 'A hundred pounds it is.'

Max grinned. 'On Thursday I'll have a one-to-one with each of you when we can discuss goals, expectations and the way forward. But in the meantime I'd like to suggest something to use as a mantra – if you believe it, you can achieve it. Now, together, what d'ya say?'

'If you believe it, you can achieve it,' Jenny and I repeated obediently, though in my case reluctantly.

I'm not into chants and subservience to a guru. And if he was thinking of moving on to air-punching hoorahs or group hugs, he could count me out. I also possess a finely tuned bullshit detector which, over the session, had emitted several bleeps.

Max was collecting up the mats and skipping ropes, and fitting them inside a large holdall, when Tina returned.

'That was Joe, Joe Fernandez,' she told us, as giggly as a teenager. 'He's offered me a job on his next series, introducing the guests – if I want it. The series is scheduled to start next January, but before then he'd like me to appear on one of the current shows, to remind everyone I'm still around. And still tasty, so Joe says.' She giggled again. 'He's arranging for his agent to contact me, with a view to bringing my name back into the limelight.'

'Way to go!' Max exclaimed. 'And remember, success is not a doorway, it's an elevator. You could end up a star.'

'Would you like to be on television again?' Jenny enquired.

Tina pouted. 'Don't know. Maybe when I'm feeling better.'

Maybe when you know you're looking better, I thought, for this morning her face was still a little drawn, as if she could still be having sleepless nights. But what was she worrying about – Duncan's demise or her paucity of cash? Or had a second spider infiltrated the bathroom?

'It'd be a nice little earner,' I said.

'Did Joe mention me?' Max enquired, placing the music system inside his holdall. 'Did he say if he'd spoken to those TV guys, the ones who might be able to put in a good word? And the ones who're looking for fresh talent?'

Tina shook her head. 'Sorry. Next time he calls, I'll ask.'

'Please do. I'm willing to audition at any time. Happy to discuss ideas. Their ideas and some I have of my own.' Lifting the holdall, he placed his free arm around her waist. 'How's the grieving process going, babe? Bereavement is one heck of a shock to the system, but bear in mind that you'll survive and be stronger,' he declared, and steered her out of the conservatory.

'Where do you reckon he finds his words of wisdom?' I said. 'Christmas crackers? Pop songs? Oprah Winfrey?'

'Some of them made sense,' Jenny protested.

'Come on, the guy's full of flannel. When he said denial is not just a river in Egypt, it's something we must use to our advantage, I wanted to puke. And as for him claiming he can stop me smoking, who does he think he is, a miracle worker?'

'You'd have to co-operate and give him a chance. Remember 'if you believe it, you can achieve it'.'

I groaned. 'You're not hooked on Max, too, like Tina? Still I must say he is exceptionally well-hung, unless he has a pound of salami Sellotaped into place. I noticed you were fascinated.'

'I wasn't,' Jenny objected, but her face reddened.

She walked over to look out at the garden, and I joined her. With a large oval lawn edged by flower beds which drifted into trees, it had patches of spring colour. Daffodils grew beneath a silver birch, a flowering white cherry spread wide branches, a carpet of snowdrops surrounded a statue, which made a focal point to one side of the garden. For the first forty years of my life I couldn't have told a dahlia from a geranium, but I've developed quite a lust for horticulture. I even watch gardening programmes and – don't laugh – take notes.

'Is that a tennis court?' Jenny asked, peering down the length of the lawn to a low hedge and land beyond.

'It is. And it's unused, judging from the weeds. It could do with a complete overhaul, like the house.'

I knew from my previous visit that the hall and kitchen were down-at-heel, but the living room and conservatory were also dilapidated. The conservatory could have, should have, been filled with lemon trees and orchids and other exotic plants – at least, that's what my TV watching would've prompted me to do – but all it contained were two sagging wicker chairs and a rusted metal waste-paper basket. Shabby stuff. Presumably the upstairs was the same.

Jenny nodded. 'I expected the house to be stylish and beautifully decorated, but it's a big disappointment. Plus it needs a real good clean. Have you noticed the dust and all the cobwebs? The scuff marks on the carpets?'

'Seems the housekeeper has departed –'

'She must've been a lazy sort. It's obvious the place hasn't had a good top and bottoming for years.'

'I guess – and I doubt Tina is much of an expert with a damp rag and a Dyson.'

'No, though she probably can't face the thought of housework right now. She says she's coping, but she comes over as… delicate. Still perhaps Max's counselling will help.'

'Perhaps,' I said, and we listened to the rumble of his voice as he continued to give his pep talk. 'The hundred pounds was a shock. If you ask me, the guy's got an eye to the main chance. I bet he doesn't miss a trick when it comes to cash and I bet the mention of wanting to run his own health club and needing a backer was a hint that he's looking for a sugar mummy.'

Jenny laughed. 'One of us?'

'Why not? I don't have the wherewithal and you're not in the market, but he doesn't know that. Or maybe he thinks Tina can be persuaded.' I hadn't told Jenny about the widow's money troubles. I hadn't told anyone. As promised, I had kept my lips tight-zipped. 'Seems Max got her husband to pay for some of his equipment. He probably spotted him flashing a roll of notes, which Duncan used to do, and decided to muscle in. Pun intended. And now he'll be working on Tina.'

'Cynic.'

'You don't fancy having a handsome virile younger man drooling over you, even if it is your cash he's after? I wouldn't mind stringing him along for a while and checking out the salami.'

Jenny chuckled. 'Carol, you're dreadful. I didn't realise Max was an actor,' she went on. 'I've never seen him in anything and I'm sure I'd remember. Never read about him.'

'Me neither. Call me cynical again, but I reckon you can

take his acting career with a large pinch of salt. Though the guy is pure Hollywood. Did Victoria ring?' I asked, recalling her anxiety.

'Yes.' She frowned. 'She was in some backpackers' hangout. I could hear music and voices in the background and, well, she sounded merry.'

'So you're wetting your knickers? Jen, Victoria is a big girl and allowed to sip the amber nectar from time to time. And if she gets tipsy – haven't we all?'

'Not me,' she said. 'When I was nineteen I rarely drank alcohol and I never got drunk. In fact, I've only been drunk twice in my whole life. And I wasn't staggering then, just a bit squiffy.'

I shook a wry head. There are times when it feels as if Jenny and I live in two different worlds. Although compared to today's ladettes, my intake had been modest, I'd consumed cocktails and beer in my late teens, enjoyed spirits for a while and now relaxed with wine. And, on occasion, I have been known to slur my words and suffer dead-head hangovers.

Our sex lives are different, too. I lost my virginity to a fellow journalist and regularly slept with Tom before we were married. I can remember telling Jen how, as girl and boyfriend, we'd once gone to a hotel for a dirty weekend – and how horrified she had been.

'Don't know what you've missed,' I told her, and listened.

In the distance there was the sound of a door closing, then the pad of footsteps as Tina returned.

'What did you think of Max?' she asked eagerly.

'Well, larger than life –' Jenny began.

'And how,' I inserted.

'– but very pleasant and informative. He certainly knows his stuff.'

Tina nodded. 'He does. And he is so wise. He was just telling me that, sad though it is, Duncan's death should be viewed as a release. A release from him sliding into dementia and a release for me, not having to cope with him dribbling, feeding him with a spoon, the accidents in his trousers.' She shuddered. 'Duncan always said that if he dropped down dead tomorrow, he'd had a charmed life, so –' She smiled, but a moment later her smile collapsed. 'I hate being without him.'

'Of course you do,' I said.

Like Steve, I couldn't help feeling sorry for her. Yet I was also impatient with the way, at times, she seemed to cultivate the helplessness and play the frail Ophelia. Indeed, it was difficult to separate her genuine feelings from the play-acting.

'Funnily enough I don't mind sleeping in the house on my own – Duncan snored and I spent lots of nights in the spare room – and it's nice to be able to watch 'Footballers' Wives' and 'Ab Fab' without him grumbling, but when I sit down to breakfast and there's just me –'

'Recovering from his death will take time,' Jenny said, then, as if afraid Tina might burst into tears, and desperate for a diversion, carried on, 'We noticed you have a tennis court. Do you play?'

'No. Last summer, when the weather was good, I worked out there with Max, but that's the only action the court's seen in years.' She giggled. 'Duncan used to remark on how whenever I went down there to exercise, Peter, from next door, always seemed to find a reason to be busy in his garden. But now he's going to be busy in mine. I've paid off the gardener and I'm going to look after the flower beds myself, though it'll wreck my nails, and Peter will cut the grass. He's done it once already.'

'That's kind of him,' I said.

'It is. Beryl, his wife, doesn't know. He cut it when she was out at one of her bridge games and that's what he'll do in future. Wait until she's gone and the coast is clear, then come round.' Tina giggled again. 'Beryl would be spitting mad if she found out. And the best part is Peter doesn't even cut his own grass, he has a gardener in. But he's sweet on me, so –' She smiled, then became thoughtful. 'I could probably get Peter to marry me.'

'He's already married,' Jenny protested.

'And he has a huge nose and tufts of white hair sprouting

from his ears,' I said.

'He's no oil painting,' Tina conceded, 'and a younger guy would be nice the next time. Especially one who didn't snore. But Peter's very well-off.'

Was she serious about wanting another husband, and so soon? She seemed to be. Did this rate as a calculating desire for a meal ticket... or a sad lack of self-confidence?

'Is that Peter there now?' Jenny asked, looking out of the window.

'Where?' Tina said.

'On the left-hand side, halfway down. A pale man, pale hair, standing still. You can just see him beyond the bushes.'

I followed her pointing finger. 'I think you're looking at a statue of David the giant slayer, Jen.'

'Am I?' She narrowed her eyes, then hooted with embarrassed laughter. 'Oh, yes. Sorry, my long sight isn't as good as it used to be. I really ought to get glasses.'

'Contact lenses are more flattering,' Tina said. 'I wear them all the time.'

Jenny grimaced. 'I wouldn't fancy putting them in and taking them out.'

'It's simple. I've got coloured contacts, too. Blue ones, green and hazel. I wear different ones to go with different outfits.'

Hah! I thought. All is explained.

'Want to come upstairs and see?' Tina suggested to Jenny. 'And I can show you how easy it is to put lenses in and take them out.'

'Okay,' she agreed.

'Coming, too?' Tina asked me.

I shook my head. Although I wear spectacles for reading, I'm happy with them. I like to think I look professorish, but cute. Though I'm probably kidding myself.

'No, but I could murder a drink of water. Alright if I help myself from the kitchen?'

'Go ahead.'

I was gulping down a refreshing glass of cold water when

the doorbell rang. I listened for sounds of my hostess coming downstairs to answer it then, when the bell rang again and there was still no response, went to open the front door myself.

'Hello,' I said, finding Max stood on the porch. 'You've forgotten something?'

He shook his head. 'Tina told me you're a reporter with *The Dursleigh Siren* and I was thinking that you might like to write an article about me? Or about how people are using personal trainers and how life-enhancing they can be,' he continued quickly, when I looked dubious. 'I have several clients in Dursleigh and –'

'How many?'

There was a pause. 'Three.'

'But you think exposure in *The Siren* could bring you some more?'

He grinned. 'A dash of publicity never goes amiss. And if my photograph appears in the paper and Tina shows it to old man Fernandez, maybe it'll jog his memory and encourage him to speak to the TV guys.'

'Or a talent scout could spot it and, stardom here you come?'

'Stranger things have happened. How about it?'

I considered the proposition. On the one hand, he would be using me. On the other, our female readers would slaver over his picture which would add va-va-voom. And hadn't Steve suggested I write something about aerobics?

'Done,' I said. 'Do you know where the newspaper office is?'

'Yes, but we could meet at The Barley Mow this evening and do the deed there.'

After a million-pound refurbishment which included a new Spanish restaurant and an expanded, ultra-classy, bar area, The Barley Mow had become Dursleigh's 'in' place. Village bigwigs and the trendy young flocked there, while the ageing pop star was a regular. When Lynn and Justin had taken me to the restaurant for my birthday, he'd been sat at the next table. Sat with a girl young enough to be his granddaughter, I might add, and wearing a naff green leather suit.

'In public, so that you're seen being interviewed,' I said. 'You've worked this out.'

'Sure.' Max was smiling and unrepentant. 'Dinner is my treat, babe. Table already reserved for eight o'clock.'

'As if.'

'It's true.'

I spread my hands. 'I'm easily bought.'

'*Ciao,*' he said, and left.

I had returned to the kitchen to refill my glass with water, when Tina and Jenny appeared.

'Max came back to suggest I write a piece about him for *The Siren,*' I told them, 'so we're meeting at the Barley Mow tonight. Dinner at his expense.'

Tina looked sulky. 'He's never taken me out.'

'It isn't a date, it's business. I'm interviewing him.'

'And you were married until very recently,' Jenny reminded her.

Tina nodded. 'That's right,' she agreed, then continued, 'I've been explaining to Jenny how I've been left with very little money and living in this flea pit.'

'So difficult. Such a shame,' Jenny said sympathetically.

'Did you and Duncan never consider updating the house, renovating it?' I asked.

'I tried to persuade him. So many times, I said we needed a new kitchen, new bathrooms, new furniture, new everything. But his sons always objected. They claimed the house was a shrine to their mother and it would break their hearts if anything was changed. Crap! They just wanted to stop me spending money, but Duncan believed them and was used to things as they were. He didn't fancy any upheaval, either. So, here I am. The money I got for the Merc won't last long –'

'You've sold it already?' I said.

'The dealers where Duncan bought it took it straight away. Joe reckoned I would've got a better price if I'd sold it privately, but I needed the cash. Max is helping me sell my brooches.'

'Max?' I queried.

'He has all kinds of contacts and he's going to show the brooches to a man he knows who'll give me a fair price. But whatever I get, the money won't last long.' She heaved a sigh. 'I'm not into scrimping and saving.'

'If you modelled again that would bring in some money,' Jenny suggested.

Tina shook her head. 'I couldn't.'

'Why not?'

'I'm not as young as I used to be,' she muttered.

'Sixty isn't that old these days,' Jenny said.

'Sixty?' Tina's chin lifted, her spine stiffened. 'I'm not sixty, nowhere near.'

'One should never trust a woman who tells one her real age. A woman who would tell one that would tell one anything,' I recited. 'To quote Oscar Wilde.'

Tina gave me a puzzled look, then said, 'If I did the rounds of the agencies chances are I'd be offered jobs advertising back ache pills or mobility scooters or those pads you can buy if you're afraid you might wet yourself.' She shuddered. 'I couldn't bear to be photographed using geriatric stuff.'

'I have no experience of the modelling scene, but, to me, you look too young and too sophisticated to appear in that kind of advertisement,' I protested.

'Far too young,' Jenny agreed. 'But you could at least go along and see what work the agencies have to offer.'

Tina shook her head. 'No.'

CHAPTER SEVEN

I WAS SURE MAX had been spinning me a line when he said he'd already booked a table at The Barley Mow, but when I arrived he was installed at one with a 'reserved' ticket on it, while all the other tables were taken.

'Aren't you the peacherino,' he said, rising to greet me.

To demonstrate I could aspire to more than a sweaty T-shirt and shorts, I was dressed in a white satin tunic over slim black pants. Golden hoops hung from my ears, my strappy black sandals were vertiginous and I had taken special care with the eyeshadow, mascara, lipstick. I'd considered I looked pretty glam when I had swanked in front of the wardrobe mirror.

'Thanks. You, too.'

He wore a well-cut silver grey suit with a white shirt. The shirt had generous lapels and was open at the neck, revealing a silver medallion nestling amongst dark curls of chest hair. Add his muscled physique and the dreadlocks, and Max was one cool dude. On the flashy side maybe, but definite eye candy. It wasn't just me who thought so. Our table was in full view of the entrance to the bar and over the evening it was noticeable how almost everyone who came in registered his appearance. Some, usually women, though there were a couple of guys, gaped in open admiration.

We ordered drinks and food from a young waitress with a nose ring who became his instant fan, then I took out my notebook. In public, I find it is often easier to use shorthand than run a tape recorder.

'Before we start, there's something I need to tell you,' Max said gravely. He hesitated and frowned, as if about to impart thunderbolt news.

'Which is?'

'I'm not really an actor.'

'You could've fooled me,' I said.

'But I didn't?'

'No way, Jose.'

'I told Tina and Joe Fernandez I acted, because I thought it'd impress them and give me a better chance of getting on TV. And, fortunately, they haven't asked what parts I've played or where.'

'So I'm not to describe you as an actor in my article?'

'Please don't. Someone could ask for evidence, my acting history and –'

'I won't.'

Max took hold of my hand and, to my great surprise, and the surprise of the waitress who was arriving with white wine for me, a lager for him, raised it to his lips and kissed it.

'Thanks, babe.'

'You're soft-soaping me,' I said.

'I'm trying.' He smiled. 'But you liked having your hand kissed.'

I had. It was gallant. Fun. Different. And a young blonde who had just walked in had looked choked with envy.

'I think we understand each other,' I said.

'I reckon so, too.'

'Do you want to be an actor?'

'I want to be famous, whatever it takes.'

'What about running your own health club?'

'I want to be famous and rich. I *will* be famous and rich. And you writing about me in *The Dursleigh Siren* – well, the longest journey begins with a single step.'

'Come out with another cringeable quote, buster,' I said, 'and that step could land you in a pothole, deep and filled with muddy water.'

Max laughed, showing his strong white teeth. 'Yes, ma'am. Though I reserve the right to use quotes in my classes. You may not go a bundle on them, but plenty of women do.'

'And you're looking for a woman to sponsor you? A wealthy woman?'

'It'd be a help if one came along.'

As we waited for our meals, I started to question him and

take notes – about his qualifications, why working in physical fitness had appealed, any anonymous case histories of clients who had benefited from his training which he could give me. By the time the waitress appeared, I had ample information for an interesting piece. I had also requested a sexy photo to accompany it.

'Is being a personal trainer a lucrative occupation?' I enquired, as we began to eat. I had chosen hake in white wine sauce, while Max had opted for fillet steak. Both, we told each other, were delicious. 'Does it support you? Off the record and for my ears only.'

'It supports me, but only just. Because hiring a trainer is expensive –'

'Which is part of the appeal?'

He nodded. 'We're talking display wealth here and personal trainers rate alongside a swimming pool in your back garden or driving a Maserati – because I'm exclusive and expensive, building up a clientele takes time.'

'And you've been doing personal training for around eighteen months,' I said, remembering what he had told me. 'What did you do before?'

'All sorts. I was a shopping mall security guard, a bouncer at a nightclub, got involved in some wheeling and dealing.'

'Which is how you're able to help Tina sell her brooches?'

'Right.'

'I won't ask if it is strictly legit.'

Max grinned. 'Wise decision. But I'll be straight with her.'

'I know that.'

'Thanks. Until I get established as a personal trainer, and to bring in extra cash, I've been trying to find work at sports centres,' he went on. 'I get to run occasional classes when instructors are ill or on holiday, but the only way I'll land a permanent job is if an existing instructor leaves. Which is something they never seem to do.'

'Have you tried the Garth House Hotel?'

'No. They have a sports centre?'

'A new one, just opened. I did an article about it in last

week's *Siren*. You could call in and ask if they need anyone.'

'I will.' Reaching across the table, he squeezed my hand. 'Thanks, babe.'

'I was right,' a reedy voice declared, and I looked up to find an elderly lady in a maroon paisley-patterned woollen dress stood beside us. 'I told my husband I felt sure you were Carol, the girl from *The Siren* and Jenny's friend. Jenny and I work in the charity shop together. I'm Eileen.'

I smiled up. 'Hello. Jenny's spoken about you.'

Eileen had a pointed nose, crêpe-lined lips and an alert expression. She looked like she didn't miss much.

'Is this your boyfriend?' she enquired, her gaze fixing on Max's hand which was still covering mine.

I laughed. She may have called me a girl, but she must see I was in my fifties – while my companion languished in his mid-twenties. Jenny had described Eileen as a 'dry old bird', so presumably this was a stab at humour.

'My occasional other,' I said. 'Isn't he gorgeous?'

'A good-looking young man,' she agreed.

Max grinned. 'Thank you.'

Eileen gave a trill of high-pitched, almost giddy laughter. 'But you are. And you –' she spoke to me '– are a very lucky woman.'

I cocked a brow. 'Don't I know it!'

'Hold on to him.'

'I intend to,' I said. 'Like glue.'

'So very nice to meet you both.' She started to move away. 'Goodbye.'

'You could've asked if she wanted a personal trainer,' I said, as the old lady returned to a table where she began gabbling away to the old man who was sat there, obviously relaying our conversation.

Max shook his head. 'I think not.'

'But she took a shine to you.' I grinned, 'Seemed to be mentally undressing you.'

He winced. 'Stop it.'

'Tina said you'd given a fitness demonstration at the golf

100

club, but how else do you find customers?' I asked, returning to our previous conversation.

'By word of mouth and by pushing leaflets through doors, though the leaflet response rate is so low it's hardly worth the effort.'

'The manager of the sportswear shop on the High Street is a friendly sort, you could ask him if you could put some of your leaflets on the counter. Or I could ask him,' I offered.

'Would you? That'd be brilliant.'

'Do you only have yourself to support? There's no partner? No offspring?'

'Just me.'

'How about a ma and pa?'

'My pa went out to get a Chinese take-away when I was three and hasn't been seen since,' he said, and gave a wry smile. 'Though it's a long walk to Beijing. And my ma is living in Italy with her latest guy. I rent a flat with my two brothers. The flat is small and cramped and, being over a fish and chip shop, it's also smelly and noisy.'

'What do your brothers do?'

'Paul's a taxi driver and writes poems in the bath. Calvin works in the fish and chip shop in the evenings and spends his days painting watercolours of mice.'

'Why mice?'

'He likes them. So far no one wants to publish Paul's poetry and Cal's paintings don't sell, but they're both convinced that by this time next year they'll be rich and famous.'

'Same aims as you.'

'Yes, though they're not like me, not physically that is. We each had a different father and Paul has red hair and freckles, whereas Cal is short, squat and swarthy, so persuading folk that we're related can be tricky. Once we went into a pub together and got talking to a couple of guys who –'

While I suspected his tales contained a fair dose of fiction, Max displayed a wicked sense of humour which had me laughing out loud. He was also determined to succeed in life. I

101

respected that, especially in view of his background, though I wasn't too sure about his methods. Throughout the evening we talked and talked – and there were no more cringeable quotes.

'You were having a good time at The Barley Mow last night,' Steve said.

I looked at him in surprise. 'You were there?'

It was the next morning. I had just settled down to work when he had walked into the general office.

'I called in for a quick drink and a word with the barman – the guy used to work at a pub in Ringley, so I know him from way back – but you were so busy chatting to your companion you never noticed me.'

'You should've come over.'

'And disturbed the *tête à tête?* Heaven forbid.'

'My companion –' I repeated his arch delivery '– was Max, the personal trainer I told you about. I was interviewing him for the piece about aerobics which you suggested.' I indicated my computer screen. 'I'm writing the article now. And Melanie has the photograph which is to go with it.'

The girl held up the print which Max had provided, dropping it through *The Siren's* letterbox before the office opened. 'The guy is awesome.'

'The two of you looked chummy,' Steve said.

'He was telling me about his life and it was interesting. I had a good evening. He's good company.'

'And virile with it?'

Should I point out that Max must be around thirty years my junior and saw me only as a useful contact? That we'd been sharing a meal, not caught *in flagrante delicto* on the table? What the hell, as I'd done with Eileen, I decided to go along with the joke, with the ego boost of the idea that the kid Max and I could be romantically involved.

Looking over my reading glasses, I smiled the kind of smile which hints at everything and says nothing. 'I can't argue with that.'

'He is sex on legs,' Melanie declared, making her way

over. She showed Steve the photograph, which was of Max in his bodysuit striking a tigerish pose. 'See.'

He frowned. 'Do we need a photograph?'

'For definite!' the girl insisted.

'Our female readers would appreciate one,' I said.

'Too muscle-bound for my taste, but your choice. And how does this Max rate as a personal trainer?'

'Ten out of ten. He knows what he's about and fires you with enthusiasm. Tina Kincaid swears by him.'

'Is he going to try and stop you smoking?' Steve enquired.

'Not only is he going to try, he'll succeed,' I declared.

I would give up the nicotine habit, I vowed as I half-watched yet another *Vicar of Dibley* repeat on television that evening. My assertion earlier had been spur of the moment and inspired by defiance, but I'd been annoyed that Steve should mention me smoking. He must have noticed how, from time to time, I exit to the fire escape for a quick drag. Yet giving up made sense. It would be advantageous to my health and for my purse. The money I saved could buy all kinds of treats. Such as a manicure – amazingly I've never had one – the knee-high black leather boots in the shoe shop window which I'd been lusting after, a selection of heathers for my front garden.

I reached for the packet of Marlboros. I would stop tomorrow and Max would help me. Max, who Steve seemed to believe could – well, just might – be my lover. No way. He may be good fun, but he was too juvenile and immature. Despite what I'd said to Jen about checking out the salami, I'm not into boys. Toy or otherwise. Handsome as he was, Max didn't turn me on. And although we'd established a certain rapport, I knew I didn't turn him on, either.

But I do miss sex. Vibrators and Richard Gere fantasies may have their joys – that's the forty-something Richard Gere in *Sommersby* – but there's nothing to beat the real thing. The feel of strong male arms around you, of skin on skin, of bodily warmth. Which was why, a few years ago, I had embarked on a couple of relationships. At the time I'd been stricken with a feeling of life passing me by, that I may never be naked in bed with a man again. And I had longed to fall in love a second time. Deeply in love with a man who would love me, for ever.

My first amour was the owner of a local garden centre whom I'd met when I had interviewed him about the centre extending their facilities. We'd liked the look of each other, flirted and he'd bought me a coffee in their café. Later, when I had gone in to purchase slug pellets – hoping I might see him – he had asked me out for dinner. On leaving the restaurant, he'd taken me back to his house and we had made love. The lovemaking had been awkward. Because I hadn't been expecting it first time out, I was wearing run-of-the-mill underwear – well-washed bra, white cotton knickers – so had needed to undress furtively. Then the guy had lain on the different side of the bed to where Tom had always lain, so no matter where I put my arms and legs, it felt wrong. Later, as he approached his climax, he had emitted hee-haw noises which reminded me of a donkey and made me want to laugh. My desire had been killed stone dead.

Afterwards, I had told myself that our lovemaking hadn't been wonderful because it had been the first time. Things would improve. They didn't. Although I wore black lace and we swapped sides, the guy had still hee-hawed and I had still wanted to laugh. Yet, out of bed we had got along fine. We had the same sense of humour, liked the same books and films, were interested in many of the same activities, in particular gardening. After three months of donkey sex, I said a reluctant farewell. He didn't understand why.

The second liaison was with a man who worked alongside Bruce and who Jenny had invited to a barbecue where – guess what? – I had been invited, too. This time, things were the other way around. Out of bed we had nothing in common, between the sheets all was lusty rapture. But if you're intimate with someone you need to respect them as a person, and I didn't. I thought he was long-winded, self-opinionated, too much the wise guy. And because I thought that and yet slept with him, I didn't respect myself, either. I had begun to wonder what I was proving by partaking in this meaningless sex, when Jenny told me that his colleague had informed Bruce I was 'randy-arsed' in bed – which made her laugh, and blush crimson, but probably confirmed me in Bruce's mind as debauched. The remark finished the relationship. Maybe today's young women would consider it a compliment, but any man who could be so indiscreet, so coarse, was not for me.

After that I had, I decided, kissed my last frog. If my eyes met the eyes of a prince, or better yet a king, across a crowded room and violins played and waves crashed – fantastic. Otherwise, I couldn't be bothered. I'm not willing to settle for something less than perfect, for Mr Anyone, simply in order to have a man.

Since then I've met a few guys whom I have considered to be 'maybes', only to discover that either we quickly ran out of conversation or disagreed on basics. For example, one bloke asked me out for dinner and at the end of the meal suggested we should split the bill. No thanks. Quaint little old me likes the man to pay, at least on a first date.

If I was twenty years younger maybe I'd happily jump into bed with every available male – but I'm not and I don't. In my middle-aged opinion, only hookers have sex with strangers.

CHAPTER EIGHT

MY STOMACH WAS FIRM and motorway flat, and the flesh on my upper arms had tightened. I felt well-toned, fit, in great shape. A regular babe, as Max would say. Smiling, I stretched, a full body stretch in deference to the maestro. Whatever his hokum, a month of his work-outs had produced results. A builder had still to let rip with a wolf-whistle, but one would, I assured myself. One would.

I climbed out of bed. I usually indulge in a lie-in on Sunday mornings, but my father and Dilys were coming for lunch and I needed to prepare the food, set the table and have a general tidy-up. If it had been my dad here on his own, I wouldn't have gone to so much trouble.

Looking around the bedroom, I had to admit I was not the world's best Molly Maid. Jeans dangled over a radiator and there was a pyramid of waiting-to-be-washed underwear on the carpet. The papery clutter of last week's weekend papers fanned out from beneath the bed, while two mugs containing dregs of cold coffee sat on the bedside table. Not that my house is dirty. I clean the kitchen, bathroom and loo every Saturday, and dust and vacuum elsewhere whenever I have the time. And the inclination. But I'm not as methodical as Jenny. More laid back. Alright, a bit of a slob.

As I peeled carrots, I thought of how, when I'd visited my father earlier in the week – after obediently phoning him first to obtain clearance – he had asked if he could bring a guest along today.

'You mean Ernest?' I had said. 'That's fine.'

Ernest, who also lives at the Bridgemont flats, is another widower, and he and my dad are friends. A timid, though determinedly inquisitive gentleman, Ernest had come for lunch twice before. On the first occasion he had asked so many questions about my house – the size of the bedrooms, if they had fireplaces, was there an attic? – that I had felt obliged to get my father to take him on a guided tour. The second time he had wanted to know if I had private health insurance – I don't, but he does – then proceeded to list his health problems which included a weak heart, mild age-onset diabetes and constipation, the latter described in embarrassing detail. He and Eileen would get on well. But he had soon reverted to his questioning – now about my job. Did I meet any anti-media aggression? Were people always honest in what they told me? Had I ever gone into situations where I had felt afraid? All three answers were negative.

My father had shaken his head. 'No, not Ernest, Dilys. Just the once. Won't make it a regular occurrence.'

'That's fine, too,' I had replied. 'I'd like to meet her.'

'She'd like to meet you,' he had said, then added with a chuckle, 'and it'll keep her sweet.'

So the invitation was, I had gathered, a ploy in him stringing the woman along. One Sunday lunch from his daughter in return for her making him his evening meal for the next couple of months. Or was it in thanks for Dilys joining him in his bed? He had made no further reference to seeing her in the black chiffon nightgown. Neither had I. But I still wondered about the implications. Still felt a wary curiosity.

Whatever my father's motives, I was determined to serve an extra-special lunch. Not only did pride insist I keep pace with Dilys who was 'a dab hand' with food, but reports of the lunch were bound to circulate around Bridgemont and I wanted my hospitality to be spoken of with praise.

'Have you heard about George's daughter? What a cook! Puts that Nigella Lawson right in the shade.'

So we were having prawn cocktail, followed by gammon with a home-made honey sauce, roast potatoes, broccoli and carrots, with a home-made pudding of crème brûlée with fresh raspberries. There may be a lack of the 'jus', 'purées' and 'tassell-tied chives' which are promoted as posh nosh these days, but, considering how rusty I was at producing three-course meals, it had seemed wise not to be too adventurous.

Throughout all the peeling, chopping and stirring, I did not smoke. I hadn't stopped completely, but I was down to ten cigarettes a day. It had not been easy. In fact, it had been hell. I had suffered withdrawal symptoms when I'd been frantic for a nicotine hit, but I had overcome them – most of them – thanks to Max and the encouragement he gives at the workouts, and the warning-off e-mails he sends.

As I am grateful to Max, so he is grateful to me. The piece I wrote about him brought in several phone calls from would-be clients asking for more information. And when he went to speak to the manageress of the health club at Garth House, he took my article with him.

'She was impressed,' Max had reported. 'I swear it got me the job.'

His job is running two aerobics classes, three evenings a week and I'd learned about it in dramatic fashion. I had been on my way along the High Street to buy a cheese bap one lunchtime when I'd heard the yell 'Carol, babe!', followed by an ear-splitting squeal of tyres. Looking round, I had seen Max skidding to a halt in his white van. When he had leapt out, dashed along the pavement and swept me up in an eager embrace, he had almost brought Dursleigh to a halt. Pedestrians had stopped in their tracks to stare, traffic had slowed, the Post Office Jezebel had abandoned her customers and rushed to the door to monitor the proceedings.

'You're the best, babe!' Max had proclaimed, as he had told me of his success. 'She's a wonderful woman,' he had informed the bug-eyed spectators and I'd received more appreciative hugs.

When he had finally released me, I'd been pink-faced and dizzy. Our audience had looked bemused, too.

'Where did you find a dish like him?' the Post Office Jezebel had wanted to know, the next time I went in.

'Oh, around,' I had said casually.

She had looked at me with new respect. 'He's a knockout.'

'Packs a punch,' I had agreed.

'Bet he's hot stuff in bed?' she had said, black-lined eyes

agleam with interest.

I had pretended not to hear. Given the chance, Jezebel will happily discuss sexual acts – her own and anybody else's – in uninhibited and graphic detail.

My approach to the sportswear shop had also paid off. When I had spoken about Max and produced my article, the manager had asked if he would go along and speak to him in person. He did. The manager, it turned out, had been wanting to jazz up his window displays. He arranged for a photographer to take shots of Max in various sports gear and now there is a life size cut-out of him in their window. A cut-out which is changed every few days and which, as the flesh and blood Max does, has women stopping to drool. It also prompts more customers to enter the shop and purchase.

By the time the ring of the doorbell announced my guests' arrival, the table was set, everything which needed to be in the oven was in the oven and the red and white wines were 'breathing' and 'chilling' respectively.

'Hello, how are –' I began, as I opened the front door, then my voice dried.

Because my mother had dressed conservatively and, in her later years, had been forever conscious of preserving dignity and looking respectable for her age – which meant silver hair, discreet make-up, neat two pieces, sensible court shoes – I had assumed Dilys would be the same. Regardless of the black chiffon nightie. It was not so.

Although the woman appeared to be in her late seventies, or more, she had yet to hear the baaa! which warns of mutton dressed as lamb. She wore a purple shellsuit with silver and white stacked trainers. Her hair, which was squid ink black, carried a purple satin bow. Her eyebrows were plucked and drawn in again in thin black arches, her eyelids shimmered silvery blue with eyeliner *à la* Cleopatra. Rouge enthusiastically peppered her cheeks, while her mouth was a splodge of crimson gloss. My father may have described her as 'a snappy dresser', but my word would be 'eccentric'. She reminded me of someone from a *Carry On* film or the kind of wacky old dame I had imagined becoming.

'Dilys, this is my darling daughter, Carol,' my father said. 'Carol, this is my dear friend, Dilys.'

'Hello,' I said again.

'Delighted to meet you, doll,' Dilys declared.

My father turned to indicate a sleek silver car which was accelerating away down the road. 'William, Dilys's son, brought us. First rate car, a Jaguar, automatic with leather upholstery, satellite navigation and park control, cost the earth. I told him he could come for lunch, too. That it would easily stretch and you wouldn't mind – indeed, you'd love it because you're short of male company – but seems he has some business to attend to. He'll be picking us up again around four.'

I nodded. 'Fine. Please come in.'

I ushered my father and Dilys into the living room then, while they settled themselves, went to check the progress of the food. Although it would have stretched to four, I was grateful not to be saddled with a blind date. The rapidly departing William would not, I suspected, have relished the prospect, either. I was 'short of male company'? My father had made me sound like some go-nowhere, do-nothing frump who would fall to her knees in gratitude if a man, any man, deigned to set foot inside the door.

'You have a lovely view,' Dilys remarked, as we drank pre-lunch sherries.

'Thank you.'

I live in a semi-detached cottage in an older, more rural part of Dursleigh which, so far, has escaped the march of building progress and trendification. A backwater of small Victorian houses, an untidy farm with tumbledown barns and, bizarrely, a sewing machine repair shop which garners few customers, it possesses a feeling of by-gone days when life was slower and uncomplicated. The back of my house faces west, looking out across fields currently planted with growing corn to tall woods beyond. Today the sky was a peaceful blue and when evening comes the sunsets can be dramatic, slashed with violet, crimson and gold. In my youth I never noticed sunsets, or fields and trees, but now the splendours of nature can fill me with wonder.

I am not, however, enthusiastic about birds, unlike my mother who used to wax lyrical about some two-a-penny robin perched on a branch. But maybe a keen interest in ornithology will arrive with age.

'Hear you've been dining out at The Barley Mow with some fellow,' my father said.

'That was a month ago,' I told him. 'The Bridgemont rumour mill must be turning awful slow.'

'Fellow with a touch of the tar-brush, I believe. Not canoodling, are you?'

'I was interviewing him for the paper, that's all. Though if I was canoodling you should be pleased. You did tell me to play the field.'

My father scowled. 'Seems that, another time, he stopped his van in the middle of the High Street and jumped out and hugged you.'

'He did.'

'But he's just a lad. A big lad, too, judging from his photo in the sports shop window.'

'You've seen one?'

'Went along specially, as soon as I heard about it. Never imagined you'd go in for someone so much younger.'

'You can be such a fuddy-duddy, George,' Dilys chided. 'Haven't you read about Joan Collins and her whatsisface, and how younger men are just the thing? If you're having a bit of leg-over, Carol, good for you.'

I smothered a smile. My mother had never used the term 'leg-over' and would have been appalled if anyone did. My father looked stunned by the notion, too. Could that mean his relationship with Dilys was purely platonic? He was not wearing the red and white waistcoat she'd bought him – I had never seen him wearing it – so might that, too, hint he was less than in thrall?

'Max is a personal trainer,' I said, 'and Jenny and I and

Tina Kincaid, she's Duncan Kincaid's widow, do classes with him at Tina's house –'

'You do classes with Tina?' Dilys cut in. She frowned. 'With Tina Kincaid?'

I nodded. 'Twice a week. I've told you about the classes, Dad.'

'Yes, but –'

'I do fitness training with the guy. End of story.' I was impatient. Several other people had inferred that Max and I were a pair and it was starting to annoy. 'Shall we go and eat?'

The meal went well. Both my guests had hearty appetites and were appreciative. As Dilys chatted away, telling a couple of slightly bawdy jokes, I began to understand her attraction for my father. She had a vivacity which was appealing. An energy which you had to admire. This was a woman who had no intention of growing old gracefully and would party until she dropped.

'That trellis of yours looks wobbly,' my father remarked, as we drank coffee in the living room afterwards. Rising, he went to the window to take a closer look. 'Suppose I firm it up?'

The trellis was fixed to the fence at the bottom of my small back garden. It supported a rambling rose and whenever the wind blew – today there was an intermittent breeze – it had a tendency to sway.

'Now?' I said.

When he had attempted to fix my temperamental loo, at a lunch when Ernest had been a guest, he had been gone for ages, leaving me to face Ernest's inquisition alone. On his return, my father had admitted defeat and declared that I needed a plumber.

'Why not?'

'Do it, George,' Dilys told him, 'and I'll help Carol clear the table.'

'There's no need,' I started to say, but she was already on her feet.

'Never imagined I'd be getting married again. Not at my age,' Dilys remarked, as my father exited and she walked through to my small front dining room.

'You're getting married?' I blinked. 'You don't mean to my dad?'

'Sure do, doll.' She began gathering up dessert bowls. 'In the summer I thought.'

'The summer?' I repeated, and heard myself squeak.

Although each time we met my father usually made some mention of Dilys, the mentions had been casual. Often about the tastiness of a meal she'd prepared. There had been no hint of their relationship becoming serious. And what about my lovely mum? It was less than two years since she had died and for him to have so swiftly swapped his affections to another woman – it seemed like treachery.

I frowned. 'My father hasn't said anything to me about you getting married.'

As she carried the bowls into the kitchen, Dilys chuckled. 'He hasn't got around to proposing yet, but he will. You know what men are like, you can see how their minds work, what they're gearing up to long before they know it themselves. It were just the same with my other husbands.'

'Other husbands?' I queried, following with the wine glasses.

'I've been widowed twice and divorced once,' she began to explain, as she went to and fro between dining room and kitchen. 'My first husband were a soldier and the silly bugger got himself killed before we'd had much time together.' Dilys sighed. 'And before he could get to know our daughter. Second bloke were a wrestler, called himself Concrete Charlie and liked to wear my camiknicks he did.' She cackled maniacally. 'But he were always down the boozer, so I gave him the heave-ho. Though I'd already met William's dad. Real smasher, he were. We lived in Bermondsey for years, then he suddenly decided he wanted to be in the country. Bought a house not far from here, but out in the sticks. Didn't suit me. Fields for miles and I can't drive, so I were really stuck.'

'Awkward,' I sympathised.

'Bloody boring with only cows to look at. Minute he

kicked it, I moved into Bridgemont. Thanks to my Billy. William,' she corrected herself. 'He doesn't like me to call him Billy now, says it brings back memories.' Her brow furrowed fleetingly, as if the memories could be unhappy. 'You see I were able to buy a flat in Bridgemont because William and his wife bought the house from me, cash on the nail. Good job they did, too, because no one else would've wanted it. Falling to pieces it were, but they had plans for a big renovation. Marble floors, billiard room, a swimming pool which their kids would've loved. Going to be a real rock star pad. But then William and his missus got divorced.'

'So the renovation didn't happen?'

Dilys shook her head. 'William still owns the place, but it's still falling to pieces. He lives in London now.' She looked out of the window. 'I'll go and see how George is getting on.'

As she disappeared into the garden, I stacked the last of the dirty dishes beside the sink. I was wondering furiously how much credence I should give to her claim of my father planning to propose – I couldn't imagine him as someone's fourth husband – when the door bell rang. Answering it, I found a man in white shirt and jeans stood on the path. He was shortish and slim, with close-cut brown hair silvering at the temples. Good-looking in a rough diamond sort of a way.

'I'm William. Dilys's son,' he announced, smiling. 'I know I'm early, but I'm pressed for time.'

'Come in. I'm Carol. Your mother's in the back garden with my dad. He's fixing a trellis, but it shouldn't take long.'

'I believe you work on *The Dursleigh Siren,*' he said, making conversation as I led him through to the living room.

I nodded. 'I've been there for quite a while.'

'You enjoy it?'

'Very much.'

There was a pause, then he said, 'Your father also told me how your ex-husband is the political editor on a national paper.'

I gave a silent groan. I could imagine the talk of 'my' Tom's success. 'Yes. I used to work for a national, too.'

114

'Your father never said that. Did you cover politics?'

'No, I did news reporting in general. Wrote about everything from IRA outrages to streakers at sports fixtures to break-ins at gold bullion warehouses.'

'When was this?' he enquired.

'Back in the Dark Ages, the late seventies when I first started out and then again during the eighties and early nineties. What line are you in?'

Crossing to the window, he looked out at the garden where my father was inspecting his work on the trellis. William knocked on the glass, and my father and Dilys turned and smiled, acknowledging him.

'I have business interests in London. Import and export. Seems like the folks are ready to go,' he said, as they began walking towards the house.

William was greeted and urged by my dad to stay for a while and have a cup of tea or coffee or something stronger.

'Carol enjoys socialising,' he said.

'No time,' William declared, and headed for the hall.

'Surely you can spare ten minutes?' Dilys appealed.

'Sorry, no.'

He was determined to leave. Did he fear my supposedly desperate desire for a male might result in his entrapment? Whatever, William's eagerness to depart seemed less than flattering.

My dad kissed me goodbye. 'Thanks a lot, pet. Lovely lunch.'

'Delicious, doll,' Dilys said, 'and so nice to sit down to a meal prepared by someone else.'

As the Jaguar disappeared down the street, I frowned. There had been something about William which revived a distant memory. Either I had seen him before or he reminded me of someone. When and where? Who? He had said he worked in 'import and export', but that meant nothing and offered up no connection. I thought and thought, but the memory remained elusive.

I had finished the washing-up and returned to fretting about the depth of my father's relationship with Dilys – should I phone my brother and tell him? – when the doorbell rang again. Walking down the hall, I saw an outline I recognised through the frosted glass of the front door. It was Lynn. An unexpected visitor.

'Howdy,' I said, smiling. 'I've just had Granddad here for lunch. And not only Granddad, but –' I stopped. I had caught sight of Beth, tucked in behind her mother. She wore an embroidered denim dress, white tights with short denim boots and had a Groovy Chick haversack on her back. She was sucking her thumb. Usually she runs forward to hug and kiss me, and to be hugged and kissed in return, then she asks for a chocolate lolly. But today there were no hugs or kisses, no request. Today she was subdued. 'Hello, my darling,' I said, touching her glossy brown curls. Curls she has inherited from her father. 'I didn't see you. How are you?'

'She's tickety-boo, but I'm not,' Lynn said tersely. 'I'm here to ask if we can stay with you for a while because I've left Justin.'

'Left him!' I shrilled.

Over the past month Lynn had made intermittent complaints about her partner, but I hadn't taken them seriously. They were, I'd believed, the usual niggles that occur in all relationships – and my daughter does have a tendency to make Himalayas out of earth mounds. She can also act rashly.

'Don't bust a gut. I've had enough. Can Beth and I stay?'

'Yes, yes, of course. Come in.'

'You're a star, Mum.'

I'm not. If I'd lived in a broom cupboard I would have welcomed them in, that's what mothers do. When your children are small, you look after them and innocently imagine that once they reach the age of eighteen or so, they will be off your hands. Ha ha. What you don't realise is that children are around, in one way or another, for the rest of your life. And you never stop thinking about them, worrying over them, relishing their successes.

But my cottage has two bedrooms; mine which contains a

double bed and a smaller room with two singles. The smaller one used to be Lynn's room and Beth has slept there when Lynn and Justin have been out late to dinner with friends or at a party, and I am babysitting. I enjoy looking after her and hearing her news, sharing her secrets; though the responsibility of being in charge of a grandchild is surprisingly wearing. I'm always secretly relieved when her parents arrive to collect her – alive and happy, with no cuts, grazes or broken bones – and I only have myself to worry about again.

'Beth, go with Gran,' Lynn instructed. 'I'll bring everything in.'

I shepherded the little girl through to the kitchen and poured her a glass of her favourite apple juice – another item which, like the chocolate lollies, is specially bought. All the while, there were glimpses of Lynn carrying an assortment of cases, travel bags and plastic supermarket carriers up the stairs.

'Daddy's been naughty,' Beth announced, as Lynn went out to her car again. 'Mummy shouted at him.'

'It was just a little quarrel,' I said soothingly. 'Like you sometimes quarrel with your friends. They'll soon make it up.'

'But Daddy shouted back. They both shouted really loud.' Her lower lip quivered. 'It hurt my ears.'

Pulling my little granddaughter onto my knee, I wound my arms around her. It upset me to see her upset and I hated the thought of her watching her parents fighting. It chilled me to the bone. Made me so angry. Had they had no thought for her distress, no consideration, no common sense?

'Mummy and Daddy will soon make it up,' I repeated.

'Mmm.' Beth sounded doubtful, then she looked out of the window. 'Can I play in the sandpit?'

I smiled. 'On you go.'

A couple of years back, I had dug a square, roughly four feet by four feet and eighteen inches deep, in the bottom corner of the back garden, lined it with polythene, bought suitable sand from a builders' merchants – my dad had told me where to go and what to ask for – and filled it. The purchase of buckets and spades had followed. It was an operation which Lynn had viewed with surprise and much amusement.

'I never saw you as the soppy grandmother type,' she had said.

'I'm not, but when Beth comes it'll be somewhere for her to play. Something for her to do,' I had defended myself.

But I am a soppy grandmother, though I had never expected to be, either. Before Beth was born, when other women had produced pictures of their grandchildren or talked about their exploits, my eyes and mind would glaze over. 'They're just kids, ordinary kids doing ordinary things,' I had wanted to say. Nothing special. Boring! Then Lynn had produced a child 'trailing clouds of glory' and overnight everything changed.

It may seem pathetic, but watching Beth grow from a baby into a toddler into a little girl has given me so much pleasure. Unimagined delight. I've even found myself telling people about the funny things my granddaughter has said. Cringe-making or what? And I have a selection of Beth's playgroup paintings Blu-tacked to my kitchen cupboards and photographs of her in the living room. The birthday and Christmas cards she's made me have all been saved. I even have one of those naff bobbing dogs on the back sill of my car, a present from Beth.

I regret not having had more children, sorely regret not insisting that Tom and I should have tried again after our son died. But, as Tom had pointed out, I had already had four years not working which, if I waited to become pregnant again, gave birth and spent time at home with a second toddler, could stretch to seven or eight – and time out in journalism is like time spent on the moon. The damage to my pension pot would also be serious. Now it doesn't seem much of an argument, but then I was unsure and biddable.

I also suspect Tom was frightened that if I had become pregnant again, I might have lost another baby. The thought had tormented me, too.

When Lynn was young, Tom hadn't been much help. He

wasn't a hands-on father like Justin, and never took her to farm parks for dad and daughter bonding – though farm parks hadn't been invented in those days. Nor the bonding concept, either. But Tom had been fighting his way up the newspaper ladder and, while I subsequently descended several steps, he continued to climb. And has reached the topmost rungs. The last time he spoke to Lynn he confirmed what my father had read – that he has strong expectations of becoming the paper's editor.

As Beth started to fill a red plastic bucket with sand, I looked for my cigarettes. I purposely don't smoke when she is around, but now I needed something to calm my nerves. No, you don't, I reprimanded myself. Be strong. You can manage.

'There are clean sheets in the airing cupboard,' I said, as Lynn came into the kitchen. 'I'll help you make up the beds.'

All the bags had been carried in and put upstairs. There seemed to be a large amount of gear to be fitted into one fairly small room.

'Already done,' she reported.

I thought of the meal situation. 'Later I'll pop out and buy food.'

'For us? Not necessary. I've brought some,' replied my efficient daughter.

'Want a coffee?' I asked.

'Please.'

After switching on the kettle, I looked in the cupboard for mugs, but the shelf was empty. A precarious mountain of crockery was stacked on the drainer – most of it from lunch, but some which had been there for eternity – and I carefully extracted two mugs. I would have a coffee, too. Remember to collect the mugs from upstairs, I instructed myself, and bring them back into use.

'You should have a dishwasher,' Lynn declared.

'It's not worth it for one person.'

'It is if that person never dries up.'

This was an old argument, one which I didn't have time for right now. A completely modern kitchen with wood-style laminate flooring was something else Lynn had promoted, but the present cord-carpeted set-up suited me fine. A new kitchen did not feature on my must-have list.

'I believe you and Justin fought in front of Beth,' I said. 'You need your heads banging together.'

'She was in bed and she heard us and came downstairs. We didn't know she was there.'

'You must've been making one heck of a din,' I accused her. 'The sooner the two of you stop playing silly buggers and get back together again, the better.'

'We're not going to get back together. Ever,' Lynn declared. 'It's over. Finished. Kaput.'

My stomach clenched and a lump of acid anxiety formed in my chest. The statement sounded definite. Horribly, sickeningly definite.

'Is there someone else involved?' I demanded. 'Have you – has Justin, met someone?'

'No! We're incompatible, that's the trouble. The big trouble. We don't communicate any more.'

I spooned instant coffee into the mugs. 'You're willing to break up Beth's family, to throw away her security and make her suffer? Aren't you being selfish?'

Lynn scowled. 'You and Dad broke up my family.'

That cut deep. It made me feel so guilty.

'But you were twenty. Beth is four.' I looked out at the sandpit where the little girl was carefully tipping out a sandpie. I loved her so much. I would do my utmost to try and protect her and stop her life from being disrupted. 'She needs to grow up with her mother and father together. It's her birthright!'

'So I'm supposed to spend the next sixteen years co-existing with Justin, wasting my life?' Lynn gave a harsh laugh. 'Thanks very much.'

I made the coffee. Should I repeat Jenny's fact that children from broken homes stand a far higher chance of having emotional difficulties and difficulties at school? And add that they are more likely to suffer from low self-esteem and drift into drugs and crime? But how could I say all that when, at base, history seemed to be repeating itself? Though I hadn't walked out and wrecked a family. Tom had.

'You and Justin have been together for six years and he's a nice guy. A really nice guy. Honest, dependable, friendly.' I handed Lynn a mug. 'Yes, he can go over the top when it comes to watching football, but even though that's irritating, in the scheme of life it's a minor irritation, and it's a stupid reason to split up.'

'It isn't just the football. There are other things.'

'Like what?'

'Him being mega tetchy. I say one wrong word and he flares up. Like him deciding he doesn't want any more kids. He's always said it's up to me, but when I suggested we have another –'

'You did?'

Eager for a second grandchild, I had spoken of how nice it would be for Beth to have a brother or a sister, but Lynn had vowed there was plenty of time.

She nodded. 'I've been feeling broody. But when I suggested another baby, he said no. Refused to give a reason, just no.' She scowled. 'I'm also fed-up with him going out and getting wasted with his mates.'

'Justin isn't that much of a drinker,' I protested.

'He never used to be, but lately –' She rolled her eyes.

'Perhaps he feels he needs a break once in a while. A break from you. And maybe that's what you need, a little space and time and then you'll start thinking straight.'

'I am thinking straight,' Lynn insisted. 'When he isn't being hyper-critical, Justin sits there in silence. A moody silence. He's not interested in me and in what I want.'

'Which is?'

'Mum, this is not your problem,' she said impatiently. 'I've left him and that's it. Naturally Beth is my premier focus, but I also have myself to think about.'

'Have you thought about where the two of you will live and what you'll live on?'

On the four mornings a week when Beth attends playgroup,

Lynn works for an estate agency in Dursleigh. She was with the firm before she become pregnant and, after a baby break, easily fitted back in. She possesses a 'magic touch with clients', so the head of the firm once informed me when we met in the village – which had me walking on air.

'Beth starts proper school in September and then I'm going to increase my hours at the agency to five a day, five days a week, excluding school holidays. I'll earn decent money, but Justin will have to cough up, too. He can afford it.'

Justin runs the Dursleigh branch of a kitchen installation company which started off small and local, but is now opening up showrooms all over the county. He earns a good wage and, thank to the sales he makes, a regularly high commission, and so was able to put down a reasonable deposit on the town house which is Lynn's pride and joy. Or should that be *was* her pride and joy?

'As for where Beth and I will live,' Lynn continued, 'don't worry, I'm not a boomerang kid.'

'I didn't think you were.'

There seems to be a growing trend for adult children to return to live with their parents. A couple of my neighbours have divorced offspring in their thirties and forties who have come back to the family home, in one case bringing their own two children with them. Not the easiest of arrangements.

'I'll put out feelers for somewhere to rent,' Lynn said, and finished her coffee. She washed her mug, dried it and put it in the cupboard. 'And now, if you'll excuse me, I'm going upstairs to unpack.'

Left alone, I watched Beth as she continued to play, constructing a circle of sandpies. Lynn had said the break-up was not my problem, but it was. The thought of my daughter as a single parent and of my granddaughter living apart from her beloved daddy knotted me up inside. It made me want to cry. To crawl under the sheets and sob. I had to persuade Lynn to return to Justin and resume their family life if, indeed, he was amenable. I must bring them back together, but how?

Justin and I had always got on well, so should I contact

him? No, that might make Lynn feel I was switching allegiance and going behind her back. Should I sit her down and give her a damn good talking-to? In her present mood, it seemed unlikely she would listen. But she had always listened to her father. That's what I would do, I would get Tom to speak to her.

On the face of it, asking a man who had deserted his own family to argue in favour of keeping another family together may seem a foolish exercise in the motes and beams department, but for over twenty years Tom had been a caring husband and father. And after our divorce, he had made sure that his relationship with Lynn, which had always been close, had continued. Later he had met Justin and liked him, and now he cared about his granddaughter. Beth has told me how Granddad speaks to her on the telephone and sends her pocket money. He would promote a reunion.

Delving into my bag, I found my cigarettes and lit one. Forgive me, Max, but this is a time of unusual stress.

Since the divorce, my contact with Tom had ceased. There had been no reason to keep in touch and once when he had suggested, via Lynn, that we should meet and take Beth out for the day together, I had refused. The idea of acting the happy united grandparents did not appeal. Lynn sees him several times a year; often on her birthday, over Christmas, for dinners out in London. She has also met her two young half-brothers and Kathryn, the slick chick. She is scathing about her. Thank goodness. I don't know what I would have done if she'd liked her.

'Wears too much make-up, is subservient to Dad – yes, Tom, no Tom, three bags full, Tom – and hangs on his every word. Whereas when he got arrogant, as he can do at times, you used to shoot him down in flames. She's also so damn twittery she drives you insane,' Lynn had said.

This had been a surprise. I had imagined that Kathryn, being one of today's young women, supposedly ass-kicking and man-chewing, would be far more assertive than me.

The last time I saw Tom was a brief, chance meeting at the

hospital when Beth was born. I had been to visit the mother and child and was on my way out, sighing over the wonder of a newborn baby – the tiny fingers, the old man grimaces, the funny little sounds – when I'd turned a corner and walked, slap-bang, into Tom. I had laughed, blushed and felt unusually nervy. It stands to reason that if you love someone enough to marry them and live contentedly with them for years, then they must have something going for them. And if you separate, and the divorce isn't too nasty, a degree of affection, of attraction, will remain.

'Carol, great to see you!' Tom had exclaimed, and kissed me on the cheek.

What is the etiquette for meeting an ex? I had had no idea, but I had not imagined he would kiss me and my nervousness grew. Cool it, I'd told myself. Be calm and collected. Casual. You've moved on in life, remember? He's no longer of any significance.

'And you,' I had said.

'When I see Lynn, I always ask her about you.'

'She's told me.'

Tom had grinned. 'You're looking good.'

'You, too,' I had said, and chatted a little too fast, a little too brightly, about our daughter and her baby before escaping.

To meet this man who was a stranger, and yet so familiar, had aroused a gallimaufry of emotions and now I wasn't keen to meet him again. But for Beth's sake, I would. Desperate circumstances demand desperate actions.

CHAPTER NINE

YET AGAIN MY ATTENTION wandered, this time to Melanie who had stretched across her desk to retrieve a recalcitrant felt-tip pen. She was clad in the usual tight-twanged top and low-rise combat pants which displayed the statutory two and a half inches of midriff and, as she stretched, she exposed her bare lower back and the top of her buttocks, waistbanded and sliced in two by a strip of scarlet nylon. Her thong. According to Jenny, over ten million thongs were sold in Britain last year, but, for me, a thong is an instrument of torture. And not something to be exhibited, which Melanie does routinely.

But in my youth – we're talking pre-history here, kids – the sight of a bra strap was deemed inappropriate, if not downright slutty, whereas nowadays displaying bra straps has become the fashion. Melanie often displays hers, which vary from black to pink to a dirty white and are substantial in order to hoist up her substantial bust. Tony speaks admiringly of her as 'voluptuous'. My description would be top-heavy.

Did the glimpse of her thong – and bra straps – raise Steve's temperature? I wondered. Might they make Captain Cool *molto agitato*? Of late, the girl had spent a lot of time with him in his office where, she said, he'd been stressing the importance of checking and rechecking facts and always making sure of people's names, because accurate reporting was essential. He had also helped her with her grammar. But could the chance of a peek at the scarlet nylon strip be an incentive in his role as tutor?

Maybe her belly button ring turned him on, too? – even though her belly is of the slightly protuberant variety. The idea of piercing your body and slotting it with metal makes me cringe. It raises visions of how, in another forty years, there could be legions of pensioners with snot constantly seeping from the holes in their noses.

No, Steve was being the efficient boss, that was all. He would never be attracted to a girl who carried around pictures of pop stars and considered mooning to be the last word in amusement. Or would he? Middle-age can be a tricky time.

Forever conscious of Steve's comment a month ago about 'not yet' getting rid of staff, I had done my best to impress on Melanie that his editorship offered her a fresh start. I had also suggested to Tony that Steve had higher standards than Eric and he'd be wise to attempt to meet them. As for myself, although I'd been forced to accept that Steve made the decisions, it still irked like hell. Should I look for another job? The idea of him losing heart and bowing out now seemed a foolish dream. It probably always had been.

I returned to the report I was writing, about how the plans to erect the mobile phone mast had been withdrawn; at a meeting where Councillor Vetch, previously great on grandstanding, had remained mute. His silence was the result of subtle suggestions in a previous piece which I'd written, a piece which Steve had agreed, the sour looks the councillor had flung my way had made that clear. I sighed. I should've been triumphant about doing my bit for the integrity of local government, but there were more pressing matters on my mind.

After a night spent tossing, turning and wallowing in despair – there's no gloom as inky black as three a.m. gloom – the morning had brought no reprieve. I was unhappy, restless. Couldn't concentrate. I needed to speak to Jenny. Putting thoughts into words can often help clear the mind and provide a firmer grip on a situation, and I needed to talk to her about Lynn.

Although she may well think 'I told you so', Jenny would never say it. She would be sympathetic. Comforting. And I was in desperate need of comfort. She isn't judgemental though, in truth, our generation can't afford to be. We're the ones with the kids who may be drug addicts or who live in squats, with sons who shout 'show us yer tits' and daughters who oblige. When I hear of the agonies, great and small, that other parents are suffering, I think 'there but for the grace of God go I.' But now I had my own agony to contend with.

After deciding my speech and tone – friendly, but brisk – I had taken a deep breath and rung Tom at his office, only to be informed by a snooty secretary that her boss had left that morning for the States and would not be back for ten days. The woman had asked if I would care to leave a message which she would endeavour to pass on, but I had declined. I could, I suppose, have telephoned the slick chick and asked her to ask Tom to telephone me, but I didn't. Since she commandeered him we've never spoken and I had no wish to start. But also I would have needed to explain why I wanted to speak to him and the idea of revealing troubles in *my* child's life did not appeal. I was damned if I would give her any reason to gloat.

'There's a new cut-out of Max in the sports shop window today,' Melanie said. 'He looks, like, really really way-out. Are you two still involved?'

I shot her an impatient glance. The idea that Max and I could be more than just associates or, at most, platonic friends, had not only lingered, it seemed to be gaining ground. Amazingly. Incredibly. And for no reason. Although I had come clean to the Post Office Jezebel and explained the reality, she persisted in calling him my 'hunky bloke' and talking of how 'young bucks hook up with more worldly women'. Other people had also, in a nudge-nudge wink-wink way, referred to us dining together. I'd even been invited out and pressed to bring him.

Word travels fast and far in Dursleigh. And inaccurately. The next time they'd met in the charity shop, Eileen had informed Jenny that she had seen me with my boyfriend.

'He is not Carol's boyfriend,' Jenny had insisted, and had later explained how, because I'd assumed Eileen had been joking about Max and me being a pair, I had joked, too, but the old lady refused to believe her. And, so Jenny has since reported, never misses a chance to pass on the news.

I had, I recalled, wanted a walker, a pretend boyfriend to fool the masses. No longer. Not when I was continually having to explain that Max and I were not, repeat not, in a relationship – and my explanation went ignored. Yet a part of me couldn't help feeling flattered by the notion that folk imagined such a young, handsome man would be smitten by a golden oldie like me.

If I had suggested another evening out, would Max have agreed? I think so. Not only did I possess useful contacts, but there's a touch of the little boy lost about him which could find solace in the company of an older woman.

'I attend his classes twice a week, if that's what you mean,' I said to Melanie.

'No more intimate evenings?' a male voice asked.

I turned, Steve had poked his head around the door.

'None.'

'Or none you're prepared to tell us about. Can I have a word?'

'Sure,' I replied, and followed him into his office.

'When is Tina Kincaid due to appear on television?' he enquired. 'We could mention it in the 'Morsels' column. People are always excited to think there's a celebrity in their midst.'

'Any time now, though, as of last Thursday, she hadn't been given the exact date. But who told you about it?'

A couple of weeks ago, Tina had announced at a work-out that she had agreed to join Joe Fernandez' series in the new year and would be a guest on one of the current run of shows 'sometime soon'. The comedian had been continually persuading and urging her.

'Tina did. She stopped me in the street last week and told me how Joe Fernandez was keen to have her on his show. I can understand why. Then she mentioned the trouble she was having with some bolts on a door. Seems they were so stiff, the poor girl could hardly move them. I suggested a drop of oil or WD40, and she was so grateful.' He grinned. 'Praised me to the skies, then wrapped her arms around me and hugged me.'

He sounded amused and yet, personally, I felt Tina's response went way over the top. Though, remembering her performance at the wake, it seemed to be her usual behaviour with men. She laid on compliments with a trowel and they were beguiled.

'Do you think she'd be happy if we mentioned her TV appearance?' Steve went on.

'I'm sure she'd love it. And she's loving the idea of going on television again. Last Thursday she was full of it, wondering what to wear, if she should go for elegance or be more up-to-the-minute trendy – seems she gets a dress allowance – agonising over whether or not she should have her hair restyled.'

'Speaking of hair, my hair growth seems to have gone berserk,' he said. 'I never used to have hair around my nipples, but now it's as thick as grass and I'm gathering a veritable pelt across my shoulders. Turning into a baboon,' he declared, lifting his elbows and dangling his arms.

I laughed. I could, I suppose, have told him about my chin hairs, but depicting yourself as an old hag is a bit different to equating with King Kong.

'I've raised a smile. Thank God,' Steve said. 'You've been looking so bloody miserable this morning.'

'I'm worried.'

'About what?'

'Lynn, my daughter.'

'And?'

Did I want to reveal my family woes? It was not as though we were buddies. All we did was rub along, grittily. Besides, wouldn't he be bored? Tom had had little patience with other people's personal anxieties.

'Come on,' Steve encouraged. 'I told you my troubles.'

'Lynn arrived at my house yesterday,' I began slowly. 'She announced that she'd left Justin, her partner, and asked if she and Beth, her little girl, could stay for a while. Lynn and Justin had quarrelled and she'd walked out.'

My pace quickened, and I found myself explaining in detail and at some length. I had never imagined Steve as a confidant, yet knowing of his torment over his divorce – and also the

129

mention of his hairy nipples – had knocked down a barrier or two. And he didn't look bored. On the contrary, he was receptive and reassuring.

'Lynn'll soon realise she's made a mistake,' he said, when I ground to a halt. 'It's easy to rush out in the heat of the moment, but when she's had time to think things through it'll all look different. She'll return.'

'I hope so. And thanks. Thanks for listening.'

He smiled. 'Anytime.'

I rose to leave. 'By the way, does the name William Langsdon ring any bells?'

'Nope.'

'He's fiftyish, slim and around five-nine, with cropped brown hair going grey. Bit of a tough guy in the good-looking football manager mode.'

'He's another of your men?'

'No! And I don't have 'men'.'

Steve grinned. 'Not even the muscular Max?'

'Especially not Max! Our dinner at the Barley Mow was a one-off and so I could interview him, that's all. We are not a couple. I met William Langsdon yesterday,' I continued. 'He's the son of someone my father knows. It's just that I'm certain I've seen him before, or perhaps I saw his photograph. In the past. Distant past. But I can't remember where or when.'

'Sorry, can't help.'

Following Max's dictum of walking instead of driving, shortly after noon I set off down the High Street and towards the river. The sunny weather had continued and high above in the clear blue, jumbo jets swanned up and out from Heathrow and an eye-in-the-sky helicopter tracked the motorway for snarl-ups. As I walked, I scanned the shop windows. Dursleigh has shops which, in my youth, would have been considered bizarre. There's the party shop, selling balloons and masks and paper trumpets. A shop dedicated to tiles, another to flooring and an angel shop dispensing – would you believe? – angel memorabilia, including gilded angel statues. And, of course, there are the charity shops.

Although Jenny was not on duty in her shop, that did not mean she would necessarily be at home, but if she wasn't I would retrace my steps to the office, picking up something for lunch on the way. Whatever, I was getting exercise.

In listening to my outpouring of anxieties about Lynn, Steve had revealed a surprisingly caring side, I reflected. The guy did have some good points.

Where the road curves away from the High Street and down alongside the river, there is a stretch of a hundred yards or so where it is wider. Here, on the side next to the river bank, cars park, bumper to bumper. Because it's handy for the shops and free, it's a popular spot. Vehicles come and go all day.

I was walking along, wondering if Beth had been happy at her playgroup today or if, poor little soul, her parents' quarrel meant she'd been sad – I hoped not – when a horn blared. Someone had freed up a parking space and another car was attempting to draw in, forcing the vehicles rounding the corner to brake, stop and wait. *Attempting* was the operative word. I saw the car, a low dark car, slowly manoeuvre into the gap, then reverse into the road again. Head into the space at a slightly different slant, only to pause, back out and hover. Traffic was stacking up in both directions.

The horn blared again. It came from a four-by-four at the front of the queue which, losing patience with the fruitless ins and outs, was giving warning that it was swinging past. Four-by-fours are the vehicle of choice among affluent families in Dursleigh who, you can guarantee, never ever go off-road. Come school run times, the roads are full of them. Often driven by reckless young mums.

Seconds later, tyres squealed. The four-by-four, a huge metallic blue job, had met a motor cyclist in black leathers and space-age helmet coming head-on. The motor cyclist swerved, narrowly missing the four-by-four which braked sharply. Juddered. The young woman at the wheel, a hatchet-faced brunette, rolled down her window and poked out her head.

'Turd!' she yelled.

The motor cyclist raised a middle finger.

A final try, and the car made it into the space and stopped. At an angle with the rear protruding, it was not parked prettily, but at last the traffic flow could resume.

As I drew closer I saw it was a BMW and realised from the back view of a blonde clad in light beige that the driver was Tina. She had switched off the engine and was sat straight-backed. Her shoulders looked tense. Intending to commiserate, I bent and peered in through the passenger door window. Tears were trickling down her cheeks.

Pushing on the handle, I opened the door and slid into the seat beside her. I patted her arm. Tina may annoy and exasperate me – there are times when I could give her a damn good shake – but I didn't like to see her so distressed.

'Don't cry,' I said. 'It's not the end of the world.'

She turned to look at me through tragic, blurry eyes. 'No?'

'I'm no crack-shot at parking myself and so what if you held up the traffic for a couple of minutes.'

She blinked rapidly. 'Held up the traffic?'

'While you did the samba, but you managed it in the end.'

'I samba-ed?'

'You're not crying because of the parking,' I said, as Tina took a tissue from the door pocket. Not only was she oblivious to the chaos she'd caused, but, I realised, the redness of her eyes and stash of soggy, discarded tissues indicated she had been crying for a while. Yet she didn't look ugly. When I cry my nose and my mascara run, my face gets blotchy, I resemble a deranged Pekinese. Tina just looked... sad. A distressed heroine. 'So what's wrong? What's the matter?'

'It's –' She was unable to get out the words.

'A bad day and you're missing Duncan?' I suggested.

Over the past couple of weeks, she had looked better and seemed happier. Indeed, her excitement about appearing on television had dominated her conversation and she had not mentioned her husband. She had also, I'd noticed, removed her wedding ring. But perhaps she was suffering from delayed shock and, suddenly and cripplingly, his death had hit home.

'It's – it's not Duncan,' she managed.

'Then what is it?'

Tina sniffed, peered into the mirror and dabbed at her eyes. Gathering her composure, which took time, she faced me. 'This morning I had a phone call from the producer of Joe's show. He said that me taking part was not Joe's decision, it was his. Seems he had only just heard what Joe was planning and he'd vetoed the idea. He doesn't want me on because –' She reached for another tissue. Tears were brimming again. '– because I'm past my sell-by date.'

'The guy didn't actually say that,' I protested.

'He did! He said he would cut the crap and tell it as it is. That Joe might think I was a wet dream in high heels, but so far as he was concerned I was way past my sell-by date and if he let me on as a meeter and greeter I'd turn the programme into a laughing stock. The Joe Fernandez' fucking old fogeys' parade.'

I raised my brows. The producer had not minced his words.

'Does Joe know about this?'

'No idea. I was so upset I couldn't face talking to anyone, so I put the answerphone on. But I seem to remember he's up in Walsall today opening an Internet café, or it could be a launderette, and he hadn't rung when I came out. I needed some things from the shops and thought a change of scene might help, but as I was driving along I started to think about what the producer had said. I began to cry, could barely see, so I decided to pull in before I had an accident.'

And in pulling in you almost caused one, I thought.

'The guy was probably thirty-five going on thirteen, with halitosis and zits, and what does he know?' I scoffed. 'Has he ever met you?' Tina shook her head. 'So he hasn't seen what you look like and –'

'He knows I'm in my fifties. Late fifties,' she muttered, as if the words were like poison on her lips, 'and that's all that counts.'

'To him, maybe, but not to everyone. I reckon if you went

133

on the show you'd be a big success.'

'You think so?' she said doubtfully.

'I do,' I replied, meaning it. 'We may live in an age obsessed with youth, but there is what's called the 'grey market' which is a sizeable portion of the population, the core, and they're not going to suffer a fit of the heebie-jeebies if they see an older woman on television.'

'You don't see very many.'

I couldn't argue with that. The females you get as news readers, chat show hostesses, even weather forecasters, all tend to be dolly birds. Bimbos. It is as though once a woman turns forty she automatically turns into an eyesore and, for the sake of the nation's wellbeing, must be banished from the screen.

'And why don't you see them?' I demanded. 'Because some callow youth producer says no. What d'you bet Joe will talk to the guy and get him to rethink?'

'Perhaps,' Tina said, as though the chance was minimal. Looking into the mirror again, she carefully wiped her eyes. 'If the weather's fine tomorrow we'll be working out on the tennis court and, I hope you don't mind, but there'll be three other women with us.'

'I don't mind. Who are they?'

'More of Max's clients. Seems they don't know each other, but they're all keen to have extra sessions and he said that if they could come along and I'd allow him to use the court, he'd give me my week's work-outs for free. I'd rather it was just you, me and Jenny, but the money from the Merc and the brooches is disappearing fast. After I settled up with the undertakers and Garth House, I realised there were gas and electricity bills to pay, then I saw the cutest pair of beaded mules and –'

'Economy is the name of the game,' I warned, and looked at my watch. 'Sorry, must go. I'm on my way to Jenny's.'

'I'll take you.'

'No need.'

'It's no bother. And Carol –' She smiled, a genuine smile as though she meant it. '– thank you.'

Driving me the few minutes to Jenny's house may not have been a bother, but getting back onto the road was. Tina had taken six shunts, in and out, to park, but it took her eight to un-park. Once again she held up the traffic and received glares from other motorists – which had me sinking low in my seat and trying to pretend I was invisible – but she seemed gloriously immune. When she finally extracted us, I offered up a prayer in grateful thanks. And I said another when I saw Jenny's car parked on her drive. She was in. Tina let me out at the kerb, executed a ragged and rapid five-point turn, and shot back off in the direction of the village.

'Hi,' I said, smiling when Jenny opened the door. Then I frowned. She looked strained and tense, not at all the usual cheery Jen. 'Is something wrong?'

'Yes. I don't know. Maybe. I've just got back from Guildford and – oh, Carol,' she said, 'it was terrible. Such a shock. So unexpected. I'll get us some lunch and then –' she made a noise which sounded like a sob '– I'll tell you about it.'

What had happened? I wondered, as she efficiently, but morosely, produced ham and tomato sandwiches, and cups of coffee. Could she have been mugged? Witnessed a distressing road accident? Become caught up in an argument in a shop? The latter seemed unlikely because Jenny will agree to almost anything rather than cause a fuss. Yet whatever it was, it had seriously shaken her.

Lunch prepared, she sat down opposite me. 'In the past six weeks, Bruce and I have only made love eight times,' she stated.

'Oh,' I said.

Over the years, the two of us have shared all kinds of secrets, worries and joys, fears and grumbles, delights and aspirations, but Jenny has never ever spoken about her sex life. Divulgences of such an intimate nature are not her style. She's never talked about lust or desire or how she'd like to get down and dirty with, perhaps, the postman or some charmer from the telly. I, on the other hand, have reminisced about passionate couplings with Tom, extolled the relief of having lovers and, more recently, complained of frustration. And shocked her rigid.

Fellatio and cunnilingus are not words which feature in Jen's vocabulary and initially I had to explain what they meant. Much to her embarrassment. Nor had she ever set eyes on, let alone used, a vibrator. Though she had been able to tell me, courtesy of her lunchtime newspaper perusal, that Britons buy as many vibrators as washing machines and tumble-dryers, and a third of homes contain one. Also that in 1883 a man named Joseph Mortimer Granville had invented a treadle-operated vibrator which was offered to doctors as a medical aid for women suffering sexual tension.

But now Jenny had shocked me.

I had no idea how often she and Bruce made love – they could restrict themselves to Christmas Eve and Easter Sunday or be at it twice nightly, like rabbits – but the 'only' combined with her expression indicated that eight times in six weeks was a pretty poor show. For them, maybe. I'd be in heaven.

'Is that because of you… or him?' I enquired gingerly.

'Him. He always claims he's too tired.'

'It'll be because he's working out at the gym,' I said, adopting the soothing role of agony aunt. 'Bruce is – what, fifty-six?'

'Fifty-seven.'

'– and exercising after a day in the office is bound to take it out of him.'

'That's what I thought, too, but then this morning in Guildford I saw –' She broke off, finding it difficult to continue.

'What did you see?' I prompted.

Jenny drew in an unsteady breath. 'Bruce with a woman. A young, well, youngish woman. About forty she was, smart, with fair hair cut in one of those long swinging bobs and wearing a dark jacket and skirt.'

'She'd be a business colleague.'

'But she kissed him! I'd gone to collect my contact lenses –

remember I told you I'd been for an eye test? – and as I was walking along the cobbled street towards the opticians I saw them coming out of a coffee bar together.'

'This was before you got your new lenses, so are you sure it was Bruce?'

'Positive.'

'But he didn't see you?'

'No. He had his arm around the woman and he was looking down at her and talking.' Jenny gulped. 'He was totally immersed in her.'

'And she kissed him?'

'On the cheek.'

I flicked a dismissive hand. 'Social kiss. Means nothing.'

'But Bruce is still exercising, still losing weight and last weekend he bought a new tie, an expensive silk tie, and you said shedding weight and new clothes means –'

'It was a joke.'

My sense of humour was causing trouble. Big trouble. First, Eileen had taken me seriously and now Jenny.

'He's started cutting his toe nails far more than he used to. He did them again last night. And he's taken to trimming the long hairs in his eyebrows.'

'That means he's having an affair? No way. Bruce isn't the type. He's a good husband. A devoted husband who can be trusted. He loves you, Jen.'

'Then what was he doing on a Monday morning in the middle of Guildford with his arm around a woman?'

'Ask him. There'll be a simple explanation. You're reading far more into this than it merits. You have no reason to worry. Absolutely none.'

'Bollocks!' Jenny retorted, and shocked me again. She virtually never uses bad language or swears.

'If you should have reason to worry, which I am cast-iron certain you do not, then you should still ask him,' I said. 'Better you know what's happening sooner rather than later.'

She stared down at her hands which were gripped tightly in her lap. So tightly, her knuckles had drained white.

'Is it?'

'Yes. If Bruce has only just started… something, then it'll be easier to finish. Think of me and Tom. He'd been canoodling with the slick chick for six months before I found out, so she'd had time to build up a pretty tight hold over him. But if I'd discovered after only a month or two, she wouldn't have been so powerful – or pregnant.'

'You're right,' Jenny decided. 'I'll speak to Bruce when he comes home this evening.'

'And don't worry.' I patted her shoulder. 'An arm around someone is insignificant. Likewise a kiss on the cheek. Your imagination's running wild and you're jumping to conclusions, but they are the wrong conclusions. Totally wrong.'

I was determined to reassure her. Jenny is a good person and a dear friend, and I hated her to be so distressed. I hated her to be unhappy. Especially about nothing.

'You didn't see them together,' she said grimly. 'How're things with you?'

I gave a casual shrug. 'Same as usual.' With her so immersed in her own troubles, this was not the time to load her up with mine. Reaching down to my bag, I took out a catalogue. 'I sent for this, thought you might like to see it, especially as the weight's falling off you.'

The catalogue was for fitness wear. We had both been saying how we ought to get something snazzier for the work-outs and try to bring ourselves up to Tina's level.

'Thanks,' she said, but her response was tepid.

There was no reaction, either, to my comment on her losing weight, yet up until now she has proudly informed me of every shed pound. To be truthful, it isn't exactly 'falling off'. Jenny has confessed that, despite Max's twice weekly incantations of 'you can do it', she isn't good at self-denial and still eats the occasional chocolate bar, so her loss rate is around a pound a week. Which isn't bad, but isn't gold star status, either.

'Have you got your contact lenses in now?' I enquired.

She shook her head. 'I'll try them later.'

Silence.

'Any more job interviews lined up?' I asked, for once having to make conversation. A fortnight ago, Jenny had attended another interview, but again had been unlucky.

'None.'

'Heard from Victoria recently?'

'Yes. She's coming home in two weeks' time.'

'You'll be looking forward to seeing her again,' I said encouragingly.

'It'll be lovely,' Jenny agreed. 'She was talking about an Australian lad called Shane, who she's palled up with. How much she'll miss him.'

'Is he her boyfriend?'

'Victoria says they're just mates, whatever that means. I do hope she's behaving herself.'

Another silence.

Five minutes later, I left. Jenny was in no mood for talking.

As I walked back to the office, I thought about what she'd told me. While I accept that none of us are ever what we seem, the idea of Bruce having 'a bit on the side' was hard to imagine. Even if he had become over-active on the toe nail cutting and eyebrow tidying. He was too solid, and too stolid, to be a love rat. And he and Jen were such a comfortable fit that I would wager millions – if I had them – on him being loyal. Yet was he? I had never expected my own husband to cheat, so how could I be certain of someone else's?

CHAPTER TEN

I FROWNED AT MY reflection in the bathroom mirror. The hairs which had flowered on my chin were still a pest. I would yank them out one morning and yet a couple of days later they would be back, full grown and defiant. Fooled ya! And now here was a third of the same ilk; rigid, jet black and lengthy. I hunted in my make-up basket for tweezers. I had visualised myself ageing into a white-haired, apple-cheeked grandmother, not some cut-price Bin Laden. Get me to retirement and I'd be able to apply for a job in a freak show as a bearded lady. Looking on the bright side, it represented an alternative work opportunity if that best-seller failed to take off.

'I hate CocoPops!'

Beth's shriek rocketed up the stairs from the kitchen. I smiled. I don't know what time it was – just coming light so probably around six a.m. – but I had been awoken that morning by a little hand tapping on my shoulder.

'Excuse me, Gran,' a voice had whispered, 'please can I come into your bed?'

'Hop in,' I'd mumbled, moving over.

'I love you, Gran.'

'Love you, too, my darling.'

Until I'd babysat and Beth had been old enough to crawl into my bed, I had forgotten how good it feels when small children snuggle up, warm and ruffled and affectionate. If you're a parent and it happens every night you want to wring their bloody necks, but when you're a grandparent and it only happens from time to time, it is delicious. A joyful reminder of family and generations, and how a part of you will live on for ever. When Beth is a grandmother, maybe she'll tell her grandchild how she cuddled up in bed with me, great-great-grandmother Carol, a funny old bird who dug a sandpit and used to give her chocolate lollies.

With Beth alongside, I had dozed. While she had talked to herself and to me, wriggled, sung songs, wriggled some more, become fascinated with the scratching sound of her fingernails on the pillow. When Lynn had awoken and ordered the child back to her own bed, I had felt deserted.

When I went downstairs, Beth was sat at the kitchen table with an untouched bowl of CocoPops in front of her. On the opposite side, Lynn drank mint tea – she'd brought her own supply of herbal teas – and read a chick-lit paperback.

'Why are you dressed like that?' Beth enquired, subjecting my T-shirt and shorts to a critical gaze.

'Because this morning I'm going to my exercise class.'

'Can I come?'

'No, you can't,' Lynn told her. 'You're going to playgroup and, besides, the class is for ladies. And you mustn't go into Gran's bed so early again. She needs her sleep. Now eat up.'

A rebellious lower lip jutted. 'Don't like CocoPops.'

'Have something else,' I suggested. 'What about Frosties?'

'I hate Frosties.'

'Rice Krispies?' I asked hopefully.

Thinking Beth would enjoy a choice of cereal, I had bought a Variety Pack. Big mistake. The selection process she went through – this one? that one? yes, no, perhaps? – would drive a saint to frenzy.

'You spoil her,' Lynn said. 'She eats the CocoPops or nothing. You like them,' she told Beth. 'You had them last week and said they were your very best favourite.'

As the little girl denied any knowledge of such a claim, I reached for the muesli which sits on the worktop, alongside the toaster. It wasn't there. I looked around, my gaze crossing over the wiped-clean worktop with no coffee rings, an empty drainer, Beth's Bart Simpson 'character lunch box' filled with fruit and other healthy food, which sat ready for her to collect on her way out. While I err on the side of domestic chaos, my daughter does not. Maybe it's a backlash against the parent, but, like Jenny, she believes there's a place for everything and likes everything in its place. She wasn't too bothered when she lived with me, but having her own home has released squeaky-clean tendencies. And since she moved in two days ago, my kitchen has never been so tidy.

Lynn is into 'minimalist' and the townhouse where she lives – lived – with Justin is all wooden floors, bare white walls and clean-lined furniture, with a vase of lilies ingeniously placed. There is nothing surplus and no detritus is allowed to settle. At least, not after seven-thirty p.m. when Beth goes to bed. Lynn had a real go at me once when I went round one evening and slung my jacket over the end of the stairs, dropped my bag and a newspaper onto a coffee table, then kicked off my shoes. I was, she informed me, turning the place into a tip.

It's funny how roles change and daughters start bossing mothers about. I wonder if it is the same with sons. Do they find fault, become prison officer strict and dispense unwanted advice? I must ask Jenny.

'Seen the muesli?' I said.

Lynn glanced up from her book. 'It's in the food cupboard.'

She didn't add 'where else, twerp?', but I heard it. And what had she been inferring when she had talked of me 'needing my sleep'? She'd made it sound as if I was ancient and decrepit. On my last legs.

I had located the muesli and was pouring some into a bowl, when Lynn closed her book.

'Time to go, Beth,' she said.

The little girl pouted. 'I haven't had my CocoPops.'

'Leave them.'

'But I want them.'

Lynn shut her eyes, appeared to silently count to ten, and opened her eyes again. Then, using a level tone which I had to admire, said, 'Eat them quickly.'

She is a good mother. She always listens to Beth, has patience and is protective of her welfare. She has brought her up to say 'excuse me' and 'please' and 'thank you', and to respect her elders.

'I don't mind Beth coming into my bed,' I said, joining Lynn at the sink, as she washed up her cup and saucer. The child was busy shovelling CocoPops into her mouth and I spoke quietly, so she could not hear. 'As for spoiling, I reckon that, given the current circumstances, a little spoiling, a little comfort, won't do any harm.' I paused. 'Don't you think you should get in touch with Justin today?'

'He can get in touch with me. He knows where I am.'

I sighed. Emphatically, with feeling. 'Neither of you speaking to the other is infantile. You need to get together and –'

'Leave it, Mum,' Lynn ordered.

Hearing her mother's sharp tone, Beth looked up and so, reluctantly, I left it.

I had parked on Tina's forecourt when Jenny drove in.

'All clear with Bruce?' I enquired, as she got out of her car. After my troubles with Lynn, I was in need of cheerful news. Desperate for something up-beat and positive.

'No.'

My heart shrivelled and I looked at her in dismay. 'Oh my God, Jen, you mean he is –'

'I didn't ask him. I was going to, but then I thought of how a kiss on the cheek and his arm around the woman means nothing and I'd got everything out of proportion and he'd only tell me I was being silly, then I'd feel a fool and –'

'You chickened out.'

''Fraid so. Feeble, but –' She gave a shamefaced shrug.

'And you're still worrying?'

'All the time.'

'If you want peace of mind, you must speak to Bruce. Tonight. You must. It might be difficult, but it's the only way.'

'I know, and I will.'

'Promise?'

'I promise. It's a lovely morning,' she declared, looking up at the cloudless blue sky. 'Perfect.'

'It is, so we'll be working out on the tennis court and there'll be three other women with us,' I said, and told her about meeting Tina the previous day. 'I meant to mention it when I called in to see you, but I forgot.'

'Poor Tina's going through such a hard time,' Jenny sympathised, when I had finished my recital about the television job falling through, and why.

'She's not the only one. Lynn and Justin have quarrelled, so she and Beth have moved in with me. Hopefully their split is temporary, but Lynn arrived on Sunday and she and Justin haven't spoken to each other since.'

Jenny looked anguished. 'Oh Carol, I'm so sorry, and what a worry.'

'I feel half demented. They're acting like a pair of kids.'

'They are a pair of kids. Academics have redefined adolescence for their generation as lasting to the age of thirty-four.'

'Seems about right.'

'They'll get back together,' Jenny said. 'It's just a hiccup.'

I was wishing I shared her certainty when I heard the thump-thump of music which indicates a radio inside a vehicle, turned full on. It was Max, coming up the road in his white van. The van was battered, but had a newly-painted logo of two exercising figures on the side, underscored by his website. Could Calvin, the mouse-addicted brother artist, be responsible? Following the van were two four-by-fours and an acid yellow sports car. Max and the four-by-fours stopped outside, but the sports car swung onto the forecourt, spraying up sheets of gravel and forcing Jenny and me to jump back. It came to a halt beside my Ford Focus, a little too close for comfort.

'Hi, babes,' Max called, and, after collecting his holdall, walked towards us. 'Listen up everyone, it's getting to know you time. This is Carol and Jenny, and here we have Pippa, Gerri –'

'That's Gerri with a g, two r's and an i,' cut in the young woman who had emerged from the sports car. Emerged as in slithered snake-like, an operation which I noticed had had her door a bare half an inch off touching my car.

'– and Dee. Everyone say hello.'

The newcomers were sun-bed bronzed – or maybe it was fake tan – and young, somewhere between late twenties and early thirties. Gerri and Dee, who carried a sleeping baby in a portable cot, were slim, while Pippa was plump. They all had dark hair with blonde streaks, cut in variations of a style which I understand is called 'the shag', which meant their hair looked as if it had been hacked about with garden shears. Dressed in black leotards cut high on the thigh, with matching headbands and Nike trainers, and wearing designer sunglasses, they were interchangeable fashion statements. I was about to make a comment on their similarity to the Beverley Sisters, when it struck me that they might not know who the Beverley Sisters were. And if they did, would not appreciate my wit.

Although Jenny and I said a cheery 'hello', their only acknowledgement was a vague nod.

'Carol's a reporter with *The Dursleigh Siren.* She wrote the article about me, the one which encouraged you to get in touch,' Max told them.

There was another vague nod, before they clustered around him as he set off for the front door. It is said that when women reach their fifties they become invisible to men, but Jenny and I were invisible to Pippa, Gerri and Dee. Our T-shirts and baggy Eric Morecambe shorts had not impressed them, either.

When Max introduced the trio to Tina, they showed a fraction more interest and even managed smiles; though whether that was because she was their hostess or because they approved of her outfit was anyone's guess. Tina wore a gunmetal-grey tank top and bootleg flares with ankle zips, which screamed 'expensive'. I hadn't seen them before and hoped they weren't a new purchase. I would have enquired – and discreetly asked if she had recovered from yesterday's disappointment – but Max declared he was running late and ushered everyone out through to the garden.

Down on the tennis court with reggae blaring, we launched

into the work-out. Would Beryl hear and march down to complain about the noise? Might Peter discover an urgent need to hoe? Time passed, but there was no sign of either of them. Though Tina's lawn was, I noticed, mown short in ruler-straight stripes.

Considering we could give our classmates a good twenty years, Tina, Jenny and I disported ourselves well. We kept pace with all the exercises, did not gasp, creak or rupture ourselves, and were not too visibly exhausted by the end. While a little red in the face, Jen and I didn't sweat profusely, either. A month of working out meant both of us were fitter.

Afterwards everyone gathered in the conservatory, where Tina had provided glasses of iced water. Her hostess skills were improving.

'Generous-sized garden,' Pippa remarked, looking out of the window. 'My husband and I have recently moved into a new property and we have a generous garden. Not as big as this, but –'

'How big?' enquired Gerri.

'Around a third of an acre.'

Gerri smiled. 'Ours is half.'

'We're fortunate, we have a full acre,' Dee announced. 'Ideal for the tinies.'

And so the point-scoring began. All three, they claimed, had husbands or partners who performed vital work in various industries and earned vast, vaster and vastest amounts. All three women followed their own 'motivations'. Pippa marketed natural remedies to health food shops, Gerri counselled unfortunates who had lost their jobs, while Dee was concentrated on bringing up her children.

'I have four, the other three are at school. A private school,' she explained. 'So many people employ nannies and, of course, I could do, too, but I prefer to nurture my children myself. As I did with the others, I take Nathaniel everywhere with me. It's 24/7. We're never parted.'

'My perspective is completely different,' Pippa declared. 'I've got three kids under five, but for the sake of my sanity I

146

need a life outside home. Anything less would be a dreadful waste of my brains. I've found a superb girl and I have absolutely no worries about leaving my children with her.'

As they banged on about their lives, Tina, Jenny and I were ignored. It was as though we didn't do and could never have done anything of the slightest interest, and were totally out of the loop.

Next they moved on to how much they appreciated Max.

'He's allowed me to freely shape my time and direct my energies,' Pippa pronounced. 'I've demystified myself and I'm like, hey, great.'

'The warm, supportive place he provides has enabled me to move forward with a new clarity,' crooned Gerri. 'We really resonate.'

'So insightful,' cooed Dee, 'and so today. I had self-esteem issues, but no longer. And he's done wonders for my pelvic floor.'

'Pass the sickbag, Alice,' I muttered.

But Max appreciated the trio, in return. He soaked up their flattery and, while he did not ignore us, was far more attentive to them. He joked, he flirted, he smiled his white, white smile. This switch of allegiance didn't bother me – they were of a similar age and it was natural – yet Tina seemed peeved. Then he put his arm around her and asked how she was feeling, and she cheered up.

The girls had hurtled into one-upmanship prattle about who had taken the most select, expensive, trendy holiday, when the telephone rang.

'This could be Joe, I haven't spoken to him since – you know,' Tina told me, and went to answer it.

If it was the comedian, there were no squeals of delight and when she returned a few minutes later her expression was grave.

'Problem?' Max asked, as the trio bandied descriptions of tropical islands and Italian castles and kids' clubs in the South of France.

'The producer doesn't think I'm right for the show, so I'm

out.'

He frowned. 'But Joe's the star so surely he can override him?'

'Seems not. He says he's tried, but the producer won't budge. For now, though Joe reckons there's still time for him to change his mind.'

'So all is not lost,' Max declared, then turned to the trio. 'We're talking about Joe Fernandez. He and Tina are friends. And, as I may have mentioned, Joe's wheelering and dealering on my behalf.'

'Anything in the pipeline?' Pippa asked him eagerly.

'I'm considering various projects.'

'So we'll soon be seeing you on the box?'

'Hope so.'

'If you believe it, you can achieve it,' I recited, but Max was not amused.

Dee studied Tina. 'You used to be on television,' she declared.

Tina smiled and put a hand on her hip. 'That's right.'

'It was when I was a child. A small child.'

Tina's smile tightened.

'My grandma had a thing about Joe Fernandez,' Gerri said. 'She used to reckon that when he sang 'My Way', he made her go all shivery. Old gal's gaga now. Been gaga for ages and has incontinence issues.'

Tina's tight smile froze.

'Before she appeared on television, Tina was a top model,' Jenny announced. 'Similar to today's supermodels. She was photographed by all the leading photographers and appeared on the covers of the most stylish magazines. She may decide to model again.'

'She's got the looks,' I said, before Tina could object. 'Let's be honest, girls, most of us are pretty standard stuff, but her bone structure – classical!'

'Will we be meeting here again on Thursday?' Pippa demanded.

She had drained her glass and was ready to go. That

another woman's achievements and beauty might surpass hers did not seem to be something she wanted to hear. Especially an older woman's.

'I suppose so,' Tina said flatly.

'It's my birthday on Thursday,' Gerri declared, and acted out a shiver of dismay. 'I'm dreading it. I shall be thirty. Me! Thirty! Imagine!'

'I hated turning thirty,' Dee said. 'I mean, it's like you're not young any more. For six months, I was really, really depressed.'

'You had it easy,' Pippa told her. 'Thirty pushed me to the edge of a nervous breakdown. How I'll cope when it comes to forty, I do not know.'

Should I tell them about the menopause? I wondered, and describe bed sweats and hot flushes and how your mind can turn to jelly? It was tempting though, in fact, I had suffered relatively few problems, thanks to the magic of HRT.

'Forty will be a major issue,' Dee declared, and agonising over how they would ever survive the onset of middle-age, the trio exited.

'Must be off to my next client,' Max declared, and he went, as well.

'If that crew made you feel as if you came out of the Ark, they did the same to me,' I told Tina.

'And me,' Jenny said.

Tina looked at us. 'Honest?'

'Honest,' Jenny confirmed. 'Though I don't think they were being deliberately hurtful, it was more a case of them just not thinking. You don't when you're their age.' She shrugged, then went on. 'But you're slim and blonde, Tina, so you should worry, whereas I'm overweight and have cellulite and my hair is going grey and –'

'Why don't you tint your hair?' Tina suggested. 'Tint it yourself. For years I've gone to a salon in Knightsbridge, but I can't afford it now so I bought hair colour from the chemist and used it at home and –' she flicked her ponytail '– it's great.'

Jenny considered the idea, then nodded. 'I'll try it,' she said, and asked for the product name. 'Though we shouldn't feel down about getting older. Winston Churchill didn't become Prime Minister until he was sixty-five and Sarah Bernhardt –'

'Who?' Tina enquired.

'Sarah Bernhardt, she was a French actress who lived around the turn of the last century. She played Juliet in 'Romeo and Juliet' when she was seventy.'

I grimaced. 'Sounds like a sight for sore eyes.'

'Maybe she was a bit ancient,' Jenny conceded, 'but the point is, she did it.'

'The experienced woman can be a potent sex symbol,' I said, rallying to her argument. 'Who do you remember in the film *The Graduate,* the seductive Mrs Robinson or her dishwater daughter? And any number of older women have posed in the nude for, say, a W.I. calendar or on the cover of *The Radio Times.*'

Tina giggled. 'You reckon I should do that?'

'I reckon you could. And I reckon you should have another shot at modelling, with your clothes on.'

She looked doubtful. 'Well –'

'I agree,' Jenny said. 'People who are positive about ageing live on average 7.5 years longer than those who complain about the passing years.'

'Duncan was always positive, but it didn't help him,' Tina said, and frowned. 'I ought to empty his wardrobes and clear out his clothes, his shoes, the gorgeous cashmere coat I bought him for Christmas, but what do I do with them? And what do I do with his books, his shaving mug, the magnifying glass he used to use? Putting everything out for the refuse lorry seems heartless and such a waste.'

'Your charity shop takes men's clothes, doesn't it?' I said to Jenny.

'Yes, so long as they're in good condition. We take books, too. And if you have items we're unable to help with, I can tell you of other places which might accept them.'

'Would you? Thanks,' Tina said gratefully. 'Suppose you take a quick look at the clothes and everything now, then you can see what I'm talking about.'

Jenny nodded. 'Okay.'

As they set off up the stairs, I went with them. I had yet to see anything in the house which appeared to be of saleable value, but perhaps I would spot something that belonged to Tina – another gift from her husband – which she could turn into cash.

The main bedroom was large and, as elsewhere, the furniture was well-worn and the furnishings drab. Halfway along one wall, a door stood open. As Tina started to show Jenny the clothes in a huge, old-fashioned wardrobe, I pushed the door wider and walked into an adjoining room.

I smiled. This was one place in the house which had been renovated. Pale built-in closets filled three walls, while on the window wall was a long, low dressing-table unit with knee-hole seat, make-up mirrors and, at one end, a full length mirror. The array of cosmetics, anti-ageing creams and a box of 'facial vibrating pads' indicated that this was Tina's dressing room.

A couple of closet doors were open. Inside the first, trouser suits, day dresses and evening dresses hung on a long rail; each in pristine condition and protected by polythene covers. The second closet had been sectioned off into shelves. The three highest shelves were stacked with handbags, again looking new and carefully wrapped, while the lower ones held shoes; high heels in many different colours, strappy sandals, mules, including what could be the beaded pair which Tina had so recently bought. When I looked closer, I saw that the shoes bore names such as Jimmy Choo and Manolo Blahnik.

There is a shop in Dursleigh which deals in 'pre-loved' clothes, so long as they are in good-as-new condition, up-market and top quality. We're talking Jaeger, Basler and designer labels – M&S or C&A don't get a look in. You take your garment along and, if it meets the criteria, agree a price and when it is sold, receive half the profit. Duncan's cashmere coat sounded a suitable candidate and I was thinking I would suggest to Tina that she could sell some footwear, handbags and clothes – instead of buying more – when I heard a squeal.

'That's fantastic!' Tina cried, and, a moment later, she squealed again. 'Another!'

When I went back through to the bedroom to investigate, she was excitedly waving a roll of banknotes in each hand.

'Look what Jenny's found. They were tucked inside a pair of Duncan's brogues, brogues he hadn't worn for years.'

'Tucked up into the toes,' Jenny explained. 'I only came across them by chance.'

'All the notes are fifties and there are twenty in each roll, which means two thousand pounds,' Tina said, beaming. 'That'll keep me going for a while.'

'There could be more,' I said.

'You think so?'

'I do. As soon as Duncan spent one wad of notes, he started on another,' I said, remembering. 'Yes?'

'Always.'

'But where did he get the cash? He didn't have much in the bank, so isn't it possible he kept it hidden at home?'

Tina looked thoughtful. 'I guess.'

'Why don't we have a blitz,' I suggested, 'and go through every single pocket in his jackets, coats, cardigans and trousers? Every pair of shoes and slippers?'

'Good idea,' Jenny said.

'His underwear, too,' Tina added. 'I'll check his thermal vests, his Y-fronts. Okay, girls, let's get cracking.'

Jenny and I went to the old-fashioned wardrobe which was filled with suits, blazers and heavier winter wear, while Tina started on drawers in a tallboy.

'Eureka!' I exclaimed, a few minutes later. In the zipped pocket of a faded blue anorak was another roll of fifty pound notes.

We had returned to our labours when Jenny found another, fitted into the collar of a rainjacket which contained the hood. Both rolls were put onto the bed.

'Success!' Tina crowed, producing a further roll from the back of a drawer where it had been lying beneath a jumble of socks. 'Duncan was a sly old dog,' she said, as we continued to search. 'I asked him once where he got all his ready cash – I mean, he never used chargecards – and he told me he'd made it a habit to take cash every week from the tills in his shops. He didn't take much, but over the years it added up. And it was money which escaped the tax man.'

'But his masterstroke could've been when he sold his shops,' I said.

Tina looked puzzled. 'What do you mean?'

'You don't know?'

'Know what?'

'Well, I can't say for certain if this is true, but there was a rumour that he did a deal with the Patels. It was reckoned that each time he sold them a shop he agreed to a lower asking price, so far as the solicitors and the tax man were concerned, which meant the Patels didn't have to pay so much in stamp duty. But it was on the understanding they gave him the difference to the true value in cash, which they were happy to do.'

'I never took much notice when Duncan talked about financial matters, my brain's not geared that way,' Tina said, 'but I remember him laughing about how he and the Patels had had 'a good thing going', so the rumour could've been correct.'

'And Duncan wouldn't have wanted to put the cash into the bank where it would've been visible,' I reasoned, 'so he kept it at home. Like here.'

The roll of notes I produced came from inside the split satin lining of an ancient dinner jacket.

Over the next quarter of an hour, the three of us continued to search and by the end of that time nineteen rolls of banknotes lay on the bed. Each roll consisted of twenty fifties which meant the total came to nineteen thousand pounds.

'Where are you going to keep all this?' Jenny asked.

Tina sucked in her lower lip. 'Don't know.'

'Do you have a safe?' I enquired.

'No. And I'd prefer not to take it to the bank because, who knows, my crappy stepsons could find out I have it and demand a share.'

'Why not put the money in the drawer, underneath all the socks?' Jenny suggested. 'Presumably it's been in the bedroom for years and not come to any harm.'

'I'll do that,' Tina decided.

'Duncan could've hidden cash in other places,' I said. 'In a desk or a cloakroom, even in the garage. You should check.' I looked at my watch. 'I must go.'

'Me, too,' said Jenny.

'Thank you both so much,' Tina said, following us as we made our way down the stairs. 'If Jenny hadn't come across the money in the shoes and if you hadn't suggested there could be more, Carol, I may never have found it. But now I'm rich! And now I want to pay for the work-outs for you both for the next six months.'

I shook my head. 'That's kind, but there's no need.'

'None,' said Jenny.

'I'm paying,' Tina insisted. 'I'll square things with Max so from now until – make it the end of the year – your work-outs are free.'

Jenny and I looked at each other. It was clear Tina would not be dissuaded.

'Thank you very much,' we said.

'And I shall tell Max I'm paying for my work-outs and I don't want the terrible trio back here on Thursday, or ever again.'

Jenny and I grinned. 'Thanks,' we repeated.

That evening on my way home from work, I took a detour to the Bridgemont flats.

'You're elusive,' I said to my father, as we drank our cups of tea. 'I rang yesterday and three times today, but there was no reply.'

'I was out with Dilys. We went down to the coast on

154

Monday and into London today.' He sank lower into the sofa. 'I'm bushed.'

'You bought her an engagement ring?' I enquired.

His head shot up. 'Wherever did you get that idea?'

'Well, on Sunday Dilys hinted that things between you could be... becoming serious.'

'And that's why you've been telephoning me?'

'I – um, I wondered what the score was.'

'Things are not serious, but if they ever should be I will let you know. When I'm good and ready. In my own sweet time. Without any prodding.'

'Yes, Dad,' I said meekly. I was being reprimanded, told to mind my own business.

'What did you think of William?' he asked.

'I only met him for five minutes, but he seemed nice enough. I believe Dilys also has a daughter.'

'Yes, she's a real beauty according to Dilys, though I've never seen her. She hasn't been to Bridgemont so far as I know. William can't be short of a bob or two,' he continued. 'He's given his mother a diamond and gold bracelet. Magnificent thing, must have cost a fortune. He's told her to keep it covered if she goes out wearing it, to stop her getting mugged.'

'A wise precaution.'

'Dilys is going to do a lunch at her place and invite the two of you, just as soon as she can tie William down to a date. She finds it difficult to keep track of him. His business means he's all over the place, then he'll suddenly appear and arrange with Gillian to stay the night in the visitors' suite. Good value, much cheaper than a hotel, though it'd be cheaper still if he was in his own home in London or travelled the few miles to that house he has locally. Or if he bedded down on Dilys's floor.' My father shook his head at the extravagance. 'Be nice if the two of you clicked.'

'We're not going to click and I don't want to click,' I told him.

'Still carrying a torch for that Max chap, are you?'

155

'I am not,' I said crisply, 'and I never have done.'

He slung me a doubtful look. 'So you say.'

'Dad, it's true! How many times must I –'

'Alright, alright.'

'After you'd gone on Sunday, Lynn and Beth arrived,' I told him. 'They've moved in with me. Lynn and Justin had quarrelled and she'd walked out and –'

'Lovers' tiff. Soon be over,' he said dismissively, and took a drink of tea. 'You remember I spoke of Em who does my cleaning? She has a son who isn't married. He's just come back after years of living in Africa and he –'

'No!'

CHAPTER ELEVEN

'YOU'VE TAKEN YOUR TIME,' Max said, 'but it seems to me the belly is flatter and the hips are starting to narrow, too.'

Jenny blushed. 'Over the past week I've lost three pounds.'

'You look terrific for it,' he told her.

Tina nodded. 'Especially with the hair.'

Jenny's fair and grey mix had been replaced by a whole-head beige blonde, which had knocked off several years and made her look surprisingly glamorous.

She smiled. 'I tinted it over the weekend.'

'Dig the gear, too,' Max remarked. 'Yours and Carol's.'

Now I smiled. 'Thanks.'

The outfits which Jenny and I had ordered from the catalogue had arrived and this was the first time we'd worn them. Being unusually daring, Jen had chosen a silvery blue ensemble of a 'brakini' and bootleg flares, while I had gone for a white vest top teamed with khaki and white jazz pants.

It was Tuesday morning, a week on, and we had completed our work-out which, because the weather had turned cloudy and it was spitting with rain, had taken place in the conservatory.

'You're achieving your goal,' Max declared, praising Jenny. 'Now all we need is for Carol to forsake her beloved cigarettes.'

'I'm trying,' I said.

'And I was born in Amsterdam.'

'I am trying. Honest. I didn't smoke on Sunday or Monday and although I'm getting the shakes –' I wobbled a hand '– I haven't had a cigarette this morning, either. But I still need you to deliver a few warning kicks in the posterior, so keep on sending the e-mails. Please.'

'Yes, ma'am.' He started to pack away his gear. 'I'm sorry, babes, but I have to cancel Thursday's session.'

'Why's that?' Tina enquired, suddenly perturbed. 'Is something wrong?'

'Just the opposite.' Max beamed. 'I've been asked to do an exercise slot on morning TV.' He named the programme and the channel. 'It's five minutes, a try-out, a one-off, but if it pushes the right buttons with the viewers there's always a chance it could become regular. If that happens we'll need to rejig your days.'

'Congratulations,' Jenny said.

I nodded. 'From me, too. You must be delighted.'

'High as a kite. And it's all thanks to Tina, because she put me in touch with Joe Fernandez who, in turn, put me in touch with the right television go-getters.' Reaching for Tina's hand, the young man raised it to his lips and kissed it – in what I recognised as a practised gesture. 'I'm grateful. You're a lady worth knowing.'

Tina looked serious. 'I hope it turns out okay.'

'Will you be doing the kind of work-out you do with us?' Jenny asked.

'Pretty much,' he said. 'Three of my clients are joining me. You've met them – Pippa, Gerri and Dee. Seems the set is small, so the producer didn't want a large group. The girls are thrilled to be taking part in such an exciting gig. If you can watch, we're due on around nine-thirty a.m.'

'You could've asked us three to do the work-outs with you,' I teased, for I guessed that the reason he'd waited until now before mentioning the programme was because he felt awkward about telling us and hoped to make a quick getaway.

He looked uneasy. 'I suppose, but –'

'Too lengthy in the molars?'

'Hell, no. You're all foxy ladies – and you should each embrace the fact that you're a woman and not a girl – but the programme's cutting edge and geared towards the younger market.'

'Surely most younger women tend to be at work or busy with their kids, and it's older women who watch at nine-thirty?' Tina said.

'Yeah, well, maybe. See you next Tuesday, babes.' Max was beating a hasty retreat. 'And wish me luck.'

'We do,' Jenny and I chorused.

'He needs it,' Tina said, when he had disappeared and we had moved into the kitchen to drink the usual glasses of water. 'The slot could easily fall through.'

'But it sounded definite,' Jenny protested.

'Nothing Joe Fernandez has a hand in is definite. He and his contacts are not reliable. You believe what you're told, how everything is arranged, then it turns out the skunk's been taking you for a ride.'

'His offer of a place for you on his show wasn't kosher?' I enquired.

'No. You remember I said how he'd pushed and promoted the idea, and almost begged me to appear? Seems he'd never mentioned it to the producer. And when he did and the producer objected, he didn't argue. He'd been talking pie in the sky to sweeten me and make me feel indebted. Joe isn't reliable in relationships, either,' Tina added bitterly.

Jenny frowned. 'He's stopped ringing you?'

'No, he still rings every day. He's keen for us to resume our affair – to 'cuddle up close' as he puts it – but that's all. He has no intention of marrying me.'

'Perhaps he wants to,' Jenny said, eager to soothe, 'but he feels duty bound to stay with his sick wife. It'd be understandable.'

'I'm not convinced the woman is sick,' Tina declared. 'She lives in their house in deepest, darkest Dorset and keeps a low profile, is never photographed or interviewed, so she could be in perfect health.'

'She's recovered?' Jenny asked.

'I don't think she ever was sick.'

Jenny looked puzzled. 'But I read about it.'

'Me, too. And, when we were together, Joe always maintained she was sick and I believed him. He was forever saying that if it hadn't been for her, we'd have been galloping up the aisle.' Tina gave a curt laugh. 'But recently it dawned on me that, according to him, the woman has been ill for near enough twenty years, with no deterioration, no improvement.'

'Does seem convenient,' I remarked.

Tina scowled. 'Too bloody convenient.'

'Why don't you ask him about his wife? About her state of health?' I said. 'Demand a straight answer to a straight question.'

'Maybe I will. After Duncan died I was pleased when Joe seemed to care – and maybe he does, a little – but he doesn't care enough to be honest with me. To admit he only wants me as his mistress and not his wife.' She sighed. 'But being his bit of fluff again isn't what *I* want. I need a husband to look after me.'

'You're not inclined to go it alone? To move on and start a new life? One in three households consist of people living on their own,' I stated, quoting a Jenny fact, 'and, believe me, it isn't so bad. You get used to running things your way, to making your own decisions, to having freedom. There are advantages and living alone doesn't equate with being lonely. I'm forever out and about.'

'Maybe someone like you can cope and be fine, but I'm hopeless on my own. I need a husband,' she repeated.

'So tell Mr Fernandez he's a past number.'

Tina looked doubtful. 'You think I should?'

I thought that no matter how critical she was of the man, she would still enjoy having him chasing her. And perhaps she considered that being chased by a skunk was better than not being chased at all. She may need a husband to look after her, but she also craved constant male attention.

'I think you should make your own decision.'

'Joe isn't as helpful as Steve is,' she said, then giggled. 'Whatever problem I have in the house, Steve seems able to tell me what to do to fix it. He's so clever. Such a pet.' She flicked back her ponytail. 'And he's available.'

'But not rich,' I pointed out.

I wasn't being catty, I was being practical. Another of Tina's needs was access to ready funds, to be spent lavishly.

Besides which, while Steve might like her looks, surely he could never become the soulmate of a woman who regularly watched 'Footballers' Wives' and for whom shoes and handbags were an obsession. Yes, I'm being catty now.

'So? I've got money and I could make a lot more, if I model again.'

'You might?' Jenny asked.

'Out of bravado and, I suppose, to show Joe I could still hack it, I rang a modelling agency and fixed to see them. The appointment isn't until Thursday week, in the afternoon, but –' Tina switched from buoyancy to trepidation '– already I feel nervous. And if I'm nervous now, what am I going to be like on the day? Maybe I should cancel.'

'You don't cancel,' I said. 'No way.'

'But –'

'Would it help if I went with you?' Jenny suggested.

'Us go up to London together?' Tina nodded 'Yes, please. Having you there would help keep me calm and give me courage. Thanks.'

Taking her diary from her bag, Jenny made a note of the date and the time they would meet at the railway station.

'If Victoria and Shane want to go anywhere that day, they'll have to make their own arrangements,' she said.

'Victoria *and* Shane?' I queried.

'When we went to pick Victoria up from the airport at the crack of dawn on Saturday, the lad was with her. Seems he'd decided to come over, spur of the moment, and spend six months in the U.K. So when we got home I had to rush around, preparing the spare room and making up the bed.'

'He's staying with you?'

'Victoria asked if he could, just until he finds lodgings, but–'

She broke off. Someone was knocking at the kitchen door.

Tina went to open it. 'Peter, my darling man!' she squealed. 'How lovely to see you. Come in, come in.'

'Called round to say I'm sorry I can't cut the lawn today because it's too wet, but I'll do it the next time I have a chance. The next time the dragon lady goes off to play her bridge and we're alone. Oh!' He had noticed Jenny and me. His colour rose and he looked flustered. 'Didn't realise your visitors were still here. Don't want to intrude.'

Tina clasped his arm, as if to prevent him from leaving. 'You're not,' she assured him. 'These are my friends. They've been doing the fitness class with me. Firming up the body beautiful.'

'And it works,' Peter declared, smiling at her.

She patted his arm. 'You flatterer!'

'Time we were gone,' I said.

Tina nodded. 'See you both next Tuesday.'

'See you,' Jenny and I echoed, and we made our way out of the house.

'You were right,' Jenny said. 'Peter does have tufts of white hair sprouting from his ears. Not a turn-on. Tina didn't mean it when she talked about him as a possible future husband, did she?'

'Who knows?'

Jenny frowned. 'But he has a wife.'

'I doubt Tina regards a wife as much of deterrent, unless, of course, she happens to be married to Joe Fernandez.'

'Probably not.'

'Are you losing weight because you're still worrying about Bruce and the woman?' I asked, as we approached our cars.

'Goodness, no! I've no idea why I made such a fuss. I mean, thinking about it again, the whole thing was so innocent. And Bruce isn't a two-timer.' Jenny trilled out a laugh. 'I've almost forgotten about it.'

I slung her an old-fashioned look. The truth was that, despite her promise of a week ago, when it came to confronting her husband she still hadn't plucked up the courage. The incident wasn't forgotten and, while she might deny it, she was still worrying – and allowing fate to weave its dubious course. Though I suppose you could also argue that by not challenging Bruce, she might be preserving her marriage.

'You're lying, Jennifer,' I said.

She sighed. 'You know me too well. Yes, I'm so wound up I don't feel like eating, not even chocolate – which isn't like me, at all. And yet common sense says there isn't any reason to be wound up or to fret. We made love last night and it was –'

'Spectacular?' I suggested, when she hesitated, modestly lowering her gaze.

'Satisfying. Having Victoria and Shane in the house makes both of us feel a little inhibited. But if I still appeal, if Bruce still wants to make love to me, then he can't be interested in anyone else. Can he?'

'Impossible,' I said, providing the answer she needed to hear.

Though Tom had continued to partake in our sex life at the same time he had been sleeping with Kathryn. The frequency may have tapered a little, but I had not noticed any decrease in his passion.

Opening her car door, Jenny slung her bag inside. 'Maybe I should find myself a boyfriend and have an affair. That'd teach him.'

I grinned. 'What type of guy do you have in mind? Mean, moody and a millionaire? Bearded intellectual? Hard-bodied beach bum with –'

'I mean it. Bruce is away on a business trip for the next couple of days, so –' She tossed her newly blonde head. '– I think I'll look around. Flutter my eyelashes, wiggle my hips and see what happens.'

'You're joking.'

'I'm not.'

She wasn't. She was straight-face serious.

'That's crazy,' I protested.

Her weight loss and new look may have boosted her confidence, but in even thinking about a flirtation Jenny was going too far.

'Why? I've only ever slept with one man. I'm missing out. I'm a freak. If a campaign was launched to discover whether there are any sad souls left in Britain who've only been shagged – unpleasant word – by just one person, I'd be a sure-fire winner.'

'And bully for you! Jen, you have a good relationship with your husband and a good sex life – usually. That's what every woman wants. It's every woman's dream. It's what we all hope for. The universal desire. Sleeping with some bloke you hardly know is a waste of time. It's also dangerous, demeaning and, in your case, would be horribly disloyal.'

'But exciting.'

'No! You mustn't even consider it. You don't know that Bruce has cheated on you and, even if he has, two wrongs don't make a right,' I said urgently.

She ignored me. 'What's happening with Lynn?' she asked. 'I assume she's still with you?'

I sighed. Jenny was simply sounding off and – surely? – would have second thoughts. Sensible thoughts. She wasn't the type to give men the come-on. She wouldn't know how to start. Her talk of 'looking around' was baloney. Imagination running riot. A total pretence.

'She is,' I replied, 'and she's still refusing to sort things out with Justin. How's Victoria?'

'Heavier by at least ten pounds and never stops talking about what a wonderful time she had in Oz. Shane's on the heavy side, too. And noisy.' She grimaced. 'They've been here three days and already I'm back to acting as a chauffeur, expected to run them all over the place.' Her chin jutted. 'I'm not going to do it. The worm has turned. Would you like to come and have dinner tomorrow evening, around seven-thirty? I won't be cooking, I shall ring for a pizza.'

'Yes, please.'

Beth opened the fridge and looked inside. 'Please may I have that can of orange?' she asked.

Lynn shook her head. 'No. You had a fizzy drink this morning and, as you know, one a day is your ration. So please close the fridge.'

'Why?'

'Because I'm asking you to and because you're letting warm air in.'

'I want to let it in.'

'The food will go mouldy.'

'I want it to go mouldy.'

'But I don't, so please close the fridge.'

Long seconds ticked by; rebellious seconds, can't make me seconds. Then, finally, the fridge door thudded shut.

'Orange is stinky and –' Beth stuck out her tongue '– you're stinky.'

Lynn sighed. 'That's silly talk.'

It was cheeky talk. The fashion in these politically correct days may be to insist that children should never be physically disciplined or even told they are naughty – 'you've made a bad choice' is apparently the phrase to use – but I still believe there are times when a short sharp slap can work wonders. I've longed to administer one to kids in public who have answered back; brattish, brazen and obnoxious. Yet if I had, I could've ended up in prison and the excuse for the kids – tomorrow's delinquents – would be that they were suffering from Attention Deficit Disorder.

I wasn't advocating a slap for Beth – the little girl is going through a confusing time and you can't blame her for acting up – but I considered Lynn could be firmer. Or perhaps it was just me, getting tetchy.

After less than two weeks of my guests being in residence I was, on occasion, becoming a trifle stressed. I didn't like sharing the bathroom – someone either seemed to be always in there or wanting to come in – and the wonky loo was getting worse. Where before it had flushed one time out of two, now it required repeated attempts. I must, I reminded myself, contact a plumber and get it fixed. My wardrobes were also a problem; packed tight with clothes I usually kept in the spare room.

Yet there was a plus side. It was good to come home after work and be greeted. Good to be able to talk to someone about the events of the day. Good to know that if I should trip, fall headlong down the stairs and be knocked unconscious – a

165

depths of the night scenario – there would be someone to hear me, rescue me and to care. Perhaps when Lynn and Beth go I should get myself a lodger? Or perhaps not.

My guests were showing signs of stress, too. Beth seemed to take a dislike to every last thing, which was unswervingly termed 'stinky', while her mother struggled to keep calm. Poor Lynn, she was trying so hard not to appear forlorn. And yet, as she had yet to meet Justin and discuss their troubles, this could be said to be her own fault.

At least they had spoken on the telephone. First he had rung her and then she had rung him, but apart from giving Beth an opportunity to chat with her daddy, both calls had been unproductive and, from Lynn's terse account of them, bitter. She had told him he needed to attend a course of anger management classes. He had informed her that she was a darn sight too critical. Stalemate.

However, help was at hand. I had spoken to Tom at his office and he was driving out to Dursleigh on Saturday afternoon. If we could manage it, I wanted him to have a quick word with me first and be filled in more fully on the situation, then he would speak to Lynn and – I hoped and prayed – persuade her to consider a reconciliation. Lynn was not aware of her father's forthcoming visit. I had reasoned that if she didn't know, she wouldn't have time to build up resistance to his persuasion.

The prospect of meeting Tom again was also raising my stress levels. I knew it shouldn't bother me, knew I shouldn't *let* it bother me, but it wasn't so easy. I may have reclaimed my life and the wounds may be well and truly healed, but… Whenever I thought about him, I was aware of emotions – mixed emotions – sneakily erupting inside me.

'Spaghetti. I hate spaghetti!' Beth declared, eyeing the pan which her mother was stirring.

Because she doesn't approve of pre-prepared meals – though she consumed plenty during her teenage years – Lynn was making dinner for her and Beth, while I ironed the top I would wear for going over to Jenny's house later.

'You like spaghetti,' I said.

'Spaghetti is stinky.' Beth stuck a finger up her nose, took it out and inspected it. 'Joeys are stinky, too.'

'You are being disgusting,' I said sharply. 'Now wash your finger and don't –'

'Chill, Gran.'

I laughed. I couldn't help it. The little girl's tone and the look she gave me were just so world-weary, so cute. Putting down the iron, I washed her finger myself and then hugged her. If Lynn hadn't been busy spooning spaghetti bolognaise onto plates, I would have hugged her, too. We may be a messed-up family, but we were still a family and I loved them both, so much. So very much.

After they had eaten, Lynn took Beth upstairs for her bath. Before she went, I kissed the little girl goodnight.

'She says please can Gran go up and kiss her again,' Lynn reported, when she returned to the living room where I was all set to depart. 'Sorry, but she does seem rather keen.'

Upstairs, Beth was lying in the subdued glow of her nightlight. A curly-haired angel in a pale pink nightdress, cuddling her teddy. When she saw me, she smiled. ''Lo, Gran.'

I bent to kiss her forehead. 'Hello, my darling.'

She wrapped her arms around my neck, so tight they almost hurt. 'I love you. And I love my daddy. I want to go back home and live with my daddy,' she said.

'I know.' I also knew that was why she had needed a second kiss, so she could tell me. Unwinding her arms, I sat down on the bed beside her. 'You will do, soon.'

'My daddy carries me around on his shoulders so I can touch the ceiling and he plays Snakes and Ladders.' She giggled. 'He isn't very good. I always win.' The giggles faded and, in one of those quicksilver changes which kids are so good at, her big brown eyes were bright with tears. 'It's my fault my mummy left my daddy. I was naughty, I spilled crisps all over the floor, salt and vinegar crisps, and –'

'It isn't your fault, Beth,' I said. I had read of how children blamed themselves for family break-ups, yet never really believed it was true. 'Mummy and Daddy falling out has nothing to do with you. Nothing at all.'

Her brow crinkled. 'You're sure?'

'I'm sure. I'm positive. And everyone spills crisps sometimes. I once spilled crisps when I was out with some friends *and* I spilled my drink. It was a glass of wine, red wine, and I knocked it off the table and onto the floor. The glass broke and the wine splashed everywhere. Onto people's clothes and even onto a cat.'

'A cat?' Beth said, round-eyed.

'A black and white cat, only the wine made most of the white parts pink. When it got splashed, the cat miaowed and jumped up in the air in surprise. Then it licked some of the wine off the carpet, gave a big hiccup and fell fast asleep under a chair with a smile on its face.'

The little girl giggled, then became serious. 'I want to see my daddy. I want to give him a big hug and a big kiss. The biggest hug ever and the biggest kiss ever.'

'You will see him,' I said. 'Very soon. I promise.'

'Cross your heart and hope to die?'

'Cross my heart –'

'You have to do it.'

I made the cross. 'Cross my heart and hope to die.'

Beth clasped her teddy, stuck her thumb into her mouth and turned on her side. Already her eyelids were drooping. 'Night, night, Gran.'

Kissing her again, I tucked the bed clothes up around her. 'Night, night, my darling.'

Determined to move mountains, part oceans, talk sense into my pig-headed daughter, I marched down to the living room. To hell with not interfering. To hell with letting other people make their own mistakes. To hell with being a know-all. And never mind if I was late at Jenny's.

'You have to arrange for Beth to see Justin,' I said. 'You must. If you don't then I shall –'

'A meeting is fixed for Saturday afternoon.'

168

'It is?'

'While you were upstairs, I rang him. Beth has been going on and on about how much she misses him, so the three of us are going to Harley's farm park.'

'What time?' I asked, thinking that Tom had said he would arrive between two-thirty and three.

'Justin's picking us up at two-fifteen.'

'What time will you be home?'

'Around four-thirtyish, I guess. Why?'

'Just wondered. You and Justin could bury the hatchet?' I suggested, daring to hope.

'Not a chance! I'm meeting him because Beth is desperate to see him and he wants to see her, but that's all.'

'The two of you need to sit down and have a frank and honest discussion,' I told her, 'and don't roll your eyes. Incredible though it may seem, there are times when mother does know best. Part of the problem when your dad and I split was that we didn't talk. Not in any depth. I never asked what was so lacking in our relationship that he'd felt a desire for someone else. Or if there was a way we could've improved things. And afterwards I tried so hard to think if there was something I'd missed. Any signs of your father's dissatisfaction.'

Lynn frowned. 'And?'

'I couldn't come up with anything. Anything serious. We'd had our grumbles with each other, the occasional ding-dong argument, but everyone does.' I went to close the door. I didn't want the sound of our voices to carry upstairs and disturb Beth. 'I know he'd met Kathryn and she was younger and prettier and a much better cook —'

'She isn't prettier. Never was, and the last time I saw her she'd put on quite a bit of weight. Sticky-out tum and too fat thighs for the satin trousers she was wearing. Sumo wrestler thighs.'

I smiled. Whenever Lynn criticises her stepmother, it is music to my ears. A ha-ha-ha! concerto. But the slick chick had had no qualms about sleeping with my husband. She had shown not the slightest remorse at trashing a marriage. So many times I had imagined how she must have pinpointed him and gone for him. Zoom! like an Exocet. She was the original scheming bitch.

'But when your dad first told me about her, I should've said that if he fancied someone younger and –' I paused '– moderately pretty, who laughed at all his jokes, it worked two ways. That I'd like to come home to a tall, dark, handsome and adoring stud who strolled around stripped to the waist.'

Lynn grinned. 'With a six-pack torso and giant-sized prick?'

'You got it.'

'But now you wish you'd tried to work things out?'

'Yes. I was stupid in that I gave up, gave in too easily. Far too easily. I should've begged and pleaded to save our marriage. Grovelled.'

'Grovelling sounds out of character.'

'Maybe, but I should've pointed out that in divorce everyone is a loser, and they are. Your dad lost out financially in that he had to support you, me and his new family. You suffered in that you were without a father around the house and also had to move house, leaving your friends behind.'

'I soon made new ones.'

'Yes, but it was an upheaval you could've done without. As for me –' I shrugged '– I missed the bastard so much. Missed him for years.'

'Even though Dad had cheated on you, you still cared about him?'

'For ages and deeply. Insane, yes? But what I'm trying to say is that all relationships need perseverance. And all relationships have their ups and downs. So don't rush into ending things with Justin. Please, please think it over. Think of how you've always got on so well together and been so happy. How delighted you both were when you realised you were pregnant. How he's a demon in bed.'

Lynn laughed. 'I've never told you that.'

'You didn't need to. But think –'

'You're going to start singing 'Always Look on the Bright Side',' she said.

'I'm tuning up. But think of Beth and how you and Justin separating will affect her. Think of everything.'

'I will.' My daughter was silent for a moment, then she fixed me with a speculative look. 'You've never shown any real interest in any man since Dad. Not long-term interest. Do you think you ever will?'

I hadn't told her about my two brief relationships, though I'm not sure why. Maybe because I'd sensed from the start that neither of them was destined to survive, maybe because I was afraid she might consider the notion of me being keen on sex at my great age was tacky, or maybe because I'd wanted her to believe I was forever faithful to her father. Freudian, that.

'Don't know, but if I did would you mind?'

'No. Why should I? In fact, I'd be delighted. But shouldn't you start looking? Time's passing, Mum, and –'

'Not you, too,' I complained. 'People, usually women, are forever trying to pair me off.'

'You know why? They think you're out there living it up in the fast lane and they're afraid you might steal their husbands.'

'I very much doubt that,' I said, though it was a new idea. I collected my shoulder bag. 'I'm off. Don't wait up.'

Could my unattached status make other women feel threatened? I wondered, as I climbed into my car. I'd never considered myself a *femme fatale* nor aggressively flirted with 'other halves', yet might they want me settled down because then I'd be out of the running? Did Jenny's desire to marry me off spring from a terror of Bruce and me combining? I grinned. She knew that her husband did not provoke the slightest sexual interest in me – or much of any other kind of interest – and *vice versa*. Indeed, I felt sure Bruce had criticised and grumbled about 'your mate Carol' on endless occasions.

Sliding into gear, I drove off. While I may not be actively on the look-out for a man, I do notice them. I notice attractive men in the street, in the supermarket, at various meetings I attend. Some of the attractive men I notice even have grey hair. I must be getting old! Will nose hairs be a turn-on as I age?

That Victoria and friend were in residence was evident the moment I stepped into Jenny's hall. A bomber jacket hung from the newel post, a pair of flip-flops lay in a corner, and the sound of pop music reverberated from upstairs.

'Sorry I'm a bit late,' I apologised. 'I've been trying to talk sense into Lynn, but no luck. However, Tom's coming to speak to her on Saturday, so keep your fingers crossed.'

'Tom's coming to Dursleigh? You contacted him?'

'I did and I just hope he'll be able to help.'

'It'll be odd for you to see him again,' Jenny commented.

'Very,' I agreed, and followed her into the kitchen.

'Victoria has turned the house into a pigsty,' Jenny complained, as she poured us glasses of wine. 'She was untidy before she went away, but she's a million times worse now. Shane isn't hooked on tidiness, either.'

'You're forever picking up after them?'

'No. I've decided that my days as a slave are over, so if something gets dropped it stays there.'

'A woman after my own heart,' I said, though I doubted she would be able to let the clutter lie for long. Knowing Jenny, it would get on her nerves and she would feel compelled to clear it. 'How's Shane progressing with locating a lodging?'

'He hasn't even begun to look. So far, the two of them have spent most of their time holed up in Victoria's room, drinking milky coffee, eating Mars Bars and listening to C.D.s. I've suggested they go into London, so he can look for digs. I've suggested they jump on a train and visit Hampton Court or the Brighton Pavilion, and show Shane some history. I've suggested they simply go for a walk and get some fresh air. But they look at me as though I'm stupid.' The music stopped, a door opened and there was the heavy clump of feet

172

descending the stairs. 'Speak of the devil.'

The kitchen door opened and Victoria came in, followed by a shaven-headed, deeply tanned youth with a stripe of dark hair down the middle of his chin. He stood around six foot four and was of rugby player proportions.

''Lo, Aunt Carol,' the girl said.

I smiled. 'Hello.'

Victoria, who has long curly mid-brown hair and hazel eyes, had always dressed in prim blouses and short skirts, but now she wore a loose top, baggy trousers and trainers. As did her companion.

'This is Shane.'

'Great to meet you, Carol,' the young man boomed, and enfolding my hand in a massive paw, he vigorously shook it.

'And you,' I said, then, extracting my hand, turned back to Victoria. 'I believe you had a good time Down Under?'

'It was beaut. Fantastic. I went to Alice Springs and Ayers Rock – to see the Rock at sunset is life-changing. Another wonderful place is the Daintree Rainforest and –' She was off, rolling out her itinerary in an Australian-tinged accent, until the energetic hooting of a car horn sounded outside. 'That'll be Mick and Mo. Didn't fancy pizza, so we're going with friends to The Rabbit Hutch.'

The Rabbit Hutch is a public house located a few miles from Dursleigh in the middle of countryside, which attracts the younger, wilder crowd. There are slot machines, a juke box and, according to notices which I've seen stuck on lamp-posts, minor pop groups with weird names often play there. The food served is cheap and cheerful.

'Soft-pedal on the burgers and the ale. Think of the calories,' Jenny cautioned.

Her daughter stiffened. 'Are you saying I'm fat?'

'I'm saying your stomach's not too bad, but you're stacking the pud onto your bottom and thighs. Which is fine if you want J-Lo *gluteus maximus* –'

'What?'

'Buttocks – but if you don't then go easy on the intake.

173

What time do you expect to be home?'

Victoria looked sour. 'Dunno, but I've got my keys.'

'No worries,' Shane boomed.

'Come in quietly.'

'We will. Bye.'

'Bye, ladies,' Shane said breezily.

The front door banged shut, there was the revving of an engine and the sound of a car drawing away down the road.

'Victoria is chunkier,' I remarked, as we took our wine through to the living room.

Jenny nodded. 'She drinks too much beer. She got into the habit while she was away and every evening since they arrived she and Shane have gone out to one of the pubs, to 'sink a few' as he puts it. And as my critical daughter used to comment on my figure defects, now it's my turn.'

'What does she think of her new blonde streamlined mum?'

'She's impressed, though she only admitted it because William and Patrick went on about me looking so good when they were here at the weekend. Patrick's accepted the New York job by the way. Starts next month. Maybe when he's settled, you and I could fly over for a few day's sightseeing and shopping? Bruce is forever jetting off to places, so I reckon I deserve a treat, too.'

'Um... yes. Sounds a good idea,' I said, startled by her initiative, but thinking that the money I was saving from cutting down on smoking could help finance a trip.

'Bruce is impressed with the new Jenny, too,' she continued. 'And yesterday one of the dustbin men winked and told me I was a cracker.'

'A short, weedy guy who wears a grubby Manila Gorilla T-shirt?'

'The same. You know him?'

'I know him.'

'And this morning Shane said he'd had no idea Victoria had such a sexpot for a mum.' Jenny chuckled. 'She was not best pleased.'

'He seems a nice enough lad.'

'He's okay. Messy and lazy, but friendly. Bruce reckons he and Victoria are just friends and not –' she searched for a suitable word '– sweethearts, though I'm not so sure.'

'You haven't heard the scurry of feet from one bedroom to another at night? Or moans of passion?'

'No, thank the Lord!'

'But you have lain awake and listened?'

'Yes,' she admitted. 'And during the day, I make a point of going into Victoria's room at regular intervals.'

I grinned. 'Spoilsport.' I was about to ask if she had had any more thoughts about conducting an extramarital affair – perhaps with the dustbin man – when the telephone rang. 'Bruce?' I suggested.

'Probably,' she said, and went off to the study to answer it. 'Carol, can you come?' she called, a minute or two later. When I joined her, she had her hand covering the mouthpiece. 'It's Max. He wants to know if we can do him a huge favour and do the work-out with him on television tomorrow morning.'

'Us and the painful three?'

'No, just us. You, me and Tina. The painful three have cancelled. I'll explain later. Max says a driver will pick us up from our various homes at around seven-fifteen a.m. and deliver us back home by eleven. The exercises will be what we usually do. How about it?' Jenny asked, smiling. 'He's already spoken to Tina and she's willing.'

I hesitated. I wasn't sure I wanted to work out on television and I would need to let Steve know that I wouldn't be in the office: there was an interview I'd arranged which would have to be postponed.

'You're willing, too?' I said.

She nodded. 'It'll be different. Max said Tina said to tell us that going on television is nothing to be scared of. That we'll enjoy ourselves.'

I could see how keen she was. 'Okay.'

Jenny spoke into the telephone. 'We're on, we'll do it,

175

we'll help. Do we wear what we normally wear?'

'Or Age Concern T-shirts?' I suggested.

'We do and we can change at the studios. You'll meet us there?' Jenny listened again and laughed. 'See you in the morning.'

'So what happened to the painful three?' I asked, as she replaced the receiver.

'Gerri pulled out first because her grandmother – the old bat who's gaga – died and she has to fly over to Ireland for her funeral. Then Pippa and Dee got together to polish up their routine, but Dee made a comment about television adding pounds and Pippa looking like a carthorse. Pippa took the huff and refused to appear. Dee was all set to exercise on her own, but Nathaniel has developed a cough and needs her attention.'

'She can't leave him with someone else for a couple of hours?'

'Apparently not.' Jenny laughed. 'So it's our chance for stardom.'

'At ultra short notice. Would you mind if I ring Steve? I need to sort things with him.'

'Go ahead. Use the phone in here.'

Left alone in the study, I dialled his mobile. If he said I was demanding too much – which would be a fair comment – I could always take half a day off as holiday.

'It's me, Carol,' I said, when he answered. 'Sorry to ring out of hours and I hope I'm not disturbing anything.'

'Like what?'

'Riotous sex?'

'I should be so lucky.'

'You're not going to like this, but the thing is I've been asked to go on television tomorrow morning and –'

'Why?'

'To do a work-out with Max.'

'Oh yes?'

I heard the insinuation in his voice. 'Not just me. Tina and my friend, Jenny, are doing it, too. But I have an interview fixed for ten o'clock. It's with the manageress of the care home that's being threatened with closure and –'

'Melanie can do the interview,' Steve said, after I had explained. 'Her writing is improving and it'll be a good exercise for her. Which show are you on?'

I told him and gave the time. 'I should be in the office by noon.'

'No problem. Just one thing, I'd like you to write about going on TV.'

I sighed. 'I should've guessed.'

'You'll do a piece? The inside story by our ace reporter?'

'Yes, sir.'

'You're getting there.'

'Getting where?' I asked.

'Unquestioning obedience,' he said.

CHAPTER TWELVE

MAX LOUNGED IN ONE corner of the purple leather sofa, deep in conversation with Cheryl, the female presenter of the morning show, who was snuggled into the other. The male presenter, Ray, a pock-marked ex-jockey and Cheryl's live-in lover – the relationship with its history of slanging-match break-ups followed by tearful reunions had been endlessly publicised – perched upright beside them on the edge of an armchair, listening. The pseudo wall behind the sofa which, presumably in a stab at bestowing a faux-literary air held two short shelves of books, was lime green, while the floor glistened a shiny orange.

Jenny, Tina and I were in a waiting room at the studios watching Max on a small television set fixed up high. Jenny and I watched with avid interest, but Tina was sulky. On our arrival and when Max was in the process of detailing which exercises he would be taking us through, an officious young man with a clipboard had appeared. He had explained that the reformed alcoholic footballer who had been booked for the show had failed to turn up – seemed he'd toppled off the wagon, yet again – and, to fill in time, the producer required an interview. Hearing this, Tina had placed a hand on her hip in a 'come and get me' gesture and smiled expectantly. But the producer had wanted Max to be interviewed, only Max.

He looked good on the screen. Well-built, smooth-skinned, handsome. And, stretched out in his black bodysuit which advertised his assets, as sexily exotic as usual. His screen manner was good, too. As he talked about the advice he could give on stress, fatigue and weight problems, he was easy and full of charm. Cheryl, a gushy girl with a strident 'sarf London' accent, pixie-cut hair and lips like sausages, was leaning towards him and laughing at something he had said. It was obvious she'd love to make a grab for his groin. And

Ray's scowling silence said he knew this.

'So who are the lucky ladies who're working out with you today?' Cheryl enquired, and Tina sat straighter.

'They're three of my regular clients. Great gals. I call them my vintage babes.'

'Vintage babes?' Tina repeated, turning to Jenny and me in wide-eyed horror.

'Let's face it, we are,' I said.

'But classy with it,' Jenny added.

After speaking with Max, we had been taken to a dressing room where we had donned our exercise gear. Jenny and I were in our usual outfits, while Tina wore a zebra-striped all-in-one which had been specially purchased for the occasion. 'It cost a mint,' she had said, giggling. We had then proceeded to make-up. Tina, who had done her face at home and was glossed, buffed and toned to covergirl perfection, was deemed to require no attention, but Jen and I had been painted and powdered. Inspecting the finished results in the mirror, we had both agreed we looked remarkably swish.

I'd wondered if the presenters would come in before the transmission and introduce themselves – even a quick hello would add sparkle to my *Siren* write-up – but we were not considered to be that important. I had also wondered if we might meet other – famous – guests, but again we were out of luck. The drunk footballer was a no-show, the gangsta rap band who were to play their current hit were signing autographs for the teenage fans who had massed outside the studios, while the American movie actress who rated as the star of this morning's programme – and whom I'd never heard of – had requested a private room with white walls, white lilies, grapefruit-scented candles, a supply of vanilla yoghurt and no visitors.

'Time to go, ladies,' announced the officious young man, marching into the room. 'Take any handbags with you, to be on the safe side. And, by the way, my name is Crispin.'

Tina may have vowed that appearing on television was nothing to be scared of, but as Crispin led us off through a maze of corridors, I noticed her hands were trembling. Jenny looked tense and I was gripped by a sudden attack of the collywobbles. Suppose I messed up. Suppose I lost the rhythm or fell over or, even worse, noisily broke wind. 'Ageing Hack Farts on TV'. I could see the gutter press headline.

We were directed onto an empty expanse to one side of the sofa set, which had the same lime green walls and retina-bruising orange floor. The colours may have been garish, but it was the lights which dazzled. They were so bright. It was like standing in the glare of brilliant sunshine or facing spotlights to be interrogated by the KGB.

After a minute or two, Max appeared. 'Right, babes,' he said, 'positions as usual. And let's knock 'em dead.'

Our usual positions meant Tina in the middle and to the front, with Jen and me behind her on either side. The reggae beat started to sound and we moved into action. Within seconds all nervousness fled for, trapped in a circle of white light with darkness beyond, it felt like being in a private world. Isolated. Unreal. There was no sense of the presenters or studio staff standing by. No awareness of cameras. No thought of being watched, assessed and – who knows? – ridiculed by millions of viewers all over the country. It was just us and Max; marching on the spot with knees high, doing side steps and heel curls, slowly circling our heads.

The cringeable quotes flowed. 'The difference between a flower and a weed is judgement', he recited, at one point. Next came 'Reach not just for the sky, but for the stars and the moon.' Though he surpassed himself with 'A cat in gloves catches no mice.' What insight was that supposed to impart?

Then it was over. As we ended the routine, Cheryl came to bathe Max in smiles, say how meaningful she had found his words and briefly thank us, before returning to the sofa where Ray was ready to introduce the actress. A cameraman stepped out of the dark to raise a congratulatory thumb. Another technician mouthed 'Fab!' Tina waved and tiptoed over to talk to them. As a one-time TV personality, she had moved into 'gracious star' mode and was accepting the acclaim as hers.

Only hers. Jenny and I rated as mere spear carriers.

'Being back in front of the cameras again felt so right, so natural,' Tina informed Crispin, as he walked us along to the canteen where we were to be provided with a refreshment before changing into our normal clothes and departing. 'Just like the old days.'

The young man looked bemused. 'You've been on television before?'

'Umpteen times. I was in a weekly show. Used to get sackloads of fan mail.'

He shot her a frowning glance, but clearly couldn't place her. 'When was this?'

'Oh, a while ago,' she said, and turned to Max. 'That was a good work-out.'

'A killer. You all looked the role,' he enthused. If he felt our performance had lacked the zap the painful three could've provided, he did not show it. He spoke to Jenny. 'You must be pleased you shed the weight?'

She grinned. 'I'm delighted.'

'Your breathing was easier,' he said to me. 'Another benefit of cutting down on the cigarettes.'

I nodded. 'Agreed and, yes, I also agree that you're wonderful.'

'Let's hope the nation's couch potatoes thought so, too,' Max said.

The canteen was a vast, utilitarian room with a black-and-white tiled floor and windows which overlooked the car park. A self-service counter ran along the back wall and there was a sea of plastic-topped tables, about a quarter of which were occupied. Following Crispin's command, a woman in a white cap and apron poured out cups of coffee and filled a plate with croissants.

'I'll be back for you in ten minutes,' Crispin declared, and departed.

None of us had eaten breakfast – and the bacon and eggs that other people were devouring looked delicious – but our coffee and croissants were welcome. We had settled around a table, when a man in a black polo neck sweater and modish spectacles appeared beside us. It was Joe Fernandez.

'Happened to be in the building, caught your segment and felt I must come and tell you that it was tremendous,' he said.

Although his gaze flickered across Max, Jenny and me, his words were meant for Tina. We all looked at her, expecting her to respond, but she was silent. Silent, concentrating on tearing open a sachet of sweeteners to add to her coffee and patently ignoring him.

'Thanks, Joe,' Max said.

Jenny nodded politely. 'Yes, thank you.'

'You were a smash hit, Max,' the comedian said.

'You think so?' he asked eagerly.

'I do. You possess the wow factor in spades. And what a lovely trio you had with you.'

When, again, Tina did not react, Jenny smiled. 'You're very kind.'

Putting a hand on the back of Tina's chair, Joe Fernandez bent over her. 'More apologies that you joining me on my show fell through, but it wasn't my fault. And all's well that ends well, eh?'

'How well is your wife?' Tina enquired.

He readjusted his spectacles. 'My wife?'

'What exactly is it that she suffers from and how bad is she? Does she require constant nursing or does she gallop around on horses by day and go jitterbugging at night?' Lifting her head, she stared into his eyes. 'Tell me. Tell me the truth.'

The comedian cleared his throat. Frowned. Coughed. 'Although there've been plenty of theories, her illness has never been fully diagnosed –'

'In twenty years? Piffle!'

'– but it's debilitating and she never knows from one day to the next how she'll be feeling.'

'Piffle and rubbish! There's nothing wrong with her,' Tina proclaimed.

Atta girl! I thought.

Straightening, Joe shot a hasty look around. People at other tables had paused in eating their meals to listen.

'Sweetie pie,' he murmured, bending down to Tina again and moving into top smarm. 'Why don't you and I talk about this in private and –'

'Your wife isn't ill. Not seriously. Never has been.' With each word, Tina's voice became louder and more dramatic. She had realised she had secured an audience and was playing to them. 'It's quite likely she's been in rude health all along.'

'Now, you adorable creature, you mustn't –'

'We are over. Finished. Through,' she announced, in the tragic tones of a damsel in distress. She was a woman wronged and angered, but regretful, too. 'I do not want to see you again or hear from you again. Ever.'

Once more Joe Fernandez straightened, checking out the other diners who were rapt and attentive. Even the counter assistant had stopped in the throes of stacking plates to listen. Joe frowned. If he accepted such a public defeat, he could be ridiculed. Someone might even blab to the press. So should he launch another charm offensive? Would Tina succumb to his persuasive powers and his lies? She had succumbed in the past. The thoughts flitted, as if written on ticker-tape, across his eyes.

When he bent over her again, she stared regally ahead.

'Go away,' she instructed. 'Leave me alone!'

'But sweetie pie –' Joe began.

'Please!' The word was a theatrical sob.

Max rose to his feet, towering over the comedian. 'You heard the lady,' he said, and, after a wary assessment of the younger man's size, Joe turned and walked swiftly out.

Tina smiled up at Max. 'My hero,' she declared, then she stood and hugged and kissed him.

The canteen erupted in a round of applause.

Max took a bow, which provoked cheers and whistles, then the pair of them resumed their seats. There came the clatter of cutlery as feeding resumed and a buzz of eager gossip as the contretemps was discussed and dissected. Tina had given quite a performance, I reflected. Maybe she should forget about modelling and switch to acting.

'I agree with Joe Fernandez,' pronounced a man, one of two who were sitting at a nearby table. 'You girls are a lovely trio – and great little movers.'

Jenny arched a brow. 'You saw us working out?'

'Saw you on that –' he indicated a television screen, one of several sited around the canteen walls '– and was riveted.'

'Likewise,' added his companion.

Both were middle-aged, with greying hair. Dressed in shirts, ties and dark trousers, with well-polished shoes and expensive watches strapped around their wrists, they had the confident air of men who are successful in their careers. Executives of some kind, though they could've been biscuit salesmen.

'Glad you enjoyed it, gents,' Jenny said. 'Enjoyed us.'

She was casting sidelong glances. She was smiling, seductively stretching in her 'brakini' and flares. She was *flirting*. And Tina, who had murmured her thanks at the compliments, was being ignored. I didn't get a look-in, either.

I stared. In all the years I'd known her, I had never seen Jenny act this way. I would never have believed she *could* act this way.

The second man edged his chair closer. 'Do you live in London?' he asked her.

'In Dursleigh, Surrey. Not too far away.'

'You come up to town much?'

'No, though all I need to do is hop on a train. There's a frequent service and it doesn't take long. Excuse me,' she said, as the frog croak tones of her mobile sounded.

They were tones which her son, Patrick, had installed. Jenny may be proficient with a computer, but she has yet to fully master her cell phone. Installing tones remains a mystery. Likewise text messaging. Must be an age thing because I'm not too clever at texting, either. I need to poke and painstakingly prod for ages, whereas kids of eight can produce reams of words with a flash of stubby fingers.

'Hello?' Jenny demanded, impatient at being interrupted.

'Oh, Bruce. You saw us?' A pause while she listened. 'Thank you. Yes, it did go well.'

Should I be a killjoy, a sneak and protector, and make a comment about how she was speaking to her husband, her beloved husband? Not much point. She wore a wedding ring on her finger. As did both the men. JLFAS, I recalled, and my heart sank.

'Victoria rang you to say I'd be on and she's videoed it?' Jenny continued. 'Yes, I forgot. Yes, we can. In a rush. See you later.'

As she ended the call, Crispin returned. 'Your driver is ready and waiting,' he advised us.

'Sorry, I have to go,' Jenny told her admirers.

'We must be off, too,' the second man said, and taking out his wallet he passed her an address card. 'I hope we'll meet again.'

Glancing at the card, she gave a smile which teased and hinted and was positively *wicked*. 'Who knows?' she said.

Where did you learn that, Jen? I wondered. What other man-killer skills do you possess? How have you kept them hidden for all these years?

As the two men departed, Crispin spoke to Max. 'The phones are going mad with viewers ringing to say how much they liked your slot and the producer's wondering if you'd be willing to do a repeat sometime soon?'

Max grinned. 'You bet.'

'Anytime,' Tina said.

Crispin shook his head. 'Max with the other women.'

'You don't want us?' she protested.

'No. Nothing wrong with the work-out – and there've been a couple of calls from folk who remember you from way back when – but the producer feels the younger trio would be more to the minute.'

Seeming torn between tears and foot-stamping temper, Tina shook her head. 'That's not fair!' she said loudly.

Once again, the canteen's hubbub stilled and all ears were pricked.

Jenny looked embarrassed. 'Don't get upset,' she implored. 'We've had our moment of glory.'

'Very nice it was, too,' I said. 'But enough is enough.'

'Everyone's agreed that we're a class act,' Tina declared, her words directed at her audience, 'and we came at short notice, and we should be asked back. We deserve it.'

'Hear, hear,' someone shouted.

'I'm very sorry,' Crispin said.

'No, you're not. You don't give a toss. But you can tell that producer of yours that the more mature woman is a potent force in the world today and his judgement is crap!' she announced, and, snatching up her bag, she flounced off through the tables and out of the canteen in her zebra pattern suit.

It was a grand exit. One which provoked another round of applause.

As Crispin and Max hurried ahead to catch Tina and try to placate her, Jenny and I followed.

'It was good of Bruce to ring,' I remarked, wanting to remind the newly minted vamp that she had a caring and attentive husband.

'Mmm. He said we could watch the video together this evening.'

'He showered compliments?'

'Reckoned I was so sinuous and seductive, he can't wait to get me into bed.'

'Which means he loves you. Only you,' I insisted.

Jenny did not reply.

Steve let rip with a whistle, a long low wolf whistle. 'Be still my beating heart.'

'You watched?' I asked.

'Me, and everyone else at *The Siren* and most of Dursleigh, judging from the phone calls which have been coming in. I-saw-Carol-strutting-her-stuff-and-was-blown-away type phone calls. When you do your write-up, we'll need to print a photograph of you in your exercise gear to please the punters.'

He made a low growl in the back of his throat. 'Sexy or what?'

'Sexy with a capital S,' Tony declared.

I grinned. 'No need to overdo it.'

'I never realised you were, like, so supple, and had such a really, really neat figure,' Melanie said. 'I mean, like, for someone of your age.'

Steve grinned. 'Carol's pretty frisky for an older woman.'

'Watch it, mate,' I told him.

Melanie adjusted her bra strap, a black one which was half an inch wide. Industrial strength. 'Maybe I should take up fitness training.'

'I can recommend it,' I said.

After being chauffeur-driven home, I had showered, changed and come on to the office where I was greeted with applause. The advertisement crew downstairs had given me a standing ovation, which was being echoed by the editorial team. There is a television in the interview room and apparently everyone had crowded in to watch on that.

'Max looked great, too,' Melanie added, then stopped as the switchboard rang. She went to answer it. 'There's a guy who says he's a refuse collector and he knows you and he'd like to speak to you.'

I shook my head. 'Tell him I'm not in the office.'

She did as instructed, but seconds later the switchboard rang again. This time the caller was a woman who described herself as a life-time reader of *The Siren*, so I took the phone. It makes sense to keep our regulars sweet.

'I wanted to tell you, my dear, how thrilled I was to see you and your young man on the television this morning. Such a surprise –' there was a squawk of delighted laughter '– and hasn't he got bedroom eyes?'

'Max isn't my young man,' I started to explain, but the woman, who sounded elderly and subscribed to 'if in doubt, shout', talked over me.

'Others might criticise you for cradle snatching, but not yours truly. You snare what you can get while you still have the opportunity, that's my advice, and never mind if people snigger. They're only jealous and –'

'I'm pleased you enjoyed the work-out,' I cut in. 'I shall be writing about it, so keep on buying *The Siren.* Goodbye.'

When the phone immediately rang again, Steve grimaced. 'Oh, the demands of fame. I'll speak to you later when the fan club's grown weary,' he said, and went off to his office.

'I'm out of here, too,' Tony said, and he exited.

The next call was from my father. I had rung the previous evening to tell him to watch the morning show. If he had missed seeing me, I would never have been forgiven. Lynn had been unable to watch because she was at work, but I'd set the video so that we could view together later. I was eager to see how the performance had gone myself.

'I thought you were splendid, pet,' my father said. 'And so did all the folks at Bridgemont.'

'You told your neighbours I'd be on?'

'Slipped a note under everyone's door last night.'

I cringed. 'Dad, you didn't!'

'Of course. Having your daughter appear on national television is something special. And we all watched together in the residents' lounge.'

My cringe deepened into a squirm. I could imagine the old folk sat in rows, hearing aids adjusted and eyes peering through bi-focals; assessing, criticising, secretly wondering what on earth George was making such a fuss about.

'Everyone loved it. Thought you were so active and so slim. Most of the ladies went a bundle on that Max fellow in his tight rig-out. Didn't leave much to the imagination. Dilys reckons he must be dynamite in bed.'

'I wouldn't know,' I said impatiently.

'That's what I told her. What I told the other ladies who'd picked up the gossip about the two of you having a thing going. I explained you were just friends and there was no jiggery-pokery, if you get my drift. That you were old enough to be the lad's mum or near enough his grandmother. But you did me proud. Don't suppose you came across that Les Dynam when you were at the television centre?'

'No.'

'Shame. He seems such a friendly chap, just wondered if he was the same in real life. How about Gloria Hunniford?'

'Not a glimpse.'

'I've always liked her, but never mind. Look forward to hearing about it in due course. Oh, and by the way, pet, I'm afraid I'll have to say thanks, but no thanks to lunch on Sunday. One of the couples here is celebrating their Ruby Wedding and everyone's invited. But I'll be at home if you come on Tuesday, around midday.'

'I'll see you then,' I agreed.

'Lynn and Beth still at your place?' he said, as an afterthought.

'They are.'

The three following calls were straightforward congratulations on a job well done with, mercifully, no mention of Max. But the next was from a Dursleigh hair stylist who coyly referred to the trainer and me as having an 'understanding'. Again, I explained there was no 'understanding', but, again, my denial fell upon stony ground.

'Bugger, bugger, bugger,' I muttered, as I replaced the receiver.

Being mistakenly linked with Max had been irritating enough before, but our television appearance seemed to have provided fresh impetus and provoked even more interest. I frowned. If I was being bombarded by phone calls, many of which assumed we were lovers, what was it going to be like when I went out and about? Would strangers stop me in the street to chat about the imagined romance? If I went to interview someone, might they attempt to turn the tables and interview me about my sex life? When I attended council or healthcare meetings, would there be the hum of whispers and knowing looks? In my role as a reporter, I needed to be seen as sensible, reliable and trustworthy, but such scurrilous gossip could ruin my reputation.

And what about me as a woman? The thought of being envied by half of Dursleigh, but maybe viewed as a laughing stock by the rest made my skin crawl. The joke had gone too far. I hated my private life being a source of lascivious speculation. Yet what could I do about it? For weeks now, at every opportunity I had plainly stated that a relationship did not exist, but I might as well have been talking to a brick wall.

For the next hour, the telephone rang repeatedly and every time it was concerning the televised work-out. Most of the calls were from folk saying how much they'd enjoyed seeing me – anyone who referred to a romance was given short shrift – though there were a couple from local females asking how they could engage Max as their personal trainer, while another woman was eager to know if I knew where Tina had bought her zebra outfit.

'It's not every editor who has a television star on his staff,' Steve said, when I finally managed to escape into the peace of his office. 'I feel very humble.'

'Please keep quiet,' I said. 'Or words to that effect.'

'Are you tempted to change careers?'

'Is this you hoping I might be about to resign?'

'Me hope that? Never.'

'Just as well, because a career change isn't about to happen. Max has been asked to do a work-out on the show again, but with other, younger, women.'

'Younger being the appeal?' I nodded. 'Do you mind?'

'No. I'm happy with my fifteen minutes of fame,' I said, then sighed as the telephone rang on his desk.

I had been anticipating yet another 'well done' message with some reference to a liaison with Max, but although the call was for me it came from Roger, my friendly policeman. He thought I would be interested to know that the previous day, in a nearby town, another jeweller's shop had been robbed and goods to the value of over a quarter of a million pounds had been taken.

'The raid was carried out with military precision and planning, the same as at Gifford's,' I told Steve, when Roger had given me the details and rung off. 'It was another sedate family firm and the thieves are believed to have been the same

190

three men. Seems this is the fourth such robbery in the past month and the police reckon a gang which has local knowledge must be operating in the area, selecting shops which offer easy pickings. The odd part is that each time the thieves have driven away and vanished into thin air. There's been no sighting of their vehicle.'

'They don't head for London, they go to ground somewhere around here?'

'That's how it appears.'

'They need to be stopped,' Steve said. 'The robbery has destroyed old man Gifford's nerves and his son isn't much better. I called in the shop the other day to see how they were coping in the aftermath –'

'That was kind.'

'– and they're not coping well. Both father and son are constantly on edge and the assistants are the same. They're wary of every customer and –' There was a knock at the door. 'Come in,' he called.

'Hope I'm not interrupting,' Tina said, smiling at him. 'Oh, hi, Carol.'

'All recovered from this morning?' I enquired.

She nodded. In the car coming back from the studios, she had been fretful and unsure. She had talked of how, despite giving Joe Fernandez his marching orders, she would miss him. Yet again, she had insisted she needed a man. A husband. And now, blonde and sleek in a white trouser suit, she looked all set to charm Steve. Was that her plan? Was he willing to be charmed? If so, more fool him.

I stood up. 'Better get on,' I said.

Back in the general office, I asked about the interview which Melanie had done earlier with the woman from the care home. Listening to her, she appeared to have asked all the right questions and acquired all the necessary information.

'It went fine and it'll be a good piece. An accurate piece,' the girl assured me. 'Eric never cared about what I did, but Steve does. Okay, he criticises and can really blast you out at times, but that makes you try harder. Makes me try harder.'

She smiled. 'He says my work is much improved and I have potential.'

'I agree with him,' I said.

Her smile widened. 'Thanks.'

Later, when Melanie went out to buy her lunch, I began to jot down notes about my television experience in readiness for an article. I was wondering if I should ask Tina for her observations, when I heard her walking quickly back along the corridor and towards the stairs.

'Bye, Carol,' she called.

'Bye.'

'What a woman!' Steve exclaimed, a minute or two later, and I turned to find him standing in the doorway. I had assumed from his words that he was praising her, but the scowl and thin line of his mouth indicated otherwise.

'Problem?' I asked.

'She wanted to know if I'd seen her on television and what did I think of her? When I said she was good, that all three of you had been good, she rushed around the desk and hugged and kissed me.'

I grinned. His voice reeked of distaste, of horror.

'You liked it last week, when she hugged you in the street. And, as I recall, the first time you met her, here at the office, you were besotted.'

'Never. As I recall, you were being so shitty that Tina made a welcome diversion. So I welcomed her.'

'Me, shitty?'

'You can be, on occasion. But her kissing me.' He shuddered. 'She was so clingy. Like a bloody limpet. Then she told me how her central heating's gone on the blink and asked if I would go round to her house to take a look. No chance. If she kisses me here, heaven knows what she'd do if she got me on my own.'

'Handcuff you to the bed and have her wicked way?' I suggested.

'She might try.' Steve made a face. 'And her husband's barely been dead two months.'

'You're not inclined to be Tina's next man?'

'Heaven forbid! I'm not setting foot inside her house, but how do I keep the woman at a distance?'

I grinned. 'Tricky one, Moriarty.'

'It isn't a joke. What I need is for her to think I'm interested in some other woman. That'd cool her down. Otherwise –' He grimaced again.

'How about saying you're getting back with your wife?'

'No. The kids'd love us to get together again, but it isn't going to happen. And I couldn't risk them getting wind of the wrong idea. It wouldn't be fair.'

'Pretend you have the hots for Melanie?' I suggested.

He gave me a *get real* look. 'Now that is a joke. The girl's years younger than me and she doesn't appeal.'

'Max is years younger than me and he doesn't appeal, either, yet so many folk seem convinced we're having an affair. It's weird! It's a pain! I'm sick and tired of it!' I complained, my frustration bubbling over.

'And you're not? Not having an affair?'

'No!'

'Oh, I thought in view of the talk that maybe, just maybe –'

'Everyone thinks 'maybe', but there isn't a 'maybe'. Never has been and never will be. I may've given a mixed message at first, but I was joking. I had dinner with the lad once and today we appeared on television, together with Tina and Jenny, but –'

'Right,' Steve said. 'We'll act like we're a pair.'

I blinked. 'What?'

'It'll end the Max gossip for you and keep Tina at bay for me. We'll go out to dinner a couple of times, be seen together, pretend to be love birds.'

'This is a wind-up, right?' I said suspiciously.

'No. But it's a purely business arrangement.'

'With no hanky-panky?' I said, then wondered if I was asking or telling.

A smile tugged at his lips. 'Wash your mouth out with soap. What do you take me for, a gigolo?'

'But I've never shown the slightest interest in you. I've never spoken to Tina, or to anyone, about fancying you – in fact, just the opposite.'

'You've told folk what a thorn in the flesh I am?'

'Not just a thorn, a rottweiler.'

Steve frowned. 'Maybe I was on the fierce side when I first took over here, but I was determined to do things right.'

'You're a bit more amicable now,' I said.

'Only a bit?'

'A lot.' I returned to the main thread. 'But if we suddenly appear as a couple, no one's going to believe it.'

'They will if we say it's instant love. Bolt from the blue stuff. It happens. I saw you on television this morning, noticed your cute backside and, wham, slavering devotion. It is cute, by the way. And as for you –' He paused, thinking.

'I noticed that you have a cute backside, too?' I suggested.

'Do I?'

'Stand up and turn round.' Steve stood up and turned round. He was wearing dark grey slacks which fitted neatly around his buttocks. 'Real cute,' I told him.

I wasn't lying. Funny I'd never noticed his bum before, but then I'd never regarded him as a man I could fancy. I'd been too busy resenting him as a usurper, I suppose.

'So what do you think? Shall we give being a pair a try?'

I considered the idea. Did I want to spend even more time with him and have my name linked with his? It would be an improvement on having my name linked with Max's and yet… but we could talk shop, were more of an age and had things in common.

'Okay, but only on the understanding that either of us can opt out at any time.'

'Sure. We'll start after the weekend, when I've had time to warn my kids.'

'And after I've explained things to Lynn and to my dad.'

'Done,' he said.

CHAPTER THIRTEEN

'HE'S HERE! MY DADDY'S here!' Beth's delighted cry sounded and she came running into the kitchen, where Lynn had just finished washing the lunch dishes and I was drying them. 'I saw his car stop outside. He's here!'

'He's early,' Lynn said, frowning, 'and I need to change. Will you let him in?'

'Of course.'

As she vanished upstairs I went to open the front door, with Beth dancing a jig for joy beside me.

'Daddy!' she yelled, when she saw him and hurled herself into his arms.

As she kissed him and told him how very much she loved him and that she had missed him 'lots and lots and lots', Justin hugged her tight.

'Some welcome,' he said to me, and he blinked.

I nodded. Maybe I'm getting soft in my old age, but I was close to tears, too.

'This is for you,' Beth said, handing him a card which was plastered with silver stars and had 'DADDY' in wavering green felt-tip capitals on the front and 'LOVE FROM BETH' in wavering red felt-tip capitals inside. 'I made it and stuck on all the stars and did the kisses, but Gran helped with the writing.'

'Only a little bit,' I said.

'It's lovely. I shall keep it for ever,' Justin declared.

'Until you die?' Beth asked.

'Until I die.'

'And then you'll be very old, as old as Gran.'

'Maybe even older.' Justin looked at me and grinned. 'Though not many people are.'

'You mean, like a hundred?' the little girl said.

His grin widened. 'In that region.'

'Up yours,' I said, *sotto voce*. 'Lynn's getting ready, she won't be long. It's good to see you,' I told him, being demonstrably friendly and kissing his cheek to show I bore no grudge.

We've always got along and I hoped he knew me well enough to know I wouldn't automatically take sides and denounce him. I hoped he knew I was aware that my daughter had faults.

'I went round to my mum and dad's last night. They were saying they'd like to see this monster.' Justin tickled Beth, making her giggle. 'See if she's still as horrible.'

'I'm not horrible,' she said indignantly.

'No, you're not, you're gorgeous. Utterly butterly gorgeous,' he said, and tickled her again. He looked out at the sunshine. 'And it's a gorgeous day for visiting the farm park. Perhaps we'll see the pigs racing and –'

'And I can stroke the baby lambs and the little tiny baby rabbits,' Beth said. 'Like last time. And I can go on the trampoline and the climbing frame and –'

'Hello.' Lynn was walking primly down the stairs. 'Shall we be off?'

Justin nodded. 'Suits me.'

'Bye.' I kissed Beth and Lynn, then kissed Justin's cheek again. 'I hope you can sort things out,' I said quietly to him.

When they'd gone I finished drying the dishes and put them away. If I left them on the drainer, Lynn would be sure to comment. I also wiped down the work surfaces. If my daughter stays here long enough, she'll scare me into domestic perfection.

Going upstairs, I changed into a black cotton top with three quarter sleeves, and white jeans. I didn't want to look overly smart, as if I was trying to impress, but I wanted to show I could still cut it. I studied myself in the mirror. Why is it you can look so different in different mirrors and look different in the same mirror at different times? And which reflection is the true you? Sometimes I see a sophisticated, fine-featured brunette of uncommon beauty, but at others I see a gargoyle.

Today, the day I was meeting Tom, I veered towards the gargoyle. Dammit.

As I waited for my visitor to arrive I thought of how I had told Lynn that I had never asked him where he felt our relationship had gone wrong. Why hadn't I asked? I'm usually curious, normally up-front. All I could imagine was that I had been so busy extracting myself with dignity, I hadn't got around to it. Or perhaps, deep down, I'd been scared of what he might say. But now I needed a full, nothing-held-back explanation.

Two-thirty came and went, then three o'clock, but there was no sign of Tom. Would he ring and belatedly cancel, or simply not turn up? When we were married, the demands of his career had often intruded on our private life and he had not been too clever at keeping me informed. I could remember waiting at home for ages, dressed in my best and ready to go, then being forced to ring friends at the last minute to apologise profusely because we wouldn't be able to join them for dinner. Or supposedly meeting Tom at some event, only to discover I was there on my own. At the time it had seemed par for the journalistic course and I had accepted it, but now I began to feel annoyed. Family matters more.

I lit a cigarette and stood, gazing out of the kitchen window and thinking. Thinking of how our marriage had ended…

The receipt had been for an asparagus kettle. It fell out of a 'Thirty Miles Around London' road map which I had borrowed from Tom's shelf in the study. That afternoon I was driving up to Waltham Abbey to interview a businessman who had made millions marketing flatpack cardboard coffins for pets and I needed to check the route.

What on earth was an asparagus kettle? Something to cook asparagus in, obviously, but was the kettle flat and long or did the spears stand upright? Was there a basket, a lid, a whistling spout? Did twenty five pounds buy the de luxe version or was it dirt cheap? I had no idea. Kitchenware didn't grab me. Cooking, neither, though as an eager to please newly-wed I had aspired to the role of domestic goddess. I had made pies with shortcrust pastry and cut-out leaves on top, produced a strangely textured strawberry jam, even baked my own bread. The culinary kick hadn't lasted for long. And now that we lived in Kensington with a Marks & Spencer selling pre-prepared meals just a five-minute walk away, who needed to cook?

At that point I had had no idea, either, that my husband was having an affair. If the receipt had been for French perfume or expensive lingerie, my suspicions might have been aroused. Though only might. After being happily married for so long, I had trusted him to be faithful. It hadn't occurred to me that Tom would stray. Not seriously occurred. Though he had warned that if Cher should ever crook a manicured finger, he'd be off like a shot to be her sex slave. There's no accounting for tastes.

I had decided he must have bought a leaving present for some secretary at his paper – we worked on different papers – and dismissed the receipt from my mind when, one night in bed, Tom called me Kath instead of Carol. When I'd laughed, raised my head from his groin and asked who the hell Kath was, he swore I'd misheard. He was so determined, I believed him.

Then the receptionist at his paper rang and left a message on the answerphone. The message was innocuous, about a cancelled meeting, but her tone was not. It was husky and intimate. Her 'It's Kathryn here –' pause '– Mr Webb' was vocal seduction. Pure 'come up and see me sometime.' Had she spoken like that on purpose, thinking the muggins wife might hear? Later, I believed so.

I had seen the girl sat at her desk in the lobby of Tom's building and once when I'd been waiting for him, we'd chatted. She had told me how she had studied journalism at college and that her aim was to work on the fashion pages – 'as soon as a vacancy occurs'. Fashion figured. Kathryn was a curvy blonde who wore the latest styles, did a busy line in lip gloss and had false eyelashes with blue mascara. A slick chick.

I'd been surprised when she had mentioned that she was taking a course in Cordon Bleu cuisine.

'The way to a man's heart is through his stomach,' she had declared, tritely, but with the arch of a plucked brow.

After hearing the message, I thought of that brow and the number of meetings and dinners Tom had recently had to attend, going out in the evening all dressed up and smelling of aftershave, and not returning until late. After midnight late. When I was in bed, fast asleep. Which meant we hadn't been making love as often. The signs seemed scarily obvious.

Yet when we did make love, it was just as good – passionate and satisfying – as ever. The pressures of our careers meant we didn't have much spare time to spend together and maybe our marriage was going through a humdrum stage, as marriages do, but we were still in tune. We kissed, teased, discussed, argued and made up. He told me regularly that he adored me. And vice versa.

I had decided I was adding up two and two and making a ridiculous five – it's amazing how you can refuse to connect the dots when you don't wish to see the full picture – when, one evening, Tom had poured me the usual glass of white wine and himself the usual whisky and water, then announced he needed to talk.

'I've been foolish,' he had said. 'I'm very sorry, but I've become involved with the receptionist at work, Kathryn.'

All of a sudden, I had found it hard to breathe. Working in London's newspaper fraternity, I was aware of the flirting which went on, the illicit fumbles, the secret liaisons. But I had never participated nor imagined that he would, either. And now he was 'very sorry' – well, thanks, mister.

'Kathryn must – must be twenty years plus your – your junior,' I had stammered.

Tom had bristled. 'So?'

'You bought her an asparagus kettle? I found a receipt.'

'Yes.'

'How romantic.' Should I request a description of the kettle? No, this was not an apt juncture.

'Actually, her asparagus is superb. Melts in the mouth.'

'You don't say. How long has this 'involvement' been going on?'

'Six or seven months.'

A layer of ice seemed to settle over me. I had always believed that a wife must know, or at least suspect, if her husband was straying – even if she didn't admit it – yet until I'd heard the husky message a day or two earlier the idea had not crossed my mind.

'Good God, Tom!'

'Thing is –' he had shifted awkwardly in his seat '– it's become... tricky. Serious.'

I had looked at him in horror. When a fellow reporter's husband had had an affair and she had taken him back, I had privately condemned her as spineless. Where was her self-esteem, her pride? If Tom should ever do the dirty on me, I would, I had told myself, be straight out of the door. That simple. But it wasn't simple.

I had wanted to burst into floods of tears. I had wanted to thump him for inflicting such a grievous hurt. I had wanted to yell, 'but I love you!' That he should be having a fling, a six month fling, had been disaster enough, yet I would have forgiven him. Not necessarily with good grace – on the contrary, I would've made his life hell – but I would have got over it. Eventually. More or less. Maybe. Put it down to a mid-life crisis and the stupidity of men. How we can all make mistakes. But his 'serious' meant this wasn't just a fling.

And this wasn't the way it was supposed to be. In a few years' time we would be celebrating our Silver Wedding and already we'd talked of indulging ourselves and jetting off to a five-star hotel in Rome or Mustique or Bangkok. But now...

'Then you must do what you want to do,' I had said, briskly and painfully. 'If you want a divorce, I won't stand in your way.'

My heart might be breaking and my life collapsing in ruins around me, but I had been determined to be civilised. To act with dignity. Other women I knew had retreated gracefully from failed marriages – at least, they had appeared to on the surface – and I would, too. Decorum was all.

What an idiot. I should have swallowed my pride and begged, pleaded, battled. Peppered his suits with cigarette acupuncture, boiled rabbits on the stove. I should have pointed out that he was reneging on a lifetime contract, but there are such things as loyalty and responsibility and considering others. Namely me and our beloved daughter, Lynn. I should've suggested that panacea of the age, counselling, or told him to check into a sex addiction clinic. I should have reminded him of all the good times we'd shared, and the bad times, and insisted we could work things out. And never mind that – a double whammy – he had already impregnated Kathryn, who subsequently became his trophy wife.

But I didn't.

I stubbed out my cigarette. It was too late to throw big scenes and make Tom suffer. Eight years too late. And now three-thirty p.m. had come and gone, and my visitor had yet to appear.

Filling a jug I wandered around, watering the plants which sit on windowsills throughout the house. Purple chrysanths, a poinsettia still gamely surviving from Christmas, various coleus which I have grown from seed. I had told myself I had no wish to meet Tom again and yet, while I felt a little uptight, there was also a buzz of anticipation. It would be interesting to see him, to talk to him. I moistened the soil of a cactus. Could I have fixed a get-together here with Lynn because I had wanted to see him? Did some unconscious need lurk inside me? After all, I could have asked him to arrange to meet our daughter in London, without me becoming personally involved.

When the doorbell rang, I jumped. I abandoned the watering, took a deep breath and went to greet my visitor. To my annoyance, I felt my heartbeat quicken. 'Chill, Gran,' I instructed.

'Hello. How are you? I hope you had a smooth drive

201

down,' I said, ushering Tom indoors. I was all smiles and graciousness, like an airline hostess welcoming a first-class passenger on board. 'Thank you for coming.'

He grinned. 'My pleasure.'

The intelligent blue eyes beneath thick black brows and the angular face were as I remembered, but his dark hair had become totally grey. Silver grey. Once it had flopped over his brow, but now it was cut short and lay close to his head. He wore a mid-blue linen suit with the jacket open, a pale blue shirt and a brightly coloured modern-art tie. He looked the archetypal media guy, a look which says 'I'm with it.' It was a look which may be appreciated by the metropolitan newspaper crowd, but seemed out of place in Dursleigh.

He handed me a large bunch of yellow roses. 'For the siren from *The Siren,*' he recited.

'Thanks.'

If only he knew how many times I had been called that and always by men who, like him, imagined they were being wittily original.

'Had to rush lunch with a government bod who was eager for a chinwag, eager for some advice. Needed to swill down the Chateau Latour, more's the pity,' he said, and grimaced. There was no apology for keeping me waiting, rather his visit was being blamed for making him hurry his meal. He fingered the modern-art tie. 'You're looking well.'

'And you.'

I was being polite, rather than strictly truthful. In the four years since I had last seen him, he had put on weight. Tall and rangy, Tom had previously kept in shape, but now there were the beginnings of a paunch and his complexion was florid. He looked like a man who wined and dined a little too often. The Cordon Bleu cuisine he was fed at home wouldn't help, either.

'Coffee?' I asked, leading the way into the kitchen.

'Please. Didn't have time for it at lunch. Politicians are always asking for my advice, off the record, of course,' he said, and as I switched on the kettle, then found and filled a crystal vase with water, he told me tales about the queue of

202

government ministers who were, he claimed, desperate for his input.

The tales were interesting and amusing – my father would've loved them – yet they also reeked of Tom's good opinion of himself. He had always liked to think he was first fiddle in the orchestra. Always name-dropped. Or could he be trying to impress me? Was he apprehensive, too? Had the prospect of meeting up with his ex-wife made him feel stressed?

'Lynn and Beth have gone with Justin to a farm park,' I explained, when he paused for breath. 'They'll be back around four-thirty, but Lynn doesn't know you're coming.'

'Fine. Smoke,' he said.

'Sorry?'

'I can smell cigarette smoke. I used to smell it when I walked in the door of our place in Kensington and smell it on you.'

'You complained bitterly,' I said, arranging the flowers. By 'arranging' I mean I removed the cellophane wrapping, snipped off the rubber bands and stuck the roses in the vase. The artistic arrangement of blooms is something else, like cookery, that has never grabbed me. 'You used to go on about it *ad nauseam.*'

He looked disgruntled. 'No, I didn't.'

'Come on, Tom, I can remember you giving me long lectures about how repulsive the smell was to people who weren't 'nicotine junkies' and how I ought to give up. How you'd set the death penalty for anyone who took cigarettes into restaurants. How I smoked like a chimney and stank like one. Your nagging made me want to scream.'

That he should walk in and refer to me smoking had irritated me now. I had only had one cigarette all day, so any smell must be faint. Very faint. Certainly faint enough to be disregarded.

'You're right, I did go on a bit,' he conceded, and grinned. 'We had a blazing row once where I took off your sweater and made you smell it, and next thing we were rolling around naked on the carpet.' He slid an arm around my waist. 'We were so great together, Carol.'

I stepped away. Him holding me close felt so familiar, far too familiar. It opened up a multitude of memories. But I was no longer his wife. No longer to be taken for granted. Neither did I appreciate his reminder of our sex life, which had been good. Bloody good.

'Black, two sugars?' I said.

'You remember. Now the smell of smoke is your smell. It's a sexy smell.'

'Pull the other one.'

'I mean it.' Taking the mug of coffee I handed him, Tom looked me up and down. 'You're sexy. Still drinking from the fountain of youth and slim as a reed – whooarh!'

I laughed. He had always gone over the top with compliments, but, like most women, I'm a sucker for compliments. Though as for drinking from the fountain of youth – I wish.

'Thanks. But Kathryn's slim, too,' I added.

I was deliberately stirring things, yet why not? I reckon I'm entitled to some small revenge.

'Not any more. She's a fat cow. When she rolls down her roll-on and her belly flops out, God, it's disgusting!'

'That's a bit harsh,' I protested. I never thought I would hear myself defending the slick chick, but the woman had given birth to two children. His children. 'And you're not exactly a sylph-like figure yourself these days.'

Tom scowled. 'Bless you for your honesty.'

'You should exercise. I do. I attend a fitness class twice a week.'

Should I tell him how I had worked out on television? No, I didn't want to get into all the whys and wherefores.

'Don't have the time to exercise, though Kathryn could and should. The sex isn't much cop these days, either,' he continued. 'Kathryn lives in perpetual fear Benedict will walk into our bedroom while we're at it, so she's scared of making any noise and as for us indulging in –'

'How old is Benedict now?' I asked.

I didn't want to hear about their love-life and as for being regaled with a description of their sexual practices – no thanks. The Tom I remembered would never have been so indiscreet, so brash, and I decided it must be the wine which was talking.

'Six. He's son number two. Cameron is coming up to eight.'

'Do you have a photograph of them?'

'Not on me.'

It would have been interesting to see what his sons looked like. Lynn has described them as having dark hair, brown eyes and cheeky grins – which is how I visualise Michael. My son. I've imagined him at every age and now he would have been twenty-five, almost twenty-six. A handsome young man who would entrance the girls. Another journalist maybe, but brilliant at whatever he did. And his mother's darling.

'Benedict gets up in the night?' I said.

'Almost every bloody night. Claims he feels lonely and wants to see his mum. I've threatened to put a bolt on his bedroom door and lock him in, but Kathryn won't agree.'

'I don't blame her,' I retorted, defending the slick chick again.

'You've got this place nice and tidy,' Tom declared, as if needing a diversion. 'You should see our kitchen in Islington, it's a tip. Kids' trainers left lying around for days, piles of unwashed cutlery and the damn cat walking over everything. Why we haven't all died of food poisoning, I'll never know.'

I smiled. This was a recital I had heard before. 'You used to complain that the kitchen was a tip in Kensington.'

'Never.'

'Think back,' I said, then, indicating we should sit at the kitchen table, I got down to business. 'As I told you on the telephone, a couple of weeks ago Lynn and Justin quarrelled and she walked out. Since then, she and Beth have been living with me. Basically, her reason for leaving is that Justin has been short-tempered, bad-tempered, moody and they're not getting along. But –'

'Happens all the time.' Tom shrugged. *'C'est la vie.'*

'But if they discussed why things have gone sour, maybe they could sort them out and get back together again. There's Beth to consider and –'

'And you're doing your marriage guidance bit, 'cept they're not married.'

'I want to help,' I said heavily. 'As you know, Lynn can act the drama queen and I don't want her to do anything rash, something she might regret for the rest of her life.'

As we drank our coffee, I explained what I knew of the situation and how I wanted him to talk to our daughter and try to persuade her to think again.

'I understand and I'll do my best to mend things,' Tom said, when I had finished. Taking hold of my hand, he squeezed it. 'You can rely on me.'

'Thanks.'

I looked into the blue eyes which I knew so well. He may have put on weight, but he was still an attractive man. The silver grey hair suited him. He had impact and an inner spark. I understood why he appealed to the politicians and why, for all those years, he had appealed to me. And yet... He had sounded a little glib about Lynn's split with Justin. Might family troubles rate as trivial in his scheme of things?

'If you thought we were so good together, why did you start the affair with Kathryn?' I enquired, withdrawing my hand. 'I know all about infatuation with someone new and 'middle-aged man craves younger woman', but what did you feel was lacking with us? Okay, you didn't like the smell of cigarettes and you considered I was chaotic in the kitchen and I never cooked asparagus, but what else was wrong?'

'There was nothing wrong. Nothing lacking.'

'No?'

'No. People have been unfaithful since time began.'

I frowned. This was true, yet... throw-away. 'Maybe, but –'

'I didn't regard the canoodling with Kathryn as serious. In fact, I'd decided to end it, but then she announced she was

206

pregnant and –' he spread his hands '– no way out.'

I stared. I had not been aware of this. 'Why didn't you tell me you'd been all set to end it with her?'

'Didn't see the point and what difference would it have made? Kathryn was determined Cameron wouldn't be a bastard – though the kid can be a real bastard at times – and insisted we must be married. She kicked up such a stink about it and I was so relieved when you didn't – kick up a stink about us divorcing, I mean.'

'What would you have done if I had?'

He moved his shoulders. 'Ended it with Kathryn. Probably. Don't know, though now I wish to hell I had. I realise I caused you a lot of distress, Carol –'

'And caused Lynn distress.'

'And caused Lynn distress, too, and I'm sorry. So very sorry.' He swallowed hard. His eyes were wet with tears.

'Oh, Tom,' I said.

To feel sympathy for the man who had dumped me may be illogical, yet I couldn't help it. I wanted to put my arms around him and hold him tight.

He swallowed again. 'When I think back I'm appalled at what I did, but if you operate under pressure that's often the way it goes. You're at the heart of the action, living the high life, hobnobbing with famous people and it's unreal, so you do daft things. A kind of madness descends. It goes with the territory. Virtually all my colleagues had affairs. Playing around was accepted and, because I didn't, for a long time I was the odd man out. A dullard. A real square.'

I looked at him in disbelief. Was he saying what I thought he was saying? Many of his contemporaries were onto their second – or, in some cases, third – younger wives. Had he viewed his affair with the slick chick as something expected of him and a way to prove himself a swinger?

'You mean you committed adultery because you wanted to be one of the boys?' I demanded. 'You went with Kathryn because you needed to show you were with-it?'

Tom frowned. Shrugged. 'Well –'

'What juvenile reasoning and what a facile bloody excuse!'

'Carol, you're not in the big-time now, you've forgotten what it's like. You've forgotten the strains and stresses, and how, if a guy is a go-getter, the girls throw themselves at him. I accept I was weak, but –'

'Did Kathryn approach you or did you approach her?'

He hesitated. 'Well, she'd been fluttering her lashes at me for quite a while and it was obvious she was eager –'

'So you approached her.' I had always condemned the girl for making the running, but I was mistaken. 'Did you have other affairs before the one with her?'

'No!'

I studied him. He looked offended and outraged. 'I believe you.'

'Thanks. And how is life on *The Siren*?' Tom enquired, clawing desperately for an escape. 'Dog barks in the night and you have your headline?'

'Piss off!'

He laughed. 'That's what I like about you, you have balls. Lynn's told me how you're settled and happy in Dursleigh, but you must regret quitting the London scene.'

'I did at first, briefly. But not any more. The people are nicer here, not so cut-throat, not so narcissistic and self-obsessed. Far more human.'

'Mmm,' he said, as if my remarks were a criticism of him. 'Are you okay for cash?'

'I am.'

'I can always let you have some if you're short.'

'Thanks, but no need.'

I would not accept money from him. And why must he always give cash to Lynn and Beth, instead of taking the time and trouble to choose a present?

'If you should ever need, I'll just tell Kathryn that Harrods is out of bounds. The way that woman can spend. Clothes for herself, things for the kids, for the house. And she pays top dollar.' He grimaced. 'Remember the early days, how short of cash we were?'

I nodded. 'We bought a new bed when Lynn got too big for her cot and paid it off at a pound a week.'

'And we had a holiday in that grotty rented cottage in North Wales.'

'Where we lived on Smash mashed potatoes and tins of Campbell's meat balls.'

Tom laughed. 'Those were the days. Do you remember –'

Off we went, sauntering down memory lane, reviving this incident and that. We had reached another cheap holiday, at a guest house in Devon where the beds had been rock-hard and it had rained all the time, when the doorbell rang. It was an unwelcome intrusion. Memory lane had been fun, a reminder of the times, places and events which we had shared. Just us. Our lives may have diverged, yet there were still years of past pleasure which could never be erased. Years when we'd been a young and happy couple.

I looked at my watch. 'This'll be the gang.' But when I opened the front door, Lynn was stood there alone.

'Justin's taken Beth to see his folks,' she told me, walking in. 'He'll bring her back around six.'

'You had a good time?' I asked, mentally crossing my fingers.

'Not bad. Beth enjoyed stroking all the long-suffering animals and Justin and I managed not to garrotte each other. Hello, Dad,' she said, in surprise.

Tom came along the hall. 'How's my favourite daughter?' he enquired, and hugged her.

'I'm well. Beth will be sorry she's missed you.'

'Ditto,' he said.

'But what are you doing here?' she asked him, then looked at me. 'I know, you've called in reinforcements. Dad's been summoned to give me counselling, too.'

'You don't mind?' I had wondered if she might resent my interference and march out, but instead she was smiling.

'Of course she doesn't mind,' Tom said, and spoke to Lynn. 'How's about you and I go for a walk?'

She shrugged. 'Whatever.'

'Back in half an hour,' he said, and they went off down the path.

As I waited for a second time that day, I didn't smoke. I refused to invite any more comments on Tom's return. Why had I been so uptight about his visit? I wondered. It seemed foolish now. We may have once been man and wife, but that had ended eight years ago. They were eight years during which I appeared to have air-brushed out many of his faults. Eight years when I had been wearing rose-coloured spectacles. Though maybe if Tom had had me to tell him to 'piss off' now and then, he would not have become quite so pompous.

Yet, whatever his faults, a scintilla or two of affection, of attraction, still remained.

The half an hour stretched to almost an hour and when they returned, Tom was looking at his watch.

'I won't come in,' he said. 'Cameron's in a concert this evening and I daren't be late.'

'What is he doing in the concert?' I asked.

'Not a clue. Hope you've listened to your old dad's words of wisdom,' he told Lynn, and took his wallet from the inside pocket of his jacket. He handed her some notes. 'Pocket money for Beth.'

She smiled and kissed him. 'Thanks. Bye,' she said, and went off upstairs.

'It's been great to see you again, Carol,' Tom declared, and pulled me close. He hugged me and I hugged him back. 'I'll be in touch to see how it goes with Lynn. Take care.'

'And you.' I waited until he had climbed into his car, a gleaming new registration Lexus, then waved him goodbye. As I went back into the house, Lynn was coming down the stairs. 'Have the words of wisdom prompted a change of heart?' I asked hopefully.

'No, and actually there weren't so many wise words. Dad spent most of the time talking about himself and Kathryn. Grumbling about her, saying how she's obsessed with the boys and how the two of them are in a constant state of warfare. How she makes his life a misery and he'd be better off without her. Then he'd be free to shack up with Cher.'

'He's not still hooked on her?'

'Sad, isn't it? And Cher must be well on the the wrong side of fifty. Poor old soul.'

'Watch it.'

Lynn smiled. 'Yes, Mum.' Her smile faded. 'Dad was asking if you had a man in your life, so I said there'd been a couple of brief encounters a few years ago, but –'

'You knew?' I said, in surprise.

'Victoria told me. She'd overheard her mum telling her dad how she wished you would settle down, but you'd ended two budding relationships.' Grinning, Lynn tilted her head. 'What I didn't reveal to Dad was that you're on the brink of starting a new romance with your boss.'

'It's a pretend romance, to end the gossip about Max and me and to help Steve escape from Tina Kincaid's pursuit,' I said earnestly. 'As I explained to you last night, we'll just be going through the motions.'

'I bet.'

'It's true! I agree I'm not as anti Steve as I was, but it's not as though either of us lusts after the other and we're certainly not going to jump into bed.'

'No?'

'No!'

Her grin widened. 'Relax, Mum. I'm teasing.'

'Oh.' Why had I risen to the bait and where had my talk of jumping into bed come from? 'But what matters is you and Justin,' I said. 'You should stick with him.'

Lynn frowned. 'You think that, but I'm not so sure.'

'Look –'

'Enough,' she said, and turned and walked away.

I clenched my fists. Once again I wanted to hit Tom, hard. As, all those years ago, I had trusted him to be faithful, so I had trusted him to talk sensibly and responsibly to our daughter. But instead he seemed to have devoted the time to telling her that if you wanted to break up a family, you did. And to hell with trying to resolve any differences.

CHAPTER FOURTEEN

WE WERE FINISHING BREAKFAST on Tuesday morning, when the door bell rang.

In a flash, Beth had slid down from her chair. 'That's my daddy,' she said. 'He's come to see me.'

'No, not today,' Lynn told her. 'Not now.'

'It'll be Mr Lingard, the man I work for,' I began to explain. 'He's driving me to my exercise class and –'

Too late. The child had gone, running along the hall to reach up on tip-toe and open the front door.

'I thought you were my daddy,' we heard her say, full of disappointment.

''Fraid not,' a familiar male voice replied.

'Come in, Steve,' I shouted, swallowing a last bite of toast and rising from the table. 'Won't be a minute.'

'My daddy has curly brown hair and he works at the kitchen showroom in Dursleigh. There are lots of pretend kitchens in there and he's the manager.' Beth was chattering as she and Steve appeared from the hall. 'My daddy plays Snakes and Ladders with me.'

'I used to play Snakes and Ladders with my little girl,' he said.

'Did she win?' Beth demanded.

'Every time. And she used to stand on my feet and we'd dance together. Twirl around and around. She liked that. But she's a big girl now.'

'How old is she?' Beth asked.

'Fourteen. She's called Debbie.'

'That's a nice name. My name is Beth and this is my mummy. Her name is Lynn. This is my gran. She's called –' there was a moment of face scrunched-up thought '– Gran.'

Steve grinned. 'Hello, Gran.'

'Hello,' I said.

'Pleased to meet you, Lynn.'

'Likewise,' Lynn said, smiling. 'I've heard a lot about you.'

'Good, bad or indifferent?' he asked. 'On second thoughts, don't answer that.'

'Bad and not so bad,' I told him.

'Could be worse, I guess. Just.'

'So, you driving Mum to this morning's work-out is the first move in Operation Rebuff Tina Kincaid?' Lynn said.

He nodded. 'I thought that if Tina saw us together, casual and out of the office, it'd be a good way to start. And if we're spotted having dinner, the gossip brigade will need to unscramble your mother's supposed affiliations.'

'Steve didn't get a 2.1 in Deception Studies for nothing,' I said, and headed for the stairs. 'Must fetch my bag.'

I combed my hair, reapplied my lipstick and found my bag. When I returned, Lynn was telling Steve about a house her estate agency had for sale, which hadn't been touched since it had been built in the nineteen twenties. The original wallpaper was hanging in shreds, the minuscule kitchen had an uneven brick floor and a deep, cracked porcelain sink, there was even a mangle in an outside wash-house.

'It's mid-terrace, on a busy road and doesn't have a garage, but you can bet someone'll snap it up,' she said. 'Even though it is priced at almost three hundred thousand.'

Steve shook a wondering head. 'Madness.'

'Sorry to interrupt, but we should make a move,' I said, and we departed.

'You have a very nice daughter,' Steve remarked, as we drove towards Thyme Park.

'Thanks. So do you.'

'Lynn's still objecting to playing happy families?'

I sighed. ''Fraid so. And poor little Beth is still pining for her daddy.'

'I gathered that.'

'It's breaking my heart,' I said, then pointed ahead. 'That's Tina's house.'

As we pulled onto the forecourt, I saw that Jenny and Max had just arrived. Jenny was stood on the porch, chatting with Tina, while Max ferried in his gear. Perfect timing.

'Steve!' As we climbed from the car, Tina waved, all smiles, and rushed down the steps to greet him. I received a quick nod, then was ignored. 'Good to see you, Steve. Such a nuisance, but my central heating's still not working properly. I was wondering if you could come round, perhaps this evening, and –'

'You need a heating expert,' he told her.

'But I'm sure you can fix it.' She opened her eyes wide. They were green today, to match the emerald green top she had teamed with white pants. 'You're so clever at that kind of thing.'

'You should contact a specialist,' he said.

'You could take a look at the boiler now,' she appealed. 'Quickly.'

'Sorry, no time.' He put an arm around my shoulders. 'I'm just delivering Carol.'

I smiled up at him. 'Thanks.'

'I'll see you later at work and then –' Steve smiled his bobby-dazzler smile '– this evening.'

'This evening?' I queried.

He gave me a hug. 'Head like a sieve, at times. You remember, we're having dinner at the new French restaurant on the High Street.'

We were? Although he'd talked of us eating out and I had agreed, this was the first I'd heard of a definite arrangement.

'Oh… yes.'

'Their fish is said to be out of this world,' Jenny enthused.

Steve bent and, to my great astonishment, kissed me on the lips. 'Take care, sweetheart.'

'Um. And you, too,' I gabbled, then watched as he strode back to his car. It was years since a man had kissed me, and my heart was racing and I had gone weak at the knees. But what about no hanky-panky? Steve had broken the rules. Get a grip, I told myself. It was only a kiss. A public kiss, bestowed for a reason. He had startled me, that was all. As he accelerated away, I drew in a steadying breath. 'That was Steve Lingard, my boss,' I told Jenny.

'I realised that, but —' She laughed. 'You sneaky thing, what I didn't realise was that the two of you were —'

'Will you run me home when we're finished here?'

'With pleasure.'

'Then all will be revealed,' I told her.

'Are you and Steve... an item?' Tina demanded, sounding none too pleased.

She had never referred to any possible link-up between me and Max, but as she didn't appear to have friends to chat with, she wouldn't have heard the gossip.

'Early days,' I replied breezily.

'You never said the two of you had something going.'

'No, because we didn't. But you know how it is when you work with a guy, one thing can lead to another and...' I spread my hands and smiled, suggesting all kinds of possibilities.

'I've been wishing Carol would find herself a boyfriend for ages. For years. And at last it's happened,' Jenny said. 'Isn't that lovely?'

'I guess.' Tina looked peeved. Then she turned to Max, who had slammed shut his van door and was carrying in the last piece of equipment. 'Ready?' she asked.

'Ready,' he confirmed.

'It was an act?' Jenny protested, as she drove me home after the work-out. 'Oh, Carol, what a shame. How disappointing. Steve came over as such a nice fellow and he seemed so fond of you, really affectionate, and —'

'An Oscar-winning performance to get Tina to back off,' I said.

'But the two of you are going out to dinner this evening?'

'Yes. If we're seen together, not only will Tina leave him alone —'

'She can be a man-eater at times.'

'You've noticed?'

Jenny nodded. 'The way she was all over Peter from next door and him married, too. But when you consider how her husband's death has left her entirely on her own, with no family to give support, you can understand if she feels emotionally insecure and needs –'

'I accept she's going through a tough time, but the truth is that Tina's number one interest is Tina. Yes?'

There was a pause. 'Yes,' Jenny acknowledged.

'If Steve and I are seen together, not only will she leave him alone,' I continued, reverting to my earlier thread, 'but the gossip about Max and me will cease.'

'The gossip is ridiculous and untrue, as I have told Eileen time and time and time again.'

'She still doesn't believe you?'

'No, and I'm afraid she's still spreading the tale.'

'Crazy old windbag.'

'She is, and the idea that you and Max would ever get together is crazy. Laughable. Absurd. How anyone in their right mind could imagine that you would cosy up with a boy who –'

'Okay, okay. It seems absurd to me, too.' Jenny may not have been about to remark on me being old enough to be Max's mother, or grandmother, but I preferred not to risk it. I do have some pride. 'I wonder how long it'll take before Eileen informs you that I have a new boyfriend, i.e. Steve?'

'A week,' Jenny prophesied. 'At most.'

'Have you been in touch with the guy who gave you his card when we were at the television studios?' I enquired.

'No. Not yet.' She paused. 'But I still have the card.'

'You've ditched Dilys?'

'Not ditched,' my dad objected. 'We've just gone our separate ways.'

'At whose suggestion?'

It was lunchtime and, as arranged, I had called in at my father's flat to see him. Because I know he likes a change from his usual lunch of soup or salad, I had brought along a couple of cheese and smoked ham brochettes and two strawberry tartlets. He had pounced on these as 'just what the doctor ordered', and we were sitting at the dining table at one end of his living room, tucking in.

'The decision was mutual,' he said, and steered a stray crumb of cheddar into his mouth. 'We had a fall out. Well, actually I had a fall out with William, her son.'

'What about?'

'The way he arrives any time, morning, afternoon or evening, and expects his mother to keep her garage constantly clear so that he can drive straight in.'

I took a sip of the Earl Grey tea I had made. My father was frowning, grouchy and aggrieved, but, to me, the matter sounded small potatoes.

'Dilys doesn't run a car,' he went on, 'so, as several of the ladies do, she uses her garage as a store. Keeps all sorts in there; pieces of carpet, old lampshades, suitcases belonging to William – must be at least half a dozen, though I've never understood why he doesn't take them to one of his houses. Everything's stacked around the sides, leaving space to park a car in the middle. Anyhow, the gardener who cuts the grass here got rained off yesterday and asked if he could leave his lawnmower in her garage, just overnight. Dilys was down filling her washing-up liquid bottle, she buys washing-up liquid in bulk – makes a tidy saving, too – and she told him to go ahead. But later in the afternoon William arrived, without warning, and saw red because when he'd zapped the garage door open – he has his own zapper – there was the lawn mower sat dead centre. So, before he could park, he'd had to get out of his car and move it.'

'Big deal.'

'Must've taken him all of two minutes, though it was still raining. I happened to be in Dilys's place when he stormed up to complain and it was not pretty. The chap was effing and blinding, using words I couldn't repeat. Naturally, I stood up for Dilys and told him to watch his mouth. I said he was lucky his mother let him use her garage and that there were plenty of parking spaces for visitors, and did it really matter if his car stood outside and got wet?'

'Perhaps he was worried someone might scratch it?' I suggested.

'Oh, it wasn't the Jaguar, his 'London' car, as he calls it. Seems he does some dealing in second-hand vehicles and he often turns up in shabby, run-down things. As he did yesterday. Anyway, when I said he was making a fuss about nothing he told me I was an interfering old fool and then – would you credit it? – Dilys tells me I'm interfering, too.'

'That was unfair.'

'Unfair, downright rude and ungrateful! Granted we've each bought our own train tickets when we've gone up to London, but it's been my petrol that's taken us to the coast and out for pub lunches. And I paid for the lunches, together with a glass or two of Martini Bianco for her. Usually two, she likes her Martini Bianco. Yes, Dilys cooked dinner for me, but it was my money which bought the food and she often ate with me, so the woman was getting her meals for free and –'

'Your friendship is over?'

'Completely.' He chewed at his sandwich. 'Thinking about Dilys, I'm afraid I have to admit she is on the common side, as your mother would've said. Good company, but some of her language and her jokes –' he shuddered '– they made your hair curl. And when she chose the nightie and arrived at my door that evening to show me –'

'She arrived at your door wearing the nightie?' I asked.

'Yes, though it was beneath a dressing gown. Thank heavens! I'd cleaned my teeth and was in my pyjamas ready for bed, when there was this knock at the door. When I saw Dilys stood there, my immediate thought was that she couldn't be feeling well. Must've taken a bad turn. Indigestion or something. But in she strolls, slips off the dressing gown and poses, hands on her hips and bold as brass. 'Like it, George?' she asks.'

'And you did,' I said, remembering his comment about Dilys looking good in the black chiffon.

My father lowered his gaze. 'Well… yes, though her cleavage was a touch withered. But her coming late at night, it was after ten-thirty, and showing me the nightie. Me, a man on my own.' He had started to mumble. 'It was forward. Too brazen. Out of line.'

The woman turning up late evening in a semi-sheer nightgown sounded to me as if she had been angling to get bedded.

'You offered her a mug of Horlicks?' I joked, eager to know what had happened next.

He managed a smile. 'I told her the nightie suited her and sent her straight back home. Didn't want to risk any gossip and, so far as I'm aware, no one heard Dilys knocking on my door or knows she came visiting that night. Certainly, no one's ever mentioned it. Thank goodness because I would never've lived it down.'

'So you'll be making your own dinners again.'

'No, no, pet. There's a very pleasant lady here called Marie. Don't think you've met her. Refined, she is, used to be a music teacher and plays the piano still. Classical stuff. Chopin and that Russian fellow with the long name. Anyhow, when she heard about Dilys and me no longer being friends, she came to see if she could offer any help in the kitchen. Came round this morning.'

'That was quick.'

'We're off to the supermarket later this afternoon to stock up and –' he chuckled '– I hear she makes a wonderful gooseberry crumble.'

'The babe magnet strikes again,' I murmured.

'Pardon?'

'Never mind. Will you be coming for lunch on Sunday?'

'Yes please, pet.'

'By yourself or would you like to bring Marie along?'

'By myself. Don't intend to get too entangled this time. And if we should start going out in my car, I'll suggest she dollies up for her share of the petrol. I loved seeing you on television last week, pet,' he went on. 'I felt so proud and everyone was so complimentary. Gillian recorded the programme and gave me the video, so I'll be able to show it to folk whenever I want.'

I made a face. Although I had enjoyed seeing the work-out myself – in all modesty, I'd performed well and had looked presentable – I imagined years of visitors being obliged to watch, listen to my father's fulsome commentary and dutifully admire.

'How nice,' I said.

As I sat down at my desk, my hand reached into my bag for cigarettes. And found nothing. The usual packet wasn't there because, in a dramatic and sacrificial gesture, I had thrown it away. I would, I had vowed, never smoke again. But... I felt worried, nervous. Worried about my little granddaughter who was longing to go back home and live with her daddy – and nervous about my dinner date with Steve. To feel jittery about having dinner with a man I worked alongside day after day was pathetic, even more so when the date was not for real, but I couldn't help it. I switched on my computer. I could easily nip out to the newsagents, so should I get twenty Marlboro? Just one packet, to calm my nerves? As I dithered, cursing myself for being so weak, I logged on to read my e-mails. There was one from Max.

'Don't. Do not. Desist. Yes, it's hard, but where's your willpower? Are you going to let a dead leaf dictate your life and maybe cause your premature death? Come Thursday, will you confess to being a spineless wimp needing a tobacco security blanket? Shame on you. You made the decision to quit, so stick with it. Now. Chew gum. Get a patch. Eat raw jelly. Line dance. Be positive.'

I smiled and despatched an e-mail in return. 'Still sticking, but not dancing, Maxie-boy,' it said.

The afternoon had been busy. After leaving my father, I had gone to speak to the owner of a pet shop where there'd been a fire and twenty-four guppies had tragically expired. At least, the pet shop owner considered it was tragic. Describing how he'd found them – in a cracked glass tank and without water – the poor man had broken down in tears. Next I had driven out to a marshmallow factory where police had rounded up several illegal immigrant workers. The manager had insisted he had had no idea his employees were not legal and, maybe in the hope of persuading me to write a sympathetic report, had presented me with two boxes of marshmallows. Later, I visited the home of a woman who had discovered, in her loft, paintings of Dursleigh street scenes which her artist grandfather had done in the early nineteen hundreds.

Finally, I had returned to the office. As I entered, Melanie had been leaving to cover a job and Tony was out, too. Like Melanie, Tony's attitude to work had changed. For years he had done no more than was necessary, but now he was discovering an unexpected drive and keen interest. He had also cut down on his bar lunches and lost some weight.

'Although Eric was a nice enough bloke, I can't remember him ever praising me for any report I wrote,' he had told me. 'Whereas Steve always says when I've done a good job.'

A few words of encouragement and Tony was making suggestions, following up leads, on the alert for stories. He had also brought in some new advertising, including the Italian restaurant.

'You reckon Tina got the message?' Steve asked, walking into the general office.

When I'd arrived at work mid-morning, he had been greeting a man who could write a gardening column for the paper and their discussion was still in progress when I had left at lunchtime.

'I do.'

'And you're free to have dinner this evening?'

'I am. Though it was a big surprise.' The kiss on the lips likewise, I thought.

'Sorry, but when Tina talked of me fixing her central heating the idea suddenly occurred.'

'What you mean is, you panicked.'

''Fraid so.' He smiled. 'I've read your 'Middle-aged

baggage works out on TV' piece. It's good. Made me laugh.'

'Thanks.'

I had finished the article late morning, printed it out and left a copy for him.

'One problem, the photograph you've provided is not of you in your exercise gear, it's just head and shoulders.'

'And head and shoulders is all you're getting. I'm not into self-promotion, plus I'm way too old to be a sex symbol.'

'Not in my opinion,' Steve said. 'In my opinion, you –' He stopped at the sound of the door being opened. ''What are you doing here?' he asked, as Debbie came in. A sulky, glowering Debbie.

'I got home from school and had a bust-up with Mum, so I walked out and hopped on a bus.'

'Does she know where you are?'

'Yes, I told her I was coming here. Coming to see you.'

Steve folded his arms. 'What's the matter this time?'

'We're having lentil burgers again for dinner. Lentil burgers! They're gross! Vile! I hate them! And you do, too.'

'True,' he agreed.

'We have them so often. Like almost every week,' his daughter complained. 'And there's stacks of the horrible things in the freezer. I told Mum I wasn't eating them any more and she started to go on about how healthy they are. Healthy? They look like shit and they taste like –'

'Cool it, Debs,' he cautioned.

'Sorry. So can I move in with you? Just me, not Paul. He likes lentil burgers, stupid twit. Can I move in and eat decent food for a change? Please, Dad, I'll be no trouble. I could bring my stuff round tomorrow after school – I'm going to a disco in the Scout hut tonight – and I promise not to play my C.D.s loud or leave my bedroom in a mess, and I'll let you watch whatever you want to watch on the telly and not grumble. Give me a break, Dad, please.'

He frowned. 'Your mother won't like it. I'm not sure I like the idea, either.'

'If you won't take me in, I shall sleep on a park bench,' the teenager declared. 'Or in a doorway! I shall go to a hostel for the homeless!'

Steve sighed a weary sigh. 'I'll speak to your mother and see if we can sort something out.'

'I knew you'd agree,' she said, and wrapped her arms around him.

'But if you stay it's a one-off and only for a short time. Just to allow you to see sense. Understood?'

Debbie smiled. 'Yes, Dad.'

'Do you like marshmallows?' I asked her, when she had released him.

'Love them.'

I passed her one of the boxes I had been given. The other was reserved for Beth. 'Then enjoy.'

'Thanks. I've written another story, though I haven't got it with me. If I bring it another time, please would you read it?'

I nodded. 'I will.'

La Petite Bourriche was situated at the end of the High Street, towards the river. Previously a fishmonger's shop, the restaurant was cottagey. It had whitewashed walls and tables covered in black-and-white gingham. A collection of bright pottery fish stood on a dresser. The frontage comprised floor-to-ceiling folding glass doors which, in the summer, were concertinaed back to allow the tables to spill out onto the pavement. Now, on a cool April evening, the glass doors were closed, but, seated at one of the front tables, Steve and I were visible to anyone walking by.

'Annette and I had a long talk earlier and we've agreed that Debbie can move into my place tomorrow,' he told me, when we had ordered our meal – sole meunière for two – and the wine had been poured. 'It'll give them time away from each other, a cooling-off period. Debs knows it's temporary and, hopefully, won't make too much fuss when it's time for her to return.'

'My guess is that she'll soon get fed up with living at your place.'

He looked doubtful. 'You reckon?'

'Think about it. Apart from the lentil burgers, she's got everything going for her at home. Friends along the road, her school nearby, a decent-sized bedroom with her boy band posters pinned to the walls.'

'You're right, but how do you know all this?' Steve asked.

'Because she's told me. When we've discussed the stories she's written, she's told me all sorts of things. Also, Debbie's promised not to play loud music or leave her bedroom untidy, and to let you watch your choice of TV. Keep her to it. And when she sees the disadvantages, she'll decide she's better off back home.'

'I hope.' He took a mouthful of wine. 'For a while now, it's seemed to be a case of whatever Annette does is wrong and whatever I do is right. Though God knows why.'

'It was like that, at one stage, with Lynn,' I said. 'I had all the sulks, the moods, while Tom got all the smiles.'

'Was this before or after your divorce?'

'Before, when Lynn was in her early teens. She used to continually find fault with me, with things I'd done or something I'd said, and it would make me so cross. We had some ferocious spats. Doesn't happen now, but I think as girls reach adolescence and the hormones are establishing themselves, there can be a tension in the mother/daughter relationship.'

'You could be right. One thing which drives Annette mad is Debbie's constant nagging to be allowed to have a pet. Seems every other girl on the planet has a dog or a cat or a hamster, except poor deprived her. And now Paul's started pleading for a pet, too.'

'The stories Debbie writes are usually about some kind of pet,' I remarked.

'Thank you for reading them. I appreciate it and I know she does, too. I've looked over the occasional one and commented, but she doesn't rate my opinion. She rates yours.'

'Her stories aren't bad and they're improving. Who knows, you could have a budding J.K. Rowling in the family.'

'Then she'll be able to keep her old dad in the luxury he deserves.' Steve drank again from his glass. 'Did Lynn tell you that we met this afternoon?'

'No. She wasn't in when I got home. She and a girlfriend, who has a daughter the same age as Beth, have taken their kids to a ceramics café.'

'Which is?'

'A place where you paint your choice of pottery – a mug, a plate or a bowl – with your own design, and have it fired and glazed. Then you buy it. If Debbie hasn't been, she might like it. But you met Lynn?'

'Yes, I saw her in the street and stopped her. You remember, this morning, Beth said her daddy was boss of the kitchen showroom? It set me thinking. The firm he works for is in the process of being taken over by a larger group and –'

'I didn't know that,' I broke in.

'Neither did Lynn, when I mentioned it. I heard about the deal through a guy I know in Ringley and, so far as I'm aware, it hasn't been made public yet. But because the take-over means there's some overlapping, a number of showrooms will be closed and staff made redundant.' Steve frowned. 'When Lynn said she hadn't heard about the take-over, I'm afraid I told her that she should've done. Justin must know, and if they lived together and didn't talk about something as important to them both as his work –' He raised his shoulders in disbelief.

'People vary.'

'And how. But I'm afraid I annoyed your daughter. If looks could kill, I'd have been dead meat on the pavement. And she would've still stalked off.'

'Don't worry about it. I've told her how foolish she's being and received my fair share of 'drop dead' looks, too.'

'Lynn said you'd called in her father at the weekend to talk sense into her, but no luck. You get on okay with him?'

'Yes, though it's rare we meet.'

Our fish arrived, accompanied by side dishes of fresh vegetables.

'Me upsetting Lynn was the bad news,' Steve said, as he

picked up his knife and fork. 'Now here's the good news. You're getting a pay rise.'

'I am?' I said delightedly.

'And so are Tony and Melanie. Your rise is larger percentage-wise than theirs, because you work a darn sight harder and have done for a long time. But they're both knuckling down and the circulation figures are already showing signs of an increase, so I persuaded Mr Pinkney-Jones that rises all round were called for.'

'Steve, that's great. I appreciate it. Thanks.'

'You may kiss me, if you wish.'

I grinned. 'That's very generous of you.'

He glanced out at the street, where two elderly ladies were passing, each with a small dog on a lead. 'It'll intrigue those who may be interested.'

Laughing, I leaned forward and kissed him. On the cheek. A smooth cheek which smelled faintly of a tangy aftershave.

'The circulation figures are going up?' I said, as we ate.

'By a small percentage, but it's a start.'

'The advertising revenue must have increased, too.'

'It has. When *The Bugle's* sales began to rise, I suggested to Mr P-J that, not only should he increase my pay – which he did, thank goodness, because supporting an ex-wife and two children in one house and financing a place for myself takes a bit of doing – but –'

'You were making a fair amount of increased profit for him, so he should've upped your pay without being asked,' I protested.

'True,' Steve acknowledged. 'But I also suggested he should allot me shares in the group, tying them in to my success. He agreed and I've done well out of the shares. Maybe I should ask him to allot you shares in the newspaper group, too.'

'Why me?'

'Because you were the true editor of *The Siren* and the reality is that you kept the paper going. If Eric hadn't had you running things for him, it would've collapsed years ago.'

I smiled. 'Thank you, kind sir.'

'I'm not being kind. I'm telling it as it is.'

'I appreciate that,' I said seriously, 'and I'd appreciate some shares.'

'I'll see what I can do.'

'Thanks. Being expected to work wonders at *The Siren* must create a certain amount of pressure,' I went on.

Steve nodded. 'It does. There are nights when I lie awake worrying for what seems like hours.'

I looked at him in surprise. So Captain Cool was not so cool, after all. 'You'll manage it. You will work wonders,' I said.

'With your help.' A dark brow lifted. 'I hope?'

'You can count on it.'

'Alleluia!'

I laughed. 'Okay, when you first arrived I wasn't too pleased, but –'

'Not pleased? Jesus, I lived in fear of my life. I was forever waiting for you to push me down the stairs or deliver a sharp kick to the sweetbreads.'

'I restrained myself.'

'Only just.' The brow lifted again. 'And now you're a fan?'

I grinned. 'I wouldn't go that far.'

When we had finished our sole, Steve took a folded sheet of paper out of his jacket pocket. 'I was wondering if you would cast your eye over this? It's my first editor's column for *The Siren*; you know the readership much better than me and I'd be grateful for your comments.'

I read the piece, which was about him coming to work in Dursleigh, a new location, but recognising the usual types of people – village stalwarts who were always ready to help, incessant grumblers, women who shouted 'yoo-hoo' across the street, teenagers who refused to put two tees in 'bottle' or one tee in 'later'.

'I like it. It'll amuse the old ladies and all the other punters,' I said.

Steve smiled, putting the paper back into his pocket.

'Thanks. I feel happier about it now.'

'You value my judgement?'

'Implicitly.'

'Then may I suggest that *The Siren* sponsors the village fête this summer? Duncan Kincaid suggested the idea to Eric year in, year out, but he always pooh-poohed it.'

'Because it seemed too much like hard work?'

I nodded. 'But the paper being a sponsor would create a vast amount of good will.'

'I'll think about it,' he said.

'And have you ever thought of writing a book? 'Journalism is literature in a hurry',' I quoted, 'so –'

'Which sage said that?'

'Actually it was Richard Gere in the film *The Runaway Bride*.'

Steve grimaced. 'Oh Lord. No, I haven't thought of writing a book. How about you?'

'Well, actually –'

All through the pudding, the coffees and liqueurs, we talked. And laughed. And the time flew by.

'Great food, great company and a great evening,' Steve declared, as he deposited me at my door. 'We must do it again. Soon.'

'To deceive Tina,' I said, and wondered who I was reminding.

He shrugged. 'Why else?'

CHAPTER FIFTEEN

WHEN I ARRIVED HOME from work the next evening, Justin's car was parked outside. I eyed it with alarm. Why was he here? Had he come to play Snakes and Ladders with his daughter or – I went cold – might he and Lynn have decided to finalise their separation and were sorting out the practicalities? Were six years of loving and living together in the process of being clinically dismantled?

Turning my key in the lock, I opened the front door. I swallowed. 'It's me,' I called.

If they were trading insults as they decided who should fall heir to how many teaspoons, I had no wish to walk in on it.

''Lo, Gran.' Beth skipped along the hall looking, I was relieved to see, happy and at ease. This meant Justin's visit must be a social visit – surely?

'Hello, my darling.'

'I'm going to be a bridesmaid,' she announced, as I bent to hug her.

'At your playgroup?'

So far, she has been a sheep in the Christmas nativity play, and a belly dancer, a nurse and an oak tree in other performances. Each time Lynn had, innovatively and uncomplainingly, produced the required outfit. The oak tree, with its ribbed cardboard trunk, stuffed brown tights branches and sewn-on green paper leaves had been a particular challenge. As was subsequently transporting the forested Beth. And taking her to the toilet had been a nightmare.

'No, silly. At a wedding. I'm going to wear a pink dress and have pink and white flowers in my hair. And I shall carry a pink and white posy.' She looked down at her new trainers, which she loves because they flash a light in the soles when she walks. 'Do you think I could wear these?'

'Pink satin shoes would look better.'

'Pink satin shoes with bows?'

'Perfect,' I said. 'But who's getting married?'

'We are,' Lynn shouted. 'Justin and me.'

I flew into the kitchen to find the two of them sat at the table, surrounded by bags and suitcases, smiling.

'You?' I demanded.

Justin nodded. 'Us.'

'This isn't a joke?' I said, longing to believe and yet wary. The m-word wasn't something they had tossed around as a possibility. Or, indeed, ever uttered, at least not in my hearing.

'As if we'd joke about a thing like that,' Lynn chided.

I kissed them both. 'Congratulations!' I wanted to whoop and rejoice. Toot a horn and turn cartwheels. They were back together. Beth was going to live with her mummy *and* her daddy, and be legitimate. My cup runneth over. Although I had pretended to be modern, casual and not to care, as I'd confided to Jenny I had always hoped they would marry – though I had never told them. 'So what changed things?' I asked.

'Steve,' Lynn replied.

'Come again?'

'Steve Lingard changed things. Yesterday morning he stopped me in the village and, when he realised I knew nothing about Justin's company being bought out, he told me I was self-centred and pathetic. Well, he didn't use the actual words, but he made it brutally clear he thought I should've been a darn sight more aware. That when Justin started to get tetchy and hard to live with, instead of retaliating I should've asked questions. Found out if something was troubling him. So, after a day of thinking over what Steve had said – and what you'd said about us needing to discuss things, frankly and honestly – this morning I went along to the showroom. I asked Justin why he hadn't told me about the take-over.'

'I explained that I'd kept it to myself because I'd been worried I could be made redundant,' Justin said, picking up the tale. 'Worried sick I'd be a failure. Which is what'd made me so snappy at home and constantly on edge.'

230

'Why would being made redundant make you a failure?' I asked.

'Because I'd feel I was letting Lynn down. Not doing my best for her and Beth.'

'Rubbish! Lots of people get made redundant through no fault of their own.'

'That's what I told him,' Lynn said.

'And I agree. Now,' Justin added. 'But I'd been doing so well and to be suddenly faced with the prospect of being out of work and on the dole, with a mortgage to pay and a family to support – it seemed like disaster.'

'But Steve was right, I ought to have realised that something was upsetting him.' Lynn said. 'Justin being crabby is out of character, so I should've twigged. I should've been more sympathetic. I should've supported him.'

Beth had been raising herself up and down on tiptoe to make her trainers flash, but now her forehead crinkled. 'What does sympa – sympathetic mean?'

'I should have been kinder to Daddy when he got cross,' Lynn told her.

'Cuddled him?'

'Cuddled him.'

I turned to Justin. 'When will you know what's going to happen about your job?'

He grinned. 'I already know. One of the directors of the new company came in last week and told me that my position is safe. Actually, he praised me to the skies and said I'm in line to become an area manager, in a year or so.'

'That's because he's way clever at running his showroom and making sales,' Beth said seriously. 'And my daddy's going to get a salary increase. That means lots more money.'

I laughed. He was not the only one, I thought, though I would save my own news for later. 'Clever Daddy! And he's also going to be a married daddy?'

'We thought we'd make it legal in church in the summer,' Justin said. 'St. John's, August. With trouble here –' he ruffled Beth's hair '– as our bridesmaid.'

231

'I'm going to be the belle of the ball,' Beth informed me.

'With just a little competition from your mother,' I said. 'But why the decision to marry?'

Justin took hold of Lynn's hand. 'Marriage is the ultimate in commitment and, after being so miserable when we broke up, we both feel we want to commit to each other, for always.'

'Till death do us part,' Lynn said, smiling at him.

I hoped she was right. I prayed that my daughter's marriage would be strong and true and permanent.

My gaze went to the bags and cases. 'So you and Beth are moving out.'

'Yes, we were waiting until you came home, for us to go home. Thank you so much for taking us in and looking after us.' Lynn rose to hug me. 'You're the best mum ever.'

'It's appreciated,' Justin said.

'I enjoyed taking them in – most of the time – but I don't want to take them in ever again,' I warned.

'You won't have to.'

'Cross your heart and hope to die?'

'Cross my heart and hope to die,' he chanted, making the requisite motions.

'Just one criticism, Mum,' Lynn said. 'The loo. Please, I beg, get it fixed. Having to pump the handle half a dozen times before the contrary thing flushes has been driving me bananas.'

'I'll see to it,' I promised.

Loading themselves up, she and Justin began to carry the bags and suitcases out to his car. Back and forth they went, until the kitchen was clear.

'Will you miss me, Gran?' Beth asked, as I walked with her down the front path. She held her Bart Simpson lunchbox in one hand and a chocolate lolly in the other.

'Yes, I will, my darling, very much. But I can come to see you whenever I want, and you can come and see me whenever you want.'

The little girl nodded. 'And when I come to your house, I can watch you on your video.'

232

'Of course.'

For some reason, her grandmother working out on a television programme fascinated her and she had replayed the video many times.

'I haven't seen it yet,' Justin said. 'I believe I'm in for a treat.'

I grinned. 'Prepare to be amazed.'

'When you see Steve, please will you thank him for saying what he did and making me think again. Tell him I'm grateful. Extremely grateful,' Lynn said.

'Will do.'

'He's quite a guy,' she continued. 'Forthright, but sexy with it. I don't blame you for getting up close and personal. Mum and Steve went out to dinner last night,' she informed Justin.

'We went for a specific reason, which Lynn will explain,' I said. 'And, as she well knows, getting up close and personal was not involved.'

My daughter chuckled. 'But you kissed him! The mother of one of the guys I work with happened to be walking her Jack Russell along the High Street and she saw you.'

'I kissed Steve on the cheek, purely for the benefit of the dog walking lady and her friend.'

'Some story!'

'It's true,' I protested.

'I ought to let Dad know that Justin and I are back together again,' Lynn said, and glanced at the laden car 'but I'll be too busy to get around to it this evening. You couldn't break the news for me and warn that he'll be required to fork out for a wedding?'

'I will.'

There were goodbye kisses, then they climbed into the car. Beth was strapped into her child seat, and I waved them goodbye. Actually, I stood on one leg and wiggled my thumbs. I did this once to amuse Beth and it has become the regular farewell. Heaven knows what my neighbours must think.

Returning indoors, I poured myself a glass of wine and

raised it on high. 'Cheers, Steve. You're a saviour.'

I felt so relieved and happy. Couldn't stop smiling. Should I ring Steve and thank him? Should I call Jenny and tell her that, at long last, my daughter was embarking on matrimony and becoming respectable? Should I advise my father that he would shortly be attending a wedding where he might be able to wow the guests with his foxtrot, so he would need to decide whether to bring along Peggy, his dancing partner, or the new cook, Marie. Later I would do all this, but first I must obey my daughter's bidding and ring Tom.

Although it was approaching seven p.m., I rang his office – only to be informed by a switchboard operator that he had left an hour ago. I dialled his home number. The slick chick could answer, but so what? Who cared? Not me. Lynn's wedding could necessitate contact with the woman and her sons – I assumed they would need to be invited – but, right now, I didn't care about that, either.

'I'd like to speak to Tom, please,' I said, when Kathryn did answer.

'I'm afraid he isn't here. Who's calling?'

'It's Carol. Carol Webb.' I have retained my married name, so I could have said it was the first Mrs Webb. The original.

'Hello, Carol.' She sounded surprised, though surprisingly pleasant. 'Tom should be in any minute, but –'

'He's running late. As usual.'

'Correct. And we're going to the theatre this evening and the boys are fed, bathed and in their pyjamas and the babysitter has arrived, but Tom hasn't.'

'I know the feeling.'

'He did this with you?'

'Repeatedly. Bloody annoying, isn't it?'

'Drives me up the wall. When he does appear he's so apologetic and yet the very next week he does the same thing again. Blames work, though I'm not always sure he's telling the truth. Can I take a message or get him to call you?' Kathryn enquired. 'I hope nothing's wrong?'

'Everything is right. Very right,' I told her. 'I was ringing to let him know that Lynn and Justin have sorted out their differences and are going to be married. In the summer.'

'Married! Ooo, that's brilliant. Lynn is such a friendly girl – we get on so well together – and she's so pretty. She'll make a lovely bride. Will she be wearing white? It'd be nice if she went the whole hog – long white dress, veil, maybe a tiara, and Justin in top hat and tails. I saw a delicious wedding dress only last week. Bit expensive, over three thousand pounds –'

'Very expensive,' I inserted, recalling Lynn's description of her stepmother as 'twittery'.

'But the bodice was lace and threaded with silver, and the skirt had rows and rows of tiny pearls arranged in a daisy pattern which – hang on. I think that's Tom at the door. Give Lynn my love and very best wishes,' she gabbled.

There was a thunk as the phone was put down and an indistinct snatch of dialogue, then Tom spoke.

'Carol, how are you?'

'Never better. Earlier this evening, I arrived home and –'

'Hold a minute. Kath,' I heard him say brusquely, 'if you don't mind, this is a private conversation.' A pause, obviously while he waited for her to leave the room. 'Sorry about that. Carry on.'

I carried on and explained my good tidings. 'So I'm jumping for joy.'

'It's excellent news,' he agreed. 'And cause for us to celebrate. How about coming up to town and I'll take you to dinner at one of the finest and newest restaurants?'

I hesitated. Although the prospect of being wined and dined at a five-star London hangout did not particularly excite me, sometime we would need to meet to talk about arrangements for the wedding.

'Thanks, I'd like that. And I'd like to meet Kathryn, too. We'll both be at the wedding, I imagine, and if we get to know each other a little beforehand it'll ease –'

'No, no, I was thinking of a special dinner,' Tom said. 'Just you and me on – how about Sunday evening?'

For the two of us to dine alone struck me as odd. Why not

include Kathryn? Also Sunday evening seemed a strange choice of day and time and, because there were often engineering works on the line at weekends, I would need to check the train service. Another thought: my father was coming for lunch, though he usually departed late afternoon.

'This coming Sunday?'

'That's right. Sunday, the 27th.'

My heart twanged. Tom had referred to a 'special' dinner and the 27th was a special date. A date which had relevance to just the two of us. Now I understood why he had chosen Sunday and felt touched. Warmed. It was a caring choice.

'The 27th it is. I'll travel up by train.'

'Then I'll meet you at Waterloo,' he said, and we fixed a time – with the proviso that I could change it, if necessary.

Replacing the phone, I took a drink of wine and then rang Steve's number.

'Sincere thanks,' I said, when he answered. 'Thank you for bringing Lynn to her senses and for bringing her and Justin back together again.'

'They've made up?' I heard the smile in his voice. 'That's great.'

'They've not only made up, they have decided to get married. In church, in the summer.'

Steve laughed. 'And you're obviously delighted.'

'Walking on air. Beth's back living with her darling daddy–'

'So you're on your own again?'

'Yes, they moved out and went home about a quarter of an hour ago. And it's all thanks to you.'

Steve lowered his voice. 'I wish my daughter would come to her senses and go home, too. She's wandering around here like a lost soul. It's obvious she'd be happier back on home territory, but whenever I suggest she returns she concocts a dozen excuses.'

'It'll happen and soon,' I assured him.

He sighed. 'I hope so.'

*   *   *

236

On Friday I was walking back from the fire station where I'd been speaking to a trio of firemen who were running in the London Marathon, dressed as Teletubbies, to raise money for a wheelchair for a disabled colleague when, further along the High Street, I saw someone waving. Narrowing my eyes against the glare of the sun, I realised it was Jenny, standing outside the charity shop and signalling to me.

'You know that yesterday afternoon I went with Tina to the model agency in London?' she said, as I joined her. 'You'll never guess what happened.'

'Tina landed a booking?'

'Not just one, three, but – Got time to talk?'

I inspected my watch. 'A quick five minutes.'

'Then come inside and I'll tell you about it.'

'No Eileen today?' I asked, as Jenny led me through the deserted shop, past rails of second-hand – oops, 'pre-owned' – clothes, towers of C.D.s and a table bearing a collection of lightly chewed Beanie Babies.

'She was here, but she's gone to the doctor's again, this time with restless legs.'

'Sure it's not restless tongue? The chronic variety?'

Jenny grinned. 'Could be. Frances was supposed to be taking over when Eileen departed, but she hasn't shown up. Frances is the Green Party supporter who's a keen do-gooder. A valiant lady and utter pain. I've told you about her.'

I nodded. 'The one who volunteers to help with anything and everything, but is totally unreliable.'

'That's her. When she's here, she charges the wrong prices and gives folk the wrong change. She drives Eileen wild. Remember I said Eileen would be gossiping about you and Steve in a week at most?' she carried on. 'It didn't take that long. When she was in earlier, she announced that one of her friends had seen 'my friend, Carol, snuggling up to a new fellow in La Petite Bourriche.' Seems the new fellow is middle-aged and not such a snappy dresser as Max, but looked a bit of all right nonetheless.'

I laughed. 'I'll tell Steve.'

Reaching the small staff room at the rear of the shop, Jenny launched into her news. 'Tina was given three bookings. Two are for advertisements for clothes, designer clothes, which will be featured in fashion magazines, and the other is for vitamin pills.'

'She was given the bookings straight off?'

'No, it took forever. For one job she had to attend an audition which, fortunately, was being held not too far away. But then she had to have photographs taken, so that the agency could put her forward for future jobs. I was sat in the waiting room leafing through copies of *Hello* and *OK!* magazines for almost three hours.'

'Poor you,' I commiserated.

'At least I'm up to date with the pop scene and who's living with whom in the film world. But –' Jenny chuckled '– as I was sat there, one of the agency bosses walked through and noticed me. Seems they'd been looking for a woman to be photographed for a kitchen equipment catalogue and she reckoned I looked like I could 'dice a mean carrot'. In other words, I look your typical middle-aged, middle income, middle of the road housewife. Mrs Average.'

'You do yourself a disservice, madam! You're an alluring sexbomb who wreaks havoc in the loins of men.'

'Am I? Do I?' She laughed. 'You're a true friend, Carol. A total liar, but a true friend all the same. Anyhow, the woman asked if I was in the market for work.'

'And you said thanks, but no thanks.'

'On the contrary, the new confident Jen said yes.'

I stared in amazement. 'You're going to be a model? That's fantastic!'

'It's hardly parading along a catwalk and it could be just this one job, but I thought I'd give it a whirl. The agency boss was keen to get me 'on board', as she kept saying.'

'Great for the ego.'

'It was. It is.'

'And, who knows, it could lead to greater things. Before long you could be refusing to get out of bed for less than ten thousand pounds a day, *à la* – whichever supermodel it was.'

Jenny grinned. 'Make that twenty thou. Though I could easily decide that modelling isn't my scene. For a start, I'd need to keep a strict watch on my weight and do I really want to spend my days traipsing around London having my appearance dissected and assessed, then being turned down?' She made a face. 'Bad for the ego. So I shall continue looking for an office job.'

'I trust the news of her model girl mum rocked Victoria back on her heels?'

'It almost flattened her. Bruce, too.'

'What was Tina's reaction?'

'She was pleased for me. I mean, it's not as if I'm any kind of competition.' Jenny frowned. 'When we were travelling up on the train, I said how sorry I was that she was all on her own, without any family. But it turns out she does have a family or, at least, she has a mother and a brother.'

'So where are they, abroad?'

'I don't think so. Tina was vague, but I got the impression she could've seen her mother fairly recently, though from a distance. Apparently there was a nasty quarrel in the past, the distant past, and they haven't spoken since. She didn't give any details.'

'Her mother must be getting on,' I observed.

Jenny nodded. 'I suggested Tina should get in touch and try to mend their relationship before it's too late – before the old lady dies – but she said she doubted her mother would be willing. Though that could've meant *she* wasn't willing. Great shame. By the way, Shane's moving out this weekend. He's found a bed-sit in Croydon, so –'

'Anyone around?' a woman's voice called.

'Coming,' Jenny replied.

'I must go,' I said. 'Bye.'

CHAPTER SIXTEEN

PULLING OUT OF DURSLEIGH Station, the train trundled past council houses pinned with satellite dishes, picked up speed alongside five-bed, five-bath executive mansions where expensive garden furniture graced wide patios, cut through rolling fields and burrowed beneath a busy dual carriageway. A couple of stops, views of a rugby pitch, a multi-masted telephone exchange, tight terraces of brand new houses each oozing a conservatory and we entered suburbia. As the train duddle-dee-dered along, I reflected on Tom's choice of day. April 27th was the birthday of Michael, our son... and the day of his death.

In a repeat of how it had been when I was expecting Lynn, throughout the nine months of my second pregnancy I had felt wonderfully well. Yes, I'd suffered bouts of morning sickness and was destined to collect another phalanx of stretch marks, but my hair gleamed, my skin was as smooth as silk, I bloomed. A week before the due date, I had gone for a regular check-up and been assured that all was in order and the baby was healthy. I felt it kick.

'It's an energetic little bugger,' Tom had remarked, putting his hand on my bump. 'My guess is, we're going to have a son.'

'Or a second daughter,' I'd said.

In those unenlightened days, you didn't get to know the gender of your offspring beforehand and I didn't want Tom to be too hopeful – or too disappointed. Though, having already got a girl, I, too, felt a boy would be ideal.

The contractions started around dawn one morning, becoming definite by breakfast time and, as arranged, I had duly delivered an unbothered Lynn into Jenny's loving care. Tom drove me to the hospital, but when the usual tests were done the doctor, a middle-aged Mancunian, had looked concerned. He took me for a scan, which frightened me. When I asked if something was wrong, he squeezed my shoulder, told me not to worry and spouted banal phrases like 'funny old world' and 'at the end of the day, all down to fate'. After the scan, we returned to the room where Tom had been left to wait. Then the trite, supposedly comforting, words ceased and the doctor hit us with – 'I can't find a heartbeat.'

My first reaction was disbelief. A mistake had been made, it couldn't be true. Then I had expected to be rushed into surgery for a Caesarean. But there was no dramatic race to the operating theatre. The baby had to come out naturally.

My labour was a numb and tortured affair which seemed to last for ever, but late that afternoon I gave birth to a little boy. A perfectly formed corpse. We had already decided that if we had a son we would call him Michael; Michael Thomas Webb.

When he was born, Michael's face was wrinkled and his mouth was open, and I kept on thinking, hoping, he might take a sudden breath and curl his tiny fingers around mine. That the doctor had been wrong and a miracle could happen. It didn't. The baby lay still, as tranquil as if he might have been asleep. One of the nurses carried him off, cleaned him and dressed him in the clothes which I had brought and then they took photographs, which I still have. We were encouraged to hold him, and I did. I cuddled my son. I told him that his mummy and daddy loved him dearly and would always love him. But Tom couldn't face it. He wouldn't touch him.

Returning home without a baby and needing to explain to two-year-old Lynn that she wasn't having a brother or a sister after all, was grim. For us, though not for her. We'd bought her a Tiny Tears doll to soften the blow and she went cheerfully off to play with it. Coping with the sympathy of friends and neighbours was grim, too.

But the full impact of the grief didn't hit me until after the funeral and then I became scared, so scared. Nothing felt safe any more and it seemed as if Lynn or Tom or I might be struck down and die at any moment. That the world was awash with tragedy and lurking danger. Everyone – my parents, my

241

friends and, in particular, Jenny, was so kind and understanding. But, in what seemed a cruelly short time, the letters of condolence dried up, people talked of other things and the usual routine resumed. Tom threw himself back into his career. He had always been ultra ambitious.

I continued to grieve. It didn't help that my body reacted as if I had given birth to a living child; my breasts swelled with untapped milk and my stomach took months to shrink back.

'It could've been my fault,' I can remember saying to Jenny. 'I stopped smoking as soon as I realised I might be pregnant, but –'

'It was not your fault,' she had insisted. 'The doctor said they couldn't find out what had gone wrong, but it had nothing to do with anything you did.'

'At one stage, I had a fad for pickled beetroot. Maybe the acid in the vinegar poisoned him.'

'Carol, it was bad luck. Pure and simple. And if you try again, all will be well,' Jenny had said, full of compassion.

But when I had raised the idea of us trying again, Tom was reluctant. Indeed, whenever I tried to speak to him about the baby, he was reluctant. He didn't like talking about our son. He concealed his pain. I couldn't. For a long time afterwards, the little white coffin would appear in my mind's eye and I would break down and sob.

Michael was buried in a churchyard in Sale and every year when I drive up to Scotland to visit my brother, I call in and put flowers on his grave. All these years on, I still mourn his loss and feel that my family never was, and never will be, properly complete.

But by suggesting we meet today, Tom had shown that although, after the first trauma of his death, he had rarely mentioned him, our son lives on in his memory.

Situated on a smart Knightsbridge street, the restaurant had a polished grey marble floor, steel-panelled walls and was space-rocket sharp. Square glass tables, set discreetly apart, were lit by stainless steel lamps which hung on long poles from the ceiling, while, at the rear, chefs worked busily behind a steel and glass counter. The décor had won many accolades and the restaurant was renowned for its 'outstanding Lot Valley cooking and wines of quality', so Tom had been quick to inform me. From what I had sampled so far, I agreed. Everything had been superb. Tom was a regular customer and, judging by the warm welcome he had received from the waiters in their long white aprons, also a generous tipper. The table we had been given, in a prime position looking onto the street and in a separate, steel-barricaded booth, indicated his standing, too.

'Kathryn didn't mind you taking me out to dinner?' I asked, as we paused between the main course and the pudding.

So far, our conversation had centred on Lynn and Justin's wedding. I had explained that they had been able to arrange the church service on the day they had desired, but were now looking for somewhere to hold the reception. This was proving difficult as all the popular places around Dursleigh appeared to have been booked up at least a year in advance.

'Kathryn doesn't know,' he replied.

'Why not? You mean you didn't tell her?'

'No. She thinks I'm off on a business trip.'

I looked at him in confusion. 'I don't understand.'

'Carol, you and I should never've been divorced. I only went along with it because Kathryn was pregnant and I'm damn sure she got pregnant on purpose.'

'It takes two,' I pointed out.

'Yes, but –' Tom realigned his dessert spoon and fork. He looked serious. 'The reason I suggested we meet tonight is because –'

'I know why.'

His brows shot up in surprise. 'You do?'

'It's because today is Michael's birthday.'

'And which Michael is that? Michael 'Wacko Jacko' Jackson, maybe?' he joked. 'Michael Portillo? Or how's about Michelangelo?'

I stared. He did not know whom I was talking about. He

hadn't a clue. The name and the date meant nothing.

'Michael is Michael Webb, our son,' I said, my voice hard, though there was a lump in my throat. 'He was born, and died, on the twenty-seventh of April.'

Tom frowned, twiddled with the stem of his wine glass and then looked up. 'I'm sorry, I should've remembered. But you don't still think about that baby? Not after so many years?'

'Yes, I do, though he obviously never crosses your mind.'

That baby he had called him, not *our* baby. How could he be so detached and uncaring? We were talking about his child, his own flesh and blood.

'What'd be the point? It was sad, him dying and you going through the pregnancy for no result. But nothing to be gained from –' He stopped, as if aware of getting himself in a tangle. As if he could've been about to casually say there was 'nothing to be gained from crying over spilt milk'.

'Have you never wondered what Michael would've been like if he'd lived?' I asked. 'Haven't you imagined him growing up?'

'No.'

Turning my head, I looked out of the window. About half an hour ago it had started to rain. Light at first, the rain had steadily increased until now, as darkness fell, it was pouring down. The pavements were glossy with wet and people holding umbrellas aloft needed to sidestep to avoid puddles. Tom had not concealed his pain. He may have been upset and disappointed at the time, but our son's death had not had a serious impact. It had not emotionally gutted. For him, Michael was not a part of our family. He had never been a true entity. I watched a car drive by, creating a wash of water from the gutters. I had believed my grief to be a shared grief, albeit hidden, but I had been mourning alone.

I turned back to him. 'So why did you suggest we dine together this evening?' I enquired.

'Because it makes life easier. You see, I'm going away tomorrow, to Brussels to cover an E.U. debate, but I told Kathryn I'd got a meeting there first thing Monday morning, so I had to take a flight tonight.'

I shook my head in bewilderment. I wasn't following him. 'Why do that? Why tell her a lie?'

'Because I've booked us a room at a hotel.'

'What?'

Reaching out a hand, Tom ran his knuckles slowly down my cheek. It was a caress I remembered from the past. A caress which I had regarded as tender and romantic, but which now seemed cynically contrived.

'Carol, I love you and I want you. When I came to your house the other day and saw you again, I realised that I've always loved you. Never stopped. Marrying Kathryn was a big mistake, a complete balls-up.'

I jerked back. 'And now you expect me to – to spend the night with you? To sleep with you?'

The idea stunned me. It was not something I had anticipated. Not something which would ever have occurred to me. Though, to be honest, there was a time – years – when I would've been sorely tempted by the chance to sleep with him; for my own pleasure and to punish Kathryn. But no longer.

Tom smiled. A confident smile which said he knew I would be soft, malleable, eager. 'Yes.'

'That's one hell of a big expectation!'

'Come on, where's the harm? It'll be like the dirty weekend we spent together before we were married when we couldn't keep our hands off each other. Remember?'

'I do. But it wouldn't be anything like it.'

'Don't play hard to get, Carol,' he coaxed. 'There's no other man in your life. Never has been, not one serious guy since we split up. And do you know why? Because –'

A waiter appeared beside us. 'Would you and the lady care to see the dessert menu, sir?' he enquired.

'Later.' Tom flicked him away with an impatient hand. 'I'll let you know when.'

'May I pour you more wine, sir?'

'We'll do it ourselves.'

The waiter bowed. 'Whatever you wish, sir,' he murmured, and retreated.

'You haven't got seriously involved with any other guy, because you know he'd be second best. Because he's not me,' Tom pronounced.

I resisted the urge to blow a raspberry. 'Such modesty.'

'Carol, we were good together before, brilliant together, and we will be again. We're a pair, dammit. Nature's soulmates. Remember how you said you didn't want Lynn to act rashly and do something she might regret for the rest of her life? You were really talking about yourself, about how you agreed so quickly to us splitting up.'

I shook my head. 'Not so.'

'I was a fool, too, the biggest fool, but we all act foolishly at times. However, I'm going to leave Kathryn. As soon as I get back from France, I shall tell her I want a divorce. Then you and I can –'

'This is ridiculous!' I burst out. But it was not only ridiculous, his assumption that I would willingly spend the night with him in a hotel was tawdry stuff.

'Why?'

'For a start, have you thought about your sons?'

'What about them?'

'How they are young and vulnerable, and how they need their father.'

'I'll still see them. Still keep in touch.'

'Seeing them isn't enough. Keeping in touch would stink!' I hissed, furious and yet keeping my voice low. Tina might have relished making a scene, but I prefer my private affairs to remain private. 'You've already broken up one family, you can't break up another.'

'Believe me, I don't want to, but –'

'On the contrary, you'd ditch your wife and your kids, like that!' I snapped my fingers, though it was not much of a snap. I've never learnt the knack. 'But, flawed as you are, your family needs you. And I would never get involved with a married man.'

He smiled. 'Not even one you'd once been married to?'

'Especially not one I had once been married to! One who is a complete and utter bastard with the morals of an alleycat!'

My estimation of Tom had not just plummeted, it had hit rock bottom. His talk of leaving Kathryn and wrecking a second family had been a reality slap. It was hard to believe that someone I had loved and valued for years could be so callous and self-centred, but I was being forced to face the truth.

'Look, if I'm divorced –'

'Married or divorced or if the two of us were marooned on a desert island, I would never sleep with you!'

He took another mouthful of wine. 'You want to be alone for ever? Without a man for the rest of your life? Celibate?'

'I am not alone. As a matter of fact, this siren is going out with Steve, the editor of *The Siren*,' I declared, then rose, grasped my bag and marched over to the stainless steel coatstand where I pulled on my jacket. 'Goodnight.'

'Madam is leaving?' enquired the waiter who had arrived, too late, to help me with my jacket.

'I am. I enjoyed the meal, it's just the company which is pitiful.'

Tom hurried over. 'Carol, be reasonable. Let's sit down and talk,' he appealed.

'We have nothing to talk about.'

He glanced at the waiter who was listening, ears pricked, keen not to miss a word. 'I'll pay the bill and get the car.'

'Don't bother. I'm off.'

With head held high, I strode to the door, opened it and put up my umbrella. I walked out into the night and the pouring rain. As I walked I looked for a taxi, but there were no taxis in sight. Behind me, I heard Tom, and then what sounded like the waiter, calling for me to stop, to come back, to return. I ignored them. Walking quickly, I traversed a corner and strode on.

CHAPTER SEVENTEEN

'I TAKE IT NONE of you caught the morning show yesterday, the show we went on?' Max said.

Three heads were shaken. Tina, Jenny and I had completed our Tuesday work-out in the conservatory and were recovering.

'Why?' Tina asked.

'Because I was on again, doing an exercise display with the other girls. We were called in at real short notice, so there wasn't time to tell you.'

'But you don't need to tell us how it went,' I said. 'A squillion viewers phoned in to say how they'd fallen head over heels in love with Pippa, Gerri and Dee, and the producer was ecstatic.'

'Nope. They didn't hit the spot at all. The producer was mega disappointed.'

I looked at Tina and Jenny, and grinned. They grinned back. Revenge is reputed to be sweet and this news was like honey on the tongue.

'What was the matter?' Tina enquired.

'Before we exercised, Cheryl and Ray talked to me and the girls on air – just had a general confab – but it turned out the watching public were not smitten. Not smitten with the girls, that is. The main criticism was that they were too pleased with themselves, too full of themselves. Apparently the word 'smart-arses' was used.'

I raised a brow. 'Surely not.'

'But in addition to ripping the girls to tatters, most of the people who rang said how they'd much preferred you three. They thought you were better at the exercises and asked when could they see you again and, please, could you be interviewed.'

Jenny laughed. 'Never!'

'It's true,' Max said, and his forehead furrowed, as if he, too, found our popularity hard to fathom. 'Seems ever since the Vintage Babes appeared –'

'We're being called that?' Tina demanded.

He nodded. 'It's become a tag.'

She considered the notion for a moment or two, then she shrugged. 'I suppose we have got a few miles on the clock.'

That's a first, I thought. Tina accepting she's getting older.

'Ever since you three appeared,' Max carried on, 'the studios have been receiving phone calls, e-mails and letters requesting a repeat. And before I came out this morning, I had a call from the producer asking if you would consider doing regular work-outs on the show.'

'This is the guy who felt younger women would be more to the minute?' I enquired.

'The same.'

'Then I hope he said please.'

'He did. You'd get paid,' Max continued. 'The amount to be agreed at a meeting with the producer, and transport would be provided, as before.'

Tina smiled delightedly. 'Sounds fantastic.'

'You were mentioned in some of the phone calls,' he told her. 'People remembered you from being on Joe's show and remarked on how hip you look.'

She giggled. 'Thanks to you.'

'Regular work-outs means what?' I queried.

'Once a week initially and then, if the viewing figures are healthy, twice,' Max said. 'But it could be the start of something big. Gigs on other shows, interviews, a work-out video. And if the marketing guys latch on, it could result in –'

'Vintage Babes birthday cakes and frilly knickers and mouse mats. Maybe even stair-lifts.' I shook my head. 'Sorry, not interested.'

'But Carol –' Tina began.

'I already have a job which I very much enjoy and which demands my time and concentration, plus I'm not fussed about appearing on television again.'

'Me, neither,' Jenny said.

Tina looked bemused by our lack of enthusiasm. 'But it's a great chance.'

'A once in a lifetime chance,' Max declared.

'A chance for what?' I asked. 'To become a D-list celeb? To be recognised in public and spoken to by complete strangers? To be featured in newspaper articles, extolling the virtues of exercising for those past their first flush? Doesn't turn me on.'

'Nor me,' said Jenny.

Tina clasped her hands together, as if in supplication. 'Please.'

I knew how much she longed to be in the limelight again and I knew how eager Max was to take advantage of this opportunity. And I felt like a heel. I had no wish to foul things up for them and yet…

'No,' Jenny said. 'Sorry, but, apart from any possible modelling, I'm still hoping to find a secretarial job and, if I do, then going up to the television centre once or twice a week would be out of the question. Besides which, I have absolutely no desire to, maybe, become a celebrity, either.'

'No?' Tina was incredulous.

'The fame game has no appeal. Carol and I don't want to be killjoys, but we have our own lives and needs to consider. Surely you can see that?'

Tina pouted. 'I guess,' she replied, though she did not sound convinced.

'Couldn't you do the exercises on your own, without us two?' I said, and turned to Max. 'Tina is the glamour girl, the one who's generated many of the phone calls, the one with TV know-how, so why don't you suggest to the producer that you do the work-outs with her, just her?'

He looked doubtful. 'I could try him.'

'I'd be happy to do whatever the producer wants, whenever he wants,' Tina said eagerly. 'And just the two of us could be successful, especially if we co-ordinated our outfits to create an image and got the look right.'

Max nodded. 'We'd need to make it stylish.'

'Why don't we go for designer gear?' she suggested. 'Two or three outfits each?'

He frowned. 'It'd cost.'

'My treat,' she told him.

Max smiled. 'A kept man at last,' he said, and slid me a wink.

'Quick word,' Jenny requested, as we walked out across the forecourt a few minutes later.

'Sure,' I replied, and when she unlocked her car, I climbed in beside her. 'I was so relieved when you explained you weren't happy to be roped in for the TV work-outs, either,' I said, before she could speak. 'I was feeling horribly guilty, a real wet blanket, but you came to the rescue. Thanks.'

She smiled. 'It's the new confident Jen at it again.'

'Good for her. You never used to stick up for yourself, but now –' I gave a mock shudder '– now you're terrifying.'

'Not quite terrifying, but I've been meek and mild for far too long and I've decided that, from now on, if I want something I go for it. That's what I wanted to tell you about. Two things. First, at the weekend I informed Bruce that, in addition to any modelling, I was applying for secretarial posts and intended to get one soon, fingers crossed.'

'His reaction?'

'He started to chunter on about how I was being silly, how we didn't need the money – the usual guff.'

'You told him it was guff?'

'I did. I also told him to shut up and listen, and then I explained that it wasn't about what *we* needed, it was about what *I* needed. Me. Obedient Jennifer, who has spent the last thirty years ironing vests of various dimensions and who is desperate to do something new and different. It took for ever – he can be amazingly dense at times – but Bruce eventually recognised what I was talking about and agreed that if I wanted a job, I should have a job.'

'Alleluia!'

251

She grinned. 'Not that he had much choice, to be honest, because I really laid it on the line. And after he'd agreed to a working wife, I asked him about the other woman.'

'You plucked up the courage?' I said, surprised.

'It was long overdue. I told him I'd seen him being kissed in Guildford and asked what was it all about. Bruce swore it was entirely innocent. He explained that the woman is a colleague from work and they'd had an early meeting with a client at the client's office. The meeting had not gone well and afterwards the woman, her name's Ruth, declared she needed a sit-down and a drink to recover.'

'Hence the coffee bar.'

'Right. Seems as soon as they'd sat down, she started to blame herself for mishandling the meeting. And she had mishandled it. Made a complete pig's ear, so Bruce said. She'd quoted the wrong figures and then got shirty with the client when he'd questioned them. Shirty as in she more or less told him he was stupid. But as they drank their coffees, she really beat herself up. Talked about being inadequate, out of her depth, how her partner never stopped criticising her, and then became tearful. Noisily tearful.'

'Bruce would've hated that.'

Jenny nodded. 'He's not good with displays of emotion, especially if they should happen in public. Seems he tried to reassure her and, in time, she wiped her eyes and calmed down. Much to his relief. But then, as they were leaving the coffee bar, she pulled his arm around her, declared undying gratitude for his empathy and concern and, as he was praying she wasn't about to burst into tears again, the woman kissed him. Which I chanced to see. But after that she drew away and there's been no physical contact since. Bruce has made certain he stays well out of touching distance.'

'You believe this?' I asked.

'I do. I'm sure it's the whole truth and nothing but the truth.'

'Me, too.'

I was sure. I could imagine Bruce's dismay, if not disgust,

at having to deal with a volatile and sobbing woman. I could also imagine how he would be determined to keep her away from him, ever after.

'I should've listened when you told me there'd be a simple explanation. Seems this Ruth is a touchy-feely type who's made a grab and kissed other men at the office, on occasions when she's told them her woes. She put the fear of God into them, too.' Jenny laughed. 'I told Bruce he should've been flattered.'

'But did you tell him that when you thought he might have misbehaved, you'd considered misbehaving yourself?'

'Yes.'

'You did?' I said, surprised.

'I explained how upset I'd been at seeing him with Ruth and how I'd flirted with the man at the TV studios, but that it had been bravado.'

'What did he say?'

'That it was understandable, though I'm not sure he believed me. That I'd flirted, I mean.'

'He should've seen you in action!'

She laughed. 'I amazed myself. But I'm not the type to have an affair, Carol. I would never have rung the guy, never followed through. Honest.'

I nodded. 'I know.'

'I was stupid,' Jenny declared. 'Stupid in thinking Bruce had another woman and stupid to flirt with that man.'

'You're not the only one. I've been stupid, too. Stupid about Tom.'

'In what way?' she asked, and I explained about us having dinner in London and how he had expected me to spend the night with him and had spoken of leaving Kathryn and their sons.

'I used to have a certain amount of respect for him, but not any longer. Now my eyes have been opened,' I said. 'Tom reckoned I hadn't found another man because anyone else would've come second to him. Talk about arrogance!'

'You don't think he was speaking the truth?' Jenny said. 'I

253

do.'

'You – you do?' I faltered.

'Yes. I think that for the past eight years, you've still been in love with him. You may have been divorced, the two of you may have rarely met, but, as far as you were concerned, Tom remained the man in your life. The one you cared about.'

'I never said I still cared for him,' I protested.

She gave a gentle smile. 'You didn't need to. Have you never wondered why you haven't felt the urge to marry again? Or become involved in a proper romance? I think it's because, subconsciously, you still regarded Tom as the ideal companion, husband and lover, and felt you couldn't replace him. You didn't want to replace him because, deep down, you still loved him. So no other man has stood a chance.'

'You reckon?' I said wonderingly.

'I'm sure,' Jenny declared.

For a minute or two I was silent and pensive, considering what she had said, then I nodded. She was right. All of a sudden it seemed so obvious: alarmingly, glaringly obvious. Yet the Tom I had loved post-divorce had been an imagined Tom. A Tom who had cared about the sanctity of marriage, about the wasted life of a stillborn child, about the emotional security of his two living sons. He did not exist and now it was over. The next time we met I would be civil, but unaffected. I smiled. I had finally, as the current jargon goes, 'drawn a line in the sand' and 'achieved closure'.

CHAPTER EIGHTEEN

THE CLOCK ON THE wall showed six p.m. Melanie had only just departed and I remained busy. I was determined to finish a piece I was writing, about how Dursleigh's shopkeeper community had warned the council they would fight the hourly parking fees which it was rumoured could be imposed on the village's general car park – and that they had the backing of many local residents. I wrote the last sentence. Re-thought and re-wrote. Then I read through the entire article and nodded. All done.

Steve was also working late, so should I suggest we go out for a meal together? Debbie was at a girlfriend's house for a sleepover this evening.

'She's fed-up with being forced to watch the current affairs programmes and documentaries that I like on TV,' Steve had told me, grinning. 'The night away is an escape.'

So he was on his own. Even if Tina no longer seemed to pose an immediate threat, another night of chat and socialising would be good.

'I was wondering –' I began, as Steve came into the general office. I broke off. The telephone on my desk had started to ring and I lifted the receiver. 'The Siren, Carol Webb speaking.'

'Your dad lives in the Bridgemont Retirement flats, doesn't he?' asked Roger, my friendly policeman.

'That's right.'

'Thought so. And thought you might like to know that the house manager from there has just rung in, reporting a disturbance.'

'What kind of a disturbance?'

'Raised voices in one of the flats and rumours of some aggro. Sounds like a domestic. Though I don't recall any trouble there ever before.'

'And the police are attending?'

'Someone'll be along a.s.a.p., but an accident's caused a snarl-up on the roundabout and a mysterious package has been left under a railway bridge, so we're stretched thin right now.' I heard an authoritative voice in the background. 'Must go. Bye.'

'Bye.' I replaced the receiver, then lifted it again and pressed out my father's number. 'There's some kind of an upset at the retirement flats where my dad lives,' I told Steve. 'I'm just calling him to see if he can tell me anything about it. 'Pensioner puts false teeth in wrong glass and wife goes berserk'. How's that for a headline?'

He smiled. ''Pensioner attacked by feral sets of false teeth', would sell more copies.'

I waited as the tone rang and rang and rang. 'No reply.'

'Your father wouldn't be involved in the upset?' Steve said, as I put down the telephone.

'No. No, it's not his style.' I recalled my scenario of the old ladies fighting over him. 'At least, I don't think so. But he's usually in at this time, watching the television news, it's part of his regular routine and –' I frowned. Although the flats were fitted with emergency pull cords in every room in case of illness, it was always possible that a resident – my dad? – could trip and knock himself unconscious or collapse. 'I think I'll drive over there and check he's okay.'

'I'll come with you.'

'There's no need,' I began, then thought of how I had been going to suggest we went out to dinner. Once I had satisfied myself that my father was in prime health, perhaps the two of us could carry on to a restaurant. 'Actually, thanks. We can go in my car and I'll bring you back to pick up yours, as and when.'

'Fine.'

'Roger also mentioned an accident on the roundabout and a mysterious package left under a railway bridge. Don't know if they're of any great importance, but –'

Steve reached for the telephone. 'I'll give Tony a quick

buzz and ask him to find out more.'

Fifteen minutes later, I pulled into one of the visitors' parking bays at the flats. As Steve and I climbed out, we heard the babble of voices, interspersed with the occasional shout, coming from around the back of the three-storey block. Taking the path which crossed the neatly cut lawn, we headed for the noise.

'Good God!' Steve muttered, as we turned the corner of the building.

Gathered on the grass in the evening sunlight was a crowd of forty to fifty people, the Bridgemont residents. One or two sat in wheelchairs, several rested on sticks, one old lady lay on a white plastic lounger, but all were looking up at a top floor balcony. Edged by a black wrought-iron railing and set with pot plants, the balcony was deserted, though the French windows which led into the flat stood wide open.

'Let him go!' a woman cried, from within the depths of the throng.

'Calm down, old chap!' quavered a stooped man in a Boston Red Sox baseball cap. Worn with the peak to the front, I'm glad to say.

'Do the decent thing,' encouraged a Santa Claus type with a bushy white beard.

As the spectators gazed up in rapt fascination – and exchanged continual comments – Gillian, the house manager, was walking back and forth in front of them.

'Please, ladies and gentlemen, move away and return to your own homes,' she appealed. 'There's nothing of any interest to be seen here. Please, go now.'

No one took a blind bit of notice.

'We've not had such excitement since Lilian said the cream was off on a trifle at Annie's birthday party and Annie, she'd made the trifle, tipped it over her,' a nearby woman remarked to a man in tartan velour bedroom slippers.

He chuckled. 'Brightened up the day, that did. And this kerfuffle, well, it's like something on the telly. In *The Bill*.'

'Or *Midsomer Murders*,' said the woman. 'I never miss

Midsomer Murders.'

The man nodded. 'Me, neither. Aren't the villages picturesque?'

As they launched into an appreciation of thatched cottages and steepled churches, I scanned the crowd and, to my relief, saw my father – fit and well and speaking to a woman standing beside him.

'There's my dad,' I told Steve and, as I was pointing him out, my father saw me.

Excusing himself from the woman – the refined Marie? – he came over.

'This is Steve, my editor,' I said, in a quick introduction.

My father nodded. 'Evening. Nice to meet you.'

'And you,' Steve replied.

'We're here because someone rang the paper to say there was trouble at Bridgemont,' I went on. 'What's happening?'

'Nasty business,' my father said. 'It's William. Dilys's William. He's up there in her place with her and Ernest, keeping the door locked and shouting abuse. William came out onto the balcony a few minutes ago and –' he expelled a breath '– my word, I've never heard such language. And in front of ladies.'

'Who are William and Dilys and Ernest?' Steve enquired.

'William is William Langsdon,' I said. 'He –'

'You once asked me if his name meant anything.'

'That's right. When I met him, he seemed somehow familiar. He's the son of Dilys, a widow who lives here. Ernest is another resident and he's a friend of my dad's.'

'Ernest has a dodgy heart,' my father inserted.

'He's a friend of Dilys's, too?' Steve said.

My father shook his head. 'He doesn't care for her. Considers she's down-market, a working class cockney,' he confided, behind his hand. 'Bit of a snob is Ernest.'

'So why is he in her flat?' Steve asked.

'William took him there, by force.'

'Force?' I protested.

'Brute force. Seems Dilys had been in her garage to get

some washing-up liquid and had forgotten to zap down the door. Ernest had noticed and was having a look inside –'

'Ernest can be nosy,' I informed Steve.

'He was having a look inside,' my father continued, 'when William arrived, saw him and took offence. Remember I told you how aggressive the fellow was with me?'

I nodded. 'I do.'

'Seems he was even worse with Ernest. Much worse. Accused him of prying, then pinned his arm behind his back, marched him straight through the lobby and into the lift. And when they reached the top floor, frogmarched him into his mother's place. A couple of folk caught a glimpse and they said Ernest looked terrified. White as paper and shaking like a leaf.'

Steve frowned. 'How long ago was this?'

'Must be getting on for an hour. They'd hardly gone through Dilys's front door when the shouting started. Seems William called Ernest all kinds of a snoop and a troublemaker, and declared he deserved to be thumped.'

I thought of how timid the old man had been. 'Poor Ernest.'

'Can't have done his heart much good. Then the shouting stopped and the folk who'd been listening decided the trouble must be over, but later on William let rip again. After his run-in with me, Dilys confessed he has one heck of a temper. Can fly off the handle about nothing. Anyway, the second time someone alerted Gillian and she went up to listen. When she heard William making threats, she knocked on the door and demanded to speak to Ernest, but William told her to mind her own business. Told her in no uncertain terms.'

'He didn't open the door?' Steve asked.

My father shook his head. 'Shouted through it. So Gillian decided she'd better ring the police, though they haven't turned up yet. Dilys's French windows were open and when they heard the racket coming through them, people started to congregate on the lawn. William didn't like that. When he came onto the balcony and saw everyone, he told us we were a bunch of cretins and ordered us to bugger off. Of course, no one moved and then he really turned the air blue. When he went inside, he slammed the French windows shut, but not much later Dilys opened them. Her place can become airless, stuffy, so –'

I pointed up. 'Activity.'

William had walked out onto the balcony. He was smiling. 'Row over. Everyone's happy. All quiet now. Time to disperse, folks,' he called in a cheery tone and flapped a hand. 'Shoo, shoo.'

'Let us see Ernest,' someone shouted.

'Yes, we want to see him,' another voice called.

'Right now,' a third person stipulated.

'Er-nest, Er-nest,' the white-bearded man started to chant, as if he was a supporter at a football match, and, within seconds, the entire crowd had taken up the refrain.

'Er-nest, Er-nest.'

Gripping his hands tight around the top of the iron railing, William scowled down. The cheeriness of a moment ago had vanished and his look was hostile. 'Sod off!' he snarled.

'Er-nest, Er-nest.' The refrain continued. Grew in volume. 'Er-nest, Er-nest. We want Ernest.'

'Shut it!' William shouted. Bending, he took hold of a plant pot and aimed it into the midst of the crowd. 'Shut the fuck up!'

There was a general gasp – some of it doubtless at the f-word – and a mass cringing back as the pot hurtled down. I watched in frozen dismay. Although William had not targeted any person in particular – he did not appear to focus on individuals, rather he saw the crowd as a mass, an infuriating mass – someone seemed destined to be hit. Hit and maybe knocked out cold or seriously injured… or killed? Thud! The missile landed between two gossiping women who, simultaneously, had each stepped aside to speak to other residents. The terra cotta pot broke into pieces, depositing a heap of black soil strewn with yellow pansies.

'Phew, that was lucky,' Steve said.

'Very lucky,' agreed my father. 'If you'll excuse me I'd better get back to Marie. Don't want her to be scared.'

I nodded. 'On you go.'

He went off and there was a minute or two of silence while the wheelchairs were moved and everyone retreated into safer positions, then the chant restarted. This time, it was even louder.

'Er-nest, Er-nest.'

William folded his arms and glared down.

In houses beyond the fenced boundary of the Bridgemont gardens, people came to peer curiously through bedroom windows. A trio of gum-chewing teenage boys ambled in off the street to find out the reason for the noise.

'Okay, you want to see the ugly old fart and you shall,' William bellowed, his voice furious. He disappeared through the French windows, only to emerge several moments later propelling Ernest, who was forced to walk backwards, in front of him. 'Here he is.'

'Christ!' Steve exclaimed.

William had one hand clamped on the old man's shoulder, while the other held a knife directed at his throat. A sharp-pointed stiletto, which glinted in the evening sun. Steering his victim to the balcony rail, William thrust him roughly against it, bending him back. One struggle for freedom, a cough or a shiver, and the knife could pierce Ernest's flesh. I frowned. It was a predicament which echoed others from a long time ago. A predicament which rang loud bells of identity. Alarming bells.

As I turned to Steve, he turned to me.

'Billy the Bridge,' we said, in mutual recognition.

Steve took his mobile from his jacket pocket. 'The police need to be here. Now.'

'It's okay,' Gillian intervened, before he could press out the number. She had come up alongside. 'I've just spoken to them again and they're on their way.'

'You explained it was urgent?' Steve demanded. 'Extremely urgent?'

'I did.' She cast an anxious look at the crisis above. 'I wish they'd hurry.'

'Likewise,' I said.

Back in the Seventies, William Langsdon – then known as Billy – had been a petty thief with a vicious streak. Growing up as a street kid meant he knew all the back alleyways to escape along, storage yards where he could hide, the crowded markets to vanish into. He had operated in the suburbs of South London and his method was to smash the windows of parked cars and snatch handbags, briefcases, anything of any value which had been left inside. Then run like the wind.

When he had broken into an expensive, much-loved sports car and been disturbed by its owner, a young athlete, he had fled, clutching a travel bag which he had found. But the athlete, who had won medals for hurdling, had gone after him. He had chased Billy from the quiet mews where the sports car had been parked and along residential streets. Chased him at speed. At intervals, when he could catch his breath, he had shouted 'stop thief!', but it was a Sunday morning and few people were around. No one came to his aid.

As they approached a railway bridge which crossed the narrow road, Billy had vaulted over a wall and started to scramble up the overgrown embankment. The athlete had followed, forcing his way through brambles and stinging nettles. By the time they reached the gravelled railway tracks at the top, he was only a yard behind. Sensing capture, Billy had dropped the travel bag and spun round, a knife in his hand. Pressing the point to the young man's shirted chest, he had forced him back against the low fretted metal bridge.

Now people began to take notice. First a cyclist had stopped on the road below to put a hand to his eyes and peer up. A couple of cars halted and their drivers got out. Children playing in a garden alerted their parents, who alerted the neighbours on both sides. Someone dialled 999. The athlete was recognised and soon the road was jammed. A local resident who worked in television notified his station. A police car arrived and, calling up, the policemen appealed to Billy to release his victim. He was not receptive.

'Come any closer and I'll stab him,' he had threatened, as the officers had clambered laboriously over the wall to scale the embankment.

There was a stand-off. A television crew appeared and began to film. Time passed and, also recognising him, Billy started to exchange comments with the athlete, who remained remarkably composed, and with the crowd. Jovial comments. Witty comments. He was playing to his audience, soaking up the attention. Eventually, as the police contingent swelled, Billy threw away the knife and surrendered.

I knew all this because I had interviewed the athlete and several of the spectators. And, as one in a team of reporters, I had covered some days of the trial. The young 'Billy the Bridge' as the tabloids dubbed him, had had dark curls, a baby face and looked so innocent. The jury and judge had been swayed by his teary-eyed remorse and insistence that he would never have used the knife, and given him the benefit of the doubt – and a laughably short sentence.

On his release, he met with the athlete and apologised. The apology took place in a television studio. The athlete hoped to become a sports commentator when he retired from hurdling, so any publicity was welcome. And Billy, who had been, he declared, 'a mixed-up kid', but was now 'strictly on the straight and narrow' had loved the fuss. Pieces about him appeared in papers and magazines, people bought him drinks in pubs, the athlete suggested he could be a useful runner if he trained – though the hard graft of training didn't appeal – but, inevitably, the spotlight had soon swung elsewhere.

Little more than a year later Billy had snatched a handbag from another car, been chased by its irate female owner and hightailed it up onto another suburban railway bridge. Yet again, a crowd had gathered, the police were summoned and Billy had basked in the furore. A television crew had skidded up. But whereas the athlete had kept his cool, the young woman was both frightened and stroppy. She had begged her captor to release her and, when he didn't, informed him he was a no-good piece of scum. That he should work for a living, not steal. Billy lost his temper.

'Shut it!' he had ordered, biting on the t's.

'Threatening a defenceless girl with a knife, aren't you the brave boy?' she had taunted.

'Belt up, slag!' he had barked.

Recognising a wildness in his eyes, her belligerence had collapsed into fear. 'I didn't mean it, truly,' she had yammered, but it was too late.

Billy had slashed the knife down her cheek, scarring her for life, then stabbed her viciously in the shoulder. This time he ran off along the railway track, but was caught the next day and arrested. This time, his sentence was far more severe. However, it seemed he must have learned his lesson, because he had not come to the notice of the media again.

Until now.

'You're over-reacting, old chap,' called the man in the baseball cap.

Gillian walked forward. 'Please don't do anything silly,' she implored.

Leaning menacingly over an ashen-faced Ernest, William ignored them. But the bally-hoo continued.

'Threatening a bloke in his seventies is pathetic,' someone shouted.

'For the weak-kneed,' declared another voice. 'You're just a coward.'

'Real lily-livered,' ridiculed a woman, who had the voice and disdain of Nora Batty, 'and not going to look so clever when the newspapers get to hear about it.'

'The newspapers have heard,' Steve murmured.

I nodded. 'You have another scoop.'

'No, you have the scoop.'

'*We* have the scoop,' I said.

A man pointed a condemning finger. 'You deserve a jolly good thrashing,' he proclaimed.

'Bring back hanging,' called another.

William glowered down. 'Another fat-arsed remark and –' He readjusted his hold on the knife, positioning the point above Ernest's Adam's apple '– he gets it!'

Once again 'Billy the Bridge' seemed to be deriving a twisted satisfaction from the crowd he had drawn and the uproar he was causing. But what about his victim? The continuing strain had to be bad for his heart... and could be fatal.

'Keep quiet, everyone,' Gillian appealed. She swung a worried look over the Bridgemont residents. 'Not another word, I beg of you. Not one word.'

'Do you have a key for Dilys's flat?' Steve asked, as she came back to where we were standing, beneath the shade of a tree.

She nodded. 'I have a master key which gives entry to all the flats. It's here.' She produced a key from her cardigan pocket.

'So I can get in,' he said, 'and distract William which, hopefully, will allow Ernest to escape.'

Gillian frowned. 'Don't you think we should wait until the police arrive and let them –'

'Waiting is too risky,' he cut in. 'The guy could lose it big time at any minute.'

'Maybe Dilys will come onto the balcony and calm her son down,' she said desperately.

Steve shook his head. 'If she hasn't tried to cool things this far, she's not going to act as pacifier now.'

'You're right,' the house manager agreed, and gave him the key. 'Dilys's flat is number 33. It's the second one along the corridor, on the left exiting from the lift.'

'I'm coming with you,' I told Steve.

'No way,' he said. 'It could be dangerous.'

'I'm coming,' I repeated. 'When William sounded off at my father, Dilys took William's side so – strange as it seems – she may be cheering him on now. When you go into her flat, she could try to stop you and to warn him, so I'll look after her, while you deal with William.'

I had no idea how I would – or even if I could – 'look after' Dilys. All I knew was that Steve must not go up there alone.

His brow furrowed. 'But –'

'Makes sense,' I insisted. 'If Dilys proves troublesome, you can't deal with two.'

'I guess not,' he conceded, though he still looked doubtful.

'So let's hoof it.'

'Be careful,' Gillian implored.

'We will,' Steve replied. 'And you do your damnedest to keep this lot silent.'

She nodded. 'I'll try.'

'We should use the stairs,' Steve decreed, as the two of us went back across the lawn and around to the main entrance. 'If William hears the lift it could make him even twitchier. Though I don't understand why the guy should be so damn twitchy in the first place. Okay, Ernest was trespassing in his mother's garage, but –'

'I reckon there must be items in there which William doesn't want anyone to see. Items he has stored which, if discovered and talked about, could land him in trouble. Serious trouble.'

'Drugs? Stolen goods?'

'Could be. He keeps suitcases in the garage and he expects to be able to drive straight in and lower the door behind him. Raises hell if he can't.' I thought back to what my father had told me. 'William will also suddenly turn up here and spend the night in the visitors' suite, although he owns a house in London and another a few miles from Dursleigh, somewhere in the countryside.'

'Odd.'

We went into the building and through the residents' lounge, heading towards the staircase.

'We don't know how Dilys will react when she sees us,' I said, 'but I'll do my best to keep her quiet.'

'Thanks, but –' Steve placed his hand on my arm, '– if there is any trouble, serious trouble, get the hell out. Don't bother about me. Just go.'

I grinned. 'You're expecting unquestioning obedience?'

'I am. Carol, I mean it. Any trouble and scoot. While you're dealing with Dilys, I'll surprise William and, with luck, grab the knife.'

'Don't be too brave. Steve, I mean it,' I said seriously.

'No, ma'am.'

In silence, we set off up one, two, three flights of stairs until we reached the top floor landing. Walking quietly, we reached a door bearing a disc marked 33. My heart pounded. I felt wary and fearful and full of foreboding. Suppose Steve's rescue mission went wrong? Suppose he got hurt? The police must be close and getting closer. Perhaps we should wait for them.

Without a sound, Steve inserted the key in the lock, turned it and pushed down on the brass handle. The door opened. As he crossed the small hall and went into the living room, I followed behind. At the end of the room where the French windows stood open, Dilys was sat on a navy leather pouffe. Clad in a white and red tracksuit of the kind favoured by the late-period Elvis, she had her back to us. Her spine was stiff and her eyes were trained on the balcony. Steve had almost reached her when she glanced back, perhaps aware of a draught, and saw us. She visibly jumped. I leapt forward, intending to clamp my hand across her mouth to silence her. But she raised a finger to her lips.

'Shh.'

I bent to her. 'Ernest has a weak heart,' I whispered urgently, 'and –'

'I know. He's told me about his heart problems and his constipation. The hours he spends on the bog.' She grimaced, then, speaking softly, went on, 'Our Billy, I mean William, is his own worst enemy. When he found Ernest in the garage he could've simply told him to get out and stay out – it's not as though he'd opened nothing, least that's what Ernest says – but instead silly bugger goes bananas.' She plucked fretfully at a black jet drop earring. 'And what happens now? There're bound to be questions asked, the police will be involved, so –

What's he up to?' she said, in alarm, as Steve looked out of the French windows.

Dilys seemed so anxious and critical of her son that I decided to tell her the truth. 'He wants to try and take the knife away from William.'

'He mustn't! William can turn nasty at times, real evil, so _'

'Then couldn't you persuade him to hand the knife over?' I suggested. 'Convince him he's making things worse, a lot worse?'

'Me? No, he won't listen to me. Never has, never will. And if I interfere, if I cross him, he won't like it and –' her face clouded '– he'll make my life hell.'

So Dilys hadn't sided with William against my father because of her own feelings, she had sided with him because she had been frightened to do otherwise.

'He didn't listen to his dad, neither,' she said. 'The only person William's ever taken any notice of is – were – his sister. You know Tina. You and her do them fitness classes together. She's such a good-looker, was from a nipper and still is. It used to make my day when I saw her on the telly with Joe Fernandez.'

I looked at her in confusion. 'Tina Kincaid is William's sister? You mean she's your daughter?'

Dilys nodded. 'Though she never tells no one and nor do I. I shouldn't be telling you now. We catch sight of each other in the village, but we're like strangers, have been for over thirty years, thanks to the prat who were her first husband and filled her head with hoity-toity ideas. But if Tina were here now, she'd be able to persuade William to cool it. He always says she can rot in hell, but, deep down, he still dotes on her and he'd do whatever –'

'Too late,' I said.

Steve had stepped onto the balcony and, leaving the old lady perched upright, I went to watch his progress. As he started on the short silent path which would position him behind William, I tensed. All it would need was for Ernest to acknowledge his approach by a swivel of her eyes or grateful smile, or someone on the lawn below to give a cheer, and the knife could be pointed at him. Plunged deep into him. Please don't let anyone react, I prayed. Please, please. Seconds ticked slowly by, but Ernest's fear meant he could see only his captor and, thankfully, the crowd made no sound.

Reaching the required position, Steve thrust out his hands, clamped them around William's neck and yanked him backwards.

'Yrrgh!' With a croak of surprise, William half fell against Steve.

Ernest gawped, amazed by this sudden turn of events, then, taking his chance, scuttled away and, passing me, sped inside.

Mouthing strangled obscenities, William punched back hard with one elbow into Steve and with the other. He hit back a suede-shoed foot, and then with a second, kicking at his shins. He squirmed and fought, but could not break free.

'Drop the knife!' Steve ordered, and received a cacophony of swearwords in reply.

There was more elbowing, followed by further kicks. Steve managed to avoid some, but those which struck home made him wince. They looked so painful, I was wincing, too, in sympathy. Then William paused, tightened his grip on the handle of the knife and half twisted around. Oh God, he was going to stab Steve.

'Watch him!' I cried, as the blade lashed through the air.

Taking one hand from his attacker's neck, Steve made a grab for his arm, but he lunged back with both elbows. The impact knocked Steve off balance and, still holding on to William, he fell against the wall and half slithered down. For a moment, the two men slumped, breathing heavily, but then the arm which gripped the knife lifted.

'No!' I yelped, and dashed forward, raised my booted foot and kicked. Kicked out hard at the menacing hand.

William swore, releasing the knife which skidded across the balcony floor, to be halted by a potted camellia.

'You might've broken something,' he accused me, nursing

his damaged fingers. He looked forlorn and pettish, ready to sob. The vicious combatant had gone, replaced by a sulky loser.

Steve stood and dragged him upright. 'If she has, you deserve it,' he said.

I was thinking how close disaster could've been when there came the pound of running footsteps. Seconds later, three policemen burst out onto the balcony, with Gillian panting in their wake. I recognised the officers, though Roger was not among them.

'That's – that's the villain,' Gillian gasped, pointing.

'And there's his knife,' Steve said, indicating the weapon as he handed him over.

Despite William's claim that his hand could be fractured and so he represented no danger, he was handcuffed. As the policemen steered him back into the living room, Gillian, Steve and I followed. Dilys, who was now sat beside Ernest on the navy leather sofa, lowered her eyes and refused to look at her son.

William was detained in the hall, while the rest of us made short statements. We would, we were told, be required to provide more detailed information the next day. In turn, everyone went to sit at the dining table to relate their story.

'Are you all right, sir?' the officer enquired, as Steve ended his account.

He put a hand to his ribs. 'I'm a bit battered and bruised, but I'll survive.'

'Maybe I should run you to the hospital and they can check you over?' I suggested. He had taken some drastic punishment and I was worried about him.

He shook his head. 'Thanks, but not necessary.'

'You're sure?'

'I'm sure.' Turning to the policeman, Steve spoke quietly. 'What is necessary,' he said, 'is that you check out the garage which Mrs Langsdon has here. You could find something of interest. Maybe drugs or stolen goods.'

The officer nodded. 'Will do.'

'William owns a house not far from Dursleigh,' I added. 'His mother can tell you where it is. That may be worth a look, too.'

'Thanks. We'll pay a visit.'

As the policemen exited with William and we prepared to leave, Dilys clasped hold of Gillian's arm. 'I'm so sorry about all this,' she said. 'So very sorry.'

'It's not your fault, dear,' the house manager replied.

'You mustn't blame yourself,' Ernest said, and took a drink from a tumbler of what looked like whisky.

'William can be kind and generous, the perfect son, but then he'll suddenly go ape and –' Dilys sighed. 'What's happened won't spoil things for me here, will it?' she asked anxiously.

'Not in the least,' Gillian told her, and headed for the door. 'Excuse me, dear. Must be off and disperse the crowd. Speak to you later.'

'And nothing's spoiled as far as I'm concerned,' Ernest said.

Leaning towards the old man, Dilys slid an arm around his shoulders and hugged him close. So close he seemed in danger of suffocating. 'You are such a lamb. A real sweetie-pie. Another drop of malt?'

'Um… yes, yes.' The hug had left him pink-faced and flustered. 'It would go down a treat.'

'How are you feeling?' I asked him.

'Tip-top,' he replied.

'No ill effects from your ordeal?'

'None. Must confess my heart skipped a few beats, but –' he took a mouthful of the fresh whisky which his hostess had provided '– it's back on an even keel now. Thanks to this gentleman,' he said, raising his glass to Steve.

Steve smiled. 'I'm relieved you've recovered so quickly.'

'Ernest was telling me how you were like Superman coming to the rescue,' Dilys said. She gazed at him in admiration. 'Arrived out of nowhere, full of courage. Can I get you a drink? And you, too, Carol?'

'Not for me, thanks,' I said.

Steve shook his head. 'Nor me. We must go.'

'I'd be grateful if you wouldn't say nothin' to Tina about me letting on that I'm her mum,' Dilys whispered to me, as Ernest started to thank Steve once again. 'She don't want folk to know we're related.'

'Would you like to be friends with her again?' I asked.

'Sure would, doll. It's my sweetest dream.'

'But you've never spoken to her?'

'Didn't want to risk any nastiness, besides it's up to her to make the first move.' The old lady sighed. 'Which she ain't going to do.'

We said our goodbyes and Dilys showed us out.

'Many thanks for kicking away the knife,' Steve said, as we walked towards the lift. 'For a moment there, I thought I could be a goner. But you saved my life.'

'Not really.'

'Yes, really.' He pressed the lift-call button. 'I didn't know you'd been in a chorus line. I mean, with a high kick like that. Wicked!'

I laughed. 'I gave myself a shock, though it was rather splendid. And so were you.'

Steve put his arms around me, drawing me close. 'We were both rather splendid,' he said, and kissed me.

At first our lips were closed, but they quickly parted. The kiss deepened. I shut my eyes, wound my arms around his neck and was lost in the feel and the taste of him. He felt hard, strong, male. He tasted good. I had told Lynn that we did not lust after each other, but I had been wrong.

Ponk! A soft noise sounded and a light flashed, white bright even beyond my eyelids. Startled, Steve and I jerked away from each other and looked round. It took me a moment to realise what had happened, then I saw the lift had arrived and the door was wide open. Outside stood a man with a goatee beard, wielding a camera. A professional type camera which he had pointed at us.

'Who are you?' Steve demanded furiously. 'And what the

272

hell do you think you're doing?'

'I'm a freelance working for –' The photographer named a tabloid. 'Someone from the flats here rang our London office to report a life or death incident, so they despatched a reporter. He's downstairs. I happened to be in the area – went to snap a package left under a railway bridge, turned out to be a Chinese carry-out – and I've just taken a picture of the valiant couple who rescued –' He broke off to grin. 'It's Steve Lingard, isn't it?'

Steve gave a curt nod. 'Correct.'

'I was there when you were presented with your Scoop of the Year award. I won a prize that evening, too. Perhaps you'd like me to take another shot, with the two of you stood together, side by side?' the photographer suggested.

'Yes, please,' I said.

CHAPTER NINETEEN

SHOULD I TELL TINA that Dilys had told me she was her mother? I wondered, as I dropped *The Siren*'s bundle of post onto my desk the next morning. The old lady may have asked me to keep quiet and yet she longed for a reconciliation. If I attempted to bring them together, would Tina be receptive? Or hostile? Could my interference make a bad, sad situation even worse? Tina would surely hear about the previous evening's crisis, but would she want to be associated with Dilys – and with her violent jailbird brother?

I began slitting open envelopes. After a broken night when I had been beset with thoughts of Dilys and Tina, William and Ernest, Steve and me, I had risen early and arrived at work ahead of time. The cleaner had finished mopping the upstairs floors and was now busy on the downstairs.

I had sorted the mail into 'Advertisement' and 'Editorial' heaps, when the door opened and Lynn rushed in.

'Have you seen this? she demanded, waving a newspaper. It was the tabloid which the photographer from last night had said he worked for.

As I ate breakfast I had rung Lynn to tell her about 'the William incident', only to discover she already knew. Her grandfather had telephoned at crack of dawn and given graphic details. He had, she reported, been 'buzzing'.

'No, though –' I gestured to a copy I had bought, but had not yet got around to opening.

Leafing to an inside page, she showed me a report headed 'Known Knifeman Attacks Pensioner' and the two accompanying photographs.

'That'll knock the birds off their perches,' she declared, with an impudent grin.

'But it gives totally the wrong impression,' I began. 'We –'

'Sorry, Mum, can't stop. Short of time. See you later.'

As Lynn dashed out, I opened my own paper and read the account which detailed Ernest's plight, how his release had been effected and William's subsequent arrest. Steve and I were named, his Scoop of the Year award got a mention, and Gillian was lavishly quoted. She had been 'overwhelmed by the rescuers' public-spirited determination to help', 'in awe of their selfless courage' and would be 'eternally grateful'. I was marvelling at her description of us as 'fearless modern day saints', when Steve arrived.

'How're the ribs this morning?' I asked.

He put a hand to his chest. 'A little tender, but not too sore.'

'And the shins?'

'Similar.'

'Your health in general?'

'Fine.'

I handed him the newspaper. 'So much for your obliging photographer,' I said.

While one photograph which accompanied the report was of William in his younger days, the other showed Steve and me with our arms around each other kissing: kissing passionately, locked in a close embrace. 'Plucky hero and heroine celebrate their success,' the caption read.

Steve gave a dry smile. 'If Tina wasn't convinced about you and I being –' his voice lowered to Barry White deep '– 'in lurrve', she will be now.'

'But the paper should never've printed this,' I protested. 'The guy took the second shot of us standing together and implied that that was what would be used. Though a picture of Ernest would be more appropriate. Presumably the photographer regards this as a joke, but it's trickery and an invasion of privacy and –'

'At least we didn't make it to the front page.'

'Thank God! But this is tantamount to criminal and –'

What else could I say? Steve might appear relaxed, but I remembered his anger with the photographer and knew he must be feeling compromised, embarrassed, aggrieved. It was

275

one thing to be spotted being kissed on the cheek in a local restaurant, but quite another to have a picture of your seemingly ardent clinch circulated throughout the nation.

And the clinch was 'seemingly' ardent for, in the clear light of day, I recognised that the kiss had been spur of the moment, inspired purely by relief and, while it had stirred me, of little consequence. We had spent the remainder of the evening together, but there had been no repeat. Steve had not morphed from autocratic boss to good friend to ardent lover. How could I have been such a klutz as to imagine he had?

I was taking a breath, ready to resume my protest, when Melanie walked in, followed by Tony. She had a copy of the tabloid tucked beneath her arm.

'I was buying my Smints when Ravi suggested I might find this of interest. And it is interesting,' she said, wiggling her eyebrows.

Ravi, a Patel son, is the manager of one of the newsagents' shops along the High Street.

'Did he tell you whether the photograph of us is in any of today's other papers?' Steve enquired.

'It isn't,' Melanie replied. 'He's checked and it's just in this one. Though the rest of the papers have reports of the trouble.'

Steve looked at me. 'I guess we should be thankful for small mercies.'

Melanie giggled. 'The two of you do –' She broke off, the switchboard telephone had started to ring and she went to answer it. 'Mr Pinkney-Jones for you,' she informed Steve.

'I'll speak to him in my office,' he told her, and departed.

'How come you and Steve were at the retirement flats when the old chap was being held captive?' Tony enquired.

I explained, described the scene and unfolding of events, and had finished answering Tony's questions when Jenny came in.

'Carol, are you all right?' she demanded, her voice tight with worry. 'I'm on duty in the shop this morning and Eileen's just told me that someone told her you were caught up in a knife attack last night.'

'I wasn't attacked and I wasn't hurt,' I assured her, and, leading her through to the quiet of the interview room, I quickly related the facts.

'How frightening for everyone,' Jenny said. 'I feel sorry for the old lady, too, having such a nasty piece of work for a son.'

'She also has a daughter, one she's proud of. This is confidential, but Dilys told me she is Tina Kincaid's mother.'

Jenny gave a startled laugh. 'What?'

'You'd think the idea was even odder if you saw Dilys. Her dress sense is… colourful, she's not the most demure or elegant of old ladies. Her language can be colourful, too.'

'Tina comes out with the odd 'crap' from time to time.'

'She does. Dilys would love for them to meet and make up, yet she's asked me not to let Tina know I'm aware of their relationship. She only mentioned it due to the stress of the situation,' I said, and explained.

'Given a push, perhaps Tina would welcome a chance to make up, too,' Jenny suggested.

'I'm not sure. They've both lived in Dursleigh for years and have had ample opportunity to build bridges, but it hasn't happened, so –'

'Let it mull.' Jenny turned towards the door. 'I must get back to the shop. So relieved you're safe, Carol. I'll see you at Tina's tomorrow and we can discuss further. Cheers.'

'Cheers.'

I had taken the 'Advertisement' stash of mail downstairs and was on my way back when Steve called me into his office.

'Mr P-J is delighted we've got ourselves in the national press as the editor and chief reporter of *The Dursleigh Siren*,' he said. 'He reckons it's valuable publicity and –'

'Did he say anything about the photograph?' I broke in.

Jenny had not mentioned it, though I felt certain she would see it – courtesy of Eileen? – sooner or later.

'Not a word. He must've read the story in another paper – and he was full of praise for the 'dynamic duo' and said there'd be a bonus with our next month's wages.'

I smiled. 'Nice!'

Back at my desk, I was preparing to write a piece about the controversial clearing of local woodland when Dursleigh's Member of Parliament strode in. He wanted to congratulate Steve and me on our derring-do and hear about the William incident firsthand. His visit turned out to be the first in a procession and, if people didn't come into the office, they rang. A surprising number of Dursleigh residents, including the Giffords, *père et fils*, the firemen I'd interviewed and the lady mayor, were eager to praise us and learn the full story. Some commented, with amusement, on the photograph. My response was a casual dismissal. Determinedly casual.

Late morning, after non-stop fielding of visitors and telephone calls, Steve and I went along to the police station to give the required fuller statements. This done, we called in at a coffee shop for a quick lunch and some welcome peace – until a fellow luncher realised who he was sitting next to.

When we returned to *The Siren,* three reporters from assorted national newspapers were waiting to speak to us. The reappearance of 'Billy the Bridge' had aroused interest – the athlete, now a leading commentator, had already relived his Seventies ordeal on breakfast television, so one of the reporters informed us – and they wanted to hear our account of the fracas. Two of the interviews were straightforward and relatively swift, but the third journalist, a sombre intellectual who worked for a Sunday quality, was, he stated, preparing an in-depth article discussing the theory of 'once a villain, always a villain'. His in-depth article necessitated an in-depth interview with the pair of us, which centred on William's words, actions and presumed feelings.

The afternoon was fast disappearing when I settled back down to work on the felling of the woodland article. I had written a couple of paragraphs when the public door swung open, yet again. This time, the visitor was Debbie.

'I was hoping you would read this for me. Please,' she appealed, taking sheets of paper from her rucksack. 'I'm on my way back from an after-school swimming practice and I made a special journey. Could you read it? I'd be way grateful. It won't take long. Just a few minutes.'

I hesitated. My day had been far from productive and even a few minutes were precious. But Debbie was so eager.

'Alright,' I agreed. Both Melanie and Tony were out, so would not be disturbed by our conversation.

She smiled. 'Thank you.'

Entitled 'A Sticky Hero', the story had been typed on a typewriter smitten with shadowed 'a's, 'e's and 'o's'. The paragraph indents varied, the double spacing narrowed to single halfway down the third, and last, page and there were several spelling mistakes. The plot concerned a teenaged girl and her adventures with a pet. To date the pets in Debbie's stories had been two dogs, a Persian cat, a rabbit and a three-legged gerbil, but this time it was a stick insect. An accident-prone and exceedingly affectionate stick insect called Kyle.

'It's good,' I declared, as I reached THE END. 'Funny, touching – never imagined I'd get emotional over a bunch of mobile twigs – and keeps you wondering what's going to happen next. Your best yet.'

Debbie beamed. 'One of the mags I read prints short stories, so I could send it up to them. What d'you think?'

'Do it. But any manuscript you submit must be properly presented and, frankly, this is a shambles.'

'I know. I use the computer and printer when I'm at home, but all Dad has is a portable typewriter which belongs in a museum.'

'Another reason for considering a return,' I said.

She nodded. 'Is the spelling correct? I'm not too clever at spelling. ''Scuse me,' she said, as a ringing sounded from her rucksack and she took out her mobile. 'Paul, what is it?' she demanded, in the impatient tones of an older sister plagued by a younger brother. Then she sat upright. 'What? She's said yes? You lucky devil. When?' As Debbie listened, a smile stretched slowly, wider and wider, across her face. 'Tell Mum I'm coming with you to collect it.' From her subsequent scowl, I guessed that her brother had objected. 'Yes, I can. I can be home in loads of time. Like in half an hour. And it won't be just yours, it'll be mine, too, because I'm moving back. I've decided. Hold on.' She got to her feet. 'Need to speak to Dad,' she informed me, and sped away to his office.

I had corrected the faulty spelling, when Debbie returned. She looked happy.

'Thanks for reading my story,' she said, collecting up the pages.

'Best of luck with it. I've sorted the spelling,' I told her.

'Ace. And now I'll be able to sort the typing.' She hooked her rucksack over her shoulder. 'In a hurry. Got packing to do. Dad'll explain. Bye.'

'Goodbye.'

The girl was halfway out of the door when she stopped. She giggled. 'By the way,' she said, 'I dug the photo of you and Dad in the paper.'

I frowned. I didn't want her to get the wrong idea and imagine the kiss might indicate a serious involvement. 'You do realise –' I started, but the door had swung shut.

Consoling myself with the thought that Debbie had seemed amused rather than concerned, I resumed my writing. Concentrate, I instructed myself. Concentrate. I was wondering if I should include some of the history of the woodland, which was reputed to have been part of Henry VIII's stamping ground, when Steve came in.

'Great news,' he said. 'This evening I'm to drive my daughter and all her belongings back to her mother's house where she will be living from henceforth.'

'I rather gathered that from her phone call with her brother, but why?'

'Because, after years of Debbie and Paul nagging and pleading and wearing her down, Annette has agreed to accept a pet into the household. One of her New Age chums owns a Dalmatian which has produced a litter and there's a puppy going spare. And Debs is determined not to miss out, so back she trots.'

'Regardless of the lentil burgers?'

He grinned. 'Regardless. Though I suspect she was on the brink of a return anyway, thanks to you.'

'Me?'

'Debbie said just now that, on several occasions, you'd pointed out advantages to her being back home.'

'Never missed a chance.'

'Thanks. I appreciate it.'

'Hope we're not intruding,' a familiar voice said, and I looked round to find my father walking into the office, accompanied by Ernest.

'Not at all,' Steve replied, and went to greet them.

I welcomed them, too, though with a degree of reluctance. Would I ever complete the woodland piece? It had gone five and I was beginning to weary of it, and to feel weary myself.

'My brave girl,' my father declared, hugging me. 'Everyone at Bridgemont thinks you're wonderful.'

I gave a suitably modest smile. Had everyone at Bridgemont, my dad included, seen the newspaper photograph? If so, was he about to comment on it? Joke and infer and assume? Please don't, I begged silently.

'We'd planned to come earlier,' my father continued, 'but this one –' he jerked his head at his companion '– nodded off after his lunch and was asleep for ages.'

'It's a reaction,' I said, wondering if my weariness could be reaction, too. 'He suffered an extremely stressful experience yesterday.'

'That's what I told him,' Ernest declared righteously, and brandished a plastic supermarket bag. 'I have a presentation I wish to make.'

'Then how about we all go into my office?' Steve suggested. 'It'll be more comfortable in there.'

As he escorted the visitors along the corridor, I locked the public door and dealt with the phones. Then I joined them.

With a flourish, Ernest produced a magnum of champagne from the carrier and handed it across the desk. 'For my deliverer from harm,' he said.

'Thank you. That's very generous.' Smiling, Steve

accepted his gift.

'It's just a token. You deserve so much more. Both you and Carol. Don't they, George?'

'They certainly do,' my father agreed.

'People have been telling me how you took some nasty blows and digs in the ribs yesterday,' Ernest said, speaking to Steve. 'Painful, are they?'

'Tender rather than painful,' he replied, 'though I'm a mass of technicolour bruises. However, I can still drink champagne. We'll need to swig it out of mugs, but shall we open it now?'

'No, no, it's for you,' his benefactor said hastily.

My father gave a wry laugh. 'And he couldn't take one more drop of alcohol. He's still recovering from all those whiskies Dilys fed him last night.'

'I have had a bit of a hangover,' Ernest confessed. 'I've been drinking tea all day to try and clear it.'

'Perhaps you'd like a cup of tea now?' I said, for that was plainly the message.

'Medium strong, dash of milk, two sugars,' he replied, and my father nodded.

I looked at Steve. 'Coffee, as usual?'

'Please.'

When I returned with a tray bearing the teas and coffees, plus a packet of shortbread biscuits, the visitors were eagerly relating how a team of police officers had spent most of the morning at Bridgemont.

'You remember how you two suggested to the policeman that they'd be wise to inspect Dilys's garage?' Ernest said. 'And to visit her son's house out in the country?'

Steve frowned. 'You heard us?'

'Sharp ears,' he declared, pulling at a lobe, 'though it passed Dilys by. Anyhow, the garage turned out to be a real Aladdin's cave. Suitcases crammed full with jewellery, figurines, silver salvers and –' his eyes gleamed '– every bit of it stolen.'

'So we understand,' Steve said. 'We were at the police station earlier and they told us how William and his accomplices had been robbing shops in the area for the past few months and that his mother's garage was where William stored the loot. Stored it temporarily, until he could dispose of it. Which is why he panicked when he found you in there.'

'I was only being neighbourly, checking to see there were no leaking water pipes or any evidence of mice,' Ernest defended himself, then changed tack. 'Did the police thank you for suggesting they take a look?'

Steve nodded. 'They were grateful.'

'So they should be, because it was a monster of a find! I got talking to one of the officers this morning, a sergeant, lives in a semi opposite the church and plays ice hockey in his spare time, and it seems there were also a couple of very valuable oil paintings, still life miniatures they were, and clocks and watches and –'

As the old man listed the haul, I handed round the teas and coffees and indicated that everyone should help themselves to biscuits.

'Apparently one of the shops William robbed was Gifford's,' my father said, when Ernest ended his recital. 'Remember, Carol, I told you about a bracelet he'd given his mother? Gold inlaid with diamonds. Turns out it was pinched from there.'

I grimaced. 'Oh dear.'

'Though Dilys didn't know,' Ernest put in quickly.

'Maybe not,' said my father, 'but the fact that she showed the bracelet to the police makes you think she'd suspected it wasn't kosher. And she must've suspected that whatever it was William was keeping in her garage wasn't kosher, either. Alright, she never ever looked inside a suitcase – that's what she told the police and I believe her, she would've been too afraid – but she had to have guessed he was up to something fishy. Especially considering his history.'

Ernest grunted, then took a mouthful of tea.

'Seems that after they'd done a robbery, skedaddled, and removed their paper suits, William dropped his accomplices off and carried on to Bridgemont with the spoils,' my father continued. 'And no one's likely to suspect a block of retirement flats of harbouring illicit goods.'

'It was smart thinking,' Steve said.

Ernest took up the tale. 'Then, after a robbery, William usually spent the night at the guest flat and drove out to his house in the country the next day. Often transporting some of the loot because, of course, by then no one was looking for the getaway car. He kept several old bangers in a barn there and used them in turn for thieving.'

Steve looked at me. 'We weren't aware of that.''

'Like I explained, I was talking to an officer about William's methods this morning and –' the old man took a second biscuit '– he revealed all.'

I could imagine the questions Ernest would have asked, on and on and on, and how the policeman could have told him more than he should, in an attempt to silence him.

'And,' my father said, 'a couple of the ladies at Bridgemont have provided dates and times for when William arrived in one of his old bangers, together with the colour of the car –'

'They weren't so smart on the make,' Ernest inserted, spraying out shortbread crumbs.

'– and they fitted with the dates of various robberies, so the case is virtually sewn up.'

'The ladies knew the dates and times he arrived? How come?' Steve enquired.

'Nora, a pleasant woman who used to clean for me and suffers from an ingrowing toenail – very painful – could remember William arriving on a couple of Fridays, after lunch, because on Friday mornings she went to the chiropodist's and in the afternoons she rested. Two of the robberies took place on Friday afternoons. Nora's flat overlooks the entrance and the garages, and if she hears a vehicle she often has a quick peek to see who it is.'

I sipped my coffee. She *always* has a quick peek, I thought, recalling the twitch of curtains whenever I visited.

'And another lady who has a view of the entrance could pinpoint the times William arrived by what television programme she'd been watching. *Countdown* around three or *Richard & Judy* at five p.m.' My father shook a bemused head. 'Imagine being glued to the box like that.'

'With short breaks to monitor arrivals,' I said.

'Nora is also almost sure of the colour of the car William was driving on which day,' Ernest added. 'Seems she has dresses in similar shades.'

Steve laughed. 'Some memory!'

'Have you spoken to Dilys today?' I asked my father. He nodded. 'How is she?

'Doesn't seem too bothered about the idea that William could be locked up for years and delighted with the way everyone's rallied round her. Folk have been constantly knocking on her door to wish her well. She's so grateful. But they know she can't be held responsible for her son being a bad 'un – could happen to any of us – and, besides, she's a friendly character.'

'Very friendly,' said Ernest. 'She's invited me for dinner at her place this evening, to say sorry for William's behaviour.'

'Play your cards right and maybe she'll offer to cook your dinner for you every evening,' my father remarked.

Ernest's cheeks pinkened. 'I wouldn't mind that.'

'Marie was saying she wouldn't mind being able to kick like you did,' my father told me, 'when you kicked the knife out of William's hand.' He chuckled. 'You reminded me of that woman who wore the black leather rig-out in *The Avengers* and got up to all kind of antics. It's years ago now, but what was her name?'

'Emma Peel,' Steve provided, and grinned. 'Carol could be her twin. Same fire, same merciless aggression, same agility.'

'Same smooth-talking sidekick male,' I said.

'Carol's agility is due to her work-outs with Max,' my father declared, 'as I told the reporter from –' He named a downmarket and often luridly sensational tabloid.

I stared at him. 'I beg your pardon?'

'There was a reporter at Bridgemont this morning and I told him the reason you were so agile was because you'd been

285

doing exercise classes twice a week with Max, who is on TV. I said you'd been on television with Max, too, and I played him the video. He loved it.'

I groaned. The photograph of Steve and I had been bad enough to bear, but now… 'Knife Attack Heroine Was Hot, Vows Personal Trainer' was one headline which flashed through my mind. "If You Believe It, You Can Achieve It', Vintage Babe Chanted,' was another.

'I expect you also told the reporter that I used to be married to Tom?'

'No. Forgot, actually. Nor did I say anything about you and Max being a pair, because –' he winked at Steve '– it's obvious you have another chap in tow. Pity the papers have stolen your thunder,' my father went on.

'Meaning?' Steve said.

'They've already written about William taking Ernest captive, and how you and Carol came to the rescue, whereas it won't be in *The Siren* until next week.'

'Ah, but then the story will be straight from the horses' mouths,' Steve told him. 'We can provide the low-down. The nitty-gritty. And while it may not rate exactly as a scoop, appetites will have been well and truly whetted.'

'Perhaps you should get the printers to produce extra copies next week?' I suggested.

He nodded. 'I was thinking the same myself.'

Ernest looked at his watch. 'And I'm thinking it's time we were off, George. I need to get washed and changed, dressed in my finery before I go up to Dilys's for dinner. Do you think I should wear a suit?'

My father shook his head. 'Sports jacket and flannels will be adequate.'

'With a tie?'

'Yes, a tie. The ladies always like a tie. Shows respect. You could take her a bunch of flowers, too.'

'Good idea, I will. So long as the florists' is still open.'

'Thanks again for the champagne,' Steve said, as we all rose to our feet.

'It's not much. Nowhere near enough, considering you saved my life,' Ernest told him. 'I believe you were the editor on *The Ringley Bugle* before you came here. How long were you in that job?'

'Around six years.'

'You started there as editor?' he asked, as they walked out onto the corridor.

'Yes.'

'How many reporters did you have working for you?'

As Ernest continued his quizzing and we followed behind, my father leant towards me. 'He's sweet on Dilys,' he whispered. 'All of a sudden, she's God's gift and can do no wrong. So watch this space, Ernest could be husband number four. And how about this chap –' he indicated Steve '– as your second hubbie?'

I slung him an impatient glance. 'Dad, you've got the wrong idea.'

'I know what I see.'

'You see nothing,' I hissed.

'Good picture, the one of you and Carol in the paper,' he said, as he shook Steve's hand in farewell. 'Gillian pinned it up on the notice board in the residents' lounge this morning and everyone's been admiring it.'

Though tempted to tear out my hair and give a manic scream, I restrained myself. And to think, I had regarded the house manager as a friend.

'Nice to be appreciated,' Steve said drily.

With Ernest hurrying to get to the flower shop and my father smiling a smile which could only be described as irritating, the visitors departed.

'So, as your dad's been spilling the beans, we'll need to watch out for another dose of publicity tomorrow,' Steve said. 'Plus maybe a re-run of the shot of the 'luvverrrs'.' He made a face. 'Still, it gave Debs something to tease me about.'

'She didn't mind that you were photographed... embracing me?'

'No. It seems to have finally dawned that her mum and dad

287

are now separate entities, will stay that way and are thus allowed to have other –'

'Friends?' I quickly provided, when he hesitated.

'Quite so.' He inspected his watch. 'I must go. Need to get ready to perform my removal man duties. I'll be too busy tonight, but suppose I fix your lavatory tomorrow evening? I should've found a new lock nut by then.'

'Tomorrow I'm out at the council meeting –'

'Sorry, forgot that.'

'– so how about Friday?'

'With scratch dinner again?' Steve asked.

'Sure.'

When we had left Bridgemont the previous evening, I had suggested we should go to my house for a drink and to recover. Once there, we had become so involved in talking over 'the William incident', that time had flown. Suddenly we were both hungry, yet had felt disinclined to venture out, so I had knocked up a quick omelette. And during the course of the evening, Steve had gone upstairs, discovered the wonky loo and offered to repair it.

'And on Friday we can drink Ernest's champagne,' he said.

'Remember you suggested I speak to the producer about Tina and me doing the work-outs as a duo?' Max asked me, as we took our places in the conservatory the next morning. 'I did and he's in favour. We start our regular slot on the show next week, probably Wednesday.'

I grinned. 'Congratulations.'

'And to you on your vigilante performance.' Lifting a couple of newspapers from his bag, he spoke to Tina and Jenny. 'I assume you're aware you're in the presence of a wonder woman.'

'I am,' Jenny confirmed.

Tina nodded. 'Me, too. I read about the trouble at the retirement flats and how you and Steve came to the rescue, Carol, and –' She hesitated. 'Mrs Langsdon must've had a difficult time and I wondered if you had any idea how she is.'

'She's in good spirits. My father lives at Bridgemont, too, and it seems all the residents are supporting her.'

Tina smiled. 'That's kind.'

'So is this,' Max said, opening a copy of a tabloid. He spoke to me. 'Don't know if you've seen it, but I want to thank you.'

'I have seen it.' On my way over to Tina's, I had stopped to buy those papers which seemed likely to print a follow-up report on the William incident and looked swiftly through them. I needed to know what was being published. 'But it's my father you should thank. He's the one who gave the reporter all the info.'

The piece Max indicated had used my knife-kicking as a hook into writing about him. He was named as my personal trainer and the source of my prowess, his exercise regime was described and there were references to his television appearances. To my relief, the report was matter-of-fact, did not make mock and came with no tacky headline. And the fuzzy photograph which accompanied it was of Max, Tina, Jenny and me on the morning show.

'Then tell him I'm grateful, real grateful, because it's already proving to be one hell of a plug. I was only just out of bed when the TV studios rang to say they were getting calls from women asking how they could enrol for my classes, and wanting to know if I was agreeable to them passing on my number. You can bet I said yes. A couple of calls came through before I left home and since then I've received six more messages. And the day has only just begun.'

'It could also encourage people to watch our TV slot,' Tina said.

'And how.' Setting aside the first newspaper, Max opened the second. It was yesterday's tabloid and he displayed the page which carried the report of the William incident. He grinned at me. 'Some snog!'

Jenny stepped forward to see the photograph. 'Interesting,' she murmured.

'That's what happens in office romances,' Tina remarked

casually. If she felt irked or jealous, she did not show it.

Should I explain how Steve and I had been carried away by relief and only for a moment? But it could sound as if I was protesting too much, so it was probably wiser – and was certainly easier – to say nothing.

I shrugged.

'Right, babes, action,' Max instructed, and we started the exercises.

After a good night's sleep I felt fit and refreshed, and I worked hard.

As soon as we had finished, Max checked his mobile. 'Four more messages!' he announced delightedly, and gathered together his gear. 'Must go home and answer them.'

'Are you intending to raise the mother/daughter situation?' Jenny asked me, as Tina accompanied the young man to the front door.

I nodded. I had spent a lot of time wondering whether to remain silent or if I should speak out, weighing up the fors and againsts. 'I think I will, in view of the fact that Tina wanted to know how Dilys was.'

'I agree. I think we should at least see how the land lies.'

'We?'

'I'm happy to help.'

I smiled. 'Thanks, Jen.'

When Tina returned, we went through to the kitchen.

'Jenny told me how you and your mother don't speak,' I said, as she filled glasses with water. 'Have you never been tempted to get in touch and put matters right?'

Tina blinked, surprised by the question. 'Well... yes. And actually –' She broke off.

'Actually what?' Jenny encouraged.

'Actually, I first came to Dursleigh because of my mother. I knew she lived in the area and I hoped we could revive our relationship.'

'But you didn't,' I said. 'Why not?'

Tina handed out the glasses. 'Because before I could pluck up the courage to approach her, I started seeing Duncan. I felt that if he knew about my family he'd disapprove and would end things with me. So I fed him a tale about being an orphan, though I owned up later. After we were married.' She hesitated. 'You see my mother is Dilys Langsdon, the lady at Bridgemont, and William Langsdon, who found fame as Billy the Bridge, is my brother.'

'We know,' I said.

She gawped. 'How do you know?'

'When William was holding Ernest hostage last night, Dilys told me. In confidence. She said you were the only person William would listen to, had ever listened to, and she wished you were there.'

'Poor Mam,' Tina muttered. 'Billy didn't play the hard man with her?'

'No, she wasn't threatened.'

'Thank goodness.'

'What was Duncan's response when you did tell him about your background?' Jenny enquired.

Tina took a sip of water. 'Initially, he didn't seem bothered. Talked about how none of us can choose our family and said it made no difference to him loving me. But a week or so later, he told me straight that I wasn't to let anyone else know I had an ex-convict for a brother, nor was I to visit my mother. Seems he'd checked up on her and didn't fancy her being identified as Duncan Kincaid's mother-in-law. And certainly not by the golf club crowd!' She sighed. 'I obeyed him. I allowed my first husband to call the shots, too.'

Jenny frowned. 'How ? What happened?'

'He liked the way I looked, but not much else. Nigel was a toff, or thought he was, and he sent me to elocution classes, lessons for deportment, how to dress, which knives and forks to use. If there was a means of improving me, he'd find it. Then he suggested I shouldn't see my folks so much. I was young and I doted on him, and I agreed. One Christmas I didn't visit or send presents, and my mother was so hurt. When we did eventually call round, there was a big row during which Nigel called them garbage and Billy turned vicious.

Everything fell to pieces.'

'You didn't try and mend things?' I asked.

'Nigel wasn't willing.'

'After you and Nigel were divorced, didn't you feel tempted to go and see your mother?' Jenny enquired.

'Yes, but soon after I met Joe Fernandez and I didn't think he'd be thrilled by my family, either.'

'There's nothing to stop you getting in touch with your mother now,' I said. 'If you did, she'd be over the moon.'

'I'd like it, too.' She hesitated. 'But first I'd better have a word with Max.'

'Max? Why Max?'

'Because I wouldn't want to do anything which might put our TV slot at risk. And if it came out that I was related to Billy – well, you never know how the television bigwigs or the producer or the viewers would react.'

'Nobody's going to blame you for the way your brother behaves,' Jenny protested.

'It wouldn't make one bit of difference,' I declared. 'And if you went to see Dilys, you'd make her so happy.'

'Perhaps I will.' Tina chewed at her lip. 'Sometime.'

I carried the melon and Palma ham starters through to the dining table. Steve had arrived and was upstairs, acting as plumber. The salmon had been placed in the oven, while assorted vegetables were prepared and waiting to be simmered on the stove. A lemon and sultana cheesecake, admittedly bought, would be served, with cream, as dessert. Call me proud, or foolish, but having been given notice I was damned if I was going to stick with a scratch dinner.

I had set out two champagne flutes and was wondering whether I should light the scented candles which floated in a bowl on the table, when the telephone rang.

'Carol here,' I said, answering it.

'Hi, this is Tina. Wanted to tell you that Max and I are going to be on television on Saturday evening, this Saturday, tomorrow, at nine-thirty, prime time. Isn't that mind-blowing?'

'Certainly is, and all good wishes, but why Saturday evening?'

'Because Joe has arranged for us to go on *Sats with Zachs*.'

'Wow!'

Sats with Zachs was a chat-come-variety show compèred by Zachary Clegg, a popular young comic. It regularly numbered amongst the 'most viewed' programmes, even surpassing some of the soaps.

'And it's definite,' Tina continued. 'Joe is keen to get back into my good books, so he pulled in a few favours, twisted an arm or two. Besides which, the producer is taken with Max. Reckons he has razzle-dazzle.'

'You're doing a work-out?'

'A short one, and we'll also be interviewed. I've bought us these trendy outfits which Max says guarantee we'll make an impact.'

'I'll be watching,' I told her.

'Thanks. Max also asked me to say thanks again to your dad for the mention in the paper. As well as a stampede of folk enquiring about his classes, a major snack foods company has rung to say they're interested in him appearing in an advertising campaign. I must give –'

'Did you speak to Max about contacting your mother?' I interrupted.

'Yes, and he suggested I leave it for now. I must give Jenny a quick ring,' she continued, 'and tell her about the show. Bye.'

'Bye, and all the best for Saturday.'

I was thinking that, for the first time in her life, Tina had friends to share things with – but how sad it was that she hesitated to share her life with her mother, when Steve came back downstairs.

'All fixed,' he declared.

'I'm grateful. You're a marvel.'

'Anything else you need done?'

I indicated the champagne. 'That opened, please.'

With a satisfying pop of the cork and a spray of bubbles, he opened the bottle and filled the glasses.

'To you,' he said, 'with very many thanks for the high kick.'

I laughed. 'And to you, with very many thanks for saving Ernest and for being a good boss. The best editor *The Dursleigh Siren* could have.'

'Praise at last! Sure you mean it?'

'Well, given the chance I might do a superior job, but –'

Steve grinned. 'Watch it.'

'I couldn't. You're definitely the best.' The doorbell rang. 'Though only because you have me around to guide you,' I added, and, putting down my glass, made a swift getaway.

When I opened the front door, Lynn was standing there with Beth. I looked at them in surprise. Why were they here? They did not usually arrive without notice, in the early evening. Nor would they come when they knew I had a guest, and I had told Lynn I would be playing hostess to Steve, unless there was a good reason. A pressing reason. My heart sank. Oh no, it was a re-run of not so long ago. Lynn and Justin had quarrelled again, separated again and my daughter and granddaughter were here to –

Justin walked in from the road. 'All well?' he enquired, with a smile.

'Um, yes. Steve's here,' I said, thankfully rejecting my fears and attempting to rearrange my thoughts.

'We know Mr Lingard is here,' Beth told me.

'Can we come in?' Lynn asked.

'Um, yes,' I said again.

Looking equally surprised to see the new arrivals, Steve greeted them and poured two more glasses of champagne. I went to get Beth an apple juice and, at the same time, turned down the heat on the salmon.

'We're here to tell you that you're being treated to a night, that's Saturday, tomorrow, at the Garth House Hotel, dinner, bed and breakfast,' Lynn announced, on my return.

'The two of you. De luxe rooms. All expenses paid,' Justin

added.

'Why are we being treated?' I asked.

'And by whom?' Steve enquired.

'The treat is from Ernest and Carol's dad, plus Lynn and me,' Justin said. 'Tony and Melanie are also making a contribution. As to why –'

'Us two wanted to say a big thank-you for the way you two helped us see sense and get back together again,' Lynn explained. 'Ernest is keen to show his appreciation for you rescuing him, and Granddad simply felt you both deserved a break. Actually, it was Ernest and Granddad who went to the hotel and fixed the booking. Seems they initially spoke to some daffy receptionist, but then the manager appeared and when he realised you were the couple who'd rescued Ernest and that you, Mum, were responsible for Max working in their health club –'

'Apparently his classes are in high demand,' Justin inserted.

'– Granddad persuaded him to knock off ten per cent. You also have free use of the health club and spa during your stay.'

I placed a hand to my brow. 'Heaven forfend.'

'When Tony and Melanie heard what we were planning,' Lynn continued, 'they said they'd like to contribute, too – because they are both getting so much more out of their jobs now, thanks to the pair of you.'

'How did they hear about what you were planning?' Steve enquired.

'Through Ernest. He decided it'd be sensible to check that you didn't have anything else arranged for Saturday and were free to go to the hotel,' Justin told him. 'So he rang *The Siren* and spoke to Melanie.'

'Seems both of you were out of the office at the time,' Lynn said.

Steve frowned. 'But Melanie wouldn't know if I had anything else arranged.'

'True, so she consulted your ex-wife who, by the way, thought the idea was a brilliant surprise. She said that on

Saturday you were going to Sussex with your son who's playing in a football league, but you should be back by around six p.m.'

He nodded. 'That's right.'

'So, folks –' Justin spread his hands '– what do you say?'

I looked at Steve. What did we say? That we might be pushed into spending time together at a hotel was a total surprise. I hadn't bargained for us being regarded quite so definitely as a pair. Steve seemed at ease, but might he object to being lumbered with me at the weekend? Could the idea of us dining together and then meeting up the next day for breakfast be a little too much?

'At dinner you can choose whatever you want from the menu and drink whatever wine you wish,' Lynn explained.

I grinned. 'You mean claret in the hundred pound range?'

'I mean within reason, though I suppose we could always take out a second mortgage or have a whip round in the village. Oh, and so far as other drinks go, Ernest discovered the bar has a choice of over seventy malt whiskies. So how's about it?'

Steve smiled at me. 'Shall we say yes?'

Put on the spot, what else could we say? With everyone being so kind and generous, to refuse the treat was impossible.

I nodded. 'Yes, and thank you.'

WHEELING MY SUITCASE BEHIND me, I walked across the expanse of marble floor towards the reception desk. It was approaching six-thirty p.m. and the hotel lobby was deserted. As I walked, I surveyed my surroundings. Gold-framed oil paintings of lords and ladies hung on the wood-panelled walls, a crystal chandelier sparkled high in the ceiling, brocade chairs formed elegant sitting areas. A log fire crackled in a vast grate and copper bowls of white azaleas stood on antique tables. Every time I visited Garth House its grandeur impressed me. I smiled. And now I was to be an overnight guest.

My worries about Steve feeling manoeuvred into us spending even more time together had been dissipated. After Lynn, Justin and Beth had left yesterday, I had been quick to suggest that if 'the treat' didn't appeal we could concoct a reason for opting out.

'We could claim some kind of a crisis at *The Siren*,' I had said.

Steve had shrugged. 'I guess, though I rather fancy living it up at Garth House. But you don't?'

'No, I do.'

'So what's the problem?'

'No problem.'

'Then let's go for it.'

But there was a problem, one I had not anticipated. While Steve fitted much of my criteria for the perfect on-call escort – he looked and acted the part, was believed by some to be my red-hot lover and had even repaired the loo – I was aware of myself doing what I had deemed to be forbidden, attaching strings. I was becoming fond of him. Too fond. Ever since we'd kissed, I had found myself fantasising about him *as* my red-hot lover. It must stop and it would stop, I vowed. After this weekend our relationship would revert to a purely working relationship. There would be no more scratch dinners, a veto on socialising. Steve had said he had no interest in a serious entanglement. As for me – falling for my boss at my age was inviting trouble. Trouble as in heartache.

Reaching the high mahogany counter, I looked over it to see a girl with a shock of frizzy ginger hair and round owl glasses staring at a computer screen. I waited, but still she stared. She must have heard the click of my high heels across the marble floor. She had to be aware of my presence. I coughed. No response. I coughed again, twice.

The receptionist scrambled to her feet. 'I'm so sorry, I do apologise, but when I concentrate –' she blinked behind the owl glasses '– I become deaf and blind to everything else. I'm not too slick on typing and I was checking a letter the manager's given me to write, but I hope I didn't keep you waiting for too long, madam. It's a dreadful thing to do, so discourteous, and I feel really bad –'

'My name is Carol Webb and I have a room booked for tonight, dinner, bed and breakfast,' I said, breaking into the effusive apology.

The girl sat down, tip-tapped jerkily at the computer keys, consulted the screen and nodded. 'Your room is The Clark Gable Room on the third floor, madam. All our bedrooms are named after film actors.'

'Film actors who've won Oscars, and that's because one of the owners of the hotel is a film buff called Oscar,' I added.

'Is that so?' She looked at me in wonderment, though I was only repeating information I had read in the Garth House glossy brochure. 'I had no idea.' There was a pause when she frowned, as if going through a mental checklist of the questions she was supposed to ask. 'What time would you like to eat, madam? Our restaurant is busy this evening and you need to make a reservation.'

'Eight o'clock?' I suggested.

Once again, the computer was consulted and more keys tapped. 'That's fine.'

'A table at eight for two,' I said, feeling a need for

confirmation.

'Two?'

'Yes. Mr Steven Lingard is also booked in for the night and we'll be dining together.'

'He is? You will?' The receptionist – a badge pinned to her jacket identified her as Poppy – returned her attention to the computer screen. She tapped for a while, then nodded. 'Yes, yes, I see that now. And I remember. You were fortunate to get a room at such short notice. The hotel is full tonight, due to an association of French travel agents who're holding a conference here. There's no need to reserve a table for breakfast, but would you like a newspaper in the morning?'

'No thanks. I assume Mr Lingard hasn't arrived yet?'

'Don't think so. I mean –' she checked the computer screen '– no.' A frizz of ginger hair was hooked behind one ear. 'I hope you don't mind me asking, but are you and Mr Lingard the people from *The Dursleigh Siren*? The people who saved Mr Ernest from certain death?'

I smiled. 'That's something of an exaggeration, but, yes, we are.'

'I thought so. I was on duty when Mr Ernest and the other gentleman came in to make your reservation. Mr Ernest asked so many questions, about the history of the building and the original family who owned it, about the wine cellar and where our produce is bought, that he got me quite flustered. You see, this is only my third week here, so I didn't know. But the manager was able to help. To some degree.' She was reflecting on this, when a thought struck. 'You need your key.'

'Please.'

Turning to squint at a framework of cubbyholes which were fixed to the wall behind her, Poppy looked along the top row, one by one, the second, the third and then recommenced her search all over again. Eventually the requisite key, one of the plastic card variety, was located and handed over.

'You're on the top floor. The lift is over there, to the left – sorry, I mean the right – of the potted palms. The porter will deliver your luggage, madam,' she told me, as I reached down to retrieve my case.

'Thank you.'

The lift was a splendid old-fashioned cage with a concertina door, polished brass handles and a stained glass ceiling. When I reached the third floor, signs indicated my required destination. Setting off along a wide, thick-carpeted corridor, I passed The Jodie Foster Room, The Tom Hanks Room, The Marlon Brando Room, The Cher Room – trust her to have received an Oscar! – until I came to The Clark Gable Room. I inserted my key, opened the door and went through a square hallway.

I laughed. 'Luxury with knobs on!'

The Clark Gable Room was a suite of rooms; spacious, airy rooms which overlooked the walled garden at the rear of the hotel and putting green beyond. The hallway led into a sitting room, which was furnished with a floral sofa and chairs, a writing bureau and coffee table. The coffee table carried a decanter of sherry, bottle of red wine and a bowl of fresh fruit. A mini bar with fridge fitted discreetly into a wall unit, which also housed a wide-screen television, DVD player and a modem connection.

On the opposite wall, double doors opened into a cream-carpeted bedroom which contained a four-poster with crimson silk flounces and was pinned with photographs of Clark Gable looking 'Gone With The Wind' handsome. Towelling bath robes, 'a gift for our guests', hung behind the door which gave way to the bathroom. Tiled in white with a lavish gold trim, the bathroom included twin washbasins and a pond-sized Jacuzzi.

As I waited for my suitcase, I began to explore – looking inside the fridge to discover more complimentary drinks, opening the bureau to find a supply of best-seller paperbacks and stainless steel pens – all stickered 'please take away'. Next I tested the four-poster, which felt seductively cosy and had, I saw, a silver coronet embroidered on the crimson duvet. In the bathroom, I admired the array of top-of-the-range soaps, shampoos and body lotions.

Exploring done, I inspected myself in the bedroom's mirrored wardrobes. Dressed in a pale green trouser suit with a navy shirt, I decided I made a suitable Garth House guest. Classy and sophisticated. Pretty, too. Today was not a gargoyle day. For dinner I would be wearing a stylish lilac and white patterned dress with a boat-shaped neck and swirling skirt. The dress was new, bought courtesy of my 'stopped smoking' fund from one of Dursleigh's dress shops that morning. In a fit of excess, I had also purchased a lilac evening bag and high heels. Everything was in my suitcase which, surely, must now be on its way?

Stupido! I thought suddenly. I should've asked the receptionist for the name of Steve's room or told her to inform me when he arrived. I had lifted the receiver to press out the Front Desk number, when there was the sound of activity outside my door. At long last, the porter had turned up.

Replacing the phone, I reached for my handbag and found my purse. I ought to tip the man, but how much should I give? Working in such a top-notch hotel, he must be used to receiving generous tips. Was two pounds sufficient or should I make that three? I've never felt confident about tipping.

'What are you doing here?' a male voice enquired, and I wrenched myself from my gratuity agonies to see Steve coming through the door, a travel bag held in his hand.

I gazed at him in surprise. 'Hi. I'm here because this is my room. The Clark Gable Room.'

'But I was told it was mine,' he said. 'And I've been given the key.'

'I have a key, too.'

He put down his bag. 'Looks like someone's screwed up.'

'The receptionist said that when Ernest and Dad came to fix the reservation Ernest bombarded her with questions and made her flustered, so maybe she made a mistake.'

'Thought they wanted only one room? Could be, she doesn't come over as the brain of Britain.'

'Anything but,' I agreed, though it did occur to me that, in his eagerness to match-make, my father could have covertly arranged for us to cohabit. The swine!

Steve frowned. 'So what do we do? The manager was at the desk just now and he was telling me how the hotel is full. Seems there's not a free room available tonight.'

'The receptionist said that to me, too.'

'Shame –' Steve glanced around '– this appears to be quite some place.'

'It is. There's a Jacuzzi you could train dolphins in and the four-poster is fit for a king.'

'The good life,' he said, and shrugged. 'I may not be able to spend the night here, but I can still enjoy a damn good dinner. And later head home, leaving my car and taking a taxi, because I dare say I'll have succumbed to a drink or two.'

'Then return for breakfast and to collect your car in the morning, after, maybe, a session at the health club?' I said. 'No. My house is much nearer, less than ten minutes away, so it makes more sense for me to go home and you to stay here.'

He shook his head. 'Why should you miss out?'

'Why should you? We could ask if it's possible to exchange tonight's reservation for another night and two rooms,' I suggested.

'The manager said the hotel was fully booked at the weekends from now until virtually the end of the summer. No, Carol, you're staying. You were here first and ladies first, and all that.'

'But you were the one who took the battering from William, who suffered the bruises. You're the real hero,' I protested, then stopped.

Someone had knocked on the door and Steve, who was nearer, went to open it.

'One suitcase, sir,' the porter told him.

Slipping his hand into his trouser pocket, he gave him a number of coins. 'Thanks.'

'Thank you, sir,' the porter said, sounding delighted.

'I owe you for that,' I told him, when the man had gone.

'Like hell. And I'm not taking any more argument. Whatever you say, you infuriating woman, you –' stretching out his arms, Steve walked towards me, as if intending to take hold and jokily shake me '– are going to spend the night here.'

I stepped back. 'Okay, okay,' I said. I didn't want him to touch me – in case I was inspired to do something foolish, like wrapping my arms around him and pulling him close. 'If you say so.'

'I do.'

'Then how's about we have a complimentary drink before I get changed for dinner?'

Steve grinned. 'You're full of bright ideas.'

I indicated the decanter and red wine on the coffee table. 'There's this or –' Crossing to open the fridge, I displayed a selection of fruit juices, beers and a bottle of white wine, '– this.'

'I'll have a beer and would you like me to open the white wine for you?'

'Yes, please.'

'I'm already dressed for dinner,' Steve said, when we were sat on the sofa with our drinks and a bowl of cashew nuts. 'I was hot and sweaty from running up and down the touch line and cheering Paul on –'

'How did his team do?'

He smiled. 'They won, by six goals to two. Paul scored two of the goals and was thrilled to bits – his dad, also – so when I got home, I had a quick shower and changed.'

'Very smart you look.' He was wearing a dark grey suit, mid-blue shirt and green, white and blue tie. 'I like the tie.' I leant forward to take a closer look. 'Dinosaurs?'

'It was a birthday present from Debbie and Paul, and the dinosaurs were chosen because, having attained the grand old age of fifty-three, they consider I'm a dinosaur, too.'

'You're fifty-three?' I said, in surprise.

'You thought I was older?'

'Just the opposite, I thought you were younger. Somewhere in your mid to late forties.'

'Flatterer, though I thought you were younger, too. When I realised from your c.v. that you were an old broad of fifty-five it was one hell of a shock!'

'Less of the old broad, you ancient dinosaur.'

Steve laughed. 'Yes, ma'am.'

With chintz green swagged curtains, green velvet-upholstered dining chairs and pale walls hung with tapestries, the restaurant was olde worlde elegant. Men in suits were sitting at a number of round white-clothed tables, interspersed with a few formally dressed women. All, presumably, French travel agents.

As the head waiter showed us to our table, I noticed that several of the men noticed me. And liked what they saw. I tilted my chin, swung my hips and strutted. Being admired – and Steve had complimented me when I'd made my entrance in my new outfit – releases the sex kitten in me. Okay, the sex cat.

When we were seated, the head waiter produced parchment menus and the wine list, then retreated. Not much later, our waiter for the evening – a polite youth called Juan – arrived to introduce himself. Steve ordered a bottle of good, though not massively expensive, Hunter Valley white, and we made our choice of dishes. Left alone again, we clinked glasses.

'With thanks to everyone who made this possible,' I said.

Steve nodded. 'It's appreciated.' He took a drink, savoured it, then gazed around. 'Seems like we could be the only home-grown types here. Or maybe not. That woman seems familiar.'

I turned to look where he was looking, at a table in the far corner of the restaurant. Here a platinum blonde was smiling flirtily at her companion, a man who was half-hidden behind a Chinese screen. The blonde wore a black sequinned boob tube and had been so lavish with the eyeliner she resembled a giant panda.

'It's Rita Smith, the Post Office Jezebel,' I told him.

'That's where I've seen her, but why do you call her that?'

'Because she's forever regaling customers with details of her lovelife, no holds barred, or speculating on what other people may, or may not, be up to in that area. I also call her

Jezebel because, despite having had three husbands and any number of 'hits' as she calls them, she never stops chatting up men.'

'When I went into the Post Office recently, she tried to chat me up,' he said.

'Tried?' I raised a brow. 'She didn't succeed?'

Steve grimaced. 'Heaven forbid. Is Jezebel married at the moment? Is that her husband she's with?'

'She's married to Number Three, has been for a couple of years, but she's forever complaining about him being a couch spud who never takes her out anywhere. And she adores the bright lights.'

'He must've decided to indulge her.'

'It'd be quite an indulgence for him to bring her to Garth House. The guy's a bricklayer, but he's out of work. Seems to be permanently out of work.'

'How can a bricklayer be out of work in Dursleigh?' Steve protested.

'With difficulty, I'd imagine.' I looked across at the table again, just in time to see Jezebel's companion, a pouchy-faced man, lean forward to tug playfully at one of her dangly earrings. 'That's not her husband. She's with Ron Vetch!'

'Ron Vetch? But our noble councillor's big song at election time is 'oh, what a trustworthy family man, I am, I am,' Steve said drily.

'Yes, though there's talk of him being offhand with his wife and not too interested in his kids.'

'I've heard the talk, but I've never heard one whisper about Vetch fraternising with other women. If word got around that he was having a bit on the side, it'd be a serious blow to his reputation and to his re-election chances.'

'Especially as the bit on the side is the Post Office Jezebel, not a respectable or respected lady. Though they are only having dinner together,' I pointed out.

'True, but why is he sat behind the screen? Did it happen by chance or could he be deliberately hiding? Anyhow, let's forget about them,' he said, as Juan appeared bearing our crab starters. 'That looks good.'

The food was delicious. And the wine. And the frappucinos which were served after the meal. Being with Steve was delicious, too. We never stopped talking, sharing opinions, laughing. I was going to miss spending time with the away-from-work Mr Lingard.

'Okay if I come up and see Tina and Max on your wide-screen TV?' he said, as we rose from the table.

'Of course.' I looked at my watch. I'd been so busy enjoying myself, I had forgotten about their appearance. 'We'd better hurry, the programme starts in five minutes.'

We had reached The Clark Gable Room and I was looking in my bag for the key, when a giggle sounded behind us. I glanced back. At the far end of the corridor, the Post Office Jezebel was in the process of opening a bedroom door, with Ron Vetch standing close behind her. He had slid one hand over her shoulder and down into her cleavage – which was the reason for the giggle.

'They're *only* having dinner together?' Steve murmured, into my ear.

'Ooh, Ron!' Jezebel squeaked. 'You are naughty! Ooooh!'

The councillor had tugged down the sequinned boob tube and was cupping her naked breasts in her hands. They were saggy and heavily freckled breasts.

'You like it,' Ron Vetch said. 'You always like it when I –' He broke off. He had looked along the corridor and realised they were not alone. With one jerk, the boob tube was pulled back up into place. 'Get inside!'

'No need to push,' Jezebel complained, as he pressed a hand to her back. Then she also saw us. Her companion might be horrified at being spotted, but she wasn't bothered. 'Hiya, folks!' she sang out.

'Inside,' Ron Vetch growled, and thrust her forward. A moment later, the door slammed shut.

Steve grinned. 'There's someone who's not a happy bunny.'

Yet I didn't feel happy about the two-way sighting, either.

As I had no doubt the other couple were preparing to embark on sexual high jinks, I knew Jezebel would believe the same about us. And would be quick to relate how she had seen us going into a bedroom together at the Garth House Hotel, etc., etc., etc. Regrettably, her imagined *et ceteras* were destined to be pornographic.

As Steve switched on the television, I sat at one end of the sofa.

'Just in time,' he said.

The signature tune of *Sats with Zachs* was fading, to be replaced with loud applause as Zachary Clegg strode through an archway. Casually dressed in a sweat shirt and jeans, the young man was smiling. He welcomed the viewers and the studio audience to his show, told a couple of topical jokes, then introduced a Brazilian dance group who launched into a hectic number.

'Would you like something to drink?' I asked.

'A beer, please.'

I poured him one and helped myself to a fruit juice. Didn't want to overdo the alcohol.

The next item on the programme was an interview with a so-called 'It-girl' and her racing driver boyfriend, a surprisingly interesting couple. After they had departed, Zachs chatted about the events of his week, told more jokes and then—

'Tonight it is my great pleasure to welcome Max and Tina, the aerobics duo,' he declared. 'First we shall see them in action and what action! Then I shall be talking to them.' He swung a hand. 'Take it away, folks.'

The beat of music sounded and the camera travelled to Max and Tina, who were stood with hands on hips and bending sideways, first low to the left and then low to the right. Both were graceful, but Max also exuded power – a seductive combination. They were encased in dark blue spandex, with white chevrons at shoulders and hips.

'With it, but not too extreme,' Steve remarked.

I nodded. 'And I like Tina's plaits.'

Her blonde hair had been drawn back and woven into corn-row braids, which were fastened with blue and white beads and swung as she moved.

Throughout the work-out, they stretched, lunged, shadow-boxed and kept in perfect time with each other. When the music finished and they took a bow, the studio audience erupted into cheers, piercing whistles and loud applause.

'I know you're a personal trainer, Max,' Zachs said, when they joined him, 'but what can you tell us about the benefits of exercise?'

Max smiled his white, white smile. 'Exercise is invaluable. It enhances self-image, relieves stress and slows down the ageing process.'

'Works for me,' Tina declared.

'Exercising has given you more confidence?' the young comic asked her.

'It has. Also I've recently suffered a personal trauma, but exercise has helped me to release my tension and recover. As for slowing down the ageing process –' she smiled into the camera. 'At my next birthday I'll be sixty.'

'Sixty?' Zachs repeated, in what seemed to be genuine disbelief. 'You have to be joking.'

'If only,' she said.

I turned to Steve in amazement. 'Tina's informing the nation?'

'Wonders will never cease.'

'Doesn't she look fantastic?' Max appealed to the audience.

'Yes!' came a general shout, and there was another round of applause.

Tina looked pleased, but modest. 'You're very kind,' she said. 'However, I'm not unusual –'

'You bloody are,' a voice yelled.

'– and don't forget that a third of the nation is now over sixty. But whatever age you are, you're never going to be younger than you are today, so live to the limit.'

'Oh Lord,' I said, 'she's started on the cringeable quotes, too.'

'You work out every day?' Zachs asked her.

'I always do a short routine, but my main sessions are twice a week, with Max and my dear friends, Carol and Jenny.'

'And Carol looks even more fantastic than Tina,' Steve declared.

I grinned at him along the length of the sofa. 'So what are you after?'

'Making love to you.'

My grin faltered. 'What?'

'Don't play the innocent.' He was moving towards me. Coming close, too close for comfort. 'I want to make love to you and you want to make love to me. Yes?'

'No.'

'Tell the truth, Carol.'

What did I do, lie through my teeth and hope to convince him? But Steve would not be easily fooled.

'Okay, yes.' I took a breath. 'But if we sleep together, it could ruin the rapport and the ease between us at work. Making love with someone changes things for ever and if we got fed-up with each other or fell out, our working relationship would be severely strained and –'

'You have to take the chance! We both know that nothing is certain in this life.'

'Yes we do, so isn't it better if we remain just friends? Good friends, but platonic friends?' I yattered. 'I know that some people already believe we're lovers, and after the Post Office Jezebel has circulated the tale of how she saw us entering a bedroom here, a lot more will believe it, but if we sleep together and it all goes pear-shaped –'

'Shut up,' Steve said, and he kissed me.

The kiss was deep, lusty and irresistible. When he pulled back, my heart was racing, the tips of my breasts had hardened and there was an ache in my groin.

'Persuaded?' he enquired.

'Persuaded,' I replied.

He smiled. 'That didn't take long.'

Standing, he drew me to my feet and we went through to

the bedroom. He kissed me again and, between increasingly urgent kisses, began undressing me. Then I undressed him – as in I almost tore off his clothes.

'Be gentle with me,' Steve said, as we lay in the four-poster. 'I still have some bruises.'

'And hairy nipples.' I licked first one and then the other.

'God, Carol,' he groaned, and we were entwined and caressing and he was tasting my breasts and – 'I've got a horrible feeling I could be falling in love with you,' he said.

'Ditto.'

Our lovemaking wasn't just good, it was bloody marvellous. Alright, I hadn't made love for years – and neither had Steve – but we were so in tune, so at ease, so aroused by each other. We woke up in the middle of the night and made wonderful love again. And again, when we came awake the next day. And after breakfast we skipped a visit to the health club and made love once more.

'Do you know the name of the film for which Clark Gable received his Oscar?' Steve asked, later that morning as we waited for the porter to collect our luggage.

I shook my head. 'Not a clue.'

Placing an arm around my shoulders, he drew me close. 'It was *It Happened One Night*.'

CHAPTER TWENTY-ONE

AT ONE END OF the trestle table, Eileen was arranging neat rows of cellophane-wrapped birthday cards, get-well cards and thank-you notes, while at the other Jenny and I swiftly set out second-hand paperbacks, C.D.s and videos. Cardboard boxes containing brand-new toiletries waited to be unpacked. Frances, who was supposed to be partnering Eileen on the charity shop stall, had so far failed to appear and, on discovering the old lady's lone-handed plight, Jenny and I had offered our assistance.

In a quarter of an hour, Dursleigh's annual fête was due to begin and the village green was busy. Sellers sped back and forth on last-minute missions; ferrying final items from vans to stalls which were laden with everything from pot plants to home-made patchwork cushions to French cheeses. A bouncy castle was being inflated, next door to a 'kiddie karts' racetrack. An old, but splendidly gleaming, Chevrolet – the last in a display of classic cars – bumped over the grass, heading for its allotted parking spot. Chef-hatted Rotarians stood chatting beside the barbecues where they were to cook chicken legs and burgers, while a genuine chef from the Tandoori supervised the organisation of his curry stall. Knots of expectant visitors hovered around the recently constructed stage.

'Great day for it!' called the greengrocer, as he put finishing touches to his coconut shy.

'Couldn't be better,' agreed the party-shop woman, who would be painting children's faces and affixing transfer-type tattoos.

After a week of cool, unsettled weather, the sun shone golden and the sky was blue. When we had awoken and seen the sunshine, Steve and I had shared a smile of relief. Shared an erotic coupling, too. We had needed a warm dry day for,

311

this year, the fête promised to draw a far larger crowd than usual and, this year, the fête's main sponsor was *The Dursleigh Siren*.

When Steve had suggested that backing the event would be good publicity for the paper, plus excellent public relations, Mr P-J had agreed. Mind you, he agreed with everything his profit-producing editor suggested. So for the past month Steve and I had been increasingly involved; conferring with members of the fête committee and, in particular, with Mr Patel who had taken over Duncan Kincaid's role as chairman, encouraging local businesses to participate, fixing for the brass band and other organisations to attend.

In our eagerness to ensure that all went well, we had arrived early to check on essentials; such as the delivery of the portable loos and erection of a large marquee where drinks and snacks would be sold. Tony and Melanie had also been active; pinning up banners advertising *The Siren* and setting out our stall. Melanie would be in charge of the stall, selling copies of the newspaper and raffle tickets, while Tony's duties were that of photographer. Next week's *Siren* would contain a special photo-filled pull-out dedicated to the fête. As for Steve and I, we were to welcome visitors and generally act as roving ambassadors.

'Still happy with your job at Garth House?' Eileen asked Jenny, as we began arranging packets of soap, tubs of bath salts and bottles of eau de cologne.

'I love it,' she replied. 'The secretarial side is a doddle and I enjoy meeting all the guests.'

The old lady slid her a look. 'I've heard you're best buddies with the manager.'

She laughed. 'I am. The previous girl was such a disaster that he thinks I'm heaven sent.'

Shortly after Steve and I had spent our night there, the hotel had placed an advertisement in *The Siren* for a receptionist. Poppy had double booked a number of other rooms – so Jenny had later learned – and when faced with a particularly irate couldn't-be guest had burst into tears and scarpered. She had left behind a fouled-up reservation system and stash of unopened, presumably forgotten, mail. After that experience, the manager had resolved to employ someone who was calm, sensible and far more mature.

'Not tempted to model again?' Eileen asked.

Jenny shook her head. 'I was approached to do a follow-up advert, but I refused. I prefer regular work with regular hours. And my first, and last, assignment was so boring.'

'Boring?'

'I went up to London and made my way to some back of beyond studio, only to have to hang around for ages waiting to be kitted out in the required clothes and for my hair to be fixed the way the kitchen catalogue woman wanted it fixed. Then there was a long argument between her and the photographer's assistant about which shoes I should wear. When I eventually got in front of the camera, I was told to stand with my head tilted at an odd angle, my hand clasped, just so, around a saucepan lid and an expression of rapt delight on my face for what seemed like hours. Next I had to bend at the waist and smile into an oven. Then I was asked to hold a casserole dish which weighed a ton. The poses went on for ever!'

'You looked very pretty in the catalogue,' Eileen told her.

'Thanks.'

'And slim.' Jenny was subjected to a beady-eyed inspection. 'You're still keeping the weight off.' The inspection switched to me. 'You're in decent shape, too. Are you both still exercising?'

'Twice a week at the Garth House health club,' I said.

'That must cost!'

'We have reduced rates. Drastically reduced, thank goodness,' Jenny said. 'When I started working at the hotel, as an employee my reduction came automatically. Then I suggested to the manager that maybe he should be generous to Carol. After all, she was responsible for Max teaching at their health club and, although he's no longer doing it, he's given Garth House some worthwhile publicity.'

Eileen nodded. 'He mentioned how he'd run classes there

in the last television interview I saw.'

'And, who knows, I could locate another aerobics smasheroo or write more glowing articles about the place,' I said.

Jenny grinned. 'I voiced both ideas. So now Carol and I exercise there twice a week, straight after work.'

'Which means that by the time Jen arrives home, her husband has set the table for dinner and peeled the spuds,' I said, with a smile.

'He did the potatoes once,' she corrected. 'Getting Bruce to prepare an entire meal is going to be a long, hard slog.'

'He'll do it, eventually,' I told her.

She nodded. 'I believe so.'

Their married life had taken on a fresh vitality and become much more of a partnership, so Jenny had reported. Enchanted with his blonder, slimmer wife, Bruce had acknowledged her need for independence, accepted her as a working girl and begun to regard her as an equal. She was no longer told what would be happening, she was consulted. And he had started to pack his own suitcase when he travelled.

'You don't suppose Frances could have forsaken her beloved bike and her principles, and decided to come by public transport?' Eileen said sourly, as a bus pulled to a stop beside the village green.

'Unlikely,' Jenny replied.

Frances was, it seemed, gravely worried about vehicles creating greenhouse gases and the erosion of the ozone layer, and only travelled on anything with an engine, under duress.

'I didn't want her as my partner today,' Eileen confided, 'but everyone else was either away on holiday or busy with their families. And now it's doubtful if the woman's going to turn up!' She studied the stream of passengers, many of them young and female, who were pouring off the bus. 'Though plenty of others are and we know who they've come to see. The gorgeous boy.' The old lady gave a high-pitched giggle. 'Never imagined when I met him with you, Carol, that he'd become so famous and such a pin-up. Didn't think Tina

Kincaid would be a TV hit again, either. Not at her age. Don't suppose you see much of them these days?'

I shook my head. 'They're too busy.'

'But we're hoping to catch up on Tina's news today,' Jenny said.

'Getting them to open the fête was quite a catch.' Eileen eyed the crowd which was growing by the minute. Families were flocking in from the High Street car park, groups of teenagers were sloping onto the grass, a mini-bus was disgorging pensioners. 'There're going to be record numbers.'

Three months ago, Max and Tina's appearance on *Sats with Zachs* had created a stir with the viewing public, inspired excited media comments and phenomenal hype. Overnight they had become box office bingo and the couple everyone was talking about. Such was the fuss, Zachary Clegg had asked them back the following Saturday, they had been given their own thrice weekly slot on the morning show – though Jenny had recently read that they were soon to have their own programme – and women's magazines had printed multi-page 'Max and Tina' features. When I had subsequently interviewed Tina about their success, she had spoken of how they were being pressed to give displays at fitness centres, to endorse products, to attend all manner of promotions and parties.

'That's A-list parties,' she had said, in delight.

These demands on their time meant that, as Max had had to relinquish his classes at Garth House, so our work-outs *chez Tina* had also been forced to end.

'Forgive me, do forgive me,' a soprano voice appealed, and the three of us looked up from our labours to see a thin woman, her straight grey hair held back by an Alice band, wheeling a bicycle towards us. 'Very sorry I'm late, but I got up this morning and decided to bake a spinach loaf –'

'Spinach loaf?' Eileen demanded, her mouth twisted in disgust.

'I use organic spinach, and the biddies at the day centre do love a slice with their tea. Then, blow me, I'd just put the loaf

315

into the oven when I remembered I'd agreed to be on duty here with you.' She smiled a weak smile. 'I do apologise.'

'And so you should, Frances.' Eileen sniffed her annoyance. 'It's fortunate Jenny and Carol came to my aid. And Steve, he's Carol's –' She hesitated. 'They live together. He's over there.' She pointed to the stage where Steve was helping to site the amplifiers. 'What a charming fellow. He carried all the boxes from my car, while these two girls got busy unpacking. However, now you're here. At last.' She sniffed again. 'When all the hard work has been done.'

'But I can't stay.'

'Can't stay?' Eileen repeated, in furious disbelief. 'And why is that?'

'Because I've promised to go and help a man who suffers from double vision with his marquetry. It's his hobby and I can't let him down,' Frances said, her eyes wary and her voice dropping to little more than a whisper. 'I'm due there in ten minutes. I'd put the appointment on my calendar at home, but not in my diary. So when you asked if I could help at the fête, I looked in my diary and saw a free day. An easy mistake to make, yes?'

She moved her hands in a desperate plea for understanding, but Eileen's expression was stony.

'You're leaving me to manage the stall by myself? And what about me taking a break? How can I go and find something to eat if I'm all alone? Or even visit the Ladies'? I can't.'

Frances hung her head. 'I'm very sorry.'

'Sorry? Pah! And I was thinking that later I'd treat myself to a curry. I like curries and especially if –' In the midst of her annoyance, the giggle gurgled out again, '– they're served by dashing young Indians.'

'I can help you to run the stall,' Jenny offered. 'And I'll help you pack everything up when the fête is over. My husband's busy with his vegetable patch, so I was planning to be here for most of the afternoon.'

Eileen smiled. 'Thank you, dear, that is most kind.' As she

swung to Frances, her smile transposed into a dirty look. 'You may not remember me saying, but, as the doctor has warned so many times, bending and stretching is bad for me, seriously damaging –' a martyred hand was placed on her hip '– and if I do too much I could end up on a stretcher. In hospital. Flat on my back for weeks. Or with a hernia, that's always a possibility. But the trouble I've had with my bones! It started in my youth when I tripped over a paving stone, the council's fault, and –'

'Excuse me, I must go, have to speak to Steve,' I said.

'And before everything kicks off, I'd like to buy myself a bottle of water. But I'll be back,' Jenny promised, and together we escaped.

I looked for Steve, only to discover that work on the sound system had finished and he was heading for the edge of the green where Mr Patel was waiting. It had been agreed that the two men would greet Tina and Max and escort them across to the stage. There the lady mayor would make a formal welcome. As Steve joined him, Mr Patel gestured towards the High Street where a long white limousine with tinted windows was navigating the bend.

'This has to be the star attractions,' I said drily. 'They have another engagement to attend later today so, as Tina refused to accept a fee, Steve offered to pay for a car and driver. Though we didn't anticipate a stretch limo!'

Jenny grinned. 'Don't know why not, it's just Max's style.'

Max had taken to fame with gusto. He was relishing every minute and never missed a chance to promote the 'dynamic duo's' image. He was also squeezing each opportunity for every last pound he and his partner could make. However, Tina – the reputed gold-digger – was not so mercenary. When Steve and I had asked her if they would be willing to open the fête – it had been my idea – she had promptly agreed, but rejected any suggestion of payment.

'Duncan would've been horrified if I charged,' she had said, then grinned. 'Besides, me being Dursleigh's honoured guest is one in the eye for Beryl and her associates.'

But when she had informed Max of the arrangement, his first question had been how much would they receive. And he had, Tina confessed, needed some persuading before he would attend the event for free.

As the limousine drew closer, people on the green also took notice. There was a general move forward and by the time the limo drew to a halt beside them, Mr Patel and Steve were backed by an excited crowd, several rows deep. When the uniformed chauffeur came round to open the passenger door and Tina stepped out, followed by Max, the crowd clapped and cheered. In front of the stage, the brass band burst into a rousing rendition of 'We Are The Champions.' Smiling, the couple paused, posed and Tony took the first of his photographs.

Tina was summery in a pink-and-white checked skirt suit with pink-fringed lapels, cuffs and hem. She wore pink killer heels and carried a matching bag. Her hair, which swayed around her shoulders, was threaded with what the media now referred to as her 'trademark' braids. Today the braids were fastened with clusters of pink and white sequins. As usual for their public appearances, Max was colour co-ordinated with his companion, though his look was casual. Casual *à la* Las Vegas. He wore a cyclamen pink, sequin-speckled T-shirt and loose white linen trousers. A silver medallion hung around his neck. When he brushed a hand back over his blonded dreadlocks, he inspired a communal female sigh.

The two of them may have been OTT for a Saturday afternoon on a village green, but their audience loved it. Me, too. Just felt it was a pity they hadn't opted for pink contact lenses.

Chatting to the new arrivals, Steve and Mr Patel led them through the throng and up onto the stage. After saying how thrilled she was to meet 'Dursleigh's very own stars' – and sounding thrilled, too – the lady mayor spoke of the 'immense privilege' it was to have them here.

'It's the best day of my life!' hollered a besotted female, and everyone laughed and applauded again.

The lady mayor moved into her thanks; thanking the committee for their efforts, thanking everyone else involved in the fête, thanking *The Dursleigh Siren* for its sponsorship. She talked of how the money raised would go to the youth music club, Girl Guides and other causes, then handed over the microphone. After Tina had declared her pleasure at being invited, Max ballyhooed their television programme which was to start in the autumn. In addition to exercise-along work-outs for the viewer, he would, he explained, be running self-help programmes for those wishing to awaken natural healing powers, release their creativity, detox etc. His spiel over, he caught hold of Tina's hand and, speaking in unison, they declared the fête open.

This brought another volley of cheers and more photographs were taken – some with Tony wielding his camera, others by the crowd. Leaving the stage, the couple rejoined Steve and Mr Patel and, surrounded by a swarm of fans, set off on a tour of the stalls.

The fans could be divided into three groups; men of all ages who fancied Tina, older women who admired Tina as a role model, and younger females who had the hots for Max. The younger females formed the largest group by far. Clearly aware of this, Max was cracking jokes, kissing hands and being the universal charmer.

As the band launched into 'Mambo Italiano' – which had Max sexily swaying his hips – Jenny went in search of a bottle of water.

Intending to see whether Melanie needed support, I had turned towards *The Siren* stall when one of the lady shop assistants from Gifford's came up. She was eager to tell me that her nerves and those of her colleague and the two Mr Giffords had recovered, they were no longer haunted by fears of another robbery and could sleep peacefully at night. Casting fond glances at the distant Steve, she declared he was so caring and thoughtful. Such a nice man.

'I think so, too,' I told her.

As she went on her way, I caught sight of Ron Vetch

buying burgers in buns for himself and his wife. Watching how he procured a seat for his wife, provided napkins, then engaged in bright conversation, I smiled. Three months ago, solemnly declaring that 'mistakes had been made, but lessons will be learned', he had resigned as a councillor. Although many Dursleigh residents remained ignorant of his 'mistakes' – he had neglected to explain – those who frequented the Post Office were better informed. Jezebel had talked freely, slamming her one-night stand as having 'a teeny todger' and being 'rubbish in bed'. But now it seemed that by nurturing his image as a devoted husband, Ron was endeavouring to get back into favour – with his wife and, no doubt, with the local community. However, judging from Mrs Vetch's lack of response and to use his politicaleze, it could be 'an uphill struggle'.

'Hello there!' someone called.

I looked round to see a wizened lady waving to me. I waved back. It was the sky-diving great-grandmother whom I had interviewed.

'Hi, Carol!'

This time Roger, my friendly policeman, had raised a hand amidst the crowd. I went to speak to him, and to his wife and toddler son who accompanied him.

My progress towards *The Siren* stall was slow. More people exchanged greetings and I stopped for several chats. I was even waylaid by Pippa, Gerri and Dee, all of whom claimed to be 'acutely stressed' now that Max had forsaken them, though they would be 'forever emotionally enriched by his wisdom' and were 'brainstorming' over his replacement. When I finally arrived at the stall, it was to discover Melanie deep in conversation with a Neighbourhood Watch stalwart. Melanie has taken over several of the evening and weekend jobs which I used to do and is a keen successor. She did not, she assured me, need any help on the stall.

I had bought a book of raffle tickets from her – one prize I didn't want to win was a year's free subscription to *The Dursleigh Siren,* though my dad would always welcome it –

when an arm slid around my waist.

'How's my favourite middle-aged baggage?' Steve asked.

'All the better for seeing you. And you, and you, and you,' I added when I turned, for Debbie, Paul and their dog were with him.

Although Debbie had made suggestions, from the start Paul had had firm ideas about what the Dalmatian should be called. As a keen football fan, the boy had wanted him to be named after one of his three favourite players, which had meant either Ruud Van or Zidane or Ronaldo. He had said Debbie could choose and she had chosen Ronaldo.

'The kids have just arrived, so I thought I'd take a break from the scrum,' Steve said, jerking his head to where Tina and Max were holding court to a group of moony-eyed admirers. He grinned down at his daughter. 'Debs has something to tell you.'

She beamed. 'My story, A Sticky Hero, is going to be published. I had a letter this morning telling me and – guess what?' – the magazine is going to pay me fifty pounds. Fifty whole pounds!'

'That's wonderful!' I said, and hugged her. 'It might be an idea to start on a sequel.'

She laughed. 'I already have.'

'Will you be giving your brother a share of the spoils?' I enquired, with a wink at Paul.

'A fiver would be generous,' Steve said. 'A tenner even better.'

Debbie gave a loud sigh. 'Oh, okay then.'

'Thanks,' Paul said, and smiled up at me.

I patted Ronaldo, who wagged an energetic tail. 'Are you going to win a medal today?'

'He will,' Paul vowed. 'We're trying to keep him calm until it's time for him to perform.'

One of the afternoon's events was a dog show with ability and obedience tests and, on hearing about this, the boy had been eager that Ronaldo should take part. When Steve had voiced doubts about the Dalmatian's ability to follow instructions – he's a little giddy and not the brightest of creatures – Paul had declared he would train him.

'Pity your mum can't be here today,' I said.

Debbie shrugged. 'Her attending the psychic fair was fixed ages ago, but perhaps she'll come next year. Has Beth arrived yet?'

'I haven't seen her, though she should be along soon.'

When Debbie and Beth had met – at a two-family lunch at my house – a bond had been formed. Beth idolised the older girl and, in turn, Debbie was amused and touched by her affection.

'Guess I should return to my escort duties,' Steve said, as Tina and Max prepared to continue their tour. 'Will you two kids be alright on your own?'

Debbie cast him a 'what a sad dad' look. 'Of course. We're going to go and enrol Ronaldo for the tests.'

Paul touched my hand. 'Will you come and watch us?'

I grinned. 'You bet.'

Although Debbie and I had always been easy together, before I'd met Steve's son I was wary. Would he resent his father caring for another woman? Might he regard my presence as an insult to his mother and hate me on sight? If he did, I could understand. But Paul – a calm, self-contained boy – had been unconcerned. Annette had no problems with Steve's new relationship and neither did he.

Also, it had helped that when he and his sister had first come to visit, I had suggested they bring Ronaldo, served lamb for dinner and afterwards given the dog the bone. As no lamb bones were available at home, it was a treat he had relished. Later I had bought him pigs' ears in a packet and a rubber chicken. The rubber chicken was a particular hit. It's kept in a polybag behind the cloakroom door and whenever Ronaldo arrives he goes crazy wanting to get at it. Yes, I can be accused of bribing my way into Paul's affections, but we all resort to subtle bribery at times. Don't we?

I was reflecting on how fortunate Steve and I were that our families got along, when the ageing pop star appeared before me. He wore a black shirt with a blue leather suit, the trousers of which were strained tight around the bulging globe of his stomach. His bleached blond hair, which was as soft and fluffy as a feather duster, showed patches of bright pink scalp. Had it never occurred to him that for a man drawing his old age pension, he looked foolish?

'Hey, Carol, how're you doin'?' he asked, grabbing hold of my hand and shaking it.

Both the mid-Atlantic accent and the mateyness were fake. Although, long ago, I had interviewed him, we were not on first name terms. A humourless character, he kept himself aloof from the village's events and when asked to lend his presence, or give a donation to projects, he always refused. Indeed, that he should have come to the fête was surprising.

'I'm well,' I replied.

'Understand it's you, gal, who's responsible for the special guests being here today and wondered if you had a famous name lined up to open the fête next year?'

'We haven't thought that far ahead,' I told him.

'Then how's about yours truly does it?' he said, and broke off to spread his chunky thighs and play a snatch of air guitar. Oh dear! 'Having had Tina and Max, you'll be wanting someone with a following, with status,' he continued. 'A guy who'll rock the chicks.'

I stage-managed a smile. 'Thanks for the offer. I'll bear it in mind.'

While the guy might still attract a small coterie of elderly hippies, he no longer possessed any status. And had never displayed much musical ability. His finest five minutes had been in the Sixties, when he had pranced to the front of his group and emitted a few 'bim-bams' and 'ya-da-der-da-doos.' It must be twenty years since he had made a record and even longer since he had had a hit. He would rock the chicks? When I'd mentioned his name to Melanie, she had never heard of him.

'Please do,' he said, and moved as if to make another grab for my hand.

I stepped back. A fire engine was drawing in off the road and onto the grass, and I pointed towards it. 'Excuse me. Must go and speak to the fire-fighters. Bye.'

As small children were lifted up into the cab of the fire engine and allowed to sound the horn, I chatted with a couple of the guys who had run in the marathon. They had told me about another charity race they would be entering, when I saw Lynn, Justin and Beth. After jotting down details of the race and asking the firemen to keep me informed, I went over.

'It's a lovely day,' Lynn remarked, when we'd exchanged hugs and kisses, and I had assured Beth that Debbie was somewhere around. 'I hope it's sunny like this for our wedding.'

'My fingers are crossed,' I told her.

After much scouring of the area for a venue, the reception was to be held at Garth House. This was thanks to Jenny, who had swiftly advised of a cancellation, and to Tom who would be footing the bill.

I bent down to Beth. 'Are you looking forward to wearing your pretty dress at the wedding?'

The little girl gave a solemn nod. 'Yes. And I'm looking forward to having a new baby brother or a new baby sister.'

I jerked upright. 'A new baby? When?'

Justin laughed. 'Relax. We haven't jumped the gun again.'

'We don't know when,' Lynn said. 'All we know is that we'd very much like one, just as soon as we're married.'

'It's about time I had a second great-grandchild,' a voice declared.

My father was stood behind us. He looked smart in a beige suit and straw panama, and was holding hands with a silver-haired woman. When I had called in to see him earlier in the week, he had told me that he and Marie would be visiting the fête. But the woman was not Marie.

He ruffled Beth's hair in greeting, then indicated his companion. 'I'd like you all to meet my friend, Grace, who has recently moved into Bridgemont. Grace, this is –' He introduced us, one by one.

'Pleased to meet you,' she said. Short, plump and dressed in a modest cream two-piece, Grace had a friendly manner.

'Do you come from around Dursleigh?' I asked.

'No, no, I'm a West Country lass. For years my husband and I ran a restaurant there. I did the cooking –'

'Won awards for it, too,' my father inserted.

'– and my husband looked after everything else. But, sadly, a year or so ago he died and I decided to move near to my son. He lives a few miles away from here, runs his own painting and decorating business.'

'You could ask Grace's son if he would decorate your flat for you, Granddad,' Lynn suggested, and slid me a smile.

We had discussed the way he benefited from his ladyfriends' various talents and his fondness for a bargain, but here was a woman who, it appeared, could offer combined attractions.

'It's already arranged. I'm on his list for September and, very kindly, he's giving me a discount,' he replied, positively smirking.

I raised my brows. 'Lucky you.'

'Grace is a bit of a bookworm, like me,' my father continued, 'and I've told her about the paperbacks which Jenny's charity shop sells. Didn't you say they were running a stall here today?'

'It's beyond the stage.' I pointed. 'Jenny's there now, with Eileen.'

He pulled a face. 'Don't care for Eileen. If I'm ever in the shop and we're on our own, she gives me the glad eye something cruel.'

'The hussy!' Grace exclaimed, as disapproving as my mother.

'I see Steve is doing his stuff. Steve is Carol's significant other,' my dad informed Grace. 'That's him, escorting Tina and Max. Tall chap with the dark hair. He's the editor of *The Dursleigh Siren* and a real bright spark. Not been with the paper six months, but has already achieved a useful increase in sales. The proprietor, posh chap with a double-barrelled name, thinks he's the bee's knees.'

'Do you and Steve enjoy working together?' Grace asked me.

I smiled. 'Very much.'

'That's nice. My husband and I always did.' She glanced towards the Rotarians' barbecue. 'Shall we have something to eat, George?'

My father nodded. 'If you wish.' He bent to kiss Beth, kissed Lynn and me, and shook hands with Justin. 'Be seeing you.'

As they walked away, Lynn chuckled. 'A demon producer of fine food who has a painter and decorator son who's been persuaded to do a cut price job,' she said. 'Beat that.'

'How about a cooking-obsessed masseuse with a banker son and a car mechanic nephew?' I suggested. 'Plus a daughter who sews inexpensive curtains.'

'Who owns a holiday villa in the Algarve,' Justin tacked on. 'And can get cheap flights.'

'That'd be competition,' Lynn admitted.

'When can I have my face painted?' Beth enquired, looking along to the stall.

'How about now?' Justin suggested.

She jiggled with excitement. 'Yes, please.'

'Coming to watch your granddaughter being transformed into a whiskery kitten?' Lynn asked me.

I shook my head. 'I'll wait for the finished product. I need to check on Jenny and see if she needs rescuing from Eileen's conversation.'

'I don't want to be a kitten,' Beth announced, as they departed. 'I want to be Spiderman. Or shall I be a dragon? Or–'

At the charity stall, many of the cards and toiletries had been sold, but a fair number of the second-hand items, including most of the books, remained.

'Hardly anyone's even glanced at them,' Jenny complained.

Eileen sighed. 'Looks like I'll be carting them all back to

the shop on Monday.'

'Do not despair,' I told them. 'My father and his new girlfriend will be along soon and, if you knock the price down low enough, he could take the lot.'

Eileen frowned, as though lowering the price did not appeal, then, as a barrel-chested man in shorts walked by, dashed out to confront him. 'Interested in a good read?' she demanded.

He tugged at his shorts, which were belted beneath his stomach. 'Well –'

'Your father has a new girlfriend?' Jenny asked me quietly, and while the old lady was hard-selling to her customer, I explained.

'Would you like to take a breather? Say, half an hour?' Eileen suggested to Jenny, when the man, who reluctantly purchased a couple of books, had made his escape. A loudspeakered announcement had advised the imminent start of the Morris dancing and people were deserting the stalls. 'Looks like we're in for a lull, so now would be a good time.'

'Thanks, I will. Fancy something to eat?' Jenny asked me.

'I can recommend the curry,' Eileen piped up. 'I had some earlier and it really tickled the tastebuds.' She giggled. 'Likewise those young Indians.'

'A drink and a sandwich will suit me,' I said.

Jenny nodded. 'And me.'

We were nearing the beer tent when we heard our names being called. Turning, we saw Tina hobbling awkwardly towards us.

'Walking on grass in brand new stilettos isn't easy and my feet are killing me,' she said. 'Is there somewhere I could sit down?'

'Come with us,' I said, and directed her into the marquee. 'How about a drink?' I suggested, when the three of us were sitting on green plastic chairs around a green plastic table.

The Morris dancers must have attracted a large audience, for the marquee was almost empty. Several tables away, a couple were cooing over a baby in a pushchair, while a trio of men consumed beer beside the back counter.

'I'd like an apple juice,' Tina said. She had removed her shoes and was gratefully wiggling her toes.

'And a sandwich? Ham or prawn or cheese and tomato or egg with mayonnaise?' I was reading from the menu board.

'Ham, please.'

'For you, Jen?'

'The same.'

I had bought the sandwiches and bottles of apple juice, together with ice in glasses, and was returning to the table when a chubby young woman peered in through the tent flap, then walked hesitantly towards us.

'I hope you don't mind and I'm sorry to interrupt, but do you think I could have your autograph?' she asked Tina. 'My boyfriend and I watch you on TV and we think you and Max are like such a wild pair and like really, really brilliant at aerobics. My boyfriend hopes that when I get older I'll look like you. But I should be so lucky.'

Tina smiled. 'You're very kind,' she said and signed the piece of paper which had been offered.

'Thank you, thank you. I shall keep this for ever,' the young woman gabbled, then she rushed back outside.

'I know you've been constantly signing autographs today, but do you often get asked?' Jenny enquired.

'It never stops,' Tina said. 'Wherever I go and whatever I do, I always seem to be recognised by someone.'

'It's the burden of fame,' I remarked.

She laughed. 'Yes, though today I am on home territory. But not for much longer, because I shall soon be moving to London. You see, I've agreed to leave Duncan's house and give up any future claim to residence, in return for a payment from my stepsons.'

'I trust it's a substantial payment,' I said.

Earlier in the month, Max had asked Lynn's estate agency to value the property and, as I had guessed, the Thyme Park plot was worth a six figure sum.

Tina smiled. 'It is. It'll be enough for me to buy an

apartment in a fashionable neighbourhood, like Chelsea. And the money Max and I are making means we'll be able to furnish the apartment in style.'

'Max will live there, too?' Jenny said. 'Like he's living with you now?'

A couple of months ago, Jenny and I had arrived at Tina's house for what was our final exercise session to find that Max had moved in. Their daily lives were, he had explained, so entwined that living together made sense; which was why he'd suggested it. After telling us of her instant agreement, Tina had enthused about how the young man had checked out her car, topping up the oil and pumping up the tyres. He was happy to despatch spiders and mix gin and tonics, too.

'He will,' Tina replied, then lowered her voice, though there was no one else within earshot. 'Every morning I do my face in the bathroom before he's awake. I don't want him to see the basic me.'

'That's silly,' Jenny protested. 'I'm sure you don't look that bad without make-up.'

'Not bad, but I look… different. This is just between the three of us,' she went on, 'but Max seeing the basic me is one reason why I'm not keen to share a bed.'

As Tina reached for her glass to take a drink of apple juice, Jenny and I exchanged a look. This was something we had wondered about.

'He's mentioned it?' I asked.

'He said that as plenty of people think we do, perhaps we should.'

'Doesn't sound very romantic,' Jenny remarked.

'It wasn't.' Tina shrugged. 'I pointed out the fact that I'm older, but Max's response was that age doesn't matter if minds and bodies connect.'

'And age is just a number?' I suggested. 'Age is purely in the mind?'

'He said that, too. But –' Again, Tina's voice dropped to confidentiality, '– to be honest, I'm not desperate about sex, never have been. Messy business and much overrated, in my opinion.'

But not in mine, I thought.

Jenny frowned. 'You didn't like it with Joe Fernandez?'

'Not with him, not with Duncan, nor with my first husband. I've spent my life faking orgasms.'

I bit into my sandwich. When I had been interviewing Max alone – Steve and I had agreed that his and Tina's popularity merited a follow-up piece in *The Siren* – the young man had confessed, strictly off the record, that living in a spacious, albeit run-down, house with Tina was a big improvement on sharing the 'over the chip shop' flat with his brothers. He had also intimated that should his hostess show signs of wanting him to sleep with her, he would oblige – though he was not smitten with overwhelming desire.

Yet a significant part of the interest in Max and Tina centred on their sexual relationship. Were they lovers, yes or no? There had been much media speculation on the subject which endlessly intrigued and which both of them – Max in particular – encouraged. One camp insisted the sexual attraction was glaringly obvious and if thirty years separated them, so what? Didn't plenty of older men have much younger partners? However, other factions felt that, no matter how good she looked, Tina was the wrong generation to appeal to such a virile young man.

Jenny had even read a suggestion that Max might be gay. It was a suggestion Max had not dismissed, though that did not necessarily mean he was. It just meant he could see greater fame and fortune to be made from appealing to all proclivities.

'How did you persuade Simon and Giles to be so generous?' I enquired.

Tina pulled at one of her sequinned braids, braids which, according to a magazine Jenny had read, were becoming the rage with woman *d'un certain age.* 'I got Max to do the negotiating. You see, we'd been talking about how travelling up and down to London was becoming a pain and –'

'You do seem to spend a lot of time there,' Jenny inserted.

'We're in London almost every day... at the television

studios or doing publicity gigs or attending meetings. Right now we're involved in talks with a chain of sports clubs which wants to use our names and we're also looking into designing our own fitness wear. And we might run life change and stress management seminars. Max is forever coming up with ideas.' She flicked a hand. 'Anyhow, I'd told Max about my financial situation and how my crap stepsons had cheated me out of Duncan's share portfolios and how chuffed they'd be if I decided I couldn't afford to live in Thyme Park any longer.'

'Did you tell him about finding the bundles of notes?' I said.

'That, too. And he's spent ages going through the house, searching for more. He found a couple wedged behind a painting, but that's all. But when Max realised the position with Simon and Giles,' she continued, 'he suggested we should speak to them and ask how much they were prepared to pay me to leave.'

'You knew the amount you wanted?'

'Max did. As you know, he had the house valued and he'd also researched the price of apartments in trendy parts of London, so he had a sum fixed in his mind.'

'Simon and Giles offered much less?' I said, knowing they would have done.

'At first. They were also unpleasant and quite rude towards me, until Max told them to show respect.' Tina giggled. 'He had them both shaking in their shoes.'

I grinned. 'Good for Max. And they agreed to pay the amount you stipulated?'

'They did. What's more, Max insisted they send me their cheque straight away, which they have done and which I've cashed, and he got them to agree that I can stay in the house until October. So we have plenty of time to look for somewhere in London. We've already viewed a few apartments and have appointments to look at others,' she said, and started on her sandwich.

'Any plans to get in touch with your mother before you leave Dursleigh?' I asked.

'No, though... do you know if she's here today?'

'She isn't. She and Ernest have gone on a coach tour holiday to the Lake District.'

'She's keeping well?'

'Very well,' I confirmed.

'I'm not planning to get together with her within the next few months, but I may do later,' Tina said. 'Perhaps next year, once our TV programme has settled down. Max says that then, if it should become known that Billy is my brother and Dilys is my mam, it won't do any harm. It could even add interest. But how are things with you and Steve? Silly question, I can tell by your glow they're still fantastic.'

I smiled. 'You're right.'

'Carol and Steve have got it bad. They're like a couple of soppy teenagers, forever smiling at each other, touching each other, drooling over each other,' Jenny said, in mock complaint. 'All we need now is for Carol to follow her daughter's example and walk down the aisle.'

I groaned. 'Here we go again. But it's not as though Steve and I will have any children and masses of people cohabit and have loyal, long-lasting relationships. We're perfectly content as we are.'

Within days of our 'treat' weekend, Steve had moved in with me. Him spending the night at my house, then driving over to his flat to pick up his post, check the answerphone or get a change of clothes was a hassle he did not need. However, he had decided he would not sell his flat, he would rent it out. Property prices continued to rise and, in the future, we might decide to sell both our places and buy one larger house.

'I'm a believer in happy endings. The eternal optimist,' Jenny said stubbornly, and looked at her watch. 'I should get back to Eileen.'

'And I have a dog show to attend. How are the feet?' I asked Tina.

'Easier,' she replied. 'So I'd better find Max.'

'Shouldn't be too difficult. You look for a crowd of breathless females who're preparing to lob their lingerie.'

She laughed. 'I'll do that. It's been lovely to see you both.'

'Lovely to see you,' I replied.

Jenny nodded. 'I hope we can get together again before too long.'

'Hope so, too.' Tina kissed us both on both cheeks. 'Goodbye, girls, goodbye.'

As she disappeared, a little unsteady in her high heels, Jenny sighed. 'So if she does eventually tie up with her mother, it'll partly be because Max reckons it could add a fillip to their fame. How calculating is that?'

'It's sad,' I said, 'though I'm sure neither of them see it that way. And, still with calculation, Max has found himself a sugar mummy.'

'And Tina's got a man to look after her who's handy about the house, which means they're both happy.'

'Though she's not keen on lovemaking. She doesn't know what she's missing. I think it's sad, too, that she needs to put on her make-up before Max can see her.'

'You're not worried about Steve seeing you with a naked face and running away screaming in horror?' Jenny asked.

'I'm not worried about him seeing my naked face or my naked body. In fact, while I don't like to boast – yes, I do – he reckons my shape is well-nigh irresistible.'

'Bruce thinks I'm the sexiest woman in Christendom.'

We looked at each other and laughed.

'What a smug pair we are,' I said.

'And what's wrong with celebrating the joy of being in our fifties? Jenny demanded.

'Nothing,' I replied. 'Not one thing.'

CHAPTER TWENTY-TWO

As I WIPED THE last of the spoons and put them into the drawer, I yawned. I was ready for bed. When the fête had ended, Debbie, Paul and Ronaldo had come back with Steve and me to my house. Annette would not be home until mid-evening, so they were to have dinner with us.

Both children had been in a joyous mood; Debbie thanks to her writing success and Paul because of Ronaldo's performance in the dog show. His first test had been 'stop and stay'. In truth, Ronaldo had not stopped and stayed well – at one point, he had run round in circles chasing his tail – but he had been awarded a 'highly commended' certificate. Although the judges' magnanimity meant that every entrant, apart from the winner, had received the same certificate, Paul had been pleased.

However, his pleasure had turned into rip-roaring delight when the dog had come first in one category and won a silver – actually chromium-plated – cup. This had been for 'Best Sausage Catcher.'

'The way he jumped!' Paul had said, reliving the moment time and again. 'So high! And he went straight for the sausage.'

Steve had grinned. 'Reminded me of his namesake, leaping for the ball.'

'You're right, Dad, it was just the same,' his son had solemnly declared.

I bolted the back door. After dropping off his children, Steve was calling in at the bottle bank to dispose of a load of empties, but he should be home any minute. Retrieving the rubber chicken from the kitchen floor, I had returned it to its polybag when I heard the front door open.

'It's me,' Steve called, and I felt a warm glow.

'Did Annette's fair go well?' I asked, when we had kissed

in the hall.

'It was very successful, apparently. Though she didn't get the chance to say much about it because the kids were so busy telling her about their day. How Ronaldo had won that goddamn prize and how Debbie's story had been accepted. She'd left before the post arrived this morning, so she didn't know.'

I hung the rubber chicken behind the cloakroom door. 'And now she has two happy children.'

'Exceedingly happy.' He followed me into the kitchen. 'When we were in the car, Debbie said there was only one thing which could make their lives better. And Paul agreed.'

'What's that?'

Steve put his arms around me. 'If you and I got married. Debbie reckons that by living in sin, we're setting them a bad example. She also said that if people love each other, she believes they should do the old-fashioned thing and get married.

'Make the ultimate commitment?' I suggested, recalling what Justin had said about his relationship with Lynn.

'Right. So how about it?'

I looked at him and grinned. I loved him so much. 'Yes, please.'

'But I thought you didn't want to marry again?'

'I thought you didn't either.'

Steve smiled. 'I've changed my mind.'

'Me, too.'

Yes, I know I said we were perfectly content to cohabit and we are, but, like Jenny, I'm a sucker for a happy ending.

THE END

About The Author

Elizabeth Oldfield started writing as a teenager, when she had articles published in magazines and newspapers. Payment was in guineas – which tells you how long ago it was! On marriage, her creative instinct was diverted into the production of a daughter, and a son. Later, when her husband's job took them to live in Singapore, she resumed writing. A chance attempt at romantic fiction proved successful and she went on to write forty genre romances for Harlequin Mills & Boon.

These were marketed in their millions, and in many different languages, around the world.

Aware of how few books explored the lives of women 'of a certain age', Elizabeth was eager to fill the gap – and *Vintage Babes* is the result.

338

ONE GLASS IS NEVER ENOUGH

By Jane Wenham-Jones

*"Delightfully sparkling, like champagne,
with the deep undertones of a fine claret."*

Three women, one bar and three different reasons for buying it. Single mother Sarah needs a home for her children; Claire's an ambitious business woman. For wealthy Gaynor, Greens Wine Bar is just one more amusement. Or is it?

On the surface, Gaynor has it all – money, looks, a beautiful home in the picturesque seaside town of Broadstairs, and Victor, her generous, successful husband. But while Sarah longs for love and Claire is making money, Gaynor wants answers. Why is Victor behaving strangely and who does he see on his frequent trips away? What's behind the threatening phone-calls? As the bar takes off, Gaynor's life starts to fall apart.

Into her turmoil comes Sam – strong and silent with a hidden past. Theirs is an unlikely friendship but then nobody is quite what they seem in this tale of love, loss and betrayal set against the middle-class dream of owning a wine bar. As Gaynor's confusion grows, events unfold that will change all of their lives forever…

ISBN 1905170106 / 97810905170104 Price: £6.99

Shortlisted for the

Barefoot In The Dark, by Lynne Barrett-Lee, is a bitter-sweet novel about taking the first steps towards trusting again. But when love at first sight is the last thing you're after, is a fairytale ending an impossible dream?

ISBN 9781905170371 / 1905170378 Price£6.99

My Mummy Wears a Wig – Does Yours?

By Michelle Williams-Huw

A diagnosis of breast cancer made Michelle Williams-Huw, mother of two small boys, re-evaluate her life as she battled her demons to come to terms with the illness. *My Mummy Wears A Wig* is poignant, sad, revelatory and deliciously funny. Readers will be riveted by her honesty and enchanted as, having hit bottom, she falls in love with life all over again.

ISBN 9781906125110   Price £7.99

HELTER SKELTER
By Della Galton

Brought up on a seaside fairground, Vanessa knows all about what a roller-coaster ride life can be. Tragedy forces her to flee but when she discovers that her husband, a property developer, is cheating on her she returns. But the fair has gone, the land, bought by her husband, is now covered by luxury flats.

Going back can be painful but this is just the start of the Helter Skelter for Vanessa. While she feels her life is spiralling ever downwards, there are the strong arms of a passion from her past to catch her at the end.

ISBN 9781905170975   Price £6.99

WANNABE A WRITER?

by Jane Wenham-Jones

A hilarious, informative guide to getting into print that's a must for anyone who's ever thought they've got a book in them

- Where do you start?
- How do you finish?
- And will anyone ever publish it when you have?

Drawing on her own experiences as a novelist and journalist, Jane, *Writing Magazine*'s agony aunt, takes you through the minefield of the writing process, giving advice on everything from how to avoid Writers' Bottom to what to wear to your launch party.

Including hot tips from authors, agents and publishers at the sharp end of the industry, *Wannabe a Writer?* tells you everything you ever wanted to know about the book world, and a few things you didn't...

ISBN 9781905170814   Price £7.99

www.wannabeawriter.co.uk

For more information about
Accent Press titles
please visit

www.accentpress.co.uk